Mercy's Prince

Katy Huth Jones

For Diane,

My sister + friend! May you always find hope and joy no matter what the circumstances in this life.

Love,

Katy Huth Jones

8 Sept 2015

Mercy's Prince

ISBN-13: 978-1514381670

ISBN-10: 1514381672

Editor—Alex McGilvery

Cover art by Colleen Clarke, of Mystique Book Designs
(http://mystiquebookdesigns.com)

Published in the United States of America

First print edition: June 2015 by Quinlan Creek Press

Dedication

This book is dedicated to my father, Walter Huth, a second son, a mighty warrior, and my hero.

Chapter 1 *He shall descend into battle, and perish.*

Something scaly crawled across Valerian's cheek. He startled awake, shivering in his cloak where he lay curled up on the bare ground. Late summer predawn in the foothills of the Dragon's Backbone was cold, especially since Valerian wasn't accustomed to sleeping out of doors.

A small warm body slid inside his cloak. Valerian flinched and managed to catch the creature, careful not to squeeze too tightly. As he suspected, it was a young burrowing dragon. Its heart fluttered against Valerian's hand.

"You must burrow elsewhere," he whispered to the dragon. "And don't let my brother or Sir Caelis find you." Valerian slipped the creature into a fissure of the smooth rock that was his pillow. Its long tail grazed his hand as it disappeared.

"Get up, you wretch." A boot nudged his back, hard.

Valerian sat up and pushed his long dark hair from his face. Crown Prince Waryn towered over him. The dim light of a gray dawn silhouetted his brother's form.

"A squire anticipates the needs of his knight. He does not oversleep." Waryn pointed to the faint orange glow in the nearby fire pit. "Kindle the fire. Now."

Valerian scrambled to his feet, avoiding another of Waryn's kicks. Blinded by tears of disappointment, he stumbled to the stack of wood he had collected the previous night, envying the men-at-arms still asleep in their tents.

With a grunt, Valerian lifted a heavy armful of wood and carried it to the fire pit. He arranged the firewood over the glowing coals and then used a stick to stir the embers to life. While he fed bits of dried grass and twigs until the logs caught fire, acrid smoke assaulted his nose. The warmth dried the dew from his face. He stared into the flames, grimacing. *No matter how hard I try, I will never prove my worth to Waryn, not as long as he remains under the influence of Sir Caelis.*

When he stood, Valerian turned and gasped. Sir Caelis stood uncomfortably close, staring at him. The knight's eyes glittered in the firelight, cold as his chain mail, and an unpleasant grin distorted his handsome features.

"Was there something you needed, sir?" Valerian forced calm into his voice. He knew not to complain, though it went against his sense of fairness that a royal squire should be required to assist any knight, especially when Caelis took advantage of the situation.

"Yes, boy, I am hungry."

Valerian bit back a retort. It was too early in the day to run afoul of Caelis. Besides, hadn't Valerian painfully learned how useless it was to fight back?

Waryn returned to stand beside Caelis. They formed a solid wall of contempt, as if daring Valerian to report their treatment of him to the king. They knew, of course, that he never would.

"I am also hungry, squire." Waryn's malicious smile mirrored Caelis' own. "But I tire of camp food. I wish fresh meat on this evening's table."

Caelis folded his arms across his chest.

"Fetch your bow, whelp, and find meat while your betters break their fast."

"Yes, sir." Valerian sighed and went to collect his bow and quiver.

The rest of the camp stirred to wakefulness while Valerian left with his bow. The glow of the rising sun barely penetrated the morning mist, making the world appear contained in this one valley. He climbed the hill. Perhaps, from its height, he could emerge from the damp fog and spot a deer or other animal grazing nearby.

Upon reaching the summit, the sun's harsh light temporarily blinded him. When his eyes adjusted, Valerian first glanced back down toward the camp. The fog was beginning to dissipate. He could make out the shapes of Waryn's men waking and milling around. Drew, Waryn's junior squire, darted toward the stream to refill water skins.

Shading his eyes from the rising sun, Valerian turned his gaze to the east. Just beyond the blood red hills lay the desert land of Mohorovia and the mysterious Horde. The king's scouts had found evidence of raids on outlying farms, and the garrisons had sent reports of Horde activity, but no one Valerian knew had actually seen a Mohorovian.

Movement caught his eye. Valerian whirled to face a copse of trees, and the bark of the nearest one shimmered. With a rustling sound, a scaly tree dragon unfurled its wings and took flight in a westerly direction. Several more flew from the other trees while Valerian watched, enthralled. He never tired of seeing these tiny cousins of the great dragons. Hoping there might be a few more, Valerian scanned the trees.

There, in the distant shadows of the wood, another movement, a blur. Had he imagined it? No, there it was again. Sunlight flashed on large burnished scales, and Valerian glimpsed multiple battle-axes.

Ambush! Valerian shouted the word inside his head, but his mouth would not open, his throat ceased to function. He managed to unlock his legs, and they propelled him down the hill at breakneck speed. He nearly knocked over Drew in his haste to reach Prince Waryn.

"There are, there are—" he said, gasping for breath.

Waryn grabbed Valerian's arms and scowled. "Spit it out, squire."

"Ambush!" Valerian pointed to the trees.

Waryn's eyes scanned the hills and widened.

"To arms," he bellowed. "Enemy sighted! Positions, all!"

They had no time to pull on surcoats or fasten greaves. Valerian gathered Waryn's helmet and shield, then his own. A bone-chilling howl filled the air. The sound vibrated down Valerian's spine, and he cringed. Clutching his spear, he heard the first clash of weapons and turned to face the enemy.

The Mohorovians were man-sized lizards striding upright on muscular back legs. Each carried a battle-ax with a razor-sharp flint blade. The spear Prince Waryn hurled at the advancing creatures bounced off their thick scales. Valerian gripped his spear more tightly, but he couldn't stop the trembling of his hands.

Every scream, every thud of battle-ax into unprotected flesh magnified itself inside Valerian's head. An arrow grazed his helmet. Blood spurted from the severed arm of the knight in front of him. In three years as Waryn's squire, the ordered drills in the castle yard had not prepared him for this melee of screaming, howling butchery.

"Caelis," Waryn shouted. "Take care of those archers before they wipe us out!"

As the best bowman among them, Caelis hurried to obey. *Poison.* The Horde used poison on their arrows. What little courage Valerian possessed shriveled.

Grunting, Waryn deflected one of the Horde's axes. He dropped his shield, gripped his spear with both hands and yelled as he shoved it between the scales on the creature's chest. The Mohorovian roared as it fell back, lashing out with its tail, but Waryn leaped aside. The creature thrashed on the ground, pulling at the spear. Green stained its fangs and it lay still.

Snatching up his shield, Waryn deflected another battle-ax, grabbed the weapon from the surprised Mohorovian and swung it around in a crushing blow. The creature's green blood spattered the air.

Waryn had been born for this moment, had dreamed of war all his life. Valerian stood on quaking legs, paralyzed. Bile rose in his throat. He wanted to throw down his spear and shield and run from the battlefield. Ashamed, he looked away from his brother, but his gaze drifted to the first Mohorovian felled by Waryn. The monster opened its eyes.

To Valerian's traumatized senses the surrounding sights and sounds moved more and more slowly, as if time prepared to stop. The Mohorovian shoved itself off the ground and snapped the shaft of the spear imbedded in its chest, then picked up a fallen ax and swung it toward Waryn's exposed side.

Valerian opened his mouth to shout at Waryn, but nothing came out. Why couldn't Valerian make his feet move? Why, oh *why* wouldn't his sweaty fingers tighten around the spear? If he could just lift his arm, he could strike down this threat to his brother's life.

The Mohorovian's muscles tensed. The flint blade glinted in the sunlight. Finally the horror of it loosened Valerian's tongue.

"Waryn!"

His brother would not be able to turn quickly enough. The ax blade swung down, down toward his blood-spattered chain mail. Waryn began to lift his shield, but the blade pierced the coat of mail and tore into his chest.

"No!" Valerian's scream released him from his paralysis. He let his shield fall and grasped the spear with both hands. He stabbed the point into one of the reptilian eyes, ramming it to the bone. The force of the blow jarred down his arms to his shoulders. The creature's hot blood spurted over him as it fell.

Valerian backed away, searching for another spear, desperate now to protect his injured brother. But the battle had moved away from them.

"Waryn!" Valerian knelt beside his brother. Waryn lay gasping. Blood seeped from the terrible chest wound, his life kept from gushing out only by the imbedded chain mail.

Valerian pulled off his gloves and pressed on the wound. He had to stop the flow of blood, or Waryn would die. In moments Valerian's hands turned red. His brother's face went white, and his skin grew cold.

"Waryn, please don't leave me." Even if Waryn heard him, he could no longer answer.

Valerian lay beside his brother, to keep him warm, to take hold of his fading life. One last breath gurgled through the ruin of Waryn's chest, and his heart stopped beating. A wail escaped Valerian's throat. How could someone who seemed invincible be so easily cut down?

"What have you done?"

Valerian sat up. Sir Caelis ran toward him and dropped to his knees.

"You could have saved him, craven whelp." Caelis clenched his fists. "You were beside him, close enough to help him. Why didn't you cut down that Mohorovian?" His eyes glared through the slit in his helmet.

Before Valerian could think of a reply, he met Caelis' stare, and a veil parted between them. Without knowing how, he could *See* the knight's desire to destroy him as if Caelis' mind was laid open, exposing his secrets. Caelis' thoughts and emotions bludgeoned him, making his head spin and his empty stomach heave.

"He died because of *you.*" Caelis picked up Waryn's body and struggled to stand. "You are no warrior. You belong in a monastery. I will not be ruled by such a weakling."

"I wish someone else could take his crown." Valerian choked on a sob. "I never wanted it."

"Be careful what you wish for, boy." With one last glare at Valerian, Caelis strode away, carrying Waryn in his arms.

When Valerian turned away, the body of the Mohorovian with the spear protruding from its bloody head was a stark reminder of his costly timidity. Death lay all around the quiet valley. The stench of it hung in the air. Where was the glory of war celebrated in the bards' songs?

Valerian pushed himself to his feet. Were there any Mohorovians left to strike him down? He had no right to live now that Waryn had died. How could he be crown prince? No one could take Waryn's place, Valerian, least of all.

“Please, take me now.” He flung his arms wide to welcome one of the Horde's poisoned arrows.

No arrows came. Valerian could not escape by his own death.

One moment of Valerian's cowardice had changed everything: Waryn the Invincible was dead. That left him, Valerian the Unready, heir to the crown of Levathia.

How could he rule a warrior kingdom when he hated war and killing?

Chapter 2 *Rule and power are with him.*

Visible from the Keep, the mountains of the Dragon's Back-bone, jagged, black, and forbidding, cut across the land and divided it in two. Instead of the North's rocky hills, evergreens, and lonely moors, a forest blanketed most of the southern half of Levathia with redbarks, shaggy beards, and black oaks.

In the far corner of the Southern Woodlands lay an isolated village of pacifists. Enclosed by forest and a wooden palisade, twenty thatched wooden huts stood in neat rows bordered by vegetable gardens and sheep pens. And in one small cottage near the village gate, fourteen-year-old Mercy ladled porridge from a blackened cauldron into a bowl, careful not to spill any on her homespun dress. She set the bowl on the table for Papa when someone knocked on the door.

"Enter," Papa called. He pushed back his stool and went to greet the visitor.

It was Mercy's older cousin, Michael.

"Uncle Joel," the visitor gasped. "Brother Gabriel is calling all the men for an emergency meeting. We have just received a summons from the king."

"A summons?"

"A general call to arms."

Papa straightened his cap and his long braid and nodded at Michael.

"Mercy," he said, not even glancing in her direction. "I shall eat later. Find Rafael and keep him out of the way." He strode out the door.

Michael's gaze followed Papa before he turned to Mercy.

"Are you well, cousin?"

Mercy gave him a shy smile.

"As well as can be." She swallowed and glanced past him to make sure Papa wasn't watching. "You know you shouldn't be here alone with me."

Michael stepped closer. His cap brushed the dried herbs hanging from the ceiling beam.

"It pains me to see you working yourself to death for a harsh father who doesn't appreciate what you do."

"Michael, don't." She backed away, bumping into the table. "Papa wasn't always like this. He still grieves for Mama."

"It's been more than four years." Michael frowned.

"I think Papa's heart turned to stone that day," she whispered.

"You deserve better. You're too young to be so ill-used."

"Please—"

"I won't apologize, Mercy." His eyes narrowed. "It's just one of the things I've been questioning lately."

"Questioning?" She swallowed, glancing out the door again, lest anyone hear them. "What do you mean?"

"Your situation, for one. There are so many things wrong with it, I don't have time enough to expound." Michael lowered his voice. "But lately I've been questioning my beliefs in our pacifist ways. I understand why murder is wrong, but I don't see how defending yourself and your family from someone who wants to kill you could ever be wrong."

"Michael! You could be flogged if anyone heard you say that."

"You wouldn't tell anyone, would you?" He grasped her hand.

"Of course not." She pulled her hand away. Didn't he realize it was not seemly to touch her now she was betrothed?

"Even Gabriel?" Michael frowned. "Even when he's your husband?"

Mercy shook her head, wiping her hand on her apron.

"I would never betray you, not even to Gabriel."

Michael sighed before speaking again.

"Thank you, Mercy. I shouldn't have said anything, but I'm so unsure of things I've believed all my life." His eyes brightened. "You know I've been going with Father to the trading post this past year, and I see men of the world. Every one of them wears a knife on his belt. I even saw a knight once. He sat upon a beautiful warhorse. He wore golden spurs on his boots, and a red and gold surcoat over his chain mail, and he carried a spear. Magnificent!"

The exultation in his voice frightened her.

"Forgive me, cousin, for causing you distress." Michael bowed his head.

"You are forgiven." But her voice trembled. Her cousin's words had touched on the doubts in her own heart she had been unwilling to acknowledge.

"Promise you won't mention any of this?" Michael lifted his right hand, palm facing her.

She placed her palm on his.

"I promise. Upon my life, I promise."

He briefly squeezed her hand.

"I'd better find out what's going on now." He paused and brought her hand to his lips. "You know, if we weren't so closely related, I'd marry you myself."

"Michael!"

He backed away.

"I know, I know. But I hope Gabriel realizes what a great blessing he's been promised." Before he turned to go he said, "By the way, I saw Rafael at the sheep pens."

Mercy rushed to the door and watched Michael run toward the meeting house, his dark braid bouncing against the back of his homespun tunic. His words made her heart heavy. They used to be such good friends, until Papa forbade contact between them. She scraped Papa's porridge back into the cauldron and hurried to the sheep pens.

At first she didn't see Rafael among all the shaggy, bleating animals. Then she spotted him sitting in a corner with a lamb in his lap. The lamb struggled to free itself from the boy's grasp.

"Rafael," she called over the din. "Let go of that lamb." She hiked up her long skirt, climbed over the low fence and pushed her way through the sheep.

"But I want to hold it, Sissy." He gripped the lamb more tightly as she approached.

"We must go home now." She bent down and attempted to take the lamb from Rafael's arms.

"No, it's mine!"

Mercy fought tears while she wrestled her brother. Though he was not five years old, he was growing stronger and more difficult to handle. She'd begged Papa for help, but he was too busy with his healing. Now she was promised to Gabriel, and upon her fifteenth birthday they would be married. She had to find a way to control her strong-willed brother by then. If only Mama hadn't died birthing Rafael, how different things would be now.

Finally, she managed to loosen Rafael's grip so the lamb could scamper away. Mercy grasped both her brother's wrists and pulled him out of the sheep pen. He dug his bare heels in the dirt and yelled the entire way.

"Having trouble, Mercy?"

Mercy lifted her head. Serene passed by with a basket on her arm. The older girl's smile was sympathetic.

"I need to get Rafael home." Mercy tightened her grip on Rafael's wrists. He howled even louder.

Serene changed directions and shifted her basket to the other arm.

"Here, let me help you." She took one of Rafael's arms. "Let's carry him."

Rafael tried to kick Serene, but she was too nimble. Together Mercy and Serene lifted the boy. Surprised, he stopped yelling and started giggling. The girls ran to Mercy's house as quickly as their burden and long skirts would allow. Once they arrived, they dropped Rafael onto his bedroll in the corner of the single room. Serene closed the door behind her and stood leaning against it. But Rafael was still giggling, all defiance gone.

"I'm hungry, Sissy," he said.

Mercy ladled porridge into a bowl and set it and a wooden spoon on the table. Rafael grabbed the spoon and began shoving porridge into his mouth.

"I miss being a girl." Mercy turned to her friend. "Do you remember when we used to play together after our chores were finished?"

"Now it seems they're never finished, doesn't it?" Serene said.

"I don't mean to complain." Mercy sighed. "I keep trying to 'remember my blessings,' as Brother Gabriel says."

Serene touched her sleeve.

"You have a heavy burden. But I suppose once we both are married it won't be any easier. Just different." Her eyes twinkled as if she were hiding a great secret.

"What is it?" Mercy frowned. It wasn't like Serene to keep things to herself.

"Nothing. That is, nothing I can tell you right now." Serene smiled, blushing. "I must go." She left so quickly Mercy had no time to collect her thoughts.

She realized after Serene was gone she hadn't asked about the summons from the king.

* * *

When Papa returned, he was even grimmer than usual.

"Are you ready for your porridge now, Papa?" Mercy picked up a bowl and ladle.

He scowled at her.

"Who can think of eating when things of much greater import have befallen us?"

"I'm sorry, Papa." Mercy dropped the ladle in the pot.

"It's not your fault you are so ignorant of the world." Papa began to pace across the room. "I do not agree with Brother Gabriel that our faith will insulate us."

"What do you mean, Papa?" He had never voiced disagreement with Gabriel, the leader of their village as well as her betrothed.

He stopped pacing and clenched his fists.

"Peace is a noble goal, but when war comes upon Levathia, pacifists are the first to suffer."

"War?" Mercy sank to the nearby stool.

"Yes. We have been invaded from the east, and King Orland has ordered all able-bodied men to join in the fight to protect our borders."

Mercy shook her head. Surely the king understood the men of their village, men who had sworn the Oath of Peace, would not, could not fight in this war.

Even the late summer sky mourned Prince Waryn's death; the low clouds leaked drops like tears. Valerian's horse plodded past the castle gates. Waryn's junior squire, Drew, and what remained of the men-at-arms followed behind. Because Sir Caelis had gone ahead with Waryn's body, everyone in the Keep wore black armbands. The guards and servants bowed as Valerian passed by on his way to the stables.

Valerian dismounted and handed Theo's reins to Drew. The squire wiped away tears and silently led both of their horses away. A messenger raced toward Valerian and fell to his knees.

"Your Highness." The boy removed his cap. "The king wishes to speak with you in the chapel."

"Thank you." Valerian made the mistake of looking directly into the boy's eyes. First that same sensation of a veil parting, then palpable waves of grief from the lad before Valerian tore his gaze away. Trembling, he ascended the stone steps leading into the Keep. This meeting could not be postponed even for an hour.

When Valerian neared the chapel, the words of the lament that monks were singing for his brother became clear. For the first time in his seventeen years Valerian wished he had not studied Latin so well, for he understood every word:

"In life he was valiant, a prince among princes
Most courageous and stalwart,
A warrior without equal on the earth,
Beloved of the people as long as time shall stand."

Valerian stepped into the candlelit chapel and saw his brother's bloody corpse laid out on a bier before the altar. The king knelt at the rail, alone. Valerian glanced around to make sure Caelis was not present and then approached the bier.

You could have saved him, a voice whispered inside his head.

Framed by short damp hair, Waryn's face was as cold and white as Valerian had last seen it. Someone had arranged his hands across the terrible wound in his chest. Why had they not removed the blood-stained mail and leathers? Of course, Valerian thought with smoldering anger, it was his brother's honorable death in battle being celebrated here. Those who died peacefully, even more than those who lived in peace, were scorned in Levathia.

Valerian took a deep breath and let it out slowly. It would not do to face his father with emotions so raw. He pushed down the grief, but the guilt was far too strong to be denied. Everything had changed. If only he had kept his wits about him, he could have saved his brother, and he would not now be standing here awaiting the king's pleasure as his sole heir.

His father, the king, sagged against the rail. He wore a black robe and no circlet on his head. With effort he stood and turned to face Valerian.

"You may approach," King Orland said, his voice breaking. He'd aged ten years since Valerian had last seen him a fortnight ago.

Valerian stepped forward and went down on one knee.

"Father, I—"

"I want to know what happened." Orland's voice shook with barely controlled rage. "Sir Caelis has told me his version. I want to hear yours."

Without thinking, Valerian met his father's red-rimmed eyes. The thoughts he *Saw* struck him more forcibly than a blow.

Why couldn't you have died instead of Waryn? It took a moment for Valerian to realize the words had not been spoken aloud. Still, they took his breath away. Valerian was able to focus instead on one of the flickering candles.

"We were ambushed. Everything happened so fast we didn't have time to properly arm ourselves." He swallowed. Then, stammering, he gave a brief account of the battle and Waryn's death. Valerian tried to downplay his role in it, but his cowardice was laid bare. He might as well have murdered his brother.

"And what shall I do with you, Valerian?"

"I—I do not know, Sire. I feel quite unprepared to take Waryn's place." His throat constricted, and he could not continue.

"Take his place? You?"

Valerian flinched and instinctively looked up again. Orland's face was terrible with grief and anger. When Valerian met his gaze, the veil parted again, and his father's thoughts pummeled him like fists: *Waryn was perfect in every way. You have always been a dreamer, a misfit, not worthy to touch the hem of your brother's robe.*

After grimacing, as if he wrestled within himself, Orland spoke aloud.

"Our line has been unbroken since Alden the Great. I will not let it end with Waryn." He shook out the folds in his robe. "You will become the warrior prince Levathia expects you to be and stay away from those priests and their accursed parchments. A warrior king needs expertise in spear and bow, in battle tactics, not history and philosophy."

Valerian swallowed the lump in his throat. His father leaned so close his hot breath touched Valerian.

"If you do not apply yourself to learning the arts of war, then I will condemn you as a traitor, personally cut off your head, and give the crown to one more worthy."

Valerian closed his eyes and swallowed again.

"Yes, Your Majesty," he managed to whisper. One more worthy. Who could be more worthy in the king's eyes than Caelis?

Caelis drained his goblet of wine and slammed it to the floor, denting the rim of the cup.

Why? Why? *Why* had Waryn died instead of his worthless brother? He slumped in his chair and dropped his head to his hands.

"Sir Caelis?" asked his page. "Can I get anything for you?"

"No," Caelis groaned. He jerked upright. "Yes. You can bring me the head of Prince Valerian on a platter."

"Sir?" The boy's eyes widened in horror.

"Never mind." Caelis waved his hand. "Just leave me in peace." He laughed bitterly. There was no such thing as peace.

“As you wish, Sir Caelis.” The page bowed and left Caelis alone in his room.

Caelis stood and began to pace. His grief focused on his anger, on his contempt for Valerian.

“How unfair,” he snarled. “How utterly unjust that the whelp survived while the greatest prince and knight in Levathia died.” All their plans, all their dreams for the future were now gone. Waryn had promised, when he eventually became king, to make Caelis Lord High Constable or perhaps even Lord High Chancellor. Now Waryn's useless, monkish brother would become heir to the throne, and what would happen to Caelis' ambitions then? His hands curled into fists as he sank to his knees, and a sob escaped him. “Waryn! My brother in every way but birth—”

Before the hot tears could flow, Caelis stumbled to his feet. He found the dented goblet and refilled it from the wineskin over and over until all the wine was gone.

Chapter 3 *It is better to go to the house of mourning, than to go to the house of feasting.*

Mercy's hands trembled while she set the table. Her apron bore the stains of the long day's work to make sure everything was perfect for Gabriel's visit. She knew Papa would be more critical than usual when he surveyed all her preparations. Thankfully Rafael had been mostly cooperative and now sat in a corner of the room making a pen with sticks and rocks to contain his clay sheep.

Papa entered the cottage in the black mood that had fallen on him ever more frequently since her mother's death. His eyes narrowed at her.

"Daughter, make haste. Brother Gabriel is on his way." He scanned the table and then the rest of the room.

If he found a single cobweb Mercy would never hear the end of it, but fortunately she had managed to make the cottage as clean as possible. Papa sniffed the air, only now noticing the aroma coming from the iron pot hung over the fire in the pit.

"What is that?"

"Savory potato pie. Isn't that Brother Gabriel's favorite?"

"It does smell good," he admitted reluctantly. Then he examined her appearance. "Turn around."

Mercy slowly pivoted. Her heart thumped unevenly. Why was Papa so determined to find fault?

"Your apron is stained. Can you not make sure you are pleasing to your future husband?"

Mercy faced Papa. His face was set in hard lines, like chiseled stone. It did no good to argue with him. He only became more unreasonable.

"Yes, Papa." She removed the apron and put on her good one, the one she only wore on holy days. Mama had embroidered the hem with tiny balmflowers to match the design of their family's hair clasps. What if she spilled something on it? She never wore this apron when cooking or serving food.

There was a knock at the door, and Mercy's gut twisted. When Papa opened the door, Brother Gabriel stepped inside. He was taller than Papa but not much younger. His brown woolen cap was one shade darker than his face, and when he turned to shut the door, his waist-length braid came into view. Gabriel greeted Papa and then faced her.

Mercy trembled. Gabriel reminded her of a hawk she'd seen up close, and she was his helpless prey. He never smiled, and his dark eyes, hooded like a hawk's, bore into hers. Mercy always dreaded the moment when he *Saw* her thoughts. Thankfully she had nothing in her mind other than worry over supper and Rafael's behavior, for Gabriel's Sight cut open her mind, exposing her innermost being and looking for flaws.

"Do I smell savory potatoes?" he asked in his deep voice. Though the words were pleasant, there was no smile in his eyes.

She dipped her head, breaking eye contact and so escaping his Sight. "You do, Brother Gabriel. Won't you be seated, please?"

He and Papa sat at the square table. Mercy had already placed two trenchers and wooden goblets of spring water. She willed her hands to still their trembling while she filled the trenchers with potatoes for each man. Then she stood nearby while Gabriel blessed the food and their home.

Home? This cottage had not been a home since Mama died, no matter how much Mercy tried to make it so. She opened her eyes when she heard the end of the blessing and stood quietly while the men ate, in case they needed more food or water.

"Did you send our response to the king's summons, Brother Gabriel?"Papa asked around a mouthful of potato pie.

Gabriel nodded and finished chewing his smaller bite. Mercy couldn't help but notice his table manners were much more refined than Papa's.

"The king's messenger returned as scheduled and added it to his pack." Gabriel's face appeared thoughtful. "If his horse is as fast as he boasts, the king will receive our answer within the week."

"And everyone signed it?"

"Yes, Brother Joel. Not one was reluctant."

Mercy remembered yesterday's conversation with Michael. *Perhaps one was reluctant.* Gabriel must have written that the men could not fight for the king in his war. If she knew how to write her name, and if she were allowed to sign, would she have agreed to disobey the king? She'd heard the whispers, the frightening word *treason.* Wasn't the punishment for treason a terrible, painful death?

"Daughter!" Papa's shout made her jump. "I said more water."

"Yes, Papa." Mercy grabbed the clay pitcher of water too quickly, and some of it sloshed onto the table.

"Must you be so clumsy?" Papa glared at her.

"I'm sorry, Papa." Mercy used her apron, her good apron, to wipe the spill.

Gabriel held up a hand. "No need to scold her. 'Tis water only and will shortly dry." His piercing gaze met her eyes.

Mercy broke the contact and carefully refilled the men's goblets. Fortunately they didn't linger over the meal, and Papa left with Gabriel to consult with the other men. Then she and Rafael ate what remained of the potatoes.

* * *

The next morning Mercy arose, earlier than usual, from her pallet on the floor. Papa and Rafael slept soundly. Mercy crept past them, grabbed her bucket, and slipped out the door without either of them stirring. By the waning moon's dim light, she walked to the gate and with a grunt lifted the bar that locked it each night. Usually she didn't leave to fetch water until the gateman arrived just before sunrise. But that was an hour away, and Mercy didn't want to wait.

She hesitated just outside the open gate, wondering if her punishment would be worth the extra hour of solitude. *Yes,* she decided, *it would.* An hour in the pillory was nothing compared with Papa's daily discontent.

Mercy hurried down to the river and turned right when she reached the bridge, her bare feet hugging the winding dirt path she knew so well. She held the wooden bucket close to her chest, which slowed her pace a little. A low branch slapped her head, knocking her kerchief askew.

She pulled off the cloth and thought of flinging it into the brambles, but practicality prevented her. It might feel good for the moment, but if she lost it, Papa would insist she make another before she could leave the house again.

"I understand about the braid," she said aloud. "But I don't understand why our heads must always be covered. In winter, yes. On rainy days, yes. But when it's hot, the scarf is binding and uncomfortable." Just once, she'd like to unbraid her hair and run as fast as she could to see if the long tresses, which fell below her knees, would fly behind her like a piece of cloth.

Mercy reached her favorite spot along the river, a quiet secluded bend. Here the village was hidden from view up on the bluff, not even a glimpse of the log wall encircling the buildings as protection from wild animals.

"I don't understand that, either." She dropped the bucket on the path. "I have never seen a dragon, large or small. Perhaps they no longer exist."

She leaned against the trunk of one of the willows, her eyes adjusted to the near darkness. The water rippled over the rocks with a cheerful sound. The willow branches whispered in the breeze. Their outline grew clearer where they hung over the water. Below them lay a fallen tree trunk she and Serene used to climb on, daring one another to jump into the river. Of course neither of them ever had.

Mercy sidled out along the rough trunk and sat down, dipping her toes in the cold water. Here she could forget there were other people in the world. No angry Papa, no exhausting little brother, no suffocating village rules, no impending marriage to a joyless man old enough to be her father. She kept her place on the fallen tree until the sky began to lighten. As tempting as it was to reflect on Michael's doubts as well as her own, she had been trained from a young child to do her duty, and she would do it if for no other reason than to honor her mother's memory.

With a sigh Mercy moved back to the bank and jumped off the tree. She filled the bucket from the river and lugged it back up the bluff. She might as well accept her punishment for leaving the gate open and get it over with. She had another long day ahead.

The funeral for Prince Waryn lasted all the following day. In the Keep's chapel, there was first a private service, followed by a ridiculous spectacle in the great courtyard. Valerian found them intolerable, both from having to sit and think about his guilt in causing Waryn's death and the certain knowledge his brother would have found the spectacle ridiculous, too.

Everyone in the Keep was present in the courtyard. Even Valerian's mother, Queen Winifred, made one of her rare public appearances, though she was scarcely recognizable in her black gown and thickly-draped veils. The more Waryn's prowess as a warrior and his leadership abilities were praised, the smaller Valerian became. He could never be one-tenth the prince his brother had been, not if he had fifty more years to prepare.

Lord Most High, he silently prayed. *Have mercy on me. Show me the way I must take, and be my strength, for I have none.*

Valerian's prayer was interrupted by a loud choral anthem, martial in tone rather than funereal, jarring him back to reality. People flowed into the great hall, probably anticipating the drunken festival that would follow the somber occasion. King Orland came toward him, the blackness of his gaze matching his mourning attire. No doubt he would tell Valerian his presence at the feast was expected. There was only one possible way to avoid attending.

"Sire." Valerian bowed, speaking before his father could. "I would like to request the privilege of standing vigil with my brother tonight."

Orland frowned. Valerian was sure his father had not expected such a request from him.

"I see no reason why you shouldn't be the one to stand vigil, Valerian, as we will lay Waryn in the family tomb tomorrow." He held out his dragon signet ring for Valerian to kiss.

Valerian bent over his father's hand and noticed Sir Caelis standing behind the king. When Valerian straightened and met the knight's gaze, he clearly *Saw* Caelis' raw grief for Waryn along with dismay that Valerian would usurp his rightful place beside his friend's body. Valerian pitied Caelis and almost retracted his request, but Valerian needed that time with Waryn more. After all, Caelis had Waryn's companionship in life and did not need to seek his forgiveness, as Valerian did.

"Then may I have your leave, Sire, to retire to the chapel for the night?" Valerian stared at the hem of his fathers' black robe so as not to risk *Seeing* his thoughts.

"You may."

King Orland moved slowly toward the great hall, followed by Sir Caelis and many courtiers. Breathing a prayer of thanksgiving, Valerian left the public gathering for the blessed privacy of the Keep's chapel, where he might finally grieve in peace.

* * *

Valerian entered the chapel and quietly shut the door behind him. Many of the candles had been snuffed, but enough remained lit to cast a soft glow on Waryn's frozen form atop the bier, now covered with a white linen shroud. Valerian advanced toward the altar and knelt at the rail, close enough to reach out and touch the bier if he wanted to.

"Forgive me," he whispered, but whether to Waryn or the Most High he wasn't sure. For as long as he lived, he would never escape the guilt and consequences of that one moment of inaction.

At first Valerian was able to focus on prayer—for his brother's soul, for the king and queen that they might be comforted in their grief, and for himself, that he might somehow find the will to step into his new role with a whole heart. Later, as the hours wore on, his knees began to pain him. He thought of looking for a cushion, but pushed that notion aside. Sore knees were the least he could suffer for Waryn's sake.

The noise of the revelers in the great hall grew loud enough he heard snatches of drunken singing and laughter, which made it difficult to concentrate. At one point he heard the door to the chapel quietly open, then footsteps, and he glanced over his shoulder. Drew approached with a small gourd.

"Drew? What are you doing here?" Valerian stood up, grateful for the excuse to allow circulation to return to his legs, albeit painfully.

The squire bowed and handed Valerian the gourd.

"I know you're not permitted to eat, but I discovered you are allowed water."

"Thank you." Valerian took a long drink and handed the gourd back to Drew. "You'd best return to the great hall. The—king may have need of you." He caught himself before he said, "the prince." Although Drew must have known what Valerian meant to say, he gave no sign.

"As you wish, Your Highness." Drew bowed again and left the way he came.

After the door closed behind Drew, Valerian knelt again. Sharp pains cut his knees like tiny knives, but he tried to ignore them. What would happen to him and Drew now that Waryn was gone? Valerian was not yet old enough to be knighted, even if he were ready for the accolade, but he had no older brother to be a royal squire for now. Would King Orland assign Drew to him? He fervently hoped so. He didn't think he could bear to have a stranger for a squire.

As the night wore on, Valerian repeated his prayers, even saying them aloud when his thoughts grew muddy. He shifted on his knees, wincing at the stabbing pains. His yawns grew more and more insistent. Valerian rubbed his eyes and then blinked to force them open, but they wouldn't stop watering. The light from the shrinking candles swam in his vision. He became light-headed.

In that place between wakefulness and sleep, a presence appeared on the other side of the bier. The faded image of his brother stood there, glowering. There was no kindness in his black eyes.

It is because of you I am dead. Waryn's voice spoke in Valerian's mind, but the image's mouth did not move. *How can you live with your cowardice? How can you ever hope to take my place?*

"I know I can never take your place," Valerian whispered. "No matter what I do, from this day forward, it will never be enough to take away my guilt."

He dropped his head to his hands, shutting out the sight of Waryn's shade. But a more vivid image intruded. Valerian stood, dressed for battle, in a grassy field. He held something in his hand—an ancient weapon rare and beautiful, a sword.

A dragon with shimmering blue-green scales came into view, towering over him. It spread its wings and opened its mouth, full of jagged teeth as long as Valerian's hand. The monster's great intake of breath pulled Valerian forward. And as the dragon exhaled, a burst of flame shot out.

Before the flame touched him, Valerian lost consciousness.

Sir Caelis stood before the chapel door with his hand on the iron handle. How dare Valerian ask to keep vigil! The whelp should not be allowed in the same room as Waryn after what he'd failed to do. Caelis should have been the one to spend this last night watching over Waryn's body. He had refrained from looking in before now because he dared not leave the king's table before Orland retired for what remained of the night.

When Caelis opened the door, the shroud-draped figure rested on the bier, and the candles had burned to stubs. And there on the floor lay the prone figure of Prince Valerian, asleep. Caelis clenched his fists. It was tragic enough that the coward had failed to save Waryn in battle. Could the feeble princeling not even stay awake for one night? Caelis itched to pull his knife from his boot and slit Valerian's throat, here in this holy place.

Instead, he closed the door on the sight and gritted his teeth. He could not allow his anger to cause him to make a foolish mistake. After all, it would be simple enough to confirm to His Majesty what the king must surely know in his heart, that his younger son was not fit to rule Levathia. Caelis need only prove by the great contrast between his abilities and Valerian's lack that it was in King Orland's best interest to name him heir instead of the whelp. In that way Caelis could still fulfill his and Waryn's dreams of ruling the people with the firm hand of a warrior and the clear vision of a superior lord.

He smiled. It would be embarrassingly easy to best Valerian. Then the weakling could be shut away with his cowardice in a monastery, where he belonged. Caelis simply had to bide his time and let the inevitable happen.

Yes, he would be patient.

Chapter 4 *The king's favour is toward a wise servant.*

Mercy sat on the bare ground just outside the cottage and opened her sewing basket, eager to try the new iron needle Papa had brought from the trading post so she could mend his spare tunic. The sun warmed her face and a songbird trilled from its perch on the thatched roof. Mercy closed one eye to better line up the thread with the needle's hole and dropped the needle when the chapel bell began ringing an alarm. Rafael jumped up from the patch of grass where he'd been playing with his clay sheep.

"What's that, Sissy?" He cocked his head. "I never heard the bell ring like that."

"Perhaps there's a fire." Mercy found the needle and replaced it in the basket. Then she stood and grabbed Rafael's hand. "We must go!"

They ran toward the chapel like the rest of the villagers who also hurried to congregate there. Mercy stopped short when she caught sight of soldiers on horseback. What were they doing here? Soldiers had never come into the Village of Peace before. Behind them, two large draft horses were hitched to a long wagon.

"Come on, Sissy!" Rafael tugged on her.

Mercy reluctantly moved closer, unable to look away from the stern men with their short hair. One of them moved his horse forward.

"Is everyone now present?" The soldier frowned. "Who is leader of this village?"

Gabriel took one step forward.

"I am Brother Gabriel."

Mercy's chest tightened. Every soldier gripped a spear and wore a long knife on his belt; Gabriel carried only the calm assurance of his faith.

"Did you not receive the King's call to arms?" The soldier nudged his horse closer to Gabriel.

"Yes." Gabriel folded his hands.

"Why did you not obey that order?" With a jerk of the reins, his horse stopped, ears turned forward.

"We sent the King our reasons why we could not accept his summons."

"You are citizens of Levathia. It is your duty to comply with the King's command."

Gabriel's face remained calm.

"We may comply only if His Majesty's command is not in conflict with our higher obligation to the God of Peace, which forbids us to take up arms against another living creature."

"These are monsters, not men," the soldier shouted. "They murder our people and destroy our land."

"We do not approve of the violent actions of the invaders," Gabriel said quietly. "But neither can we break the Oath of Peace we have all sworn."

The soldier scanned the faces around him. He tightened his jaw.

"Then you leave me no choice but to arrest every male among you of military age."

All eyes turned to Gabriel. He inclined his head.

"We will not resist you. But we will not violate our Oath of Peace."

Some of the women began to cry. The soldiers dismounted and with their spears herded the men and older boys into a tight group. Most of them remained silent. But when Mercy glanced at Michael there was a rebellious look on his face. She wanted to call out to him to be patient, to hold his tongue, but he was too far away.

"Brother Gabriel!" Michael pushed past one of the soldiers. "How can we…"

"Silence!" Gabriel gripped Michael's shoulders, stunning him into compliance. Mercy stared, unbelieving, at the man she was betrothed to marry. She had never seen evidence of this kind of force in him.

While the men were led away, many wives and daughters tried to follow, but they were held back by the captors' spears. Gabriel briefly turned his hawkish stare upon Mercy. He'd had that same stern look on the day she took her Oath of Peace when he'd used the Sight on her for the first time. It had frightened her, that baring of her soul. She understood why he had to *See* and verify the motives of all who took the Oath, but still it was difficult for her to look into his eyes.

What would happen when they finally married? She couldn't avoid his Sight then. Mercy shuddered. *If* they married. What if the men never returned? What would happen to them, to all of the Brethren?

One hour after Prince Waryn was laid to rest in the tomb beneath the Keep, King Orland summoned Valerian to appear in the throne room. Valerian chose to retain his black attire, but at the last minute added his silver circlet. Perhaps its weight upon his head would help him measure his words more carefully than usual.

Two things he dreaded: Facing Sir Caelis and being in close proximity to Eldred, the king's aged Seer. There was no way he could hide from Eldred's piercing eyes.

When Valerian entered the throne room, there were only four others present beside King Orland, and his stomach unclenched a little. Caelis and Drew, Waryn's junior squire, stood to one side of the king; an older man whom Valerian didn't recognize stood at Orland's shoulder with a much younger man near him.

Valerian kept his focus on his father until he reached the foot of the dais. He bowed low and made his voice as calm as possible.

"What is your will, Your Majesty?" Valerian ignored the looming presence of Sir Caelis and inspected the intricate hem of the king's robe, to avoid unintentionally *Seeing* his father's thoughts.

"Prince Valerian." King Orland's voice commanded his attention. "When a suitable period of mourning for the crown prince has passed, we shall confirm you as our heir to the throne. Until that day, it is our desire that you apply yourself to excellence in the arts of strategy and warfare. To that end, we are assigning an experienced squire to you."

Valerian gazed expectantly at Drew, but the king continued.

"Since Sir Caelis lost his squire to the Horde, Drew has been assigned to him. We give you Kieran MacLachlan as your squire."

After a moment of disappointment, for he trusted Drew completely, Valerian contemplated the younger of the two strangers. He stood a full two hands shorter than Valerian with a wiry build, but confidence gave him a graceful, not arrogant, posture. His curly black hair fell to his shoulders like Valerian's rather than the short bowl cut preferred by most men of war. Valerian did not trust himself to look directly into the squire's eyes, so he bowed again to his father and made the formal reply.

"I thank you, Your Majesty, and I gratefully accept the service of this squire."

Kieran went down on one knee and put his bare hands between Valerian's gloved ones in a token of submission.

"I be your man in life and in death, Your Highness." The squire spoke with a musical Highland lilt. MacLachlan. Of course.

Valerian raised up the young man but still avoided his gaze.

"Aylmer," said the king. "Verify now the loyalty of the prince's new squire."

When Kieran faced the older man, Valerian gritted his teeth. Who was this Aylmer? What happened to Eldred in the fortnight Valerian had been away from the Keep? Eldred had served as the royal Seer since the time of Valerian's grandfather.

While Aylmer read Kieran's thoughts, King Orland leaned forward and spoke so that only Valerian could hear.

"Eldred's health worsened, so he asked to be released from his position in order to move to the Southern Woodlands. He wished to spend his remaining days near a sister in one of the southern villages."

Valerian nodded. He wasn't sure whether to be relieved or dismayed. After all, Eldred had been Grandfather's closest friend. Valerian might have asked Eldred for help in dealing with his sudden acquisition of the Sight. Right now, though, he wasn't sure who he could trust.

"Your Majesty, this squire reveals complete loyalty to the royal family." The new Seer folded his pudgy hands across his ample belly.

King Orland leaned back, satisfied.

"Excellent. Prince Valerian, you will take your new squire and prepare for tomorrow's training schedule. For now, you will return to your own rooms, but be prepared to move into the crown prince's rooms when I command it."

"Yes, Your Majesty." Valerian bowed to the king and Kieran did as well.

While Kieran followed him to his quarters, Valerian swallowed his sudden distress at the necessity of living in his dead brother's rooms in the near future. It was a painful reminder that he was expected to take Waryn's place in life and responsibility.

After they entered the quiet room, Kieran shut the door. Valerian turned to speak to the squire, but he went down on one knee.

"Forgive me, Sire," he said. "I know all o' this must be more than a wee bit awkward for you, so permit me to tell you about myself."

"Yes, of course." As long as Kieran spoke, Valerian didn't have to.

"My father is a chieftain. As his seventh and last son, I have no hope of inheritance, so early in life he encouraged me to pursue the rank of knight in service to the king."

Kieran stared boldly at him, but Valerian focused instead on the embroidered collar of the squire's tunic.

"Is this your first time at the Keep, then?" he asked.

"Nay, Sire. As a wee lad I served as page for a year to Sir Walter."

"So did I." Valerian frowned. Had they met before? "How old are you, Kieran?"

"I have seventeen summers." The squire flashed a grin.

So they were the same age. Valerian tried to remember if he'd seen this open, guileless young man before.

"I do remember you, Sire," Kieran said, as if he'd read Valerian's thoughts. "You were too busy then to notice the likes of me."

"I wish I had paid more attention." Valerian shook his head. "I feel that you and I might have become friends."

"'Twas my thought as well." Kieran shrugged. "But I suppose now we're too old and set in our ways to do aught but our duty."

Without thinking, Valerian looked directly into the squire's eyes. The veil parted, and he *Saw* that Kieran was only teasing, trying to put the young prince at ease in a tense and awkward situation. With a sigh, Valerian broke eye contact and sat down in the nearest chair to regain his composure.

"Pardon me for asking, Sire, but did you just *See* me thoughts?"

Valerian jerked up his head. Guilt at invading another's privacy clenched his heart, but another possibility entered his mind.

"Are you a Seer, then?"

"Nay, me prince, but I have been told that I am too sensitive to those that be one."

Valerian put his head in his hands.

"Truly, I don't know if I am a Seer or not."

"Oh, you are one, all right. 'Tis no mistaking that." Kieran moved closer. "I take it you have not known this long?"

Valerian hesitated. He'd *Seen* no deceit in Kieran, and he needed to talk to someone.

"I had no indication of this talent until two days ago, just after my brother, Prince Waryn, was killed."

"I have heard that the Sight can appear sudden-like, at the death of a loved one or other traumatic event."

Traumatic? Valerian almost laughed out loud. Of course Waryn's death had traumatized him. The entire direction of his life had now changed, and he was powerless to prevent any of it.

While Caelis strode to his rooms, Drew's hurried footsteps echoed behind him. By the time they reached the door, Caelis had decided to set the squire straight from the beginning.

Drew rushed ahead to open the door for Caelis. As soon as they were inside, Caelis shoved the door closed and turned on the young man.

"I am telling you now, squire, and will only say this once, so pay attention."

Drew's eyes widened in surprise.

"Yes, sir?"

"When I call you, I expect a prompt response the first time. Otherwise, I want you to leave me alone. No hanging about, breathing down my neck. Is that clear?"

The squire pushed the hair away from his eyes.

"Yes, sir." He backed away as if to exit the room.

Caelis grabbed the front of Drew's tunic.

"And another thing, I will not be questioned, no matter how you disagree with my actions or methods. Do I make myself understood?"

"Y-yes, sir." Drew swallowed.

Caelis pulled the young man closer until their faces were inches apart.

"I do not," he said quietly but with purposeful menace, "I absolutely do *not* want to hear you speak of Prince Waryn in my presence." He glared into Drew's frightened eyes.

"As you wish, Sir Caelis."

"Now, go." He shoved Drew to the floor and turned away. His new squire scurried from the room as the door shut out the sound of his footsteps.

Caelis almost pitied King Orland. Of course, the king wanted a son of his own body to succeed him, especially since his own brother and the brother's only son were dull-witted, even less fit to rule than Valerian. Such a great shame, for Orland once had the perfect heir, but now everything had changed. Caelis smiled at the pleasure he anticipated in demonstrating to the king and everyone else his superiority over Waryn's pathetic brother. He was certain Orland would make the right decision for the future of Levathia, and choose Caelis to be the next crown prince.

Chapter 5 *His arrow shall go forth as lightning.*

Mercy stood helplessly watching while the men of the village were led away by the soldiers on horseback. Michael glanced back once, but Papa didn't.

"Where's Papa going?" Rafael gripped her hand. Fear darkened his eyes. Mercy had never seen her brother afraid of anything before.

"The soldiers want to talk to Papa and the other men." She forced a smile, trying to reassure Rafael. "I'm sure they will come home soon." But she didn't truly believe that, and apparently she wasn't the only one. Many women and young girls wept openly. Mercy startled when a hand pressed her shoulder. It was her Aunt Prudence, Michael's mother.

"We should meet to decide what to do." Aunt Prudence's frown made Mercy wonder if she'd done something to offend her mother's only sister. The thin woman's perpetual sour expression was such a contrast to the kindness Mercy remembered of her mother.

"Decide to do what?" Mercy could think of nothing other than the king's probable reaction to Gabriel's convictions.

"Is your head in the clouds, girl? Only the Most High knows when the men will return. Until they do, there is work to be done. That means we who remain will have to add their jobs to our own."

Sister Providence hobbled forward, leaning on her cane.

"Sister Prudence," she said, "our Sister Mercy is not yet the wife of the village leader. There is no need for such harsh words."

Though her aunt's words pained her, Mercy had long ago built a wall around her heart to protect herself from them, and Papa's too. From here in this protected place Mercy could focus on doing her duty, and she now turned her thoughts to the village. What were the men's peculiar tasks in early autumn? Farming? Fortunately the grain had been harvested. Shearing the sheep? That would not happen again until the spring. Woodworking? Smithing? Perhaps that could wait, too.

"Aunt Prudence," she said, projecting more confidence than she had. "The only men's task I can think of that might have to be divided among us is gatekeeper. The rest has either been done or can wait until the men return."

Several others had gathered around. Some nodded. Most had ceased their crying. Mercy sensed all their stares upon her, desperate for someone to lead them, to reassure them in this sudden loss of their menfolk. She trembled when she realized the women were looking to *her* for leadership. How could that be? Though her father was the Healer and her future husband the village leader, she was one of the youngest present.

"Joel's daughter speaks the truth," said Sister Glory, the eldest of the village. "We each have our own work to do. It will pass the time while we wait. Since I still remember how to write, I shall prepare a schedule for keeping the gate so it does not become a burden for any one of us."

"I volunteer to take the first watch." Serene stepped forward and smiled at Mercy.

Sister Providence broke into a toothless grin and struck the ground with her cane.

"Then hop to it, girl! The gates are standing wide open to the world!"

With a giggle, Mercy's friend lifted her skirts and dashed to the gate, closed it, and struggled to lift the wooden bar into place. Mercy hurried to help her, and Rafael tagged along. Together Mercy and Serene managed to bar the gate.

"Well, that will make it difficult for anyone who wants to slip out unnoticed," said Serene. "It's heavier than it looks."

Mercy studied her friend, puzzled at her words.

"Why would anyone want to 'slip out unnoticed,' as you say? Where would they go?" Even though she had so recently spent an uncomfortable hour hunched over in the pillory for doing just that, Mercy couldn't imagine Serene disobeying any of the village's many rules.

"Forget I said anything." Serene's face colored. "You're right; we have nowhere to go. We're trapped."

Before Mercy could reply, Serene turned away.

"You'd best get back to your chores, Mercy, and let me keep the gate, for all the good it will do."

Mercy sighed and reached for her brother's hand.

"Let's go, Rafael." Still subdued, he didn't protest.

While Mercy walked back to their cottage, she pondered Serene's strange words. Did Serene really feel trapped? If so, would she do something about it? A new sense of dread chilled Mercy, more than just fear for the safety of the men. What would happen if, once the men did return and Mercy was married to Gabriel, he were to See her deepest thoughts? How could she keep Michael's and now Serene's careless words from Gabriel? Would she be able to have any secrets ever again?

In the Keep's archery yard, all the people who'd once ignored him scrutinized Valerian's every action. His back burned from all the eyes watching him. He sighted the arrow, prepared to let it fly.

Please, Most High, let it hit the target at least.

He set himself as the archery master suggested and released the arrow. It sped to the target, embedded at the lower edge of the bull's eye.

"Well done, Sire," said Kieran with a grin.

Valerian smiled at his new squire's enthusiasm. Was there anything that could dampen it?

He glanced toward the entrance to the Keep in time to see Sir Caelis approaching, followed by Drew and a small group of lords and ladies. Having such an audience without Caelis would be enough to discomfit him. How could he continue now? Kieran lowered his voice so only Valerian could hear.

"Dinna let him bother you, Sire." He took an arrow from the standing quiver. "Here, try another."

Valerian took the arrow from Kieran and nocked it to the bowstring. But he hesitated for an instant too long.

"Squire," Caelis said. "My bow."

The sound of the knight's voice and his menacing presence never failed to fill Valerian with dread, as well as reopen old, unpleasant memories. He forgot to set his arm properly before the arrow left his fingers and missed the target completely. One of the approaching women giggled.

"Pardon me, Your Highness, if I disturbed your concentration." Caelis smirked and held out his gloved hand.

Valerian stood immobile while Caelis took the bow and arrow from Drew, pulled back, and after scarcely aiming, released the arrow. It hit the bull's eye with a resounding thump. Sighs and polite applause came from the ladies.

With all the target butts in the archery yard, why must Caelis pick *this* one?

Of course, Valerian knew the answer. A sickening image arose, unbidden, in his mind. Ten years were not enough time to banish it: Caelis holding up an infant burrowing dragon, not much larger than a small lizard, that he had impaled with an arrow. While Waryn held Valerian's head to make sure he didn't turn away, Caelis bit off the head of the struggling reptile and spat it in Valerian's face.

It took all of Valerian's self-control not to run away from the archery yard. He had to find a way to change his reaction to the knight, since there was no way to change Caelis. Bracing himself, Valerian held out his trembling hand for another arrow. Before Kieran handed one to him, Caelis drew back with practiced ease and sent a second arrow into the bull's eye.

While the ladies clapped and cooed, Caelis sneered at Valerian and took a third arrow from Drew. Since Valerian was watching Caelis instead of Kieran's hand, his own arrow slipped through his fingers to the dirt. Valerian's face grew hot. Kieran bent down to pick up the arrow while Caelis' smacked into the bull's eye.

When Kieran offered the arrow, he caught Valerian's eye and gave a slight nod. Valerian didn't need to use his Sight to understand Kieran wanted him to shoot again. He studied the target. Caelis had evenly placed three arrows around the center of the bull's eye.

Filling his lungs, Valerian closed his eyes for a moment. He shut out everything around him and honed in on the new target Caelis had made, imagined *his* arrow imbedded there. His eyes flew open; he pulled back the string and released it. The arrow smacked into the target in the middle of Caelis' three.

Kieran met Valerian's gaze again with a satisfied smile. The ladies and even the lords applauded. Valerian could scarcely believe what he'd done and waited for a snide remark from Caelis. Kieran didn't give the knight an opportunity.

"Come now, Sire." Kieran held out a hand for Valerian's bow. "Let Sir Caelis continue with the target, and we shall practice with quarterstaffs across the yard."

With a glance that revealed a scowl from Caelis and a furtive smile from Drew, Valerian allowed Kieran to lead him away from the archery range.

"Did I really make that shot, Kieran?" Valerian kept his voice low. "Or was it a dream?"

"O' course ye made the shot, Your Highness," the squire said, laughing. "You dinna give yourself enough credit."

Upon reaching the quarterstaff practice ring, Valerian took a deep breath and let it out slowly. Now was not the time for fear and doubt. Now was the time for courage and surety of purpose.

It wasn't too late for him to learn courage, was it?

Caelis clenched his jaw to keep from saying any unkind remark about Valerian's lucky shot. He would best the whelp honestly, and he needed to stay focused on that goal. He held out his gloved hand for another arrow, which Drew promptly gave him.

Calmly but with purpose Caelis placed the arrow, drew back, and sent the arrow with the force of his will. It hit the target precisely alongside Valerian's so that they appeared to be one arrow. Caelis only wished it were possible to split the offending shaft.

Remembering his audience, Caelis turned and bowed graciously before handing the bow to Drew. Leading his entourage, he then strolled toward the javelin targets attached to a wooden beam jutting out from the ramparts of the curtain wall. Caelis and Waryn had spent much time practicing here, imagining the bull's eye to be on the head of a great dragon. Indeed, the highly placed targets must have been originally designed to train men for dragon fighting. What a thrill that would have been!

After his first throw hit the edge of the target, Caelis placed the next three squarely in the bull's eye, to the delight of the growing crowd of ladies. While he decided whether or not to head to the quarterstaff field, he overheard one of the women.

"It's such a shame about Prince Waryn," she said. "I was so looking forward to his marriage to Lady Hanalah. She would have been a delightful addition to our company."

Grief lanced Caelis' heart at the casual mention of his lost friend, but he clenched his fists to control himself. He wanted nothing more than to lash out at this self-important lady and remind her that Waryn's death was a tragedy in so many ways. Instead he merely glared at her plump, painted face beneath her colorful headdress until she glanced his way. Her eyes widened, and she inclined her head.

Pivoting on his heel, Caelis strode toward the quintains set up at the far end of the castle yard. He snapped his fingers, and Drew appeared beside him.

"Yes, sir?"

"Bring my horse. I wish to break a few lances on the quintain."

"Right away, sir." Drew raced to the stables, and Caelis had to admire the youth's speed.

He made himself slow his pace so he would not lose his followers. They were vital to his plan to help the king see the obvious difference between Caelis and Valerian.

While the ladies approached like a chattering flock of birds, Caelis smiled at the notion of his cousin, the beautiful, sensuous Hanalah, being a "delightful" addition to their company. Foolish women! Hanalah had only wanted to marry the crown prince for the power and prestige it would have given their family. Oh, she would have been happy to provide a royal heir or two, but she and Waryn would not have let marriage stop them from their respective pleasures.

Then Caelis laughed as another thought entered his mind. What if the king decided to treat for Hanalah's marriage to Valerian? The thought of his flirtatious cousin with the monk lifted his mood, and he was able to complete the afternoon's performance with unaffected graciousness, to the delight of all the ladies.

Chapter 6 *The quiver rattleth against him, the glittering spear and the shield.*

"Mercy!"

The cottage door flew open without a knock. Serene hurried inside.

"Whatever is the matter?" Mercy grabbed her hands.

"You must hurry! Faith is having her baby, but it will not come."

Mercy's first reaction was panic. How could she help? She was not a Healer; Papa was. But Papa was gone, taken away seven days ago.

"I will come, but I must find someone to watch Rafael." She nodded to her brother where he sat shaping a clay pot.

Serene pulled her toward the door.

"I'll stay with him. You must go now!"

Mercy was grateful she'd assisted Papa at childbirths for several years. At the last one, just half a year ago, he'd let her deliver the babe by herself. She grabbed her carry sack and placed in it her mortar and pestle, vials of oil, and fresh bunches of dried balmflower and tongues-of-fire.

"I'm away," she said to Serene. "Thank you."

Mercy ran to Faith's nearby cottage. At the door she heard anguished moaning. Without knocking, Mercy entered. Aunt Prudence, Sister Providence, and Charity, Faith's mother, hovered around a pallet on the floor.

"Has anyone boiled water?" Mercy dropped to her knees beside the laboring woman. Faith wasn't much older than her. The poor young wife lay trembling, drenched in sweat, her face white as a new lamb's wool.

Breathing deeply to still her own trembling heart, Mercy laid her small hands on the taut belly and closed her eyes, willing herself to feel what was happening. The babe appeared to be properly turned, but she couldn't tell for sure. Under her hands she felt a contraction begin, heard Faith's groaning.

In a flash of insight, Mercy *knew* that the babe was in distress. So clear was the image in her mind, it was as if she could *See* with her hands.

"Is the water hot?" she asked hoarsely.

"Yes," came Providence's voice behind her.

"Pour it into a cup, please."

Mercy opened her carry sack and pulled out the mortar, pestle, and dried balmflower. She ground the herb into fine pieces and scraped it into the water.

"Stir this and give it to her."

While Providence obeyed, Mercy took out one of the vials of oil and poured a little into her palm. After rubbing her hands together, she came close to the laboring woman, who lay panting after the contraction.

"Faith, dear, it's Mercy. I'm here in my father's place. You must make yourself drink this tea. It will help dull the pain."

When Faith nodded, her eyes full of pain and weariness, Mercy took a deep breath. This next part would be difficult.

"I must now reach inside you to check the babe. Something doesn't feel right, but I won't know until I touch it directly."

Faith nodded again, and her mother brought the cup to her lips. Her trust humbled Mercy.

Gently, she slipped one oiled hand into the birth canal, grateful anew that Papa had used her assistance in this for the last several births. She touched the crown of the head, a large head, and something else. The birth cord was wrapped around the babe's neck like a noose, preventing its exit and possibly its breath as well.

For once Mercy was thankful she had small hands. She was able to push the baby back far enough to work the birth cord around and around, removing it from its stranglehold. She rested her fingers on the small neck until she was sure she found a pulse, and then slid out her hand. Aunt Prudence was ready with a cloth to wipe off Mercy's hand and arm.

"Thank you, Aunt." She turned her attention to Faith. "You should feel a stronger urge to push now. The babe is free to come forth."

The birthing woman's face contorted with the coming of another contraction. This time she screamed at the intensity of it. Mercy shuddered, remembering her own mother's agonized screams when Rafael was born. She'd clung to Mercy, her fingernails puncturing Mercy's hand. It had been a terrible experience. Would Faith share her mother's fate?

Mercy shook off the feeling of doom. She may not be a proper Healer, but she would do all in her power to save Faith and the babe. She oiled her hand again, and as soon as the third contraction finished, slid her hand inside the birth canal. The babe's head was so large it was unable to progress, even without the birth cord's obstruction.

With a little gasp, Mercy recalled the old shepherd Ezekiel's account of a lamb's birth, one that had been too large for the ewe to deliver alone. He'd worked it out, bit by bit. Stretching her small fingers around the babe's head, Mercy waited for the next contraction and worked with the muscles' action to coax the babe further into the birth canal. Two more contractions, and the crown of the head was ready to emerge. Now Mercy could use both hands to ease the head past tissues strained to the point of rupturing.

There was one final valiant push. Faith screamed louder than Mercy believed possible, and the babe slid out, bloody and yelling, a healthy boy. The other women took over to separate the birth cord and wrap the child in cloths. Mercy waited for the afterbirth, which took a long while to emerge.

When it did, a fountain of blood followed. Instinctively Mercy clamped down on the woman's belly, desperate to staunch the flow.

"Please, God of Peace, don't take her now!" She squeezed her eyes shut and tried to imagine where the blood was hemorrhaging.

Incredibly, she could clearly *See* the place in her mind's eye and moved her hands over the area. She pressed harder, using not just physical strength but also her will to pinch off the artery and cause the bleeding to slow and clot. Mercy detached from her surroundings and drifted, floating as if she were a leaf on the river, until strong hands pulled her away.

"Enough," said a gruff voice. "The bleeding's stopped. Don't kill yourself."

Mercy opened her eyes and focused on the wrinkled face of Sister Providence.

"Is she still alive?" Mercy whispered.

"Yes, child." Providence's voice softened. "You have saved her. But you almost went too far. You must be careful with your gift."

"Gift?" Mercy frowned. "What gift?"

Providence leaned so close Mercy could see the tuft of hair growing from the wart on her chin.

"Your Healing gift. Did you not know?" Mercy shook her head.

"Power came forth from your hands. I saw the light there." Providence's voice was reverent. "Praise be to the Most High! Another Healer among us!"

These were the last words Mercy heard before she lost consciousness.

Valerian awoke to trumpets sounding a call to arms. He nearly fell out of his high bed, but Kieran was there, already awake and ready to assist him.

"What happened?" Valerian rubbed the sleep from his eyes before raising his arms so Kieran could help him pull off the nightshirt. Then the squire deftly pulled Valerian's tunic over his head followed by the coat of mail.

"I dinna know, Sire, but I would guess a Horde attack."

"The Horde? Where?" Valerian began to tremble.

Kieran shrugged. His nimble fingers buckled the belt securing Valerian's purple surcoat.

"What about your mail?" Valerian asked. "I can put on my own boots." Kieran couldn't go into battle without wearing chain mail, for all the good it did for Waryn.

"Now, Your Highness, you must stop thinking like a squire and start acting like a prince." He grinned to show he was teasing, even while he struggled into his own mail and surcoat.

They gathered bows, quivers, and spears and hurried down the stone stairs to the great hall where men were arriving from all corners of the Keep. King Orland stood at one end of the room, also dressed for battle. A herald called for silence over the din.

"Briarwood Village is under attack by the Horde." The king's voice rang with anticipation, not fear. "We ride to intercept them as quickly as possible. Your horses are made ready. I will lead you myself."

The men cheered while they poured out of the hall and headed toward the stables. Valerian glanced at Kieran, but the squire didn't seem concerned about the king putting himself in harm's way. Unspoken words hung in the air, palpable to Valerian: *Vengeance! Avenge Prince Waryn's death!*

In the press of bodies Valerian didn't hear Sir Caelis come up behind him. His voice spoke in Valerian's ear.

"Stay away from the king. I will protect him in this battle." Before Valerian could frame a reply, Caelis faded into the crowd of men.

A groom stood holding Theo's reins. Valerian's black warhorse snorted, pawing the stable floor.

"He smells a battle, Your Highness," said the young man.

"Thank you, Conrad." Valerian slipped his bow and quiver onto the saddle and handed his spear to Conrad before he mounted Theo.

"Good hunting, Sire." Conrad gave Valerian the reins and the spear and stood back from the restless stallion.

Valerian urged Theo forward and guided him in the direction of the king's banner. He made sure Kieran followed on his bay. They cantered with the rest of the men toward the village, which lay one valley south of the Keep. The lead scout crested the hill as the bulk of the army began their ascent. Reining to a halt, the scout held up his fist, indicating arrows should be readied. Valerian slid his spear into the sheath on the saddle and secured the reins to leave his hands free. Thankfully he'd spent many hours learning to guide Theo with his knees. He strung his bow and pulled an arrow from the quiver.

Guiding Theo upward, Valerian gained the summit. Below, a battle raged between villagers armed with pitchforks and the Horde with their battle-axes. King Orland signaled the charge, and Valerian had only to hold on while Theo plunged down the hill with the rest.

The nearest cottages were ablaze. Several bodies lay nearby, but the fighting had moved to the farther side of the village. Valerian aimed at a Mohorovian within his range and shot the arrow, but the tip glanced along the creature's scales. It turned and bellowed when it saw the men of Levathia charging toward them.

Valerian nocked another arrow as he searched for the nearest target. A Mohorovian archer readied an arrow of its own, a poisoned one, and took aim at King Orland. Blocking out everything else, Valerian focused on the creature's unprotected forearm and let his arrow fly. It impaled the Mohorovian before it could shoot, and the deadly arrow fell harmlessly to the ground.

Then Valerian heard a yell beside him. Sir Rudyard MacNeil fell from his horse, clutching his leg where a Horde arrow had struck him. Valerian wheeled Theo around and slid from the saddle. He dropped Theo's reins so the stallion would know to stand still and act as a shield while the rest of the horses thundered past them.

"Ruddy! What can I do?" The shaft protruded from both sides of his friend's calf. The flint arrowhead glistened with blood.

"I'm already dead, Val." The knight's desperate eyes gazed up at Valerian.

Without meaning to, Valerian *Saw* Rudyard's fear, not for himself but for the pregnant wife he would leave behind. There had to be some way to save him!

"Me leg! Cut off me leg!" Rudyard gasped. "I dinna want tae die!"

Reeling against the horror of it but frantic to save the man's life, Valerian pulled off his belt and tightened it around Rudyard's leg just above the knee. But how would he amputate it? His only blade was a knife, and he could not bear to saw through flesh and bone while causing a man such agony.

One of the Horde's battle-axes lay on the ground, and Valerian snatched it up. Before he could think too clearly about what he was doing, he gripped the handle, raised it over his head, and brought it down across Ruddy's leg with all the strength he had.

Afraid to look at what he'd done, Valerian let Ruddy's scream fill his being. The stench of burned flesh reached his nostrils, and Valerian opened his eyes. Kieran had cauterized the stump with a burning brand. A pool of blood lay beneath Ruddy's severed leg.

"Kieran! How—"

"When you stopped, Sire, I turned back and realized what you were about to do, so I got fire from a burning cottage."

Valerian's knees turned to water, and he had to sit down. If Kieran hadn't been there, hadn't seen what was going on, Ruddy would have bled to death. He wouldn't have saved his friend at all.

Rudyard lay mercifully unconscious. What would he say when he did regain consciousness? Would he thank Valerian for cutting off his leg? Valerian shuddered.

He and Kieran stayed with Rudyard. Although they couldn't see clearly what was happening on the other side of the village, the battle did not last long. Once all the Horde were either dead or run away, the villagers tended the wounded and keened for their dead. A man-at-arms helped Kieran lift Ruddy into a wagon with other wounded of the king's men.

King Orland, fortunately, was unscathed though in a foul mood. After making sure Sir Rudyard would be cared for, Valerian mounted Theo. He hung back from the main force and the king's anger. Before he could face his father and weather the brunt of his storm, even though the anger would not be directed at him this time, Valerian had to quiet the tempest in his own breast. He could scarcely tear his gaze away from the sight of Ruddy's leg.

What had he done? In the moment it had seemed the thing to do, to save his friend's life. But how would a knight, especially one as valiant and noble as Sir Rudyard, live with the loss of a leg? Would it have been kinder for Valerian to let him die after all?

"Sire." Kieran's quiet voice pierced Valerian's numbness. "Shouldn't we return to the Keep?"

Valerian gazed up at his squire, sitting patiently on his bay stallion. How did Kieran manage it? Did nothing disturb his calm courage?

"What do you think, Kieran? Should we have saved him?"

Kieran turned his horse nearer to Theo, who snorted but did not move.

"All I can tell ye, Sire, is that I believe life is a precious gift. Once Sir Rudyard recovers from the shock of his injury, I feel certain he will nae squander that gift."

Valerian didn't answer. Words were so inadequate at times. But after a few minutes he was ready to go back, and he and Kieran rode in companionable silence.

Caelis took the long way back to the Keep, riding alone with Drew. He pondered what he'd seen today. The Mohorovians, though formidable opponents with their massive size and natural armor, were not undefeatable. They had several weaknesses that must be exploited. Their long fingers capably grasped the battle-ax, but if the men's spearheads had a grappling hook added, Caelis had no doubt those axes could be pulled out of the reptilian hands. The creatures' scales were too thick for regular arrowheads to penetrate, but if a bow could be designed that would deliver shorter, thicker bolts with more power, then the Horde could easily be defeated.

"Drew."

"Yes, sir?" Drew pulled his horse alongside Caelis' white stallion.

"Did you notice the obvious superiority of the Horde's battle-axes over our spears?"

"Yes, sir, I did."

"I have an idea that might give us an advantage. I must meet with the armorer. Should King Orland ask for me, tell him I will be in the armory."

Before Drew could answer, Caelis spurred his horse and raced toward the Keep. He crouched low over his stallion's neck, laughing. Not only would his ideas destroy the enemy, they would earn the king's gratitude and give Caelis the advantage over Prince Valerian, too.

Chapter 7 *By wisdom kings reign, and princes decree justice.*

Mercy set a bowl of porridge in front of Rafael. When he grabbed his spoon, Mercy placed her hand over his.

"We must be thankful first," she said. "Will you say the blessing?"

Rafael's eyes widened, and then he became shy.

"I never said it, Sissy. Papa always said it."

"I know, love. But Papa is not here. You are the man of the house until he comes back." Mercy squeezed her brother's hand to reassure him.

"I can do it. I know what to say." Rafael straightened, bowed his head, and closed his eyes. "For this food we are to eat, may we be thankful. Amen."

"Amen." Mercy smiled at the pleased look on his face.

While they ate, Mercy replayed yesterday's incredible childbirth over and over, but it was Sister Providence's words about her "gift" that had shaken her most. Was she truly a Healer, then? Was that how it happened for Papa? If only she could ask him about it. She placed her spoon in the empty bowl.

"Did you ever watch Papa Heal someone?"

"Only when my arm got broke." Rafael wiped his mouth and held up his right arm. "This one, 'member?"

"I do remember." Mercy felt his wrist for the knot where the break had been. Frowning, she cupped his arm and closed her eyes. With a gasp she *Saw* clearly that the bone had not healed properly and what she needed to do to make it right.

When she started to drift, Rafael shook her, insistently.

"Sissy! Wake up!"

Mercy opened her eyes. Rafael frowned in concern.

"What happened?" She glanced down at Rafael's wrist. The knot was gone.

"There was light in your hands," he said. "Like a candle. It was warm, too." He moved his wrist back and forth. "It feels better now."

"Was there a light when Papa Healed you?" Mercy shivered, suddenly cold.

"No, Sissy." Rafael slid down from the stool. "Can I play now?"

"Yes, love." Mercy tried to smile, but she couldn't stop the chattering of her jaw.

After Mercy wiped off the bowls and spoons, she went out to her herb garden behind the cottage, hoping the soil and the sun would calm her inner turmoil. She knelt among the plants and inhaled their mingled fragrances. If Healing was a gift from the Most High, then it would explain how she *Saw* things that eyes alone could not possibly see. It would also explain why something she could only describe as *power* coursed through her hands but also used up some vital part of herself. Despite the warmth of the sun, Mercy shuddered.

Rafael's mention of a light reminded her that Sister Providence had seen it, too. Had there been light under Papa's hands while he worked? She couldn't remember ever seeing it. But why would her experience be different from his? If only she could ask him about it! Before she could collect herself and think about what needed to be done in the garden, Serene appeared with a basket on her arm.

"Hello, Mercy. Can you steal away to the river for a little while? It's very important that I speak to you there."

Mercy stood and wiped her hands on her apron.

"I need to fetch water, so I might as well go now as later." She'd never seen such a radiant glow on Serene's face before. "Is there any reason you can't talk to me here?"

"Yes, but you'll have to come to the river to find out why." Serene started toward the gate. "Come quickly!"

Mercy went to fetch two buckets and a carry yoke. It wasn't like Serene to be secretive. But now she was so curious that her earlier disquiet faded. She peeked inside the cottage and found Rafael playing with his clay animals.

"I must fetch water now. Stay inside and I'll be back shortly."

"Yes, Sissy." Rafael didn't even look up from his playthings.

Mercy shrugged the carry yoke over one shoulder and walked as fast as she could to the village gate. Her Aunt Prudence was gatekeeper today, sitting in a chair and carding wool.

"Peace be to you, Auntie." Mercy opened the gate with her free hand.

"And to you, Mercy. Going for water, I see."

"Yes, ma'am." Mercy hoped her aunt wasn't in a prying mood today.

"Well, if you see Serene while you're out there, remind her of the respect she owes her elders."

"Yes, ma'am. I shall." Mercy's face became warm. Before Aunt Prudence could say any more, Mercy was outside, shutting the gate behind her.

She hurried down the path. When she reached the willow tree, Serene was pacing, anxious about something.

"What is it?" Mercy whispered, fearful that something dreadful was about to happen.

Serene's gaze bore into hers, as if she was trying to *See* Mercy's heart.

"Do you really love Gabriel?"

Mercy was so taken aback she couldn't answer right away.

"I think so," she managed to say.

"Mercy! Either you love him or you don't. I don't see how you could love him, though. He's old enough to be your father. And he's so somber all the time."

"Yes, I know." Mercy ducked her head. "But he did choose me. He and father arranged everything."

"Aren't you afraid to be trapped for life with an old man? A stranger?"

"He's not a stranger." Mercy frowned. "I've known him since before Mama died, since he first came to our village and stayed in our home. I'm sure after we're married I will grow to love him in time."

"You don't understand." Serene shook her head. "Love is more than that. It's a feeling—well, it's like having all the stars in the sky crammed into your sewing basket. It's when you want him beside you, and no one else." She smiled with a pleased look on her face.

"Do you feel that way about Ishmael?" Mercy's heart skipped a beat. Maybe Serene would be able to tell her something of the way of a man and a maid that no one else seemed to want to talk about. After all, she was to be married before Mercy would marry Gabriel.

"Of course not. That's why I don't want to marry him. It wasn't my idea, you know." Serene lowered her voice. "I wanted you to meet me here so I could tell you good-bye."

"Good-bye?" Mercy's chest tightened, making it hard to breathe. "Where are you going?"

"I'm going to marry the man I love." Serene's eyes burned with emotion.

"What?" Mercy nearly lost her balance and had to set down the carry yoke.

"His name is Jacob." Serene gazed across the river. "I met him when he came to trade with my father last year. I've been seeing him once or twice a week ever since."

"You have?" Mercy whispered, fearful the wind would hear this sacrilege and bear witness that she was privy to it.

"I love him, and he loves me." She turned back to Mercy. "How could I spend the rest of my life with Ishmael knowing that I loved another man? Would that be fair, either to me or to Ishmael?"

Mercy could not answer, but now she was curious about every detail of this forbidden relationship.

"Has he kissed you?"

"Oh, yes." She took Mercy's hand in hers and led her back toward the village. "It's so wonderful, Mercy, to love and be loved, and—to choose."

"Is it worth being banned from the village? Never seeing your family again?" Mercy didn't add, *never seeing me again.*

Serene stopped at the bridge and hugged her.

"I will miss you terribly, my dearest friend." She pulled back, and there were tears in her eyes. "But I choose Jacob over everything and everyone else."

Serene ran across the bridge where a man on horseback waited. He pulled her up to the saddle, kissed her, and they rode away without a backward glance.

Mercy burst into tears. The hole of abandonment reopened in her heart, the same emptiness she'd carried since her mother died.

Valerian entered the infirmary with trepidation gnawing at his stomach. Would Rudyard hate him? If so, Valerian would find a way to live with that. More importantly, though, could the knight use his strong will to go on with his life?

Few of the cots were occupied. Valerian spotted his friend by the contrast of his copper-colored hair upon the white linen. No one else had hair quite that shade of red. When he approached the bed, Ruddy's eyes were closed, but his face did not look peaceful. It was impossible not to notice the missing leg under the thin sheet, and guilt pressed upon Valerian's chest.

He stood at the foot of the bed, wondering whether to go or stay, when Rudyard's eyes flew open. His gaze pierced Valerian.

"What are ye doing here, Your Highness?" His voice was strained.

Valerian's feet were immobile. He wanted to come closer but couldn't make himself.

"I had to make sure you were going to survive."

"Survive?" Rudyard managed to pull himself upright. The stump moved under the sheet. "Is that what ye call this?" He savagely pulled off the cover to reveal the bandaged wound.

"I only thought—"

Rudyard's voice dropped to a hoarse whisper.

"Why, oh why didn't you let me die? How can I live as half a man?"

"All I could think was that life is precious, and with your wife expecting the babe, they would need you." Valerian swallowed.

"Shannon?" Rudyard frowned. "How did ye know about the babe? I had not told a soul about that."

Before Valerian could blurt out that Ruddy had told him, he realized he must have *Seen* it in the older man's thoughts. That was not a thing to be admitted with emotions so raw.

"I'm sorry Ruddy, I did what I believed best at the time. I pray you'll find the will to go on."

He wanted to say more, but Rudyard pulled the sheet over his stump and lay back, closing his eyes.

"Leave me, Your Highness. 'Tis nothing more tae be said."

Valerian turned away and left the infirmary. For the first time in his life he wanted to break something. At that moment Kieran ran up to him.

"Sire, the king requests your presence in the throne room immediately."

He nodded curtly and followed his squire. His fists clenched and unclenched. How could he calm himself in time? If he tried to speak, he was sure a scream would burst out. Before they reached the throne room, Kieran turned into a side room, pulling Valerian with him.

"My lord," said Kieran quietly. "Ye have moments only to calm yourself."

Was it so obvious? Valerian couldn't even swallow, his throat was so constricted.

Kieran snatched a pillow from a nearby chair. He held it between them.

"Hit it, Sire."

"What?" Valerian choked on the word.

"Hit the pillow as hard as ye can. Don't hold back."

"A prince must control such urges." Valerian shook his head. "I can't."

"Ye canna afford not to. Hit it."

Halfheartedly Valerian punched his fist into the pillow.

"Harder, Sire."

Valerian punched it once more.

"Harder!"

With a cry Valerian smashed his fist into the pillow, knocking Kieran back. A dam broke, and Valerian pounded the small target over and over, giving in to the blind rage. He stopped when the pillow vanished. Valerian came to himself and found Kieran on the floor. He held out a hand to lift the squire.

"Kieran, forgive me." His face grew warm.

"I forgive you, my lord. Feel better now?" Kieran grinned.

Valerian's eyes widened and his jaw relaxed a little.

"Yes. I truly do."

"It works for me every time. But now we must hurry." Kieran tossed the pillow on the chair.

The moment the dragon doors opened and he saw the look on King Orland's face, Valerian wished he had not taken the time to beat on a pillow. Lords and knights, including Sir Caelis, the bishop, and Aylmer the Seer were ranged around the king, all waiting for Valerian, it seemed. He reached the foot of the throne and bowed.

"What is your will, Your Majesty?"

The king gestured to the empty place at his right hand. Waryn's place.

Valerian swallowed. When he stepped onto the spot where his brother had always stood, his guilt over Waryn and now Ruddy rose in his throat, and he tasted bile. Valerian forced his face to project calm he did not possess.

"Bring the prisoners forward," King Orland said.

The doors opened again to admit a group of about forty men and youths dressed in farmer's homespun. Although the prisoners' hands were bound, they did not look as if they would offer any resistance. Before they came too close to the throne, the guards halted them. All the men bowed to the king, and Valerian saw their braids then, the braid of the pacifists' uncut hair.

"Who is leader among you?" asked King Orland.

The tallest of them, although not the eldest, stepped forward.

"I am called Gabriel, Your Majesty." Though his voice was quiet, the man showed no fear in his face or posture.

"Answer now, Gabriel, why your village has refused to take up arms in the defense of Levathia. I have received your letter, but I wish to hear it from your own lips." The king leaned forward to hear the man's answer.

Gabriel did not cower, as most would, as Valerian himself would have. Where did this man find such courage?

"Your Majesty, we are the Brethren. We have pledged our lives to peace with a solemn, irrevocable oath to the Most High God. We cannot fight, not even if it means forfeiting our own lives."

King Orland did not move or even speak. In the tense silence, Valerian studied Gabriel's peaceful face, and their eyes met. In that instant Valerian realized Gabriel was a Seer, too. He *Saw* the absolute confidence in the man and knew when Gabriel *Saw* his utter lack. Valerian averted his gaze and clenched his fists to still their trembling. Finally the king spoke, and the fury in his voice made Valerian cringe.

"Do you realize I have the power of life and death over you?"

"Yes, Your Majesty." If Gabriel had any fear he did not show it.

"And yet you are unmoved by the plight of your countrymen?"

Gabriel paused before replying, but Valerian knew what his answer would be. He'd *Seen* the man's unassailable convictions.

"We are moved, Your Majesty, and yet must remain unmoved in order to serve a Higher Power."

Beside him, Valerian sensed the king's simmering rage. He could understand it, for this man's willingness to defy the king's decree when the land desperately needed fighting men forced the king into a corner. If King Orland was lenient, it would set a bad precedent and weaken the law. But Valerian knew his father well enough to know he would find no pleasure in ordering the execution of peaceful men.

Personally Valerian sympathized with the Brethren's choice. When Waryn was alive, Valerian had chosen to live the peaceful life of a monk. But desperate times dictated that a man put aside his personal desires and sacrifice for the greater need. That was the duty he'd been taught by his grandfather and his father.

"Prince Valerian," King Orland said through gritted teeth.

"Yes, Your Majesty?" Valerian's stomach clenched. Was the king angry at him?

"As our heir to the throne," the king continued, "we desire that you decree a suitable punishment for these men, the Brethren, who refuse to fight with us according to the dictates of their conscience."

If the king had slapped him, it could not have been a greater surprise than this request. These men had to die for their disobedience, for wasn't their refusal to fight treason? But the king must have commanded

Valerian to decree the punishment so he would not have to put these men to death, for didn't the king alone have that power?

Again Valerian regarded Gabriel, who measured him calmly, without fear. Then Valerian studied the faces of the others, some of whom appeared resigned to their fate, but more than one showed alarm, especially the younger ones.

"Your Majesty, these men should be imprisoned here until I have made my decision." It was probably not what his father wanted to hear, but he was not about to make a decree of such magnitude without searching for precedent in Levathia's laws and history.

King Orland stood. He glowered down at Valerian before speaking to the guards.

"Take them to the dungeon."

Before Gabriel turned to leave, he caught Valerian's eye and smiled. Valerian looked away, unsettled. But he could not stop staring at the braids of each of the men. Most hung to their waists, a few even longer. How it would feel to wear that constant reminder of a solemn oath?

As soon as the doors closed behind the last man, King Orland dismissed the assembly. Caelis lingered, but then he glared at Valerian and strode after the others. Valerian started to leave also, but the king put a hand on his shoulder.

"A word with you, Valerian."

"Yes, sir?" He turned to face his father.

"Don't take too long to make your decision regarding their punishment. It is good not to be hasty in your judgments, but too much time breeds indecision."

"I understand, sir."

"It would be such a waste to execute those men." King Orland frowned. "I would rather find a way to convince them to fight." He turned on his heel and exited through the hidden door behind the throne that led directly to his chambers above.

Valerian clenched his teeth. He didn't see how anyone could change their minds, especially not Gabriel's. That man, he was sure, would die a terrible martyr's death before he would ever consider altering his convictions. It was a trait to be admired or at least respected. With a sigh Valerian hurried to the Keep's library. He had a lot of reading to do.

As he strode toward his room, Caelis laughed. It echoed in the narrow hall sounding maniacal, even to him. King Orland had ordered Prince Valerian to enact a punishment upon the Brethren that fit their crime of refusing to fight. No doubt the hapless prince would order the pacifists to pay in sheep or hand-crafted wooden boxes, or whatever they were known for.

"Bah!" He spat on the floor. He'd grown up with a healthy disgust for the pacifists, and seeing them now in the throne room merely solidified his contempt. How dare they refuse to come to Levathia's defense! Only parasites would refuse to defend the land that gave them life. The king should have ordered them executed, not deferred the decree to his son.

Caelis stood before the door to his room, glowering at the unadorned wood. Waryn's door was carved with dragons and intricate scrolling. How far Caelis had fallen in such a short time, and all because of that miserable princeling. Until today, Caelis believed Valerian to be an unfortunate accident of birth, and that Waryn had inherited the kingly qualities of his father. Orland's reluctance to carry out the sentence for obvious treason demonstrated a weakness Caelis had never seen before. Was it possible the younger son, and not the elder, took after the father?

He smashed his fist against the door and whirled away, heading for the armory. Only there did his bitterness fade. The master armorer welcomed Caelis' ideas and even now was implementing his design for a grappling hook. The new bow still needed work, but Caelis knew it was achievable. Even the armorer admitted to Caelis' talent for weapon design.

Smiling, Caelis took the steps down to the armory two at a time. Let the king and his son wrestle with punishment and mercy; Caelis would devote his time to saving the land from the Horde and so make King Orland permanently indebted to him. He laughed as he approached the door of the armory, startling a page who ran past him. More than the king would be in his debt; Caelis would be a *hero* to all in the land, and Orland would be a *fool* not to name Caelis his heir.

Caelis opened the door to the armory and inhaled the scents of leather and oils and metal. There was much work to be done, and no more time for grief.

Chapter 8 *I gave my heart to know wisdom.*

Mercy knew she should return to the village right away, but her heart was so heavy she didn't feel prepared to deal with Aunt Prudence's questions. Since she had two buckets on her carry yoke, she decided to look for wildflowers before the weather turned. One bucket of water would be sufficient for her and Rafael until tomorrow.

She took one bucket off the yoke and wandered alongside the river half-heartedly looking for flowers. How could Serene give up everything and everyone she'd ever known for a feeling? Wasn't love supposed to grow from the head as well as the heart? Mercy would not have chosen to marry Gabriel, but now that the choice had been made for her, it was her duty to learn to love him and honor him as her future husband. Was there not happiness, or at least satisfaction in doing one's duty?

Tears came again, blurring her vision. She glimpsed a patch of blue in the grass and wiped her eyes. Though she still could not see them clearly, she knew they had to be balmflowers. She set down the carry yoke and cupped the flowers in her hands. At that lightest touch, she *Saw* the certain knowledge of the plant's power to dull pain. She gasped at the clarity of it.

Eagerly Mercy scanned her surroundings and found a thistle. She touched the flower, then the leaves, and finally the prickly stalk. At each touch, she *Saw* what each part would do to heal. It was as if the plants were speaking to her!

It wasn't long before Mercy's bucket was crammed full of flowers, stems, and leaves. She'd collected not only balmflower and thistle, but feverfew, goldenrod, and willowherb. She even discovered a new medicinal plant that she'd always considered a dangerous weed, but upon touching the dragonwort's flower petals, she *Saw* that it would cause drowsiness.

Only the stem and leaves were poisonous. Perhaps, the dragonwort would help someone with insomnia.

After collecting several of the flowers, Mercy spied another plant, bloodroot, which Papa had always told her to avoid as poisonous. She cautiously cupped her hands around the pale flower with its frayed petals and *Saw* in the plant an urgent warning of danger. The same warning persisted with the stem and leaves. At an inner urging, Mercy dug up one of the plants to expose its fat, reddish root. As soon as she closed her fingers around the root, she was given the knowledge of its power to clot blood. Could this have helped Faith yesterday at the childbirth? Even if it were only effective on external wounds, what a blessing to have its help. Mercy dug up half the plants to collect the roots, leaving the rest to grow as Papa had instructed her.

The light grew noticeably dimmer when the sun dipped below the tree line, and Mercy gasped. She'd been out for hours. She grabbed her overflowing bucket and ran back to the river to retrieve her water bucket and carry yoke. After filling the empty bucket with water, she headed up the path to the village. Water sloshed out of the bucket, splashing her skirt and feet, but she didn't slow her pace.

Aunt Prudence opened the gate just before Mercy could knock.

"Where have you been, Niece?" Prudence only called her that when she was angry.

"I've been out gathering medicinal plants." Mercy swung the bucket closer to the older woman so she could better see in the dimming light.

"And what about your friend, Serene? Don't tell me she's still out there picking flowers."

"No." Mercy choked on the word and had to clear her throat. "She is lost to us."

"Lost?" Her aunt frowned. "What do you mean?"

"She has run away with a man from the outside." Mercy turned away before Aunt Prudence could see her tears. "I must get home to Rafael now."

Mercy walked slowly toward her cottage, leaving her aunt in stunned silence.

When Valerian entered the quiet library and scriptorium, peace settled over him. This was his favorite place in the entire Keep. Father Preston, the priest in charge, saw him and approached.

"How may we assist you, Your Highness?" The older man's voice was not much above a whisper.

Valerian kept his voice quiet as well.

"I must see the books of judgment recorded during the last war."

Father Preston frowned thoughtfully.

"That would be during the reign of your grandfather, King Theodoric, I believe."

"Yes, Father Preston." Valerian's grandfather had told him about that war. Only with great effort and loss of life had Levathia prevailed over a much larger force of men that had invaded by sea. Now the pressing question was whether any Levathians had refused to fight, and if so, how they had been punished.

Several monks worked silently at nearby tables, most copying with black ink, but one used gold paint on an illumination. A pang of grief stabbed Valerian's heart. He would never join them now.

"Brother Alban," said the priest. "Fetch the books of judgment from the reign of King Theodoric for His Highness."

The scribe disappeared among the rows of shelves and returned carrying three bound leather volumes, which he set on an empty table.

Valerian thanked Brother Alban and moved a stool to the table. He carefully opened the cover to reveal the sheets of parchment, inhaling the familiar scents of ink and leather. Out of habit he admired the even script and the small illumination on the first page, but his urgent search pushed lesser matters aside.

He scanned the pages one by one. There was nothing helpful in the first tome, and he'd almost reached the end of the second when he found one reference to a Devlin Birk who refused to fight and was hanged. But the entry implied that Birk was sympathetic to the enemy, not that he refused to fight for reasons of conscience.

The third volume also covered the time after the war, so Valerian didn't read any more after that. As he closed the book he realized how stiff his neck and shoulders had become and he slowly stretched to relieve the pressure. When he stood, he saw that all but one of the monks had left. It was Brother Alban.

"Do you need any other assistance, Your Highness?" The monk stepped forward to retrieve the books.

"No, thank you. It must be later than I thought." Valerian realized he was very thirsty.

"Yes, Your Highness. The others have just left for Vespers."

"Vespers?" No wonder his neck had become stiff. It had grown so late he'd missed his evening meal. "Thank you, Brother Alban."

He went straight to his room and found Kieran placing Valerian's personal items in a trunk.

"What are you doing?" He realized his few possessions were missing.

"If I'd known where ye were, Sire, I would have told you." The squire pulled a sealed message from inside his tunic. "The king has ordered you to move into the crown prince's rooms, so I thought tae save you time and trouble by making all things ready."

Now? Live in Waryn's rooms? To be sure, he and Kieran would have larger living quarters. But how could Valerian ever sleep comfortably in his brother's bed?

"Thank you, Kieran. I'm sorry I didn't think to send word to you. I've been in the library for most of the day, and it appears I've missed the evening meal."

Kieran shook his head.

"I dinna understand how you could read when there was food to be eaten, but I'll be happy tae go to the kitchen and find something for you."

While the squire went off to forage, Valerian tucked the unread message into his tunic and lifted the top layer of clothing in the trunk to see what Kieran had put inside. He was startled by a knock at the door and the sudden appearance of a young boy with curly brown hair. When Valerian stood, the page bowed.

"What is your will, Your Highness?"

Valerian couldn't help smiling at the high-pitched but courtly voice.

"Hello, Gannon. What do you here?"

"Why, sir, the king has sent me to be your page now that Prince Waryn is—gone." He went down on one knee, pressed his palms together and offered them as a token of submission.

Valerian wondered why his father had sent a message rather than tell him directly about the room and the page he'd inherited from Waryn. Perhaps it was how the king dealt with his grief. Valerian swallowed his own pang of sorrow and cleared his throat.

"Very well, Gannon." He took the boy's joined hands between his own. "I accept your service."

Kieran returned with a trencher piled high with meat and bread, and swallowed the bite he'd been chewing.

"I hope this will be enough, Sire." He set the food on an empty table and turned to the boy. "Who is this?"

"My lord," said Gannon, "I am the prince's page." He bowed to Kieran.

Kieran laughed and bade the boy rise.

"No need to call me 'lord,' as I am a mere squire to Prince Valerian."

"There is nothing 'mere' about you, Kieran," Valerian said. "This is Gannon, formerly page to my brother."

Kieran sent Valerian a sympathetic gaze, and Valerian *Saw* his genuine concern that this move would be difficult enough without having a constant reminder of Waryn through the boy. Valerian averted his gaze to break the contact.

"It will be all right, Kieran. But come, you and Gannon must help me eat this mountain of food so we can settle ourselves in our new rooms."

After eating, Kieran and Gannon carried Valerian's possessions, mostly books and parchments and clothing, to the crown prince's apartment next door to the king's chamber. Kieran then had Gannon show him the best places to store his and Valerian's things.

While they were occupied, Valerian explored the rooms with new eyes. He had not been here often, and those rare occasions were full of painful memories. The solar's large fireplace reminded him of the time Waryn and Caelis had threatened to throw him in the roaring flames if he told anyone they were responsible for a prank on the Keep's stable master.

The heavy trunk by the window seat had been his temporary prison more than once.

The bedchamber felt cold to him, and not because no fire burned on the hearth. His own bed was smaller but safe and comfortable. Valerian did not think he would sleep peacefully in this massive bed.

Kieran and Gannon were setting up their cots when Valerian stepped back into the living room.

"Are you going to change the bedding?" Valerian indicated the dark bedchamber.

"Yes, Sire." Kieran nodded at Gannon. "The lad has already taken care of that."

"It was one of my duties for Prince Waryn," Gannon said with a bow. "I even brought the pillows from your old bed, Your Highness."

Valerian went down on one knee so the boy could better see him.

"Thank you, Gannon. You are a conscientious page."

Gannon smiled and looked directly into his eyes. Valerian *Saw* Gannon's strong desire to please. For this boy's sake, Valerian would make the effort to accept this change with his mind and his heart.

The evening grew late by the time Valerian's possessions were put in his brother's presses. After Kieran and Gannon helped Valerian get ready for bed, they shut the door to the bedchamber, leaving Valerian alone. The small fire now burning cast flickering shadows of the bed posts and canopy. The single candle beside the bed was a feeble light to repel the darkness. He picked up the king's message and broke the royal seal.

"*Valerian,*" it read, "*the time has come for you to move into Waryn's rooms. I have assigned Gannon to be your page. This is a painful adjustment for us all.*" There was no signature, just the royal seal.

Valerian tossed the missive into the fire. He hadn't expected more from his father; they had never been close. King Orland had invested all his time and energy in Waryn, the heir, the perfect prince. Valerian had always known he was the "spare" and that no one expected he would ever have to step into his brother's role. He snuffed out the candle's flame and climbed into the bed, but he left the curtains open.

He lay back on his own pillows, thankful to Gannon for bringing them. It was the only comfort here. Valerian thought of asking Kieran to move his and Gannon's cots into the bedchamber, but he didn't want them to think him a coward. So he buried his face in his pillow and willed himself to sleep. Tomorrow he would need all his wits about him.

Caelis stood outside the door to the king's suite holding a spear with the new grappling hook attached. He raised his hand to knock but paused to study the carvings on the door. The dragon rampant, the emblem of the ruling house, was prominent of course, but the rest of the door's panels contained scenes carved with meticulous detail: a knight battling a dragon, two jousting knights, two others fighting with battle-axes, a king on his throne accepting homage from a kneeling knight. Caelis glanced toward Waryn's door just down the hall. As ornate as that door was, it was nothing compared to the king's.

For a moment, an image superimposed itself in Caelis' mind, a new door with the emblem of his house, the lion rampant. He shook himself and gripped the spear more tightly. If the king would name him heir, Caelis would gladly give up his lion and take the dragon for his own. But first he had to prove himself. He knocked on the door's frame.

A page opened the door and glanced at the spear with bulging eyes.

"Yes, sir?"

"I wish to show this to His Majesty. Will you please let him know I am here?" Caelis smiled at the boy to cover his irritation at having to ask a child for access to the king.

"Yes, sir." The page closed the door.

Caelis inhaled deeply to calm his ire. If and when the king summoned him, he had to remember the pleasantries that were so important in society. The page finally returned, and Caelis shifted his feet in anticipation of meeting with the king.

"The king cannot see you tonight," the boy said. "He asks that you leave the spear and he will examine it and return it to you with his opinion."

A growl threatened to erupt from Caelis' throat. He imagined himself running the spear through the boy's gut. Instead, Caelis handed the weapon to the king's page, sneering when he nearly dropped it.

"Can you manage it?" He forced concern into his voice.

"Yes, sir." The page wobbled, and the spear spun in his small hands. "Thank you, sir."

With his foot, the page shut the door. Caelis stood in front of it for a few moments, clenching his fists. He used to be welcome in this royal tower at any time, day or night. Of course, he almost always visited Waryn's suite, but he did accompany the crown prince to the king's rooms on many occasions. Now he was denied the opportunity to speak to the king and dismissed like a servant. By a page, no less!

Caelis slammed his fist into his palm. He would have to let the king come to him in his own time. Perhaps Orland wished the privacy of his grief tonight. That, Caelis could understand. He backed away from the door in the vague hope the page might rush out and ask him to come in, saying that the king was pleased about the spear.

By the time Caelis reached the stairwell, no one appeared at the king's door, so he quit the tower. His boots pounded the narrow stone steps, echoing in the stairwell. When he emerged, he started toward the armory, nodding at a pair of men-at-arms striding down the hall. But halfway to the armory, Caelis stopped. What more could he do this evening? The armorer's apprentices had to finish making the pieces of his new bow.

Growling, Caelis clenched his fists again. When Waryn was alive there was never any question of how Caelis would spend his evenings. Who else in the Keep was worthy company for him now?

Caelis headed toward the suite of the Lord High Constable. Lewes had recently been named his junior squire. Caelis hadn't had much opportunity to become acquainted with his young cousin. After announcing himself to yet another page, Caelis paced in the hall, fuming. At last the door opened, and Lewes himself invited Caelis inside the sitting room.

The young man bore the Reed stamp of fair skin, yellow hair, and light blue eyes. Caelis' aunt, his father's sister, had been a beautiful woman, and Lewes had inherited her comeliness.

"Shall you be seated, Sir Caelis?" Lewes said, gesturing to a chair near the fireplace.

"Thank you, cousin." Caelis sat and waited until Lewes sat as well. "Are you settling into your new duties?"

"Very well, thank you." Lewes smiled, revealing a dimple in his smooth cheek. The smile vanished while he scanned the room. Then he leaned closer to Caelis and lowered his voice. "I've been anxious to speak with you since I came to the Keep, but my time is not my own, as you well know."

Caelis sat forward and kept his voice quiet. "Are you in any trouble?" His compulsion to protect this young cousin awakened.

"No trouble yet." Lewes stared at Caelis, taking his measure. "On the honor of our family name, can I trust you?"

Caelis' eyes widened, and his belly tightened. What was going on here?

"Of course. I swear by all that is holy you can trust me, cousin."

Lewes glanced around once more and swallowed.

"I am trusting you with my life, Sir Caelis, but I believe you of all people will understand what our Uncle Reed does not." He paused and took a deep breath. "A growing faction in the south desires to be a separate kingdom. I am commissioned to discover highly placed sympathizers in the north."

"You do realize this is treason?" Caelis frowned.

"Yes." His gaze bore into Caelis', making him appear much older than his years.

"What about the king's Seer? All he has to do is read your thoughts and you are dead as well as your conspirators."

"The new Seer is one of us," Lewes smirked. "Sir Caelis, I am prepared to forfeit my life for the cause of southern independence." His gaze hardened. "I would rather die than continue to live under the House of Alden. These northerners have no regard for our concerns in the south."

Caelis sat back, studying his cousin. When had he become such a passionate revolutionary? If Waryn was still alive, Caelis would have been incensed by Lewes' traitorous contempt for the House of Alden. But Waryn was gone, and the ruling family would never be the same. King Orland had revealed a weakness for mercy, and between Valerian, Orland's brother, and the brother's son, there was no capable heir to take Waryn's place.

A page entered the room and bowed to Sir Caelis.

"Lewes, Sir Brandon has need of you." The boy did not leave.

Caelis and Lewes both stood. Caelis held out his hand, and his cousin grasped it.

"My word is my bond," Caelis said. "I will consider what you have said, and we will discuss this further."

"Thank you, Sir Caelis." Lewes bowed gravely and met Caelis' gaze once more before backing away.

The page opened the door and bowed to Caelis. "Thank you for coming, sir," he said.

Caelis nodded and stepped into the hall. His belly roiled, and his knees began to quake. What had he just done? Given his word to a traitor? He should go straight to the king, demand to be heard, and reveal what he'd just learned.

But didn't Lewes' words stir up loyalty to family and the south within him? Even though Caelis still hoped to persuade the king to make him heir instead of Valerian, he was not about to turn on his own family. If Lewes and others felt so strongly about separating from the current ruling house, perhaps Caelis could ally himself with them and demonstrate his superiority over all candidates for king, north and south. Not only would he save the land from the marauding Horde, he could unite the factions in Levathia and prove himself the one most fit to rule them all.

Chapter 9 *You shall decree a thing.*

Mercy entered the dark cottage, set down the buckets, and groped for a candle, flint and steel. She lit the candle and placed it on the table. Her brother huddled in a corner of the room, rocking himself. His braid had come undone, his hair disheveled as if he'd been pulling on it. Alarmed, she rushed to his side.

"Rafael?" He didn't look up. "Rafael! What's wrong?" She gently touched his shoulders.

He flinched as if she'd struck him.

"Rafael." Mercy forced the panic from her voice. "Come to Sissy."

After a moment he stopped rocking and turned toward her. Mercy stifled a gasp. Her brother's eyes appeared vacant. She shuddered and held out her arms in a welcoming gesture.

It seemed an eternal minute, but the light of recognition returned, and Rafael cried out, throwing himself into Mercy's embrace. She sat on the floor and pulled the child onto her lap, rocking him and crooning a lullaby until he relaxed. At last he looked up, his cheeks wet with tears.

"Sissy?"

"Yes, love, what's the matter?"

"Is Papa dead because of me?" Rafael wiped his cheeks.

Mercy's heart skipped a beat.

"Why would you think that?"

"Mama died b-because of me." His breath caught on a sob.

"No! That's not why Mama died."

"But Aunt Prudence said Mama died because I was too big." He put two fingers in his mouth.

How dare her aunt say such a thing in the child's presence! Mercy held Rafael close and started rocking again, this time to calm herself so she could carefully choose her words. She stopped and held Rafael's face between her hands so he had to look at her.

"My dearest brother, do you remember where Sissy had to go yesterday?"

Rafael nodded and removed the fingers from his mouth.

"To help Sister Faith's baby get borned."

"She almost died, but it wasn't the baby's fault."

Rafael's eyes widened.

"Do all mothers die when they have babies?"

"No! Faith lives, and most mothers live to have many babies. Please, Rafael, it was nobody's fault that Mama died."

Rafael sat in silence, and Mercy wondered, *Did I say the wrong thing?* She stroked his head and absently combed his silky hair with her fingers.

"Sissy?"

"Yes, Rafael?"

"Are you going to leave me, too?" He stared at her with a calm that chilled her.

Before she could answer, there was an urgent knock at the door. Rafael slid off Mercy's lap and together they opened the door. Diligence, Grace's young daughter, stood there, wringing her hands. Mercy stepped outside and Rafael followed.

"What's wrong, Dilly?" Mercy asked when tears welled up in the girl's eyes.

"Grandmama fell and hit her head. There is blood everywhere. Please, help her."

"I'm coming." Mercy grabbed her sack of herbs and immediately thought of the bloodroot she'd found earlier. She pulled two of the roots from the bottom of the bucket.

Then she saw Rafael's face. How could she leave him alone again? She just couldn't!

"Go on," she said to Diligence. "I'll be there as fast as I can." When the girl ran off, Mercy went down on one knee and brought her face close to her brother's.

"Rafael, would you like to be Sissy's helper?"

"Oh, yes! I can help you." He actually smiled.

Mercy picked up her sack with one hand, took Rafael's in the other, and together they ran toward their patient's cottage.

Valerian stood in the middle of a grassy field. Enormous white stones encircled it. Beyond were ancient oak trees, their leaves rustling in the breeze.

He lifted the sword in his hands when he heard the whoosh of enormous wings. The ground shook as a mighty dragon landed in front of him. It rose on its back legs, towering over him. The great mouth opened, the beast took a deep breath, and when it exhaled, fire burst from its mouth with the overpowering odor of sulfur….

Valerian startled awake and sat up in the bed. Thoughts and images flashed through his mind too quickly to grasp and examine. They pounded against him, made his head throb. It took him a moment to remember where he was.

His brother's room, his brother's bed.

He'd had that dream about the dragon and the sword again. It was a dream, but it felt so *real*. Had Waryn sent the dream to torment him? Did the dead haunt the living through dreams?

Valerian lay back and closed his eyes. He tried to breathe deeply to calm the pounding of his heart. His head threatened to crack open from all the painful things inside: Waryn's death, Caelis' hate, his father's pressing him to make life or death decisions as crown prince, his unsettling ability to read the thoughts of every person with whom he made eye contact.

One question rose above the cacophony in his mind: How could he fairly punish the Brethren when deep in his heart he agreed with them and envied their choice to follow their conscience?

Gritting his teeth against the throbbing pain, he pulled a robe over his nightshirt and put slippers on his feet. As quietly as he could, he opened the hidden panel behind the bed, identical to the one in his old room, and groped his way down the secret passageway. At the first intersection, he turned right until he came to the door under the tower staircase. From there he was able to descend to the dungeon.

The keeper sat on a chair, snoring softly. When Valerian rattled the metal grate, the man snorted, opened his eyes, and recognized the prince. He stood, wide awake.

"Your Highness? What be your will?"

"I must see the leader of the Brethren."

"Now, Your Highness? 'Tis the middle of the night, is it not?"

Valerian straightened to his full height and glared down at the man.

"If I cannot sleep, then neither shall he."

"O' course, Your Highness." The keeper fumbled with his keys and opened the grated door. "Come this way."

The door closed behind them with a clang. Valerian had never been inside the dungeon before. He hadn't realized how dark and oppressive it would be, cave-like with no windows to let in even one ray of sunlight. In the cold dampness hung the stench of centuries of unwashed bodies.

Imprisonment was intended to crush the spirit from a man. Valerian steeled his heart against compassion for the unfortunate criminals trapped inside these walls. Execution would be preferable to captivity in a foul place like this.

The keeper took a torch from its wall cresset and led Valerian down a narrow passageway. Rough-hewn walls dripped with moisture. Valerian's lungs labored to breathe in the stifling air. The way soon opened into a cavernous single room. Its only light came from the keeper's torch.

Rows of stocks held the pacifists' legs immobile, forcing them to sit on the cold damp stone. Had they been here in total darkness, seated in this uncomfortable position the entire time? No way to get up and relieve themselves? With rats and other vermin crawling over them?

Horrified, Valerian advanced to the nearest group of men.

"Why are they locked up like this?"

"Your Highness, there be many of them and only one of me." The keeper brought the torch closer.

"These are not violent men. They will not harm you." Valerian put as much authority into his voice as he could. "Release them from the stocks."

"But, Your Highness—"

"I said, release them!"

Shrugging, the keeper handed the torch to Valerian. He fumbled with his keys until he found the right one and unlocked each of the stocks. With groans and exclamations of thanks, the Brethren slowly lifted the upper pieces of wood and pulled themselves out. They had difficulty standing.

The keeper took the torch from Valerian.

"Which of you lot is the leader?" said the keeper.

"I am." Gabriel hobbled forward. He inclined his head to Valerian. "Thank you for your mercy, Your Highness."

"You may not have cause to thank me." Valerian gestured for the keeper to stand back and immediately regretted it. He could not see Gabriel's eyes in the gloom and, therefore, could not read his thoughts. He lowered his voice.

"I am ordered to determine your punishment for refusing to fight. How is it just for the king to let you live when others have died to protect their homes and families? Have you no regard for your own women and children?"

Gabriel shifted his feet but otherwise stood calmly.

"Our families understand as we do that there are things much more terrible than death. To break our solemn Oath of Peace is far worse than leaving this life prematurely. We believe that an Afterlife of peace and joy awaits us."

The horror of the two battles Valerian had already experienced flashed in his mind: Waryn's warm blood gushing through his fingers as he died, and Ruddy's severed leg twitching. A fire-breathing dragon reared up inside him.

"How dare you speak of joy and peace while other good men are made to suffer and die performing their duty to king and country? Don't you think I would prefer peace over war?"

Gabriel did not flinch at Valerian's words.

"Then why don't you join us, Your Highness? The way of peace is open to all."

Valerian clenched his fists. It took all his self-control not to strike Gabriel.

"I cannot join you because I have my duty, whether I wish it or no." He whirled away from Gabriel's maddening calmness and confidence. "Keeper! Take me away, but leave a light for these men." Valerian strode out without a backward glance at the Brethren. He couldn't bear to look at them again.

Once he regained his bedchamber, Valerian lit a candle and set it on the large table. He found his stash of blank parchments, quills and ink and sat down, willing his hands to still their trembling. Quickly he began to write in his careful, even script.

"I, Valerian d'Alden, by the grace of God, Prince of Levathia, do decree that the pacifists known as the Brethren, of the Village of Peace in the Southern Woodlands, must forfeit their lives as set forth in the King's Statutes for Times of War because of their refusal to fight to protect the citizens of Levathia against a hostile force invading from Mohorovia."

Valerian did not sign the document. He reread the words he had just penned and shuddered. What a terrible price to pay in order to stay true to their consciences, but Valerian could find no loophole in the laws of Levathia. Disobedience to the king's command was a serious breach during peacetime; it was treason and a capital offense during times of war. If the Brethren were allowed to refuse to fight, wouldn't it make it easier for others to pretend to have a "conscience" against going to war so they wouldn't have to make any sacrifices? What else could he recommended to the king other than their deaths?

He continued to stare at the words until they blurred together. Valerian rubbed his eyes and reread the phrase "forfeit their lives." Something occurred to him. Perhaps there was a way to follow the letter of the law without having to execute all those peaceful men. Valerian took a fresh sheet of parchment and began to write again.

"I, Valerian d'Alden, by the grace of God, Prince of Levathia, do decree that the pacifists known as the Brethren, of the Village of Peace in the Southern Woodlands, must labor as the land's needs dictate for the duration of the war in order to ensure that necessary work does not go undone while other men are taking up arms to protect Levathia from invasion."

There. Involuntary servitude would be sufficient punishment yet vague enough that King Orland would be able to put the Brethren to any task he deemed most needful at the time. Gratefully he signed the decree with a flourish and set his seal below the name.

The sun's rays came in the window, illuminating the parchment. Turning over the first sheet, Valerian set it on top of the stack. He would erase the ink when he returned. After all, parchment was not to be wasted. Kieran quietly entered.

"My lord, I apologize for not rising sooner. What can I do for you?"

"You can come with me to deliver this to the king and then we can break our fast together." Valerian picked up the sealed document. He wanted to get the Brethren out of that miserable dungeon as quickly as possible.

Kieran glanced down at Valerian's nightclothes.

"Do ye not want to change first?"

Valerian almost said he'd wait until after he spoke with the king, but then he remembered the sudden call to arms the other day.

"I ought to be prepared, as you are." He indicated Kieran's leathers and mail. "Then we'll be ready to go to the practice yard after we eat."

Kieran helped him fasten the hard-to-reach lacings on his leather breeches and tunic as well as pull on the mail shirt and boots. They found the page Gannon putting away his and Kieran's cots in the next room. The boy bowed to Valerian.

"Good morrow, Your Highness. What is your will this fine day?"

Valerian smiled at the earnest Gannon.

"Kieran and I must see the king. I'm afraid I've left the bedclothes a mess for you."

"I'll take care of that for you, Sire." The page grinned and hurried into the bedchamber.

Valerian and Kieran left him to tidy the rooms while they went next door and knocked. King Orland's page answered and bowed when he recognized Valerian.

"I must see my father, if he is awake."

The page gestured for them to enter.

"Your Highness, the king is in his bedchamber. Please be seated and I will tell him that you've come." The boy, who was older than Gannon, disappeared into another room.

Valerian sat on the edge of a cushioned bench. This solar was too richly furnished for him to ever be comfortable in it. A cheerful fire crackled in the fireplace, and the curtains had been opened to let in the morning light. The gold threads of one of the tapestries glinted in the light, and Valerian walked to it, seeing it as if for the first time. He'd never before noticed that amid the embroidered dragons there was a man, and the man held a sword. Just like in his dream.

The bedchamber door opened, and the page came out again.

"The king will see you now."

Valerian frowned at Kieran.

"I hope this won't take long."

"Dinna worry about me, Sire." Kieran sighed as he leaned back on one of the chair's overstuffed pillows.

Valerian stepped into his father's bedchamber. His bed was as large as the one in Waryn's room, only the curtains and bedclothes were dyed royal purple. Orland sat in his dressing chair wearing a simple white robe.

"Yes, what is it, Valerian?"

Valerian held out the sheet of parchment.

"I have decreed a punishment for the Brethren."

Orland stood, took the parchment and scanned the brief decree. He met Valerian's gaze, and to his relief Valerian *Saw* his father's surprise and pleasure.

"This is brilliant." He tapped the parchment. "I did not want to have to execute so many able-bodied men. Now I can put them to work in the mines or on a large farm in the south so others will be free to fight with us."

Before either of them could say more, there was a sharp rap at the door. Orland sighed and said, "Enter."

A squire ran in and bowed low. Kieran followed and exchanged a worried look with Valerian.

"Your Majesty, an army approaches from the east." The young man lifted his head. "The Horde is about to attack."

"Why didn't the scouts give us warning?" asked the king.

"Sir Caelis believes they must have been captured or killed."

"Sound the alarm," the king told the squire. "Prepare for battle. Have everyone assemble in the castle yard."

Valerian and Kieran rushed to gather helmets, weapons, and horses, and stood with the rest of the men. Sir Caelis led men and women from the armory, each carrying several of the newly designed spears. King Orland gestured for Caelis to speak. The knight held up one of the spears.

"Since our first encounter with the Horde, the armorers have worked day and night to improve our spears. They have added a grappling hook below the blade to aid you in deflecting the Horde's battle-axes. I regret there has been no time to practice. I will demonstrate." He nodded to one of the armorers, and the man lifted a Horde battle-ax to strike Caelis. The knight caught the blade with the hook and twisted the ax out of the man's grip.

Then Orland led the way to the Keep's gate, riding past the armorers so each man could take a hooked spear until there were no more and simple spears had to be issued instead. The army rode through the town just below the Keep, adding to their ranks townspeople armed with bows or quarterstaffs or pitchforks.

While Valerian rode out the town's eastern gate, he saw the dust kicked up by the approaching Horde. Their army appeared to number several hundred.

"Why," he muttered so only Kieran could hear, "do we keep engaging them in the field rather than force them to lay siege where the Keep's defenses would be far superior to the battle-axes and even the poisoned arrows?"

"The glory of war, Sire." Kieran's smile was grim.

"Glory?" *There is no glory here, only blood and suffering and death.* But when King Orland ordered the charge, Valerian shouted along with the rest over the pounding of his heart and the pounding of Theo's hooves while his faithful warhorse plunged into the fray.

It wasn't difficult to use the new hook on the spear and twist a battle-ax out of the scaly hands of a Mohorovian. Valerian worked with Theo to cut down one enemy at a time. They kept coming, and Valerian's arms ached with the continual effort. He struggled to get his spear in position, and a Mohorovian grabbed the grappling hook, pulling Valerian out of the stirrups. He fell off Theo hard enough to knock the wind out of him. By the time he stood up, disoriented, the Mohorovian advanced on him.

"Valerian!" Kieran shouted as he wheeled his horse to come around.

The Mohorovian swung his ax in an arc that would cut Valerian in half. Valerian backed away but stumbled on a rock, and the ax sliced across his belly with such force that it cut through the mail, the leather tunic, and into his flesh.

Kieran shouted again as his horse trampled the Mohorovian, and then he impaled the creature with his spear. He leaped off the horse and ran to Valerian.

Valerian felt no pain, only spreading warmth in his midsection. The battle raging all around seemed far, far away. As the world grew dark, the last thing he saw clearly was Kieran's horrified face.

Caelis turned his warhorse with his knees and used the grappling hook to pull yet another battle-ax from the grasp of a Mohorovian. The monster roared, and with an answering yell, Caelis impaled the creature with his spear. A handful of the Horde fled toward the east. Caelis couched his spear, prepared to go after them, but King Orland held up a mailed fist.

"Let them go," he said. The king raised the visor on his helmet.

In disbelief, Caelis started to protest, but the grim look on Orland's face prevented him. Why was the king showing mercy when it would be simple to finish them off?

Then Caelis followed King Orland's gaze. A crowd gathered around a fallen man. When some of them shifted Caelis caught a glimpse of a purple surcoat. Prince Valerian. Was he dead or merely wounded? Caelis could scarcely hide his satisfaction.

The king's squire ran to Orland and bowed.

"Your Majesty," the young man said. "The prince is badly hurt. A belly wound." Sorrow wreathed his face.

"Is the battle surgeon with him?" Orland's voice was strained to the point of breaking.

"Yes, Your Majesty." The squire wrung his hands. "They will move Prince Valerian to the infirmary as quickly as possible."

King Orland nodded. Then he sheathed his spear and removed his helmet, handing it to the squire.

"Tell the surgeon I shall meet him in the infirmary."

"Yes, Sire." The squire bowed and returned to the somber group.

After composing his features, King Orland turned his attention to Caelis.

"The grappling hook was effective in disarming the Horde, Sir Caelis." He straightened and inhaled a deep breath. "Ride with me to the Keep."

"Yes, Your Majesty." Caelis signaled Drew and gave the squire his helmet.

They rode at an easy pace past the fallen. The king stared forward, and Caelis kept expecting him to speak, but he never said a word. Though there was much Caelis wanted to say, it was enough that Orland had chosen Caelis to accompany him. After all, the sight of the two of them returning alone, both riding white stallions, would make a memorable impression on all who saw them.

When they reached the stables, King Orland reined in his horse and turned his face to Caelis.

"Thank you, Sir Caelis," he said simply. Then he dismounted and strode into the Keep, alone.

Caelis handed his horse over to a groom and took his spear to the armory for repair. The tip of the blade had broken, though the grappling hook was undamaged. Before he stepped inside the noisy armory, Caelis stopped and calmed himself. If Valerian died, it would make King Orland's dilemma easier, for then the king would not have to choose to disinherit his only remaining son. Caelis wished for the whelp's death, then, even if it would lessen his triumph.

Chapter 10 *As cold waters to a thirsty soul, so is good news from a far country.*

Mercy and Rafael raced to Sister Providence's cottage which she shared with Grace and little Diligence. The girl stood in the doorway waiting for them.

"Please hurry." Tears rolled down her cheeks. "Grandmama has lost so much blood."

The old woman lay on a pallet. Although Grace was trying to clean her mother with rags stained red, blood still bubbled from a deep gash in Providence's head. Mercy moved Grace's hand holding the rag over the wound.

"Put pressure here." Mercy demonstrated for the older woman, grateful Grace didn't question her authority. "Dilly, you and Rafael run back to our cottage and bring the bucket of water there. Careful not to spill too much."

"Yes, Mercy." Dilly grabbed Rafael's hand and they disappeared.

Mercy took a bloodroot from her carry sack. With her small knife she scored the tough outer skin until the vital sap began to flow. Then she turned to Grace.

"Lift your hands now." When Grace backed away, the bleeding began anew. Mercy placed the root on top of the gaping wound. She held it in place and closed her eyes, clearing her mind. Warmth and healing flowed from her hands through the root and into the gash. She could actually *See* the blood clotting!

Once she was sure the bleeding had stopped, Mercy breathed deeply and shook off the echo of euphoria that she had come to associate with the Healing gift. She lifted the root and saw no more fresh blood. Dilly and Rafael had brought the bucket of water, so Mercy washed the open wound before stitching the ragged edges together. Rafael moved closer.

"Sissy, are you sewing Sister Providence just like you sewed the tear in my tunic?"

"Yes, love." Mercy smiled at the comparison.

Rafael gazed up at her with eagerness.

"Will you teach me how to do that?"

"Of course I will." Mercy tied off the thread and snipped it with a tiny blade. "But you must practice on cloth before you can stitch people's skin."

"Okay, Sissy."

"I must take Rafael home now," Mercy said to Grace while she packed her carry sack. "I am gatekeeper tomorrow and must rise early. Please send Dilly if there are any problems in the night, though. I pray your mother wakes up soon."

"Thank you for your help." Grace hugged Mercy, and when she pulled back there were tears in Grace's eyes. "I praise the Most High for your gift."

Mercy and Rafael walked back to their cottage, hand-in-hand. To Mercy's relief Rafael was more like his old self, chattering on about the blood and the stitches and fetching water with Dilly. He wanted to sleep beside her, just as he had as an infant, and she gratefully held him close. They both slept soundly all night.

The following morning Mercy sat at the gate while Rafael divided his time between coming to check on her and playing around the cottage. It was a beautiful autumn day with a crisp blue sky and a slight chill in the air, though the leaves had not yet begun to change color.

A rap at the gate startled Mercy from her mending. She stood on tiptoe to peer through the small peep hole and gasped when she saw a strange man standing there. His left arm was in a sling, and he held the reins of his horse in the other gloved hand. He appeared to be alone.

"What do you want?" Mercy asked, not able to keep the tremor from her voice.

"I have a message from King Orland."

Mercy's heart lurched. Was it good news or bad? Would the men return or, God forbid, were they dead?

With trembling hands Mercy opened the heavy wooden gate. Before her stood the messenger, a young man not many years older than her cousin, Michael. His hair was cut short under his cap. At least he didn't appear to be a soldier.

He handed Mercy a sealed parchment scroll. The wax seal bore the imprint of a dragon.

"What does it say?" She ran her finger over the dragon.

"You'll have to read it to find out."

"I don't know how to read." Mercy gazed up at him.

The young man frowned and gestured around him.

"There must be someone here who can read."

"Only the men of the village, and they were all taken." Mercy remembered then that Sister Providence might be able to read the message, but the poor woman had not yet regained consciousness. She pointed to the man's sling. "What happened?"

"My horse threw me yesterday and I have not yet found a physician." He sighed.

"Do you want me to look at it? I'm a Healer."

The man studied her.

"But you're so young."

"Yes, but I might still be able to help you." Mercy turned away from his frank stare.

When he didn't answer right away, Mercy glanced up. He was staring at his arm, deep in thought.

"I'm sure it's broken, and I must confess I'm not optimistic about finding a physician anywhere nearby. The closest one is probably at Lord Reed's castle." He shrugged. "All right, have a look."

Mercy motioned to her chair. The messenger first secured his horse to the gate post before sitting in the chair. He took the scroll from Mercy and stuck it in his belt. When she removed the sling, he winced. She pushed up his sleeve and saw right away that his forearm was bent at an unnatural angle.

"It's broken, isn't it?"

Mercy heard the anxiety in his voice. It made him seem even younger, and his trust humbled her.

"Yes, but I won't know how badly until I touch it. May I do so?"

He nodded, resigned.

As gently as she could, Mercy encircled his arm with her small hands. Both forearm bones were broken, but only one was out of place. If he took care of it, the arm would heal well.

"I must set the bone in place." She glanced up at him again. "Ready?"

He nodded and steeled himself.

Closing her eyes, Mercy focused only on the two ends of bone. Firmly but gently she eased them into place. Her hands lingered until she was sure that healing blood flowed into the area, helping the ends of bone to knit together. She started to feel faint and heard the man's voice as if from far away.

"Young woman? Are you all right?"

Mercy opened her eyes. The man had a worried look.

"Your face became white, so I was concerned." He held up his arm and opened and closed his fist. "I don't know what you did, but it doesn't feel broken any more."

With a gasp, Mercy examined the arm again. The bones were straight and solid, as if they'd never been injured. Indeed, what had really happened? She'd only meant to set the bone.

He leaned closer and spoke in a reverent voice.

"I saw a light in your hands like the glow of a candle. I could even feel its warmth in my arm. There is some power at work in you."

Before Mercy could answer him, Rafael ran up.

"Sissy! Are you all right? Who is this man? Is that a real horse?"

"Hello." The messenger stood. "Who is this?"

"I'm Rafael. This is my Sissy. Who are you?"

The man took off his cap and bowed with a flourish.

"I am Flint Mallory, royal messenger of His Majesty, King Orland. And this," he slapped his horse on the neck, "is my almost always faithful Taggart."

Mercy couldn't tear her gaze away from Flint's short hair. Although it wasn't the bowl cut that most of the soldiers wore, it was still shorn to his ears.

Rafael didn't seem to notice. He moved closer to the horse and gingerly touched its foreleg. Flint addressed Mercy.

"My orders were to deliver this message. But you can't know what the message says because none of you can read." He patted his arm. "In payment for the good turn you have done for me, I would like for you to call all the villagers together and I will read the message to you. Then I can honestly tell the king I have delivered it."

Rafael turned so quickly he startled the horse.

"Sissy, may I ring the bell?"

"Yes, Rafael," she said with a smile.

He ran off. In a few minutes Mercy heard the distinct clanging and saw the women running to answer it.

"We'd best follow him," she told Flint, "or they will think Rafael has played a prank."

Though her knees wobbled, she managed to keep up with the messenger's long strides. She joined the crowd of women and girls and two young boys close to Rafael's age.

After Flint introduced himself, he broke the seal and opened the scroll. Mercy saw even symbols written with black ink and another of the dragon seals at the bottom. The messenger cleared his throat.

"This says, 'From His Majesty, Orland d'Alden, by the grace of God, King of Levathia, to the women and children of the Village of Peace in the Southern Woodlands: Greeting. This is to inform you that, as punishment for their refusal to obey the king's command to fight with the army of Levathia, the men and older youths of your village have been made subject to the king's will and are working at hard labor in an undisclosed location in the Southern Woodlands until it please His Majesty. You will not learn their whereabouts until their sentence has been completed. But be assured, they were all well when they left the Keep on the new moon last.' And then the king has signed and sealed this at the bottom." Flint held up the scroll so that everyone could see the wax seal.

Two young wives began to weep, but most of the women either smiled or appeared thoughtful. It was certainly better news than they had hoped. A few of them pushed forward and began to ask questions.

"Did you see them?"

"How long will they be punished?"

"Might they return before the winter solstice?"

"Hold your peace!" Flint held up a hand, calling for silence. "I truly know nothing more than what is written here. I am only the king's messenger."

"For this news you have brought us," said Aunt Prudence, "you must stay and let us feed you."

Flint's answer was lost in the general hubbub as daughters, wives, and mothers urged him to sit on a bench in the village green and wait for them to bring food. Rafael attached himself to the young man, pestering him with questions about his horse, but Flint apparently enjoyed all the attention.

"Will your horse let me feed and water him in the sheep pens?" Mercy asked.

"Yes, Taggart is quite gentle." Flint stared at Mercy. "Are you sure you're all right?"

She nodded, though she did still feel faint.

"By the way," he said, "I never heard your name. I'm sure it's something more than Sissy." He patted Rafael's head.

"My name is Mercy."

Flint smiled and indicated his arm.

"Thank you, Mercy."

"And thank you for reading the message to us." She curtsied to him.

While she led the man's horse to the sheep pens, Mercy pondered what it meant that she'd completely Healed the broken arm when she'd only meant to set the bone. Did she control the Healing, or did it control her?

Valerian drifted on a current of shifting darkness and light. In the times of darkness, Waryn and the dragons appeared to him, angry and accusing. During the times of light, however, he saw Kieran's face and sometimes heard his voice, though he could not understand the words.

At last he opened his eyes. When he was able to focus on his surroundings, he was disappointed that he was still alive, that he'd not yet gone on to the Afterlife. Instead he lay on a cot in the Keep's infirmary. How long had he been here?

Valerian tried to push himself upright and cried out from the sharp pain in his belly. He lay back, gasping, trying to make the agony stop.

"My lord!" Kieran appeared at his side, grinning. "You're back with us again."

It was a few moments before Valerian could contain the pain and have breath to speak.

"What happened?" His voice sounded hoarse.

Kieran's smile faded, replaced with a concerned frown.

"Ye were nearly cut in two by a Horde battle-ax."

Images of that last battle came into Valerian's mind. He remembered falling off his horse, the approaching Mohorovian and the ax swinging toward him, but nothing afterward.

"Where's Theo?" Valerian touched his bare midsection and winced at the soreness of the puffy tissue. Rough stitches ran in a ragged line from side to side.

"He's in the stables. I've had someone exercise him for ye every day."

"How long have I been here? And what about the Horde?" Valerian's mouth was so dry, it was difficult to talk.

Kieran held a flask of water to Valerian's lips.

"It's been six days since the battle. There's been no sign of the beasties since then."

Valerian drank the flask dry before speaking.

"Six days. No wonder I'm so hungry."

"Now that *is* a good sign, my lord. Ye need more than the broth I've managed to put down your throat. But you must get up and move around, no matter how much it pains you." Kieran set the empty flask on a table. "I'm here to help ye, Sire, so you can regain the strength you've lost."

How he could possibly raise himself up, much less get out of the cot?

"The easiest way is to turn on your side and roll your way out, if you get my meaning." Kieran moved closer, ready to help.

Valerian sucked in a deep breath and forced himself to turn. He cried out again when his belly threatened to split open.

"You're doing fine, my lord. Now, roll into me and I'll help ye stand."

Valerian did so, unable to contain a cry of agony. He stood leaning on Kieran, gasping.

"Why?" He could barely speak between gasps. "Does it. Hurt. So badly?"

"Possibly because that ax slashed so deeply that your bowels were exposed." Kieran's face was grim. "Only the cut edges of your mail and leathers kept them from spilling on the ground."

Sobered by the close brush with death, Valerian said no more. As soon as the pain subsided, he shuffled alongside Kieran. The squire kept him from falling more than once. How could his legs have become so weak in such a short time?

He was trembling by the time they finished walking the perimeter of the infirmary. There was a chair beside his cot, and Kieran helped him sit there.

"'Twill be easier for ye to get out of the chair than the cot," Kieran said. "I'll fetch some real food for you, Sire. Don't go anywhere 'til I return." He winked and strode from the room.

Valerian sat as immobile as possible. Even with the slightest movement, tiny knives stabbed his belly. He couldn't get the image of protruding bowels out of his mind. It appeared that the Most High was not finished with him yet.

When he heard footsteps he glanced up, expecting Kieran, but it was King Orland.

"Father." Instinctively Valerian tried to rise and cried out at the pain.

Orland frowned. "Should you be up?"

"Kieran says I must in order to heal." He gasped. "It actually hurts less sitting upright than lying in the bed."

Orland sat on the cot, still frowning. His stare unnerved Valerian. Had he done something wrong?

"I do need you mended, Valerian, but make haste slowly and heal properly." The king sighed.

"Is it true, sire, that the Horde have not returned since that last battle?" Valerian tried to take a deep breath and winced.

"Our scouts can find no sign of them." Orland frowned again. "My worry is that they have drawn back into Mohorovia for the winter to breed." He stared at Valerian. "In your reading of history, have you found any references to dragon species and how prolific they might be?"

Valerian tried to remember what he'd read about the many kinds of dragons. In most of the histories they were mentioned, but the focus of the writers was on the heroics of those who killed them.

"There's not much written, but I seem to recall that most species lay clutches of eggs. Since the Horde are obviously reptilian, it would make sense they might breed that way, too." He frowned as he remembered one odd detail. "There's a ballad about Sir Alden finding a nest of eggs after killing the she-dragon. I know ballads tend to exaggerate, but this one mentioned hundreds of eggs in one nest."

Orland took a deep breath and changed the subject.

"As you know, Valerian, I make a progress of the land every year. I wish for you to accompany me on the next one."

"I will be glad to go with you, Father." In truth, he'd always wished to see the rest of Levathia. His knowledge of the land came only from what he'd read and from a large tapestry map that hung in the great hall.

"I need information before that time, however." Orland glanced down at Valerian's midsection and winced again. "As soon as you're able to ride, I want to send you with your squire and a squad of ten men to visit each of the five border garrisons and gather whatever information their scouts have learned."

"Send me, Sire? In command, you mean?" Valerian's heartbeat quickened with anxiety. Would experienced soldiers or knights be willing to follow his orders?

"Yes, Valerian. It's time you learned command, and this is a good place to begin." The king stood. "Consider which ten men from the Keep you wish to take and we will consult together. But for now, follow the physician's orders, and Kieran's suggestions, and heal as quickly as you are able."

“Yes, Father.” Valerian watched the king leave the infirmary, his thoughts tangled with fear and excitement. Who might he choose as part of the ten? He would have to ask Kieran.

By the time the squire returned with food, Valerian was trembling with exhaustion, almost too tired to eat. Kieran must have noticed, because he served Valerian in silence and then helped him lay down. Valerian's last thought as he drifted off to sleep was that he needed to remember to tell Kieran as soon as he awakened about the king giving him his first command.

At a knock on his door, Caelis let Lewes in. He had already sent away Drew and his page on an errand.

“I don't have much time, Sir Caelis.” Lewes pulled a scrap of parchment from his sleeve. “Here are the names you requested.”

Caelis scanned the eight names and nodded. All were bowmen from the southern provinces. He crushed the parchment and strode to the fireplace, tossing it in the flames.

“I will request these men be assigned to me, to assist me while I perfect my new crossbow.” Caelis faced his cousin. “As I get to know them better, I'll make sure of their loyalty to the southern cause.”

“I know we can count on you, Sir Caelis.” Lewes put his hand on the door. “I'd best return to Sir Brandon now.”

Caelis nodded, and the door closed behind the squire. He turned back to the fireplace, leaning on the mantel while he watched the flames. The parchment had vanished, but Caelis remembered each name. Most were already familiar to him, so he did not anticipate any difficulty in securing their loyalty.

He gritted his teeth, thinking about loyalty. He'd been devoted to Waryn and thought he was to King Orland, as well. But the king continued to reveal weaknesses that were unacceptable to Caelis. First, he allowed Valerian and not Caelis the privilege of standing vigil over Waryn's body. Then, he granted mercy to the pacifists when they should have been executed. And today, when Caelis asked if he might take a squad of men to discover why the Horde attacks had not been renewed, the king informed him that he was going to send *Valerian* when the prince had fully recovered from his near-fatal wound. Sending the whelp in *command*! It would be laughable, except it was a slap in Caelis's face after all he'd done for the king.

Waryn would be horrified, if he knew the turn of Caelis' thoughts. He would have called it treason. But was not his father's weakness a betrayal of the ideals that Waryn had shared with Caelis? In their ideal society, mercy and weakness had no place. Only the strong deserved to live, and only the strongest of the strong deserved to rule. So, Caelis was not the traitor; the king and his weakling younger son had demonstrated they were undeserving of their elevated positions granted by the accident of birth.

Caelis opened the door and stepped into the hallway. His heart pounded, and he had to wipe his clammy palms on his breeches. It wasn't too late, he wasn't fully committed; he could still prove his loyalty to the king and the oath he'd sworn as knight by turning in his cousin. He sucked in a ragged breath. If only Waryn was still alive. But he was dead, and everything had changed. Caelis could not remain loyal when the one to whom he'd sworn loyalty had proven his unworthiness.

He squared his shoulders and strode toward the armory. The crossbows should be ready. Caelis need only ask for the eight bowmen. The rest he would decide when the opportunity presented itself.

Chapter 11 *There was given unto him a great sword.*

Mercy kneaded the bread dough with sure hands. She loved the yeasty smell, and the pliable softness gave her the illusion of control over something when so much in her life was beyond her control.

The door opened, and Rafael came in from the sheep pens.

"Sissy, will we have a winter feast this year? Dilly doesn't think we will."

Mercy turned to her brother. Worry creased his brow.

"Do you remember last year's feast?"

He nodded, and his face relaxed with a smile.

"I liked the games, and the food."

Mercy remembered how she and Michael had won last year's berry toss. No matter how she threw the berry, even at the limits of her throwing range, he caught it in his mouth with his hands tied behind his back. The last toss he'd lost his balance, rolled on the ground, and managed to push himself upright. She hadn't been sure if he'd caught the berry, but he stuck out his tongue, triumphantly proving that he had.

Her heart sank. Last year's feast had been her final one to enjoy as a maiden. Even if the men had not been taken away, this year she was betrothed to Gabriel and would not have been permitted to play games with her cousin. She would most likely have been serving food or sitting quietly with other matrons; she was certain the serious-minded Gabriel would never "play" at anything.

But the men were not here. And even if she was too old to play, the younger children deserved that opportunity.

"You can tell Dilly that we *will* have a winter feast this year. I promise."

"Oh, thank you, Sissy!" Rafael threw himself into Mercy's arms.

After he pulled away, Mercy went back to her bread dough.

"When I'm finished with this, why don't we plan for the feast? I'm sure everyone will be thankful to think about something happy."

"Can we play games?"

"Of course."

Rafael clapped his hands.

"And may I help you cook?"

"Of course you may. What would you like to cook?"

Before he could answer, someone knocked. Mercy sighed.

"What now?" She wiped her hands on her apron and opened the door. Diligence stood there, bouncing on one foot.

"Is your grandmother worse?" Mercy asked.

Dilly shook her head.

"No, Sister Mercy. There is a woman at the gate who has brought a sick little girl. She asked for the Healer."

"Tell them we shall be there as soon as possible." Mercy glanced at Rafael.

Dilly ran back toward the gate. Mercy washed her hands, covered her bread dough with a damp cloth, and picked up her carry sack. She held out her free hand to Rafael.

"I'm afraid our feast day preparations will have to wait until after we examine our new patient. Are you ready, my dear helper?"

Rafael sighed and nodded. He held Mercy's hand as they walked to the gate. Mercy wondered where the woman was from and how she knew there was a Healer here. Papa had had no such visits from people outside the village. Could Flint Mallory have told others about his mended arm? What would happen to their quiet isolation if more and more outsiders discovered she was a Healer?

* * *

Through the end of autumn a small but steady stream of people came to the Village of Peace to be Healed. Mercy could not turn them away, but she grew resentful that her chores went undone, and the spotless cottage which had been her pride and joy was no longer tidy.

Rafael didn't seem to mind all the needy strangers, as long as he could help her. Mercy thought she would go mad if she didn't find a moment's peace, and soon. She even began to daydream about leaving, like Serene had done, but reason prevailed. Running away would only create new problems.

It didn't help that Aunt Prudence constantly berated her for the state of her cottage or her appearance without once offering to help. Even the other women tended to avoid her now. More than once Mercy had come upon two or three of them whispering together, and when they noticed her suddenly stopped and walked away. Did they disapprove of her Healing those from the outside? But how could she turn them away? One day Rafael found her weeping and patted her arm.

"Sissy?"

"Yes, love?" Mercy dried her eyes with her apron.

"Why are you crying?"

Mercy sat down and pulled Rafael into her lap. She rocked them both for comfort.

"Sometimes the tears fill me up and they have to spill out. I'm sorry for upsetting you."

"It's okay, Sissy. We've had lots and lots of patients, and it's almost winter feast time. Dilly and me have been getting ready so you don't have to." Though his face was solemn, his eyes shone with contentment and Mercy hugged him.

"Bless you, Rafael, and Dilly too. Perhaps we can still bake some sweet bread in time for the feast."

"Oh, yes!" Rafael grinned. "I love sweet bread."

Mercy counted the days in her head.

"Winter feast is three days from now, so let's plan to make the sweet bread in two days, on Winter's Eve. All right?"

"All right, Sissy." He kissed her cheek and scurried away, happier than Mercy had ever seen him.

On his first excursion outside the infirmary Valerian entered the noisy armory with Kieran. At cluttered benches sat apprentices, as well as nimble-fingered women, hunched over arrow shafts, painstakingly fletching them. Others carved spears, sharpened blades, smoothed bow handles, worked on mail shirts, helmets, greaves.

Valerian spotted Master Murray, the chief armorer, inspecting a yew bow. He squeezed past a large wooden container, Kieran in tow, and they patiently waited to speak to the man.

"A sliver more off the side, if you please." The grizzled armorer handed the bow to another man, who saw Valerian and bent over the wood. Master Murray turned and smiled. "Pardon me, Your Highness," he said, bowing. "How may I assist you?"

Valerian met the man's gaze and *Saw* his patient single-mindedness.

"My squire, Kieran, and I were wondering if you had any ideas for weapons suitable to use against the Horde's battle-axes?"

"Ah, you are not the first to realize a simple spear is not adequate. One reason for adding the grappling hook below the spearhead. That was Sir Caelis' idea."

Valerian remembered how the force of using the modified spear had quickly tired his arms.

"Do you have any other ideas? The Horde's scales are too dense for arrows to penetrate beyond a range of about five yards."

Murray rubbed his stubbly chin and glanced about him.

"Sir Caelis is currently working with one of my apprentices on a modified bow."

"Have you thought of a blade we might use?" Valerian persisted. "Even a battle-ax with a longer reach?"

"Not yet, Sire, but I am open to any and all ideas by those in actual combat. You know better what you're facing than I do." He smiled grimly and pointed to a doorway at the back of the large room. "You and your squire are welcome to look through the stores. I throw nothing away."

"Many thanks." Valerian and Kieran made their way through the clutter to the storeroom. They took unlit torches from their cressets on either side of the door. Kieran lit his from the bellows fire and touched it to Valerian's. Together they entered the musty, windowless room. There were piles of broken spears and bows, all manner of wood and metal scraps, as well as shelves, wooden crates, and several trunks lining the walls.

"Why don't we each take a wall," said Kieran. "We could look through those containers twice as fast."

Valerian nodded and opened the nearest crate. He quickly determined there was nothing of use in that one as well as the others along that wall. After despairing that this errand was a waste of time, Valerian spied a trunk behind another stack of crates. The latch was broken, but the trunk was very old and intricate in design. Trembling with excitement, Valerian cleared everything on top of it and blew away a layer of dust settled in the crevices of the carved lid.

He gasped. There was a dragon in the emblem, the sign of the royal house.

"Kieran! Come and see."

His squire left his rummaging to stand beside him.

"That trunk looks very old indeed, my lord."

Valerian handed his torch to Kieran and lifted the lid. Inside, lay a moth-eaten fur robe lined with an embroidered hem.

"I'm sorry for interrupting your search." Valerian didn't bother to hide his disappointment. "I was sure this ancient trunk would hold something useful."

"Perhaps it does yet, Sire." Kieran lowered one of the torches. Something metal reflected in the light.

Valerian pushed aside the fur and discovered not one but two leather scabbards. From each protruded the hilt of a sword.

"I have read about these," Valerian said, remembering the tapestry in King Orland's room as well as his own recurring dream. "Swords were once widely used as weapons, but they were not effective against Levathia's many large dragon species, so they were replaced with bow and spear."

He reverently lifted the top scabbard. It had dragon designs worked into the leather. When he held it up, the shape of the hilt formed a cross. Did the design have any religious significance or was it merely functional? He took hold of the hilt below the crosspiece. The haft fit perfectly in his hand. Slowly he slid the sword from the scabbard and raised the blade upright. Kieran studied the blade by the torchlight.

"It looks clean, Sire. No tarnish after resting here who knows how long."

"I wonder if it's still sharp?" The blade was double-edged. Would it be effective from horseback as well as in hand-to-hand combat? There was only one way to find out.

They retraced their steps through the clutter and replaced the torches in the cressets beside the doorway. Master Murray conferred with an apprentice, and they made their way toward him. He turned his head and saw the scabbards. With a nod, he left his apprentice.

"Aha! I have been wondering what happened to those blades, Your Highness." He held out his hands and Valerian placed the scabbard across them. The armorer first inspected the leather and then pulled out the sword, examining it with a critical eye.

"Do you know what this is, my prince?" Murray glanced at Valerian, looking pleased.

"I know it's a sword, and a beautiful one at that." Valerian tore his gaze away from the blade. "It must be very old."

Murray nodded. "There is no one alive who remembers the craft of making them, although I have found some notes left by my predecessor." He smiled. "This very sword belonged to your ancestor, Alden the Great."

Valerian gasped. Alden himself had used this blade *three centuries* ago.

"May we take these?"

"Of course, Your Highness. Let me sharpen the blades, although I would caution you not to actually use them until you have learned the techniques."

"How will we do that if no one has used them for centuries?" Valerian stared at the blades in Murray's hand.

"Years ago I found an old scroll detailing the proper way to use a sword, and I gave it to the monks in the library for safekeeping." The armorer took the swords to the grindstone.

Valerian spoke to Kieran while he watched Master Murray.

"I'll find that scroll, and then we should find a place to practice away from prying eyes." An image of Sir Caelis came to his mind.

"I have an idea, Sire, that will give us practice time and help you get ready for a long journey on horseback."

Valerian turned to Kieran.

"Long journey?"

"Your first command, remember?" The squire grinned.

Valerian nodded, and his throat tightened. How could he forget?

* * *

Two days later Kieran had made preparations for them to leave the Keep for an excursion. Valerian found himself in Theo's stall wondering how he would pull himself up to the saddle. Since being cut open by a Horde battle-ax, he had discovered how many simple movements he'd taken for granted required intact belly muscles.

"Here, Sire," said Conrad, the groom. "I'll get ye a bucket to stand on."

That would be fine for mounting this time, but what about dismounting? And the next time he needed to get back on the horse?

Valerian stepped onto the overturned bucket, and Conrad boosted him the rest of the way to Theo's tall back. The scar tissue pulled with discomfort, but thankfully the knife pains had dulled.

"How does that feel, Your Highness?"

"It feels good, Conrad." Valerian nodded at the young man. "Very good, in fact."

The groom pulled his forelock in salute and backed away so Valerian could guide Theo from the stall. Kieran was waiting astride his bay.

"Are you ready for an adventure, Your Highness?"

"As ready as I'll ever be." Valerian shifted a little in the saddle.

They rode from the Keep, through the town, and then followed the northern road skirting the lake. Townspeople and farmers on the road saluted them as they passed.

Valerian breathed deeply of the crisp autumn air. The sky was a brilliant blue, and many of the trees had turned fiery red, orange, or yellow. He relished the outdoors after so many weeks in the infirmary. Theo's gait was steady, and although Valerian hunched in the saddle, clutching his belly to ease the jolts, it was a pleasure to ride again.

After an hour or so, Kieran turned his bay off the road, and Theo followed. The horse had to change his gait as they climbed in altitude, and once Valerian hissed through his teeth as his scar pulled sharply. By the time they reached a protected glen on a broad hilltop, Valerian was panting.

"Here we are, Sire." Kieran slid down from his horse. "You'll not find a more bonny place in all the north."

Valerian tried to take a deep breath, but he could not straighten himself in the saddle. He feared that if he tried to dismount by himself he would fall and split open his scar.

"Kieran," he managed to say.

"Right here, me prince." Kieran helped him get off the horse and braced him when he nearly fell.

"Why am I so tired?" All he wanted to do was lay down and sleep for a week.

"Just lean on me and I'll show you a place to rest."

Valerian gratefully submitted to Kieran while he led him to a nearby grove of trees. He heard the burbling of a mountain stream and the cry of a hawk overhead. Within the dappled shade lay a moss-covered fallen tree. Kieran helped him sit there.

"Catch your breath, Sire, and I'll take care of the horses."

Valerian sat as still as he could, closed his eyes, and listened to the water while he tried to breathe deeply. In and out. In and out. In time his belly muscles relaxed and the pain subsided.

"Don't move, Val." Kieran's voice was an urgent whisper that made Valerian's gut tighten in alarm.

Kieran slowly approached him, and Valerian searched the area frantically, expecting to see a river dragon, or worse. Kieran lightly brushed his shoulder, and a hairy spider the size of his hand scurried away.

Valerian exhaled in relief.

"Is that all?"

"Most folks dinna like the beasties." Kieran shrugged.

"I was expecting a river dragon, at least." Valerian turned to Kieran. "Do you realize I've never actually seen one?"

Kieran squatted down, toying with a stick.

"Well, then, we should remedy that."

A barrier had grown between them, and Valerian thought he knew what it was. "Do you realize you called me 'Val' just now?"

Kieran fell to his knees and bowed his head.

"Forgive me, Your Highness. I had no right to take such liberties. I'm not even sure why that jumped out o' me mouth."

"There is nothing to forgive." When Kieran lifted his head, Valerian smiled at him. "Only two others have called me 'Val': my grandfather, and Sir Rudyard, who was my mentor." He sighed. "I have not had many friends in my life. It's lonely being a prince. There's always an unspoken barrier between a royal and everyone else."

"I count it a great honor to be your squire, Your Highness. I hope I may also become your friend." Kieran stared boldly at Valerian, inviting him to *See* his sincerity.

Would Valerian ever deserve such loyalty? He had to clear his throat before speaking.

"It is I who am honored to have you for a squire," he said quietly.

"Well then, my bonny prince," said Kieran with a grin. "Let me show ye how a true friend helps ready you for your first command."

* * *

For the next two weeks, Kieran was relentless in his exercise program. They ran up and down the hills, swam in a cold deep pool, and rode their horses twice a day. Kieran found sticks about the length of the swords, and using the scroll Valerian found in the library, they learned basic sword positions. At first they moved slowly, learning how to attack and defend, thrust and parry, until the movements became second nature. Each of them sported bruises, but they slept well each night under the stars wrapped in their furs. Kieran taught Valerian the names of several constellations, and Valerian began to see the Archer, the Herdsman, and the Dragon as friendly lights in the velvet black sky.

Kieran had brought some provisions, but they ate mainly from the land. There were fish in the stream, small game in the woods, and late berries ripe for the picking. Valerian's strength gradually returned, though his healing muscles still protested with stabbing pains. There was even quiet time to reflect on his grief for Waryn and deal with the loss.

By the time they cleaned up their campsite and packed the horses for their return to the Keep, Valerian believed himself ready to meet the challenge of his first command. He and Kieran had even discussed which ten men of the Keep he should choose to take with them.

"If the king allows, we should give a demonstration of our sword moves," Kieran said as he boosted Valerian to Theo's saddle.

Surely not a public demonstration? Sir Caelis would have something to say about that. But Valerian pushed the knight's potential objections aside. It was time to stop letting Caelis intimidate him.

Caelis sent his fourth bolt into the bull's eye of the target in the archery yard. Even shooting three times the distance of a regular bow, he could hit the bull's eye nearly every time. He gripped the new crossbow and turned to his new men, grinning.

"Well done, Sir Caelis," said Thrane, who had made himself Caelis' shadow of late.

Even though Thrane was tall and broad-shouldered with a scar on his face from an old knife wound, he had a knack for blending in with a crowd and making himself unremarkable. He was a fair archer, but his passion for the cause of southern independence made up for any lack in fighting skills. In the course of a few weeks, Thrane had helped Caelis shape the men into a formidable unit of crossbow archers.

Unfortunately, the Horde had not attacked again so Caelis could put the crossbow to the test. Caelis chafed at the delay, but when he'd again asked the king if he could take his men and scout the border, he was dismissed. The king wanted to wait until Valerian was able to do it.

After spending weeks in the infirmary, the prince and his squire were now out somewhere, training. If Caelis knew where they'd gone, he would be tempted to follow them. Then he might be tempted to arrange an accident. No, it was best he remained here in the Keep where all the lords and ladies admired his uncanny ability with the crossbow, even if King Orland didn't.

Remembering his crowd of admirers, Caelis turned and gave them a courtly bow and a dazzling smile. Then, he handed his crossbow to Drew, directed the men to gather the bolts, and strode back to the Keep, alone.

* * *

That night sleep would not come. Caelis' discontent coiled within him, like a serpent ready to strike. He sat up on his narrow bed and raked his hair with his fingers. Beyond the door Drew and the page slept on their cots in the sitting room.

Caelis swung his legs over the edge of the bed. This bedchamber wasn't much more than an alcove with a door, but Waryn chose this room for him after they were knighted because it was situated beneath the crown prince's suite and connected to it by a secret stairwell. Waryn supposed it was originally built into the Keep as an escape route for the royal family, but during the years of their friendship it had been a fast way to contact one another.

Whether or not he should have, Waryn had shown Caelis all the secret passages in the royal tower. While the new occupant of Waryn's suites was away from the Keep, Caelis had an urge to revisit the room one more time, since Valerian was not likely to invite him.

As quietly as he could, Caelis pushed the bed away from the back wall. Then he fumbled for the latch and slowly pressed it. The door opened into the dark stairwell. Caelis thought about bringing a torch, but decided against it. He did pull on his breeches, belt, and boots and place a knife in the sheath on his belt. One could never be too careful.

He entered the stairwell and pushed the door closed. Treading slowly in the absolute darkness, Caelis steadied himself against the curved outer wall. When he reached the landing above, he groped again for a latch and pulled open the door. Waryn's bed, of course, was not pushed far from the wall, so Caelis had to sidle between the headboard and the wall to work his way around. Finally, he stood in the middle of the familiar room.

After the blackness of the stairwell, the moonlight streaming through the window made everything recognizable. Nothing had been moved. Except for the deathly quiet, Caelis could imagine Waryn striding through the door from the sitting room with a wide smile and a warm welcome. A stab of grief startled Caelis, and he gasped.

He walked toward the window seat and paused at the large table, where he and Waryn had shared many meals. Now it contained a stack of parchments, a pot of ink, and quill pens. Of course. The monk lived here now. Caelis lifted his hand to sweep all of it from the table. But he couldn't do that; Waryn's page was surely asleep in the other room and would hear the noise. He did lift the top sheet, which lay crookedly, and turned it over. To his surprise, there was writing there.

Caelis took the parchment to the window and held it under the bright moonlight. When he read the words penned by Valerian, his eyes widened in surprise. He didn't think the whelp had the nerve to order anyone's execution. Of course, he obviously didn't because the king had ordered the Brethren imprisoned instead. Then why didn't he destroy this document? Caelis grunted. Valerian had probably not been back to this room since his injury weeks ago. He might have already forgotten about it. Caelis gazed out the window.

"Sir Caelis?"

He whirled at the sound of the page's voice. The boy stood in the doorway, illuminated from behind by the light from the fireplace.

"Yes, Gannon?" Caelis kept his voice calm.

"You should not be here, sir. These are Prince Valerian's rooms now."

Caelis narrowed his eyes. He'd had enough from cheeky pages of late.

"I know that." He tried to keep the irritation out of his voice. "I just wanted to visit this room one more time before the prince returns." Caelis feigned a catch in his voice in order to touch the page's sympathy. "I grieve for Prince Waryn."

Gannon balled his fists on his narrow hips.

"Then what are you doing with the prince's things?" The page pointed at the parchment in Caelis' hand. When Caelis didn't answer right away, Gannon stepped forward and lifted his chin. "I will have to tell the king about this."

Caelis first set down the parchment with a trembling hand. Then he glowered at the arrogant page. "How dare you?" He lunged forward and boxed the boy's ears. "You are but a page!"

He didn't have the chance to finish his tirade, for Gannon's eyes rolled back in his head, and he went limp, collapsing to the floor. Frowning, Caelis went down on one knee and put his hand on the boy's chest. The small heart beat its last under Caelis' palm, and he gasped. He had only intended to discipline the boy, but who would believe him when it became known he'd let himself into the rooms of the crown prince without permission?

His own heart pounding, Caelis lifted the small body. Should he hide it? No, that would only raise more questions. He glanced around the room. The garderobe. Servants had fallen down the shafts before and drowned in the middens below. This was only a page, after all.

Caelis dropped the body head first, and seconds later heard a faint plop. No one could connect the boy's death to him. He wiped his hands on his tunic and strode back to the table. After all this trouble, he might as well take the parchment. It might later prove useful.

He left the door to the sitting room open, to make it more plausible the boy fell into the bedchamber's garderobe while using the necessary. Then he slipped into the secret entrance, closing the door behind him.

Chapter 12 *He that troubleth his own house shall inherit the wind.*

Mercy opened the cottage door and gasped. It was Papa! She rushed to embrace him, but stopped at the look on his face.

"You're back," she said timidly.

"That is obvious." His scowl deepened. "What are you doing?"

Mercy gestured to the loaves of sweet bread she and Rafael were decorating.

"Tomorrow is the winter feast, Papa. Rafael is helping me make something for the gathering."

"How can you think of celebrating at a time like this?"

Mercy blinked away the tears that came to her eyes. Papa had been little more than a slave the last few months, but that made his anger hurt even more. Didn't he think about what the women and children had suffered in the men's absence?

"Have you been released from your servitude?" she asked.

"I'll explain later. Brother Gabriel comes directly. Make yourself presentable."

"Yes, Papa." Mercy pulled on her overdress and braided her hair with trembling fingers. As she tied on her kerchief, her fingers fumbled with the knot. Rafael had not moved or said a word since Papa entered.

A quiet knock sounded at the door. Papa opened it, and without a word Gabriel stepped inside. His intense eyes met Mercy's, and he *Saw* her thoughts. It was never a comfortable feeling, but she determined not to fear her future husband.

"May the God of Peace bless you for that," he said with a smile, causing her to blush. "Both of you, be seated."

The three of them sat on the stools at the table.

"Have you told her anything, Brother Joel?"

Papa shook his head.

"I only just arrived myself."

Gabriel faced Mercy. Though his eyes bore into hers, he did not use his Sight again, for which she silently thanked him.

"We were imprisoned at the Keep while the king's son was given the task of determining our punishment."

"In prison?" Mercy frowned. "But I thought you were working somewhere in the Southern Woodlands. The king sent a messenger to tell us."

"Silence, daughter." Papa crossed his arms.

Gabriel held up a hand to Papa.

"Yes, we were sent to a large holding of Lord Reed's and have been there until today, when we were allowed to return to the village."

Mercy glanced at Papa but risked speaking to Gabriel.

"Did the king say you had completed your sentence?"

Papa scowled, but Gabriel continued before he could say anything.

"His exact words were that our three months' labor was sufficient payment for the three battles in which we did not fight, but should the fighting resume, then we will be returned to our labors."

"I don't understand why you had to labor at all." Mercy shook her head. "Didn't you explain to the king about the Oath?"

"Daughter! You speak of matters you know not of!" Papa raised himself off the stool, and for a moment Mercy feared he would strike her. She had never seen him so angry before.

Gabriel restrained him until he sat down again.

"Peace, Brother Joel. You must not allow your anger and bitterness to consume you. Sister Mercy has a right to know what we are dealing with."

Once Papa had settled down, Gabriel leaned closer to Mercy. He had never seemed so eager to share anything with her before. It was unnerving but gave her hope, too, that perhaps their marriage could become a true partnership.

"According to the laws of Levathia, we are disobedient to the king's requirement that all able-bodied subjects must fight in his army. But according to the laws of the God of Peace, we cannot fight. Therefore, we must obey God's laws over those of the king. That is what I explained to him."

"Then why did the king have his son determine your punishment?" Mercy frowned.

"Only the king himself has the power of life and death over his subjects, which I suspect is the reason he gave this task to the prince." Gabriel smiled. "I don't believe the king wanted to have us executed."

"Executed?" Mercy gasped. "Simply for following your conscience?"

"For *not* following the king's command." Gabriel's face became thoughtful. "I can understand better, I think, why the king must sometimes be harsh in his rule. If he were to allow even one man to disobey his law, would that not open the floodgate for all men to disregard the rule of law? The result would be disastrous for the entire kingdom."

Mercy tried to grasp what Gabriel was saying.

"So it was the prince who ordered you to become slaves instead."

He nodded and folded his hands upon the table.

"It was actually a quite reasonable way for the king to save face."

"Reasonable?" Papa said. "How is it reasonable for a Healer to have to dig ditches from sunup to sundown, seven days a week?"

Mercy winced and covered her ears. Papa had never shouted so loudly.

"Please, Brother Joel," Gabriel said. "You must control yourself."

Papa growled and stood. Then he went outside, slamming the cottage door.

Mercy saw the hurt in Rafael's eyes. His lower lip trembled.

"Come here, Rafael," she said with outstretched hands.

He jumped up and ran to her. She held him close and scooped him into her lap. He put two fingers in his mouth while Mercy rocked him.

"I'm sorry, Brother Gabriel," she said. "Please continue."

He stared at her with a pleased smile and continued to stare until she had to look away.

"Forgive me," he said. "It's just that, after what we have experienced in the last few months, seeing you is like a drink of cool water to a man dying of thirst."

Mercy's cheeks flushed. Gabriel had never said anything like that to her before.

"I'm just thankful that you all have come home."

Gabriel offered his hand. Swallowing, she placed her small hand in his larger one. He gripped it gently.

"Your father is having a difficult time forgiving the king and his son for the indignities he has suffered."

Mercy nodded, but her throat was too choked to answer.

"I don't believe he will lose control, but if you fear for yourself or the child, please tell me and I will talk to him. He still respects me or at least my authority."

Mercy tried to hold them back, but tears spilled onto her cheeks and she pulled back her hand, horrified for him to see her weakness. Gabriel waited quietly while she dried her eyes, still rocking Rafael.

"I'm sorry," she whispered.

He shook his head and smiled again.

"No need for that. Will you tell me what you have been doing while we were absent?"

Shyly at first, Mercy told Gabriel all that had happened, including Serene's departure, the coming of the king's messenger, and last of all that she had discovered her gift of Healing. His eyes brightened at the news.

"Praise the God of Peace!" he said, his voice exultant. He invited her to hold his hand again, and this time he cupped it between his own and bowed his head.

"Oh, God of all Peace, may You bless this Your child as she uses the gift of Healing You have bestowed upon her." Then he tenderly kissed her hand and released it.

Mercy studied Gabriel's face, seeing it as if for the first time. He was not truly handsome, not compared to her cousin, Michael. But Gabriel had a noble mien and was pleasant enough to look upon. Not, she chastised herself, that the outward appearance was as important as what was in the heart. After all, Sister Providence had long ago lost whatever beauty she'd had in her youth, but the old woman possessed so much inner beauty it put Mercy to shame.

"May I ask," Mercy said, "what 'indignities' was Papa talking about?"

For the first time, Gabriel seemed reluctant to speak about what happened.

"In the prison we were put in stocks for two days."

"Stocks? Is that anything like our pillory?"

Gabriel's mouth was grim.

"Yes, but with several great differences. The prison was underground, and there were no windows. The air was difficult to breathe."

"What other differences?" Mercy asked when Gabriel didn't continue.

"Where the pillory holds one's head and arms immobile, stocks are for the legs." Gabriel took a deep breath. "There were rats. Big ones. And because we were trapped like that for two days—"

"Two days?" Mercy gasped. How could they have endured sitting immobile with rats crawling on them for so long? "The king's son ordered that? No wonder Papa is so angry. I would hate him, too."

"Sister Mercy." Gabriel suddenly reverted to the stern village leader, and it made her want to cry. "You must not hate or it will turn and consume you, as it has your father. The prince merely ordered us imprisoned. When he came to the dungeon and discovered our condition, he immediately had us released from the stocks and commanded light be provided."

"You had no light?" she whispered. "Not even a ray of sunlight?"

Gabriel shook his head, his eyes distant.

"Truly the dungeon was a tomb of death and decay."

Mercy shuddered. Gabriel's words showed that whatever difficulties she'd endured in the absence of the men, it was nothing compared to what they'd experienced.

"How long did you have to stay in the dungeon?"

"No more than a week. It seemed much longer than seven days, but time moves slowly in a place like that." He smiled at her again.

Mercy marveled that his reaction to the situation was so different from Papa's. In fact, Gabriel was so altered by the experience she hardly knew him. Before, he had been somber, rarely smiling, and she had feared that as her husband it would be impossible to please him. But now he fairly glowed with an inner joy she found both puzzling and exhilarating. Would she have found such joy in the midst of suffering?

He stood and Mercy gently slid Rafael from her lap so she could stand also.

"I would prefer to stay here in your company, dear sister, but there are many things I must do." His eyes searched hers, and he *Saw* her thoughts again.

"I hope I may see you at the feast tomorrow?" Mercy became suddenly shy. Rafael leaned closer to her to better hear Gabriel's answer.

"Of course. A celebration will help lift everyone's spirits." He gently touched her cheek as he continued to gaze into her eyes.

For a moment, Mercy thought he might kiss her, but he merely smiled and backed toward the door.

"Until tomorrow then?" She wanted to say more; she was reluctant for him to leave.

"Yes, my dear sister. Peace be with you." He left her then, closing the door behind him.

Mercy stared at the door, marveling that Gabriel was an entirely different man. With him she knew she'd be safe and secure. This cottage was no longer a haven. She sighed and turned. Rafael stood where she'd left him, bewildered. She sat on the stool again, and he climbed back to her lap.

"What do you think of him, Rafael?"

"He is much nicer than he was before. And Sissy?" He gazed up at her.

"Yes, love?"

"I think he likes you very much." He sounded so much like a wise old man that Mercy laughed.

"I hope he likes me, Rafael. After all, I will be his wife after three new moons."

Rafael went rigid.

"Will I have to stay here with Papa when you get married?"

Mercy made sure he was looking into her eyes so he would know her words were true.

"No. You will live with Gabriel and me. We will all be together."

And Papa may visit us if he will behave himself.

As soon as Valerian and Kieran rode into the Keep, they were intercepted on their way to the stables by one of King Orland's pages.

"Your Highness," the boy said with a bow. "The king wishes to see you right away."

Valerian glanced at Kieran and shrugged. Then he nodded at the page.

"Tell His Majesty we will attend him presently."

The page bowed again and raced back to the Keep.

"He must o' been watching for you, Sire." Kieran dismounted and gave the reins to a groom.

"My father must be anxious about something." Valerian frowned. "Could the Horde have attacked in our absence?" When he handed the reins to Conrad, the groom shook his head.

"Nay, Sire. There's no sign of the Horde." Conrad waited beside Theo, but Valerian managed to slide down unaided. "Your Highness appears to have recovered." The groom removed Theo's bridle.

"Yes, thank you, Conrad. My squire has the gift of making the impossible possible."

Conrad grinned and saluted Kieran, who laughed.

"Now, Sire, dinna give me so much credit. Ye are amazingly strong to have come so far after such a dire injury."

Valerian made the mistake of looking directly at Conrad and *Saw* the admiration and respect the groom had toward him. Valerian turned away, embarrassed by the praise and uncomfortable at breaching the young man's privacy. Even though most of those he'd *Seen* did not realize their thoughts were exposed to him, Valerian desperately wanted to find a way to set limitations on himself.

While Valerian and Kieran entered the Keep and made their way to King Orland's apartment, they met many lords, ladies, knights, and servants. After their initial surprise upon seeing the prince in radiant health, each stared at the unfamiliar weapons hanging from his and Kieran's belts. Valerian wondered why the population of the Keep had increased until he realized it was the first day of the twelfth month and nearly time for the winter feast. Kieran leaned close so only Valerian could hear him.

"You are certainly making a memorable entrance upon your return, Your Highness."

"I certainly did not intend to do so." Valerian smiled at Kieran. "Perhaps it is my bonny squire who turns so many heads."

Laughing, Kieran stopped and bowed with a flourish.

"Aye, perhaps ye have it there, Sire."

They were still laughing when they knocked on King Orland's door. A page admitted them, and the king warmly greeted them.

"Be seated," Orland said. Valerian sat across from his father, but Kieran hesitated. "You too, MacLachlan." The king gestured to the chair beside Valerian.

While Kieran carefully lowered himself to the seat, Valerian adjusted his scabbard so it wouldn't scratch the wooden arms of his chair. His father pointed to the scabbard.

"What, pray tell, is that, Valerian?"

"I'm glad you asked, Father. Before we left, we found these in the armory." He pulled Alden's sword from the scabbard and laid it across his palms to show the king. Orland studied it thoughtfully. He reached for the hilt, looking to Valerian for permission.

"Go ahead, Father. This very sword belonged to our ancestor, Lord Alden."

The king raised his brows in surprise. He gripped the hilt and lifted the weapon, inspecting the blade.

"Careful, Father. Master Murray sharpened the blade. The edge is so sharp Kieran and I haven't yet had the nerve to use them." He grinned at his squire.

"What do you mean?"

"Using an old scroll from the library and sticks instead of the actual blades, we've taught ourselves the basic moves of how to use these swords in hand-to-hand combat. We believe they would be effective against the Horde's axes and would like to give a demonstration."

Orland sighed and returned the blade to Valerian.

"I'm afraid that will have to wait. I need you to leave immediately for the border garrisons. Have you chosen your ten men?"

Valerian returned the sword to the scabbard. He could not hide his disappointment. Somehow he had to show his father what marvelous weapons these swords were. But it appeared he would have to be patient.

"Yes, sir. Kieran has my list."

The squire fumbled in his belt pouch and pulled out a small roll of parchment that represented hours of discussion on his and Valerian's part. Kieran gave the roll to the king, who scanned the list of names and nodded.

"This is excellent, Valerian. You have chosen steady youths and two, no, three older, more experienced men. Sir Gregory will be especially valuable to you." He handed the list to Kieran. "Summon these men to the hall where we will dine together this evening, and then I want you to leave at first light. Everything has been prepared."

"Tomorrow?"

"Yes, Valerian. I know this means you will be away from the Keep for the winter feast, but I cannot wait until after."

Valerian inclined his head to hide his panic. He didn't mind being absent during the feast days, but he wasn't sure how he could prepare himself to take command on such short notice.

"You need only rest until this evening." Orland stood, and Valerian scrambled to stand also.

"Yes, Father." Valerian and Kieran bowed and started to leave.

"One more thing, Valerian." Orland's mouth tightened. "You will not find the page, Gannon, in your rooms."

"Why, Father?"

"The poor lad was found drowned in the castle middens." Orland folded his hands to contain his discomfort. "Apparently he fell into the shaft while cleaning the garderobe."

Valerian glanced at Kieran, stricken. Though he hadn't known the boy well, one couldn't help but like his cheerful disposition and eagerness to please.

"Thank you for telling me, Father." Valerian fled before the king could say more. He and Kieran walked to his adjoining rooms in silence. How did his father expect him to *rest* after news like that?

* * *

Later that evening, Valerian entered the hall at his father's right hand. Kieran had dressed him in a black velvet doublet. He wore a jeweled chain around his neck and his circlet of rank upon his brow, while King Orland was even more elaborately attired.

Kieran stood with the other ten men while they waited for Valerian and his father to be seated first, the king at the head and Valerian to his right. Kieran took the seat beside him, and Sir Gregory and his squire, Terron sat opposite them. Valerian noted that the five Highlanders sat on Kieran's side in order by age, since none of them held rank, and the other three men sat on Sir Gregory's side. He said a silent prayer that he would be able to lead these men without making a complete fool of himself.

While pages served heaping platters of food, Orland asked about Sir Gregory's aged father. That gave the other men permission to talk among themselves. Kieran had an animated conversation with those further down the table, and Valerian envied his easy way with people. Valerian smiled when he caught Terron's eye, for the squire appeared almost as uncomfortable as he felt. He *Saw* the young man's nervousness at traveling the length of the border after the recent bloody battles with the Horde.

"What think you, squire?" he asked Terron. "Will we see any sign of the Horde on this journey?"

"I must confess, Your Highness," Terron said, "I hope we do not run into an ambush with our small number."

"Dinna worry about that, lad." The man seated beside Kieran, Quinlan MacNeil, had a surprisingly deep voice for a man of his slight stature. "After all, 'tis not the number but the ability of the men who stand with you." He leaned back so he could see Valerian. "By the way, Your Highness, my thanks for what ye did for my cousin, Ruddy. I know 'twill be difficult for him, but ye did save his life."

"He would have done the same for me. Sir Rudyard is an excellent knight and mentor." Valerian noticed everyone had grown quiet, watching him. When he glanced at his father, the king nodded for him to speak. Valerian cleared his throat.

"I want all of you to know how grateful I am to band together with you for this scouting mission. Even though we are primarily to gather information on the Horde, we will travel prepared to fight if necessary. I'll need volunteers to ride as front and rear guards. At night, we'll take turns on watch when we camp between garrisons. The safe return of each of you is most important to me."

While he spoke, Valerian glanced from man to man, deliberately not making direct eye contact. Observing how they all listened attentively made him hope they would give him a chance to prove himself, at least, though he was younger than every man present except for Terron.

Quinlan MacNeil began to beat on the table with the flat of his hand. The rest of the Highlanders joined in his rhythmic thumping, including Kieran. When the others realized it was a sign of approval, they added their hands to the noisy accolade. Valerian's face grew warm as the king caught his eye and smiled.

Once the room became quiet again, King Orland lifted his goblet.

"I salute you and wish you success on your journey."

All the men stood and lifted their goblets to the king.

"Long live the king!" Sir Gregory shouted. The shout was echoed by the others, and as one they drained their goblets. "We should get a good night's rest now," the knight said.

"Hear, hear," added a voice down the table.

With bows and parting words, the men drifted out toward the barracks, leaving Valerian alone with his father and Kieran.

"A word with you before you go." Orland stood and addressed Kieran. "In the crown prince's wardrobe is a royal surcoat."

"Purple hemmed in gold with the dragon emblem worked in gold thread, Your Majesty?"

"That's the one." Orland turned back to Valerian. "I want you to wear that surcoat."

"Isn't it too fine for such a journey, Father?"

"Perhaps, but since you have not had the opportunity to travel much beyond the Keep, the surcoat will identify you and admit you to the garrisons with no delay."

If Valerian were going to rule this land someday, it was about time he discovered the lay of the land and the quality of its inhabitants. Would he ever have the confidence that his father, and even Kieran, possessed?

When Lewes entered Caelis' room, his wary gaze darted to every corner. Caelis could hardly blame him. His young cousin would not survive long without such caution.

"Hello, Lewes," Caelis said with a genuine smile. He beckoned to Drew and his page. "You may leave us now and fetch your supper in the kitchen." Once they quit the room, Caelis invited Lewes to sit at the table with him, where a small meal awaited them.

They did not speak until they'd eaten and Caelis refilled their goblets. Lewes leaned back and smiled.

"I know you did not invite me here merely to eat, Sir Caelis." He sipped the wine, watching Caelis over the rim.

"You're right, cousin." Caelis reached inside his tunic and pulled out a folded piece of parchment. "Read this."

Lewes set down the goblet, opened the parchment, and scanned the brief lines. His eyes widened and darted back to Caelis.

"Where did you get this?"

"I found it in the crown prince's bedchamber after the prince and his squire left the Keep for a fortnight." Caelis stared at Lewes.

"Only the king has the power of life and death."

"Yes," Caelis said.

"Then why did Prince Valerian write this? And why did he not destroy it afterward?" When Lewes frowned, Caelis shrugged.

"I can't answer your 'whys,' but I have a question for you. Are you absolutely certain the king's Seer is sympathetic to our cause?" A shiver ran down Caelis' spine, more of thrill than fear. He'd said "our" cause and meant it.

"Yes, I'm sure," Lewes said. "He may not be of much use in a battle, but he definitely will not betray us to the king."

Caelis leaned forward. "If I could find a way to sign and seal this order, I would find a way to use it to damage the relationship between the king and his son."

Lewes glanced at the parchment again. "I can sign and seal it, Sir Caelis. But I wouldn't be able to return it until tomorrow morning."

"Tomorrow is soon enough. I must see the king tonight." Caelis rubbed his hands in anticipation. "I plan to leave for the Southern Woodlands tomorrow."

Lewes folded the parchment and placed it inside his own tunic. Then he stood.

"I must leave you now, Sir Caelis." Lewes said. "Sir Brandon only gave me one hour." He patted the breast of his tunic. "I will finish preparing your weapon, and trust you to use it in the best possible way."

"Until tomorrow then, cousin." Caelis gripped Lewes' wrist. By the time the young man stepped out of the room, Caelis had decided what exactly to ask King Orland.

* * *

Caelis strode down the hall leading to the royal apartment. He was playing a dangerous game, and he relished the edge it gave him, like sharply honed blade. After climbing the tower stairs, Caelis went straight to the king's door and knocked. A page opened it.

"May I help you, sir?"

"Would you please announce to His Majesty that Sir Caelis requests an audience?"

The page inclined his head.

"Wait here, please." Then he shut the door.

Caelis fumed while he waited. It was infuriating that a boy should be allowed to give orders to him. Finally the door opened again.

"His Majesty will see you now." The page admitted Caelis and bowed. "Please, be seated."

Caelis sat on an embroidered chair. When Orland didn't appear immediately, Caelis got up and paced across the thick carpet of the sitting room. In just a few minutes the king entered the room, still wearing his royal tunic.

"Good evening, Sir Caelis. There is nothing amiss, I trust?"

Caelis bowed and pasted a courtier's smile on his face.

"Good evening, Your Majesty. All is well. I have a small request."

Orland sat in his overstuffed chair and gestured for Caelis to sit across from him.

"What is it, Sir Caelis?"

"Sire, my men are restless with no news about the Horde. I would like to take them south for field maneuvers and as an opportunity to visit my uncle Reed for the winter feast, with your permission, of course." *And coincidentally, traveling south gives me an opportunity to keep a close watch on your son.*

The king stroked his beard, studying Caelis.

"What about your project with Master Murray? The new kind of bow you mentioned before?"

"Murray has replicated several of them, and I and my men wish to test them in the field while we are away."

"Do you have provisions enough for all your men? I want no incidents with farmers or villagers along the way."

"Oh no, Your Majesty, there will be no incidents." Caelis smiled. "We will take basic rations and supplement with the abundant game in the Southern Woodlands. That is how we plan to test the new bows."

King Orland stood, so Caelis had to stand as well.

"It appears you have thought of everything, Sir Caelis. Therefore I grant you permission to take your men south for the winter. My only stipulation is that you return to the Keep before spring thaw. I fully expect the Horde to return at that time."

Caelis bowed low and carefully hid the smirk that crept to his lips.

"Thank you, Your Majesty. We will leave in a day or two, as soon as we ready our supplies."

Orland dismissed him with a wave of the hand. "Good night to you, Sir Caelis, and safe journey."

Caelis backed toward the door and left the room, well satisfied.

Chapter 13 *Better is a dinner of herbs where love is than a fattened ox and hatred therewith.*

Mercy awakened to Rafael's gentle shaking.

"Sissy, wake up," he whispered. "Today is winter feast."

She sat up on her pallet, remembering Gabriel's admiration of the past evening. Then she also remembered Papa's anger. For Rafael's sake, she tried to smile. When Mercy glanced at the place where Papa usually slept, his pallet was empty. She frowned.

"Shall we break our fast and get ready for the feast?" She unclasped her hair and undid the braid in order to comb it.

"Yes, Sissy!" Rafael scampered to the pot of cold porridge hanging over the ashes of yesterday's fire. "I'll take out the ashes."

"Thank you, love." While Rafael carefully scraped the ashes into a bucket, Mercy spent more time than usual making herself presentable. After all, Gabriel had returned, and she wanted to look her best.

Mercy dreaded facing Papa again. She rehearsed words to turn away his unkindness, hoping she might calm his anger as cool water puts out a fire. Once Rafael had taken the bucket of ashes to the pile, she started the fire and added a little water to the porridge, stirring it. Rafael climbed on one of the stools at the table.

"Sissy?"

"Yes, love?"

"Will Papa eat with us?"

"I don't know, Rafael. We'll have to wait and see."

But by the time the porridge was warmed and they had eaten, Papa had not returned. Mercy had just wiped out her bowl when someone knocked at the door.

"I'll answer it," Rafael said as he opened the door. "Sissy, it's Michael."

Mercy rushed to the door to greet her cousin, but the grim set of his mouth stopped her. He had aged years since she'd last seen him. Had his experiences damaged his soul as well as Papa's?

"I am so glad you have returned, cousin." She wanted to cry at the hardness in his eyes. Michael's eyes used to sparkle with mischief and joy.

"There's someone at the gate looking for Mercy the Healer," he said. "Do they mean you?"

Mercy hesitated, not sure what she should tell him.

"Much has happened while you were gone."

"Obviously."

She picked up her carry sack and beckoned to Rafael.

"Why do you need him?"

"He is my assistant." Mercy clasped Rafael's hand.

Michael frowned but said no more, to her relief. He did walk with them back to the gate. There was so much Mercy wanted to ask him, but something had come between them, something more than her betrothal to Gabriel. Her cousin was a stranger to her now.

Sitting just inside the gate, an old woman held her side in obvious pain.

"You are the Healer?" Her voice was strained.

"Yes, Madam." Mercy knelt down beside the woman. "How long have you been in pain?"

Before the woman could answer, Papa's voice made Mercy jump.

"What is going on here?"

Mercy stood and faced her father.

"I was about to examine her. I'm a Healer now, Papa."

"When did this happen?" The wild fury in his eyes made Mercy want to back away, but she held her ground. She had to make him understand.

"I wanted to tell you last night, but you left, and then you weren't in the cottage this morning. The gift came to me while I was helping Faith in childbirth."

Instead of the understanding and rejoicing she expected he would feel, he glared at her.

"I have never heard of a woman receiving the gift of Healing. You must be mistaken."

"It's true, Papa. I have many witnesses."

"Whether you are a Healer or no, I forbid you to assist any outsiders." He grabbed her arm and jerked her away. The old woman moaned and fell forward.

"Sissy!" Rafael stared at the woman in horror. She was vomiting blood.

"Papa! You must let me help her!" Mercy struggled against her father's grip on her arm.

"No. Let her die." He lifted his other hand to strike her.

But Mercy lifted her face to him, staring boldly into his eyes. Fear and anger warred within her, and he must have seen it in her face. He lowered his hand without striking her, but he pulled her toward their cottage without a word.

"Papa! We can't let her die, not when we can help her. Isn't that what the gift is for?"

"No. Not for outsiders. Why should we help them when they want to destroy us?" He opened the door of the cottage and pushed her inside. "Do not leave until I give you permission."

"But Papa!" She jumped back when he slammed the door.

This was too much! Papa acted as if he were possessed by demons. Mercy waited for a few heartbeats and then opened the door. There was no sign of her father, so she ran back to the gate.

No one had moved. Michael and Rafael stood where she'd left them, and the woman still lay on the ground, the puddle of blood soaking into the dirt. Mercy turned her to one side and checked her pulse. She could find none in her neck, so she placed her hand on the woman's chest. Her heart had stopped beating.

"No!" Mercy rocked back on her heels. If Papa had not interfered, or if he had only helped her, they could have saved this woman.

"Sissy?" Rafael took a step closer.

Mercy shook her head.

"She's dead, love. It wasn't your fault."

"No." Rafael's voice was choked. "It was Papa's fault."

Mercy hugged him fiercely.

"Don't say that, Rafael. It may be that even with Papa's help she would have died." But she didn't really believe that.

"What do we do with the body?" Michael squatted beside the woman. "We can't just leave it lying here."

"I don't know." Mercy fought back tears. "Did she tell you her name or where she came from?"

"No, and I didn't ask. I suppose we'll just have to bury her." When Michael lifted his gaze to Mercy, his eyes softened. "It's not your fault, Mercy. I'll find someone to help me. You'd best get home before your father sees you."

"Thank you, cousin." Mercy took Rafael back to the cottage.

Once inside they sat together on her pallet. Neither had a need for words. But Mercy's thoughts would not be still, no matter how hard she tried. She didn't understand how Papa could be so cruel. What would Gabriel do when he found out?

After many silent prayers for patience and for Papa's bitterness to be healed, Mercy discovered Rafael had fallen asleep with his head resting against her thigh. Reluctant to wake him, she stayed where she was, even though her legs began to cramp. That reminded her of the stocks in which the men had been locked while in the dungeon, and she began to cry for the cruelty of the outsiders who had corrupted her father's heart. These last few months had been a loss of innocence for all of the Brethren.

The sun's rays slanting through the window let Mercy know the passing of time. Perhaps the feast would help Rafael forget for a little while the bad things he'd seen this morning. He opened his eyes and sat up.

"Sissy? Did we miss the feast?"

"No, love. But it will be starting soon. We should collect our sweet bread and take it to the square."

After using the necessary, Rafael allowed Mercy to rebraid his hair. She loved to comb its silky softness with her fingers. As she tied the end with a strip of cloth, she imagined what he would look like when he received his own hair clasp someday at the Oath Taking. Three years had passed since she'd taken the Oath. Soon, on her fifteenth birthday, she would become Gabriel's wife. She wished they could marry today so she wouldn't have to stay with Papa.

The afternoon was pleasantly cool. By the time Mercy and Rafael approached the village square, a bonfire blazed in the fire pit. Tables were set up, and Rafael proudly added their sweet bread to the growing piles of food. Then he ran to join Dilly and Samuel and the other children in their games. Mercy longed to follow him. So far she had not seen Papa.

She found Aunt Prudence, who had put herself in charge of the food.

"Is there anything else that needs doing, aunt?"

"No, Mercy. We've taken care of it. What took you so long?"

Mercy lowered her gaze so her aunt would not notice her tears.

"I'm sorry. I was delayed."

Prudence turned away and fussed with the arrangements of food on the tables. Before Mercy could decide what to do, Gabriel appeared at her side. He gently took her arm and guided her away from prying ears.

"Are you all right? What has happened?"

Mercy shook her head, afraid to speak lest she lose control of herself.

Gabriel led her to a bench at the edge of the square. He gestured for her to sit and then sat beside her.

"Don't keep this to yourself. I need to know whether or not your father has overstepped his bounds, for his sake as well as yours."

Haltingly, Mercy told him every detail of the morning's incident. She didn't want to sound disrespectful, but there was no way to soften her father's raw anger and hatred.

She gazed up into Gabriel's eyes and he *Saw* her thoughts. For the first time she did not fear that intimate baring of her soul; in fact, she welcomed it. He was someone she knew she could trust.

Without understanding how she did it, Mercy opened herself to Gabriel, inviting him to share in her grief over Papa, her concern for the effects of Papa's anger on Rafael, and her worry about balancing everyone's needs with her own. What she did not expect was the flash of desire that passed between them, and she stood, breaking their new rapport.

"Oh," she said, her voice choked by this unexpected yearning for intimacy. "Please, forgive me." She shut her eyes, not daring to look at him.

But Gabriel slowly stood before her and lifted her chin with a gentle hand. She risked another glance at him. There was kindness and understanding and a reflection of her own longing. Mercy stared at the smile on his lips and wondered what it would be like to kiss him.

"I am thankful," he said in a quiet voice, "that you do not fear me, my sister, my almost-bride. I had worried that you would see me as too old and too familiar."

Mercy cleared her throat.

"I'm glad I have known you since I was a child. You are already part of my life. Now I can share all of myself with you." Her face grew warm. "Well, in a short time, that is."

His smile broadened, and the lines around his eyes that used to make him look stern now crinkled with joy. In that moment, Mercy forgot all her sorrow and the burdens of responsibility. She realized gratefully they could share those burdens. She need never bear them alone again! And she was determined to support and comfort him in his work as the spiritual leader of the village. Gabriel took her hand and kissed it.

"I shall endeavor to be worthy of this great gift you have given me, Sister Mercy." His smile became tinged with sadness. "I would prefer to spend the evening at your side, but it appears I must spend it with your father instead."

"I hope he will listen to you." She savored the warmth of his touch. "Will you come and eat with us tomorrow?"

"Of course. I will come every day and stay as long as possible."

They stood gazing at one another, each reluctant to part from the other. At last, Gabriel released her hand.

"Until tomorrow then?"

Mercy nodded, smiling. As she watched him depart, she sighed happily. Perhaps she didn't yet love Gabriel the way Serene had described, but she knew with all of her being that someday she would.

The red light of the rising sun reflected off the walls of the Keep and illuminated the deserted castle yard. Valerian was glad King Orland did not call attention to their leave-taking. He was self-conscious enough wearing the royal surcoat when all his men wore plain leathers. Valerian's warhorse pranced across the yard as if he realized the import of this journey, and Conrad solemnly handed Theo's reins to Valerian.

The young man known as "Hawk" led the scouting party out the castle gates, carrying the royal dragon pennon on his spear. Behind him rode Sir Gregory and Terron his squire, followed by Valerian and Kieran and the rest of the men. They made their way through the sleepy town and onto the eastern road. The Dragon's Backbone loomed to the south, and an eagle glided high above in the clear sky. All was well for the first hour. Then a grouse startled from the brush, spooking Theo, and the warhorse shied off the road. His right front foot stepped in a burrow and he stumbled painfully, nearly pitching Valerian off.

Kieran leaped down from his horse and grabbed Theo's bridle.

"Easy, easy," he crooned to the injured stallion.

Valerian dismounted and immediately crouched down to examine Theo's leg. He ran his hands down the length of the limb but discerned no break. Theo was definitely favoring it, though.

"I'm relieved his leg's not broken," Valerian said to Kieran, "but there's no chance he can continue on this journey. Thankfully we aren't far from the Keep."

The others crowded around to see what had happened.

"Is the beastie injured, Your Highness?" someone asked.

"Not seriously, thank you, but we'll need to return him to the Keep and get another horse."

"I'll take him back, Sire," said Kieran. "There's that young dappled gray Conrad has been training. I can have him saddled and bring him back quicker than a flight of arrows."

The squire Terron dismounted and brought his horse forward.

"If it pleases Your Highness, I'll walk while you ride my Ranger. That way we won't have to slow down much until Kieran returns."

"Thank you, Terron, and you also, Kieran. I see I am in good hands." Valerian stroked Theo's neck and gazed into the great horse's brown eyes. "You must heal so we can go on other adventures." With a final pat on his withers, Valerian turned away and mounted Terron's horse.

The squire adjusted the stirrups while Valerian watched Kieran ride back to the Keep, leading the limping Theo.

The eleven men made their way eastward following the road. Terron trotted alongside Valerian, not at all winded. The air was crisp but not too cold. The northern mountain range rose majestically to their left, all of the peaks snow-covered on their march to meet the taller Dragon's Backbone. Long purple grass waved in the breeze except in the cultivated fields, which contained only stubble this close to winter. Small villages lay along the road at regular intervals, and when people recognized their approaching band by the royal pennon, they came out of their cottages to see who it was. Once they spied the royal surcoat, everyone bowed. Valerian made sure to smile and nod at them, though he wished he could wear plain leathers and blend in with his men rather than be singled out by this overly ornate, uncomfortable garment indicating he was the crown prince.

They stopped at midday by a stream lined with evergreens to rest the horses and eat a brief meal. From their vantage point, Valerian could see back along the road as it wound through the hills, but he could not yet spot Kieran and the other horse. Valerian sat on a fallen tree and opened his saddle bag. He unwrapped a piece of flat bread and a small wheel of cheese. While he ate, Valerian observed the others. Sir Gregory squatted beside the stream, washing his hands. The five Highlanders sat together in the grass, sharing food and tall tales. The two men-at-arms, one older and more experienced than the other, leaned on a shelf of rock, eating quietly. Hawk had climbed an outcropping of rock and perched high above them, scanning the horizon. Terron sat nearby chewing on a piece of dried meat.

"Terron?"

The young man quickly stood.

"Yes, Your Highness?"

Valerian had to keep in mind these men were used to expecting orders from those in charge. He wasn't sure how to carry on a regular conversation with them.

"Please, be seated." Terron sat gingerly, prepared to jump up at a moment's notice. "I don't see Kieran yet. Would you like me to trade with one of the others so you can ride?"

"Truly, Sire, I don't mind running. As a boy, I used to run messages between the Keep and outlying villages because I was so fast." He grinned.

"Well, perhaps we can have a race someday."

"Do you run, Your Highness?"

"Not fast, I'm afraid, since my legs grew so long, but I was thinking about a race in general." Valerian remembered that Drew was a fast runner. "There may be others who would like to test their speed against yours."

"I would like that, Sire," Terron said, smiling.

They continued, with Terron keeping pace and showing no signs of being winded. Kieran did not catch up to them until late in the afternoon. By then the light was fading and it was time to find a place to stop for the night.

Valerian grew restless watching the men efficiently set up camp on a bluff overlooking the road. He wrung his hands, used to helping, but Sir Gregory quietly reminded him he must act like a prince now, not a squire.

Kieran was helping Parker, the younger man-at-arms, set up Valerian's small tent. Though it was barely large enough to sleep two, Valerian was grateful not to have anything finer than the rest of the men.

"Your Highness," said Parker, bowing. "This is the best of the tents, but it's not much."

"It is quite adequate, thank you." Valerian smiled at the young man. "If we had brought anything larger we would have needed sumpter horses."

Parker pulled his forelock. "Aye, Your Highness. A scouting party needs to travel light."

Hawk strode toward Valerian, inclining his head.

"Your Highness, MacAlister and I have scouted the area and see no sign of the Horde."

"Thank you, Hawk." Valerian tried to project confidence into his voice. "Do you recommend one per shift on the watch then?"

"Yes, Sire. This bluff affords a long view, and the moon will light the countryside." Hawk indicated the moon rising in the east.

Valerian leaned closer and spoke quietly.

"Who would you recommend make the schedule for the night guard?" He met the scout's piercing gaze and *Saw* no scorn there, only a willingness to help the young prince learn the usual ways of doing things.

"You'd best let Cameron have that duty, Highness." Hawk smiled. "The old soldier thinks no one else can do it as well as he can."

"Thank you, Hawk." Valerian spied the older man-at-arms setting up the last of the six tents and strode to him. "Cameron," he said. "A word with you."

The soldier stood and bowed his head. His ice blue eyes studied Valerian, who *Saw* the man's obsession with efficiency. Now Hawk's remark became clear.

"You are in charge of scheduling the night guard," Valerian said. The tone of command grew slightly more comfortable to use, and Valerian hoped it would someday come naturally. "I expect you to include me in the schedule."

Cameron inclined his head again. He did not smile, but his eyes relaxed a little.

"Of course, Your Highness. Consider it done."

* * *

After an uneventful night, Valerian and his men set off in the morning under gray skies. It took half the day to traverse the gap between the mountain ranges. Late in the afternoon it began to lightly snow. White patches formed in the ruts of the road, in the dry grass along either side, and upon the boughs of the evergreens.

Valerian's purple dragon pennon appeared over a rise in the road, and Hawk upon his brown horse materialized out of the snow and gloom.

"The garrison is just ahead, Your Highness," he said. "We'll reach it before dark."

By the time they reached the gate, it was open, welcoming them. Two soldiers stood with raised spears on the crenellated wall. They inclined their heads as Valerian rode past. Behind him, Kieran and the other Highlanders called out greetings to friends or relatives quartered there. Kieran's accent broadened and Valerian could scarcely understand him. The commander stepped out to greet Valerian. Behind enormous black mustaches dotted with snowflakes, the man's face was familiar.

"Welcome tae the northern garrison, Your Highness." His voice was loud and deep. "I am Angus MacLachlan."

"MacLachlan?" Valerian glanced back at Kieran, who was having an animated conversation with several garrison men.

"Aye, he's my wee baby brother." When Angus grinned, Valerian saw the family resemblance.

"Your brother is my squire. I would be lost without him."

"I'm verra glad to hear that, Sire. Come, let us get indoors. We have a fire in the hall, and ye are just in time to join us for our evening meal." He led Valerian inside, and Valerian had to duck under a low doorway.

"We don't wish to deprive you of supplies," he said. "We have brought provisions."

"Nonsense, Sire, 'tis our pleasure to break bread with you."

In the hall, three long tables and benches were arranged along three sides, leaving the middle of the room empty. The fireplace took up most of the fourth wall. The meal consisted of heaping platters of venison, flat bread, and a bitter mead. The men were rough and loud, not at all like the overly formal courtiers Valerian was used to dining with. These men, however, appeared to enjoy one another's company. Two large dogs vied for scraps the men tossed to the rush-strewn floor. Valerian imagined what his mother's reaction would be upon seeing that in the Keep's great hall.

After the platters were removed and cups refilled, one of the garrison men tuned a small lyre. Another pulled a flute from his belt, saluting Valerian and Angus MacLachlan before placing it to his lips. He and the lyre player began a lively tune. Kieran jumped up, grinning.

"They're calling to me feet, Sire." He winked at Valerian and hopped over their table to the open space. Three others joined him a wild dance filled with tapping feet, leaps and spins in the air. It fatigued Valerian just watching them. More dances followed with others joining them. Kieran never seemed to tire.

One of the garrison men placed two crossed spears on the floor, forming four equal quarters. Kieran stood in one with his hands balled on his hips, and Anson MacDougall, the youngest of Valerian's Highlanders, took the opposite corner.

The musicians began a measured song. Valerian watched, entranced, as Kieran and Anson moved in unison with complicated foot movements, heel and toe. They made their way through the four quarters until the end of the first verse. Then began a wilder verse full of leaps and twists as the two Highlanders made their dizzying way around the quarters. Valerian was sure they would trip on the spears or collide in midair, but their grace and precision were so finely honed they made the impossible look easy.

When they leaped away from the spears, the final note sounded, triumphant, and the hall erupted in cheers. Valerian stood with the others, clapping as hard as he could, full of admiration for his squire's heretofore unknown talent.

Kieran and Anson bowed low, accepting the applause. When Kieran returned to his place, he drained the cup Valerian offered.

"Kieran, I'm amazed. Why did you never tell me you could dance like that?"

The squire grinned at him.

"There's nae such music at the Keep to call to my feet."

"We'll remedy that when we return." Valerian smiled in anticipation.

Angus MacLachlan took advantage of the lull to lean closer to Valerian.

"May I ask, Your Highness, if there be some problem that brings you out here? Surely you didna come just so Kieran and young MacDougall could dance for us?"

"The king sent us to the garrisons for your reports on the Horde."

Angus sat back and took a drink. He wiped his mustache before replying. "Well then, Sire, there isna a report tae give you. We have seen nae sign o' the beasties for at least two new moons."

"Nothing?"

Angus shook his head. "I send scouts on a regular basis. They range far into the plains but have found nothing. 'Tis as if the Horde have disappeared from the face of the earth."

"Could the colder weather have driven them south?" Valerian frowned. "Or do they perhaps sleep for the winter like some lizards and serpents?"

"If that were true, 'twould be new on their part. We have always found signs of them before, even during the coldest winter months." Angus took another drink. "We'll keep scouting, for 'tis our job to guard this northern pass. If we find anything, we'll be sure to alert the king."

Though Valerian was happy to sleep with the men in the barracks, Angus insisted that the prince take his room for privacy. Valerian was grateful when Kieran made a pallet beside the bed. He'd half expected the squire would want to spend more time with the other Highlanders.

"Nay, Sire," said Kieran after Angus left them alone. "I dinna feel the need to dance all night. Besides, by now the others will be wanting to drink more than dance." He helped Valerian untie and remove the surcoat.

"So you don't drink with them?"

"Never. I dinna want what little good sense I have to vanish in me cups." Kieran cocked his head, listening. "If we don't fall asleep quickly, we'll soon be privy to their loud and awful singing." He shed his own outer garments and rolled up in furs his brother had provided.

Valerian climbed into Angus' roughly hewn bed. It was nearly as hard as sleeping on the ground, but he was grateful to Kieran's brother for the gesture.

"Pardon me, Sire, I forgot the candles." Kieran jumped up and began to snuff the several flames. Before the last light went out, he turned to Valerian. The single flame cast deep shadows on his face and glinted in his tousled hair.

"That last dance is called the 'sword dance,' though we've always used crossed spears." He grinned. "Now that you and I have real swords, I think I ought tae teach you that dance."

"Even your talents as a teacher will be sorely challenged by someone who tends to trip over his own feet, but I'm willing to try." Valerian chuckled.

Fortunately they both fell asleep before the singing in the hall became rowdy.

* * *

They spent an extra day at the garrison. Valerian rode out with a scouting party who showed him the lay of the land. He began to understand why the Highlanders had such pride in their country. Even with the scarcity of trees, the gorse-covered limestone hills and barren mountains appealed to him, mostly because of the isolation. He could grow used to the solitude, as long as he had his scrolls.

Valerian and his men reluctantly parted with friends old and new to journey south. The next garrison was located in a "gateway" between two peaks of the Dragon's Backbone, a range of jagged black mountains that cut Levathia in half. Valerian could visualize its location in his head from the tapestry map at the Keep, but nothing prepared him for the sight of red cliffs jutting straight up from the Plains of Mohorovia, as if giant hands had cut the land with a sharp knife and then pushed the Levathian side upward about five hundred feet.

"Did you know the border looked like this?" Valerian asked Kieran.

"Nay, Sire. I've not been this far south before."

Sir Gregory pulled up and waited for Valerian to come alongside. The knight smiled beneath his close-cropped beard and mustaches and gestured to the vista below.

"This, Your Highness, is why only five garrisons are needed to secure our border with Mohorovia. Most of these cliffs are inaccessible from the plains."

"I had wondered about that. Thank you for enlightening me, Sir Gregory."

It took three days to reach the Gateway garrison. As in the north, the commander had nothing to report on the Horde. Valerian and his men stayed just one night in order to press on to the next garrison, which was known as Midway. From here there was a better view of the Dragon's Backbone. And from the tower one could see across the plains for many miles.

"How can the Horde live there?" Valerian wondered aloud. "There are no trees, little grass, and rocks as far as the eye can see."

"Even Hawk can see nothing living," Kieran said. "Indeed 'tis a most desolate place."

Once Valerian and his men left Midway, they traveled south again. After three more days, they reached Blackwater Garrison. The tapestry map did not accurately portray the oddly-shaped lake formed by the jagged cliffs. A waterfall spilled over the western edge where a river rushed down from the tree-covered hills of the Southern Woodlands. The garrison squatted on the edge of the cliff beside the lake. When Valerian studied the lake from the tower, he was surprised that the water appeared black. He discovered the lake was considered "bottomless" because of the great tear in the land that had formed it.

Here, too, there had been no sign of the Horde, though scouting parties went out daily. The commander and his men decided the beasts had died out from some disease or predator.

The day after leaving Blackwater to ride south to the last of the five garrisons, it began to rain. The men rode into the trees to find shelter at night, though their tents did not repel all the rain. For the first time since they left the Keep, there was grumbling from the men.

"They dinna blame you, Sire," Kieran assured Valerian. "They just want to dry out."

Fortunately, they reached the southern garrison just before midday, and the rain had stopped. Hawk crested a hill and shouted back, "There it is, just below!"

The others urged their horses to plod as quickly as possible through the mud until they were all crowded together on the edge of the cliff. On a promontory ridge below them stood the stone walls of the garrison. The sound of a trumpet echoed off the cliffs.

"Sire!" Hawk pointed west. "A large band of the Horde moves toward the garrison. We can reach the gates before they do, if we hurry."

Valerian strained his eyes but could only see a dark blur on the horizon.

"Let's go."

They picked their way along the edge of the cliff while the attacking band approached. An urgency to hurry the men pressed upon Valerian, but he kept his peace lest one of the horses make a bad step on the ledge.

"Your Highness," Hawk said. "The Horde carry their bows and poisoned arrows."

"Can we still reach the gate in time?" Valerian asked. They were so near, but the Horde steadily narrowed the gap.

"If we increase our pace." Hawk shifted his grip on the dragon pennon.

"Scouting party, to me," Valerian shouted. Then he urged the dappled gray to a run. The others followed him, thundering toward the gate.

Caelis was well satisfied with the performance of his new crossbow. For a fortnight, he and his men traveled the length of Levathia within sight of several of the garrisons, though they did not visit them. Each day Caelis rode out with one of the men, alone, and during that time learned all he could about each one. Now Caelis was confident he had a small but loyal following of rabid secessionists, each convinced the ruling family had grown too soft and too distant for the south to remain in submission to the north.

Before leaving the north, Caelis and his men visited the sites of the earlier battles with the Horde and each recovered a useable battle-ax. No one questioned Caelis about taking the axes or practicing their swings upon fallen trees and the occasional unfortunate river dragon. The men had taken to beheading the game they took with their crossbows, mainly deer or squirrels, challenging one another to see who had the cleanest, swiftest stroke. Even Drew didn't mind chopping into dead meat, but the squire was still squeamish about using the ax on live animals. He was the only one, though.

By the time they reached the Southern Woodlands, Caelis had made his decision. He decided to sound out Thrane before springing it on the rest. The two of them rode out alone from camp to look for game. When they reached a clearing, Caelis reined in his horse, and Thrane came alongside him.

"Why have we stopped, Sir Caelis?" Thrane frowned. "Is anything wrong?"

"I was hoping you could tell me." Caelis handed over the folded piece of parchment and waited while the man read it. Thrane's eyes widened.

"Is this why we were sent south?" Thrane actually licked his lips in anticipation.

Caelis nodded. This was a better reaction than he expected. Thrane usually wanted to know all the details.

"We are to wait until the men return from their bondage," Caelis said. "I will determine that tomorrow. Meanwhile, I want your honest opinion: Will any of the others have a problem with this order?"

"None, Sir Caelis." Thrane smiled. The scar creased his face. "Except possibly your squire."

Caelis growled in his throat and clenched the reins.

"I'll take care of my squire. Just see that you do your part."

"You have nothing to worry about on that account, Sir Caelis."

They rode on in silence, and Caelis managed to bring down one of his uncle's deer with his crossbow.

Chapter 14 *His heart is as firm as a stone; yea, as hard as a piece of the nether millstone.*

Mercy sat on the bench after Gabriel left the feast. Her heart was too full to risk speaking to anyone just yet. Especially Aunt Prudence.

She prayed Gabriel could say something to Papa that would help her father find peace again. The more she thought about it, the more she was convinced his heart had been filled with bitterness since Mama's death, and his experiences of the past few months had only served to harden those feelings.

Mercy sighed. She really didn't want to think about Papa just now. It was much more pleasant to think about Gabriel instead. What an unexpected joy to realize she could love him, and that part of their future oneness as husband and wife would include sharing even the difficulties. She would never have to be alone again.

While she wrapped herself in these lovely thoughts, Michael came and sat beside her on the bench.

"Oh! Hello, Michael." Mercy's face grew warm. She was thankful her cousin was not a Seer.

"I've never seen you this way." He studied her face. "You look happy. At peace."

"I am." Her smile faded. "I wish you were, too."

Michael turned away. He tightened his jaw and clenched his fists, speaking in a harsh whisper.

"I shall never be at peace again."

Mercy laid a hand on his arm, but he shrugged it away.

"You're not supposed to touch me, remember?" He stood and his eyes narrowed. "I'm not supposed to speak to you without another woman present." His words dripped contempt.

"Michael, please." She stood beside him. "Don't push me away. Tell me what's troubling you."

For a moment it appeared he would open his heart to her, but he shook his head.

"You will be Gabriel's wife soon, and he would banish me if he *Saw* the hate I have in my heart toward the outsiders. I no longer agree with the isolation that keeps us from knowing them and learning how to deal with them."

Michael glared at her, his lip curling in a snarl. Before she could think of what to say, he closed his eyes in pain and ran away. Mercy held back tears with difficulty, but she was grateful she had when Aunt Prudence headed toward her.

"What did you say, niece, to so trouble my son?" Her eyes narrowed.

"Michael was already troubled. I merely asked him what was wrong."

Aunt Prudence crossed her arms.

"You had best stay away from Michael. You are almost a married woman, and you will be the wife of the village leader. You must set the example for the rest of the villagers. Your every word and deed will be measured."

While her aunt made her proclamations, Mercy grew cold, and she shivered. When Prudence strode back to the tables, Mercy was doubly thankful she and Gabriel had already begun to develop a rapport. She would need his support even more than she realized.

* * *

After Mercy helped the other women clean up, Rafael left the other children and grabbed her hand.

"I had the most wonderful time, Sissy. Everyone liked our sweet bread. And I won the egg carry race."

"I'm glad for you." Mercy hugged her brother. "Will you be able to sleep after so much excitement?"

"I don't know." Rafael grinned. "But if I do, I know I will have good dreams."

Mercy grabbed Rafael's hand and started toward their cottage. Rafael pulled ahead.

"Let's race, Sissy." He ran.

Laughing, Mercy ran after him. She didn't try to catch up to him, and he thumped the cottage door first.

"I won!"

Mercy pulled up beside him and caught her breath.

"Of course you won." Still laughing they entered the cottage together.

They stopped when they saw Papa sitting at the table. A stub of candle cast flickering shadows on his face. He scowled at them.

"You are no longer a child, daughter. You must act with more dignity."

"I'm sorry, Papa."

"You are to marry Brother Gabriel soon. I will not have you bring dishonor to our family or to him by inappropriate behavior."

"How have I behaved inappropriately, Papa?"

He pushed away from the table, glaring at her.

"You have consorted with outsiders. You have touched and spoken privately with a young man."

"Do you mean Flint Mallory, the king's messenger?"

"I don't know his name. I only know what I have been told."

"Then let me assure you, Papa, there was nothing inappropriate. He came to deliver a message from the king. I was gatekeeper that day. I discovered he had broken his arm and so I Healed him. That is all."

Papa took a jerky step closer to her. He clenched his fists.

"Whether you are a true Healer or no, you must never again touch any man, young or old. You are soon to be the wife of the village leader and must be blameless in your behavior. If you are a Healer, you will confine yourself to women and children, and then only with my approval. Gabriel may be leader of this village, but he does not command my Healing."

Mercy held back tears of frustration. She wanted to tell Papa he was wrong not to help outsiders, but she knew it would only make the situation worse.

"Why do you keep saying 'if' I am a Healer? The gift came upon me at Faith's childbirth. I have Healed several of the other women in the village. You can ask them if you won't believe me."

"I don't need to ask them," he snarled. "Brother Gabriel says I must believe you, that I must not fight against the will of the Most High."

"Then why are you so angry?" Mercy frowned. Rafael pressed himself against her, trembling.

Papa slammed his fist down on the table.

"Do I not have a right to be angry? A Healer should be respected and valued."

"But you are."

"Not by outsiders. You don't know what they said, what they did to us."

"Tell me, Papa." Mercy held out her hands. "Please tell me so I might understand."

He shook his head and gritted his teeth.

"You can't possibly understand. You're just a naïve girl. You should not have spoken to that outsider and especially not presumed to Heal him. He obviously told others about you, and now the outsiders will never leave us alone." He gestured to the cottage. "Besides, it's not seemly for you to leave your womanly tasks undone in order to do a man's job."

"But all of you were taken away. We did not know, until Flint Mallory delivered the king's message, that you would ever return to us. We had to take care of the village and do some of the men's tasks, like keeping the gate." Mercy paused, but he did not acknowledge her words. "Papa! I never desired to take your place in anything, especially Healing."

"Whether you desired it or no, you *have* taken my place. Outsiders travel here to seek you out, as they never did for me. Outsiders treated me like a beast of burden, like a dull-witted slave. I can never forgive them, no matter what Brother Gabriel says."

Mercy remembered Gabriel's words to her yesterday.

"If we hate, it will turn and consume us."

Papa's eyes widened, looking wild. Mercy shrank back.

"So, taking my place as Healer is not enough. Must you take Brother Gabriel's and preach to me as well? How dare you!"

Mercy couldn't duck fast enough. Papa slapped her so hard that she fell. Rafael managed to stay out of Papa's reach.

Mercy brought her hand to her cheek. She couldn't believe he had actually struck her. When she met his gaze again, some of the anger had drained away. His eyes still smoldered in the candlelight, but they no longer appeared wild.

"Go to bed, both of you." His voice was hoarse. "I don't want to see or hear you anymore tonight. I will not tolerate your disrespect and disobedience." Without another glance, he lay on his pallet and turned his back to them.

Mercy hardly dared to breathe. Every instinct told her to pick up Rafael and leave. She wanted to run straight to Gabriel. Hadn't he told her to let him know if Papa became violent? But if she went now, could it make Papa become more irrational? If only Gabriel were here!

She wished they could marry tomorrow, or even tonight. She wished she never had to deal with Papa again. Mercy touched her cheek. It was sore and swollen. She wondered if it were possible to Heal herself.

Rafael stifled a sob, and she instinctively covered his mouth and shook her head. They couldn't make Papa mad again. She kissed him and held him close.

"I love you, Rafael," she whispered in his ear. "Try to sleep now, and tomorrow I'll ask Gabriel to help us."

Rafael nodded and held Mercy as if he would never let go. She managed to move her pallet as far away from Papa as possible. Then she blew out the candle, and she and Rafael lay on her pallet. He curled into a fetal position, and she curved herself protectively around him. It wasn't until she heard Papa's regular breathing that she was able to fall into a troubled sleep.

Valerian wished he rode upon Theo during their mad dash to the garrison ahead of the Horde. He prayed the gray was sure-footed. The light rain finally ended, but the horses' hooves churned the mud, each horse spraying the one behind him. Terron's horse stumbled, but the squire managed to hold on. The massed Horde came closer and closer. Valerian kept his eye on the garrison gate just ahead. A guard saw them and shouted something. Hawk signaled with his pennon, and the gate opened.

"Hurry!" shouted the guard when they came close enough. "The Horde's attacking."

Once they entered the garrison, Valerian slid off his horse and grabbed his bow and arrows from the saddle. He pulled his bowstring from inside his jerkin and slipped it on the bow while he ran with Kieran up the steps to the wall.

"Your Highness," said a surprised soldier. "Are your men handy with their bows?"

"There are no better in the north," Valerian said, loudly enough that his men could hear. "We've been riding in heavy rain, so I pray our bowstrings are dry enough."

They strung their bows, and all but Anson's were taut enough to use. One of the garrison men found an extra for him.

They ranged along the wall facing east, and shortly the enemy came within bow range. None carried battle-axes. They were armed only with bows and their poisoned arrows. Valerian wondered why they were attacking this fortified garrison high on its strategic promontory. What could be the purpose of such an attack?

He soon discovered there seemed to be no purpose at all. There were at least fourscore of the brutes, but their arrows harmlessly grazed the wall or landed in the yard of the garrison, well away from their intended targets. Though most of the men's arrows bounced off the Mohorovians' thick scaly hides, Valerian managed to shoot one through the eye, and it fell into the mud. He had to look away from the sight. Others followed his example, and four archers each killed one of the monsters by shooting the vulnerable eyes.

The Horde's survivors ignored their fallen comrades and ran back the way they came. Valerian tracked their path until they disappeared over the horizon. Hawk still watched for several heartbeats.

"Could you tell where they came from?" Valerian asked.

"No, Your Highness." Hawk frowned in puzzlement. "I saw nothing other than the plains we have seen the length of the country."

Valerian imagined what his father would order next in this situation.

"Perhaps we should go after them."

"We've done that, Your Highness," said the first soldier Valerian had spoken with. "If they have a settlement, or a nest, or whatever those creatures call home, we have yet to find it."

Valerian remembered the burrowing dragons he used to find near the Keep as a boy.

"Could they live underground?"

"'Tis possible, Sire," said the man with a shrug.

"Who is commander here?" Valerian asked.

"Sir Walter, Your Highness."

"I would like to speak with him."

"I will bring him." The man bowed and started to walk away.

"No," said Valerian. When the man stopped and turned back Valerian continued in what he hoped was a commanding voice. "There is no need. Take me to Sir Walter."

"As you wish, Your Highness." The man bowed again. "Follow me, Sire."

While the man led him to the stairs, Valerian nodded at Kieran. The squire gave Valerian a two-fingered salute.

Valerian followed the soldier to one of the stone buildings. He barely ducked under the low doorway in time to keep from bashing his head. Seated at a desk near the fireplace sat his former pagemaster, Sir Walter. A familiar knot of apprehension clenched his gut at the sight of the grizzled knight. For three years, Valerian had done his best to please Sir Walter, but the older man had been a stern taskmaster to a shy young prince.

Sir Walter glanced up, and his eyes widened when he recognized Valerian. He stood and inclined his head.

"Your Highness. I'm surprised to see you here."

"Sir Walter." Valerian avoided direct eye contact, reluctant to *See* the man's thoughts.

"What brings you so far south at this time?"

Valerian stepped closer to the desk. He glanced at the stack of parchment and pot of ink beside three fat candles. Steam rose from a mug, and the scent of cloves wafted in the air.

"The king sent us to visit each of the garrisons."

"So what think you of that strange attack?" Sir Walter gestured to the embrasure in the corner. A short bow and quiver of arrows were propped against the stone wall. "Have the other garrisons been so harried?"

"Nay, Sir Walter. In fact, they all report the situation unusually quiet. The Horde have disappeared from the north."

"Hmm." Sir Walter frowned. "Perhaps it's because we're so far south and winter never grows as cold as in the north. But that doesn't explain these daily pointless attacks. To me, it suggests the Horde are mindless beasts, not nearly as intelligent as we originally feared." He gestured to an empty stool. "Please, Your Highness, be seated." Only after Valerian sat did the knight reseat himself. Then he leaned closer.

"I realize, my prince, you never expected to take your brother's place, but I'm confident you will find your strength. Your grandfather believed in your potential."

"Thank you, Sir Walter." The mention of his grandfather made Valerian miss him even more.

Sir Walter's gaze shifted from Valerian's face to his long hair. "Permission to speak as your former pagemaster, Sire?" When Valerian nodded, the knight continued. "It has been my experience that short hair is easier to keep in the field. Less trouble under a helm."

"Thank you, Sir Walter." Valerian forced a smile. Did Sir Walter disapprove of Valerian's hair because it was not military or because it reminded him of someone who would rather be a priest or a scholar?

The knight cleared his throat and took a sip from his mug.

"Did you remember that today is winter feast? We would be honored for you and your men to join us, Your Highness."

"Then we gratefully accept your hospitality. I know I can speak for all of the men." Valerian hoped there was enough food, knowing how much Kieran and the other young men could eat.

"How many do you have with you, Sire?"

"Ten, not counting my squire, Kieran MacLachlan. Father thought that a good number for my first command."

Sir Walter nodded and smiled.

"Kieran, eh? I'm sure he's grown out of the rascal he was as a page." He studied Valerian. "And how have you been getting along with your first command, my prince?"

Because he'd known the knight all his life, Valerian began to feel comfortable discussing the men and the journey with him. He *Saw* Sir Walter's grudging approval, though laced with the certainty that Valerian was not ruthless and fearless as Waryn had been. *Would people never stop comparing him to his brother?* Valerian shook off his petty thoughts and focused on the situation at hand.

"You mention you've been 'harried' by the Horde. For how long?"

"About a month, as I was writing to the king." Sir Walter gestured to the parchments. "We're never in danger, have never had a man injured, but every day about that number of the creatures run in from the east, shoot their poisoned arrows, and then run back the way they came. I've sent scouts to follow them, but even after riding for miles into the plains, they find no sign of them, as if they've melted into the ground. I don't know what to think about it."

"Indeed, Sir Walter, it is puzzling. If they were men, I'd say it was a diversion, but as you say, they seem to be mindless creatures."

"Do you have a timetable, Sire, as to when the king expects you back at the Keep?"

"No. Father did not specify. I'm sure he meant for us to return by spring thaw."

"Then would it be too much to ask for you and your men to winter here and help us solve the puzzle of the Horde's strange activities?"

Valerian paused to consider the request.

"First tell me how far it is from here to Lord Reed's castle."

"No more than a two day journey, due west." The knight pointed in that direction.

"And have you heard whether or not Eldred, my father's former Seer, has taken up residence in one of these southern villages?"

Sir Walter stroked his beard.

"I have heard mention of Eldred recently. I'll have to ask around. Why do you ask, Sire?"

Valerian did not want tell Sir Walter the primary reason he desired to see Eldred, which was to ask him about the Sight and how to control it.

"I'd hoped while I was in the south to find the old man and inquire about him." Valerian shifted on the stool. "I also owe Lord Reed a visit, but not for the same reason."

"Oh?" Sir Walter raised an eyebrow.

"He wishes to offer his daughter's hand, and my father wishes me to accept her as a future queen consort." Valerian sighed. "She would have married my brother, after all." He had overheard his father and Waryn discussing the importance of his marrying a woman from the south to diffuse the tensions between the two regions.

The knight chuckled when Valerian grimaced.

"As I recall, you could do far worse, my prince."

"Lady Hanalah is very beautiful," Valerian admitted. He had never planned to marry, but now as crown prince he would be required to produce an heir. If he couldn't avoid marriage, he wanted more than physical beauty in a wife; he'd hoped to find one with intelligent conversation, at least.

"That sounds like a more pleasant problem than chasing after phantom monsters." Sir Walter leaned back and smiled.

"Then I have a proposal, Sir Walter." Valerian folded his hands to still their sudden trembling. "What if I leave my men here to assist you while I and my squire visit Eldred and Lord Reed? If I am delayed, I can rendezvous with the men at Midway Garrison by the next new moon. If I conclude my business sooner, then I can return here and we will leave together. Is that acceptable?"

Sir Walter stood and made a respectful bow.

"That is one proposal I can wholeheartedly agree to, Prince Valerian. Shall we go to the hall and celebrate the winter feast?"

"It will be my pleasure."

While they walked to the garrison's hall, Valerian wished with all his heart he could find a way to avoid marriage to the beautiful but empty-headed Lady Hanalah.

Caelis sat upon his restless horse in the predawn chill. The gate was barred for the night, so they would have to wait until it was opened again. Not, he mused, that there would be any resistance from the villagers. But he would prefer not to damage the gate in the attack, even though they had their Horde battle-axes. If anyone discovered the bodies, he wanted them to think it was their work. He had to wait until the right moment to blame it on Valerian.

"Sir Caelis," whispered one of the men. "I checked the gate again, and it has been opened, but there is no one in sight, inside or out."

Caelis frowned. Had one of them gone outside? Or had someone merely opened the gate in preparation for something else? He growled in his throat. He didn't have time to chase phantoms. They needed to get in, do the deed, and get out as quickly as possible.

"Squire," he hissed.

Drew guided his horse closer to Caelis' mount.

"Yes, sir?"

"Pass it along for the men to dismount and ready their axes." Even in the dim light Caelis could see the frown on Drew's face.

"But sir, there are women and children, innocents--"

Caelis backhanded Drew, knocking him to the ground. "Don't you dare question me."

Drew pushed himself up and fingered his jaw. Caelis slid off his horse and grabbed Drew's surcoat.

"If you dare disobey me, I will kill you myself."

"Yes, sir," the squire whispered. His eyes glistened.

Caelis pushed him away. He strode to the next man and gave the curt order to be passed down the line. Once all the men had dismounted, Caelis left the horses tethered and led the men up the bluff to the open wooden gate.

There was no one in sight. Once all of Caelis' men had filed inside, he counted the structures and divided up his men. They lit their torches and silently approached the sleepy cottages.

Drew followed him to the first one. Caelis pushed open the door and found one middle-aged man inside. Before the man came fully awake, Caelis swung the ax around and split his chest open. A fountain of blood gushed out. While Drew became violently sick, Caelis kicked the dead man to the floor and pulled his ax out of the man's ruined chest. Then he pushed the body over, picked up the man's long braid in one hand, and sliced through the scalp with the ax.

"Now you can die a man instead of a cowardly woman," he growled.

He pulled Drew along to the next cottage. They found another man about the same age, who was fully awake and standing in front of a young boy. Before the man could say a word, Caelis cut him down.

"Take care of the boy, Drew," he said while he scalped the second man.

"I can't, sir." Drew placed himself in front of the child. "You'll have to kill me first."

Caelis lifted his ax to kill them both. But when he gazed at the boy, he checked his swing. Those frightened eyes were just like *Caeden's* on that morning long ago when he'd failed to save his drowning brother. He lowered the ax.

Outside the cottage screams shattered the peaceful morning. Caelis inspected the bloody scalp in his hand. There was no satisfaction in killing those who would not fight back.

"I'll deal with you later, squire. Bring the boy." He strode out without a backward glance.

In minutes the screaming stopped. Each of Caelis' men held at least one scalp. One had several braids draped around his neck. All of their leathers were spattered with blood, which appeared black in the dim light.

"Let's get the devil out of here," Caelis growled. He glanced behind him. Drew held the boy's hand.

They hurried back to the horses and galloped away.

Chapter 15 *You have condemned and killed the just, and he does not resist you.*

Mercy tossed and turned on her pallet, unable to return to sleep. Papa's anger frightened her, but also made her angry, too. Didn't he realize how cruel he had become? Was it her fault Mama had died? Or Rafael's?

She sat up and covered her mouth to keep from gasping aloud. Did Papa blame *himself* for Mama's death? After all, he was a Healer, and yet he'd been unable to save his own wife in childbirth. What a burden that must be to him! Even so, Mercy didn't understand why he would treat his own children with such hateful contempt. The men had only been home for two days and already Mercy found the situation unbearable.

She got up and silently pulled on her overdress and apron. She tied her scarf over her braid. For a moment, she stood motionless, listening to Papa's and Rafael's regular breathing. Then she opened the door wide enough to slip through and closed it behind her.

The village slept peacefully more than an hour before sunrise. The world was so wide without the clutter of people's voices, the clamor of their demands. Above her, the stars twinkled coldly in the moonless sky. Her bare feet padded on the chilly dirt.

Mercy approached the barred gate. She had a twist of guilt while she struggled to lift the bar and set it down without making too much noise. Whatever her punishment for this second violation of the rules, she would face it gladly; the turmoil inside her had to find release, and the only place she knew to find it was at the river.

She hurried down the winding path until she came to the willow. She heard an owl's muted call and a gentle splash in the river. Other than that the night was quiet. Mercy sat on the fallen tree trunk beside the willow. Her thoughts were too jumbled to focus on one and make sense of it, so she lay back and contemplated the stars. The sky changed from black to midnight blue, and the first rosy glow of the sun began to lighten the eastern edge.

All her senses came alive at once, and the hair on the back of her neck prickled. She sat up, listening, when a scream sounded from up on the bluff, coming from the *village*. Mercy forgot to breathe. Her feet were frozen in place. Dragons must be attacking. What could she do? Oh, God of Peace, what should she *do*?

Mercy gasped, and that was enough to unlock her paralysis. She began to run up the path, but her legs moved in slow motion. A rumble vibrated the ground, as if a thunderstorm were approaching. But in moments the sound faded, and all was silent again.

By the time Mercy reached the open gate, the gate that *she* had left unbarred, she had to catch her breath before she could enter. Her heart leaped inside her chest, frantic with fear. There was enough light to see something lying on the ground nearby. With trembling knees, she came nearer. One of the villagers lay face down. Blood covered his tunic and the back of his head. She knelt to examine him. He'd been partially scalped and his braid was gone. Gently she turned him over and a wail escaped her throat.

It was Michael. Her poor cousin lay dead from a dozen terrible wounds. She backed away from the sheer awfulness of the sight of him. Tears blurred her vision. Had anyone else been hurt?

Mercy turned and ran to her cottage. She stifled a scream when she saw the open door. But she stopped at the threshold.

"Papa? Rafael?"

No answer. Mercy stepped inside. Her father lay slumped on the floor. Blood dripped from a gash in his chest and puddled beneath him.

"Papa!" She felt for a pulse, but he was dead. "Rafael?" Her voice rose in terror. "Rafael!"

He was not there.

Mercy ran from cottage to cottage and found everyone dead, many still in their beds. Only Dilly and little Samuel were outside, as Michael had been. It appeared they'd tried to run, but they had been cut down too.

"Rafael!" She screamed. Where was he?

She ran to the sheep pens, and a whimper came from her throat when she saw they had all been slaughtered. She'd hoped Rafael might be hiding here, but she found no sign of him, dead or alive.

Desperate, Mercy raced around the village again, searching every one of his hiding places, but he was nowhere to be found.

The sun rose above the tree line, casting a harsh light on the silent village, blinding her. She turned toward the village square and tripped over something on the ground. Another body lay face down. Like the rest of the men, but not the women or children, the braid had been cut away with part of the scalp.

Mercy knew who this had to be. She gently turned him over and her hands became soaked in blood from the terrible wound in his chest.

It was Gabriel.

Incredibly, his face was peaceful, more beautiful to her in death than he had been in life. She started to caress his cheek and saw the gore on her hands. Anguished keening burst from her, turning into a scream so raw that something tore inside her throat. She fell across Gabriel's body, sobbing until there were no tears left and her swelling throat closed off all sound. The world went mercifully black.

* * *

When she came to herself, it was midday. Gabriel's face had grown stiff, his body now a hollow shell; the vital man he'd been had left this world. That certain knowledge helped Mercy return to rational thought. Her throat spasmed, painfully tight and dry, but she feared she would throw up if she drank any water now.

Already vultures circled overhead. She couldn't bear the thought of them feasting on the bodies of her loved ones. What could she do? She hadn't the strength to dig a grave large enough to bury everyone.

Most had died inside their cottages. They would be protected for a little while. It was those few who had died outside, Gabriel and Michael, Dilly and Samuel, who needed immediate attention.

Mercy ran to Dilly's small broken body and gently carried her to the chapel. She laid the poor girl on the wooden floor, arranging her limbs to appear that she was sleeping peacefully. Mercy placed young Samuel beside her. Their faces were beyond pain, and she prayed they now knew perfect peace.

Michael and Gabriel were too heavy to carry. It pained her that she would have to drag them as if they were sacks of flour. Both deserved much more dignity than she was able to give them.

Even though she knew he could no longer feel pain, Mercy gently eased Gabriel over the chapel threshold and down to the front where the children lay. She placed him beside Dilly, arranging his hands over the gash in his chest. Her eyes bled tears and she angrily wiped them away. How cruel that their feelings for one another had been awakened just before all hope of a life together had been shattered!

Last of all, she went for Michael's body. Mercy reeled in horror when she grabbed his hands and his nearly severed arm began to tear. She had to carefully pull him by his bare feet. Once she got him over the threshold, a streak of blood marked his passage on the floor of the chapel. Trembling, Mercy took a basin of water from the corner and set it down beside her cousin. She dipped the hem of her apron in the water and wiped the blood from his face and hands before crossing them on his chest.

Oh, Michael, she said silently, since her voice had failed her. *I'm sorry I wasn't here to die with you, my dear, dear cousin.* She tried to smooth his brow, but it was too late to erase the agony from his face.

Mercy kept vigil over these four as the shadows of that terrible day lengthened and darkness fell. From time to time she gave in to the tears. It was such a waste, a tragic waste of life, and she was the one who had left the gate open to whatever had killed them all. She wept for Papa, that his final words to her had been so unkind, that they would never have a chance to heal the rift. She wept for Gabriel and the love they would have shared. And she wept for Rafael. Not knowing what had happened to him was the worst of all.

How could she bear to keep living? Why had she been spared? She cried out from her heart to the Most High, but there was no answer. And sometime in the quiet hours of the night, she fell asleep, utterly spent.

* * *

Mercy woke, stiff and sore and very thirsty. Though she was numb from the horror of the violence and the crushing guilt that her careless act had been the cause of it, she realized even in the fog of her grief that she had to decide what to do with the bodies. She couldn't bury them, and she didn't think she would be able to make a proper pyre for all of them. Her only option was to burn the buildings in which the bodies lay so they would be consumed too.

Mercy fashioned several brands of wood, wrapping a piece of oil-soaked cloth around one end. Before she used Papa's flint and steel to light them, she dragged Papa's body to the nearest cottage in order to spare her own with the healing herbs drying from her ceiling beam.

Beginning at Ishmael's house, Mercy lit one of the brands. When it burned hot and bright, she tossed it onto the thatched roof, which quickly burst into flames. There were heavy low clouds and no wind, not even a breeze. The sky itself seemed to share in her mourning.

She did the same at each cottage, mentally saying goodbye to those within, shutting the door and setting it ablaze. Finally, she came to the chapel and opened the door. She gripped the last brand but didn't light it right away. The four bodies lay so still. She knew they were dead, but part of her hoped they would open their eyes, that all she needed to do was Heal them and they would be restored to her.

Tears poured from her eyes. She struggled to light the brand with trembling hands. When it caught, she told Gabriel and Michael and Dilly and Samuel goodbye, shut the door, and tossed the brand onto the chapel's thatched roof. Mercy backed toward the gate, watching the flames to make sure they didn't go out and wishing she had Gabriel's hair clasp to keep in memory of him. Whoever had killed him had taken it with his braid.

Mercy made sure all the fires were burning well, and then she turned and ran out the gate, down the path, and did not stop at the willow. She ran until there was no more path. The riverbank flattened out into a sandy cove, and Mercy fell to her hands and knees, gasping for breath.

Once she could breathe normally, she crawled to the water's edge. She washed her hands, but even after several minutes of scrubbing, she still didn't feel clean. Mercy cupped some water in her hands and splashed it on her face. Then she sat quietly until she regained control of herself.

Only after she took a long drink of the cool water did she look back. Columns of black smoke rose into the darkening sky. She covered her face to shut out the sight, but she couldn't close her mind to the images of bodies blackened by the fires.

As twilight lengthened, fear intruded on her grief. What creatures lurked among the trees? She ought to return to the village and sleep behind the barred gate. But how could she sleep there with the bodies still burning? Tears spilled onto her cheeks. She didn't bother to wipe them.

She remembered a tree that Michael used to climb, showing off. Her throat tightened at the memory of her beloved cousin. She pushed her grief aside and stood. Her feet took her to that tree. It was tall enough that she would be able to climb to a high branch, one that would keep her safe from night predators investigating the smell of death.

It took a long time to climb the tree. Her skirts kept getting in the way and she had to hike them up in the apron ties. She didn't think about how high she'd gone; she focused on one branch at a time. When she reached one that was perpendicular to the ground and large enough to straddle, she swung her leg around, sat with her back against the trunk, and glanced down. It made her dizzy to realize how high she'd climbed, and for a long moment she seriously considered letting go and ending her life.

Reason returned, and Mercy scolded herself for even thinking of squandering the gift of life. Although she did not understand why she alone had been spared, she retained enough sanity to realize there had to be a reason, whether she understood or no.

The light faded, and the night turned dark and cold. Owls hooted nearby. When the breeze blew from the direction of the village, Mercy caught the scent of smoke and death, and she shuddered.

The night seemed longer than just a few hours. Mercy feared falling asleep. Sometimes she dozed off and startled herself to wakefulness. Panic rose in her if she thought too much about the distance to the ground. Insects crawled on her, and once she heard a distant roar and imagined it must be a river dragon.

At dawn, she decided she'd had enough of the tree. There was sufficient light that she could slowly work her way down. It was more difficult going down then climbing up, and twice she made a bad step, scraping her leg and hand. When she touched the ground with her foot, she sighed.

After relieving her bladder beside the tree and washing her face in the river, she took a long drink. Her throat was still painfully constricted and she could not make a sound. She had to return to the village and decide what to do next. The fires should have burned down, even if they were still smoldering and hot.

As she neared the bluff, she saw vultures already circling, and her heart lurched. Had the fires not done their work? Had they burned the cottages but left the bodies exposed for the scavengers? Then she remembered: she had done nothing about the dead sheep. Mercy ran up the path toward the gate.

Valerian and Kieran awakened one hour after sunrise. When Kieran held up the royal surcoat, Valerian shook his head.

"I know Father said I must wear it, but he specified for the visits to the garrisons. We are visiting three people who know me by sight, Eldred and Lord Reed," Valerian paused to swallow. "And Lady Hanalah. I want no special treatment from anyone else."

Kieran frowned, but he didn't argue. He outfitted Valerian in plain leathers. While Kieran dressed himself, Valerian climbed the tower steps to greet the day. The one guard nodded his head in greeting; everyone else still slept after the night's indulgence. When Valerian faced the west, the Plains of Mohorovia changed from gray to red as the sun rose higher in the sky. Somewhere in that vast nothingness the Horde were either dying off or preparing for something sinister. Was it possible to discover the truth? Would it make any difference if Valerian were to stay and help with the search?

Valerian shook his head and shut his eyes. He had to stop putting doubts into his mind. Shouldn't he make a decision and stand by it? Even if it turned out to be the wrong decision, he wouldn't accomplish anything by wavering. He said a prayer for the safety and success of the men of the garrison, especially the ten whom he had come to like and appreciate, not as underlings to be controlled, but as fellow human beings. And he asked the Most High to watch over him and Kieran, no matter what happened next.

One by one, the men under his command awakened. As Valerian spoke to each man, they gripped forearms as comrades and wished one another well. The squire Terron held the reins of Valerian's horse while he mounted, and Valerian raised a hand to his men and Sir Walter, who had also come out to bid them farewell. Then, before he could change his mind, Valerian turned the horse toward the open gate and galloped away. He glanced back once to make sure Kieran followed.

The morning remained mild with no wind. The horses climbed the winding road that briefly turned south. As they crested the cliff, Valerian glanced back down at the garrison a final time. From this distance, it appeared small and lonely against the backdrop of the vast empty plains.

They rode at an easy pace for the rest of the day. Oddly, there was no one else along the road, and it appeared to have seen little use of late. Kieran found an elevated spot for a campsite, and they built a small fire. While they ate cold meat and bread from the garrison, Kieran stood.

"Sire, look." He pointed south.

Valerian stood beside him and saw the yellowish glow of multiple fires.

"I wonder what's burning. Was it deliberately set, do you think?"

"Difficult to say, Sire. We can investigate in the morning, if you wish."

"Let's leave at first light." The more Valerian watched the fire's glow, the more uneasy he grew, so much so that he insisted they take turns on watch.

While Kieran slept, Valerian continued to check the progress of the fire. The flames had died, but the glow remained for most of his watch. Whatever had burned still smoldered, and he felt an urgency to see what it was.

After he woke Kieran for his watch, Valerian was able to fall asleep, but he dreamed of the dragon again, and something new. A man appeared out of the dragon's flame. His face was pale, and his folded hands drew attention to the gaping wound in his chest. When his mind pierced Valerian's, he knew it was Gabriel. The Brethren leader held up blood-soaked hands, and a stabbing pain exploded in Valerian's head.

He sat up, gasping. Kieran squatted beside him, his face full of concern.

"Are ye all right, Sire?"

Valerian closed his eyes and massaged his temples.

"I thought it was just another bad dream, since it began with the dragon and the sword, but then a man came to me. It was Gabriel, the Brethren leader." He met Kieran's gaze. "He had a terrible chest wound and blood on his hands. What does that mean?"

"Would it have something to do with those fires, I wonder?" Kieran jerked his head toward the south.

Valerian stood. The sky lightened in the east.

"There's only one way to find out."

Chapter 16 *A merry heart maketh a cheerful countenance, but by sorrow of the heart the spirit is broken.*

When Mercy neared the village, the clopping of horses' hooves on the bridge made her stop. She ran back down the path and hid behind a large oak tree. Her heart pounded so loudly she feared someone would hear it.

Mercy peered around the trunk. Two riders approached the open gate. They were dressed as soldiers but wore longer hair than any outsiders she'd seen before. Even so it was only shoulder-length. They dismounted and left the horses untied while they conferred with one another. One of them was much taller than the other.

Were they trustworthy? Could she approach them for help? But how would she ask for help when she couldn't use her voice? When they entered the village, Mercy hurried after them, careful to stay out of sight. She covered her nose and mouth with her apron so as not to choke on the lingering smoke.

"What do you think happened here?" asked the tall one, coughing. He stared at the pile of ashes and burned fragments that had once been Adriel and Faith's cottage.

"Difficult to say, Sire." The shorter one poked around with the toe of his boot. He bent down and picked up a small object.

"What is it?"

"This looks like a wee bairn's arm bone." He paused. "These ashes are still warm."

Mercy blinked back tears. That would be Faith's infant, the one she had safely delivered, for all the good it had done.

The two young men didn't speak again. They split up, searching the village. The taller one turned toward Mercy, and for a moment she panicked, thinking he had seen her. Bending down, she moved behind a wood pile and peeked through a gap in the logs. The stranger's face did not look hardened and angry like the soldiers who took away the men that fateful day. His face was thoughtful, almost gentle.

"Sire," his companion shouted. "Come and see." He ran toward the sound and Mercy followed.

The first one had discovered the dead sheep. The carcasses were black with buzzing flies, but they didn't disguise the bloated remains.

"I canna be sure, my lord, but it looks as if a large blade made these gashes. They're about the size of the Horde's ax blades."

The taller one didn't answer. Mercy had seen enough.

She ran back to the gate. Though she badly needed to trust somebody, she wasn't sure she could face another person yet, even these two honest-faced young men.

Oh, God of peace, she prayed. *Please show me the way.*

Mercy glanced back to make sure they hadn't seen her, but when she stepped beyond the gate, two horses blocked her way. One was brown with a black mane and tail, and the other gray with white spots splashed across its rump. The horses regarded her, and the gray whinnied as if it were amused. The brown lowered its head, and Mercy stroked the velvet muzzle as she gazed into the large brown eyes.

"Well, what have we here?"

Mercy jumped back from the horse and saw the shorter young man standing there. He smiled kindly, reaching for the brown's reins.

"Gilly didna scare you, I hope? He can be over-friendly at times."

Mercy shook her head.

"I am Kieran MacLachlan. Do ye live here, lass?"

Mercy nodded, glancing at the gate. How could she explain what happened? She swallowed hard and tried to speak, but no sound came from her throat.

"Are ye not able to speak, then?" Kieran's speech was different than any she'd ever heard.

She shook her head and sighed with frustration. Then she shut her eyes, lest the tears come again.

When she opened them, the tall young man stood before her. His face was full of compassion as she stared into his dark eyes. She gasped when he *Saw* her thoughts, just as Gabriel had done. Without considering the consequences, she opened her thoughts to him, desperate to show him what had happened. In the space of a few heartbeats she flooded his mind with images of the massacre and how she had burned the bodies inside the buildings.

He staggered against the gray horse, and Kieran hurried to help him before he lost his balance.

"What is it, Sire? What happened?" Kieran had to lower him to a sitting position. The horses backed away so as not to step on him.

He held his head between his hands when he lifted his gaze to her again.

"How did you do that? Are you a Seer, too?"

Mercy saw the pain in his eyes as he continued to *See* her. She covered her mouth, horrified. She hadn't meant to hurt him. *I'm sorry*, she said in her mind as if he could hear her. *I'm not a Seer, only a Healer.*

"You're a Healer? I've never known one, but perhaps that's the explanation." He continued to rub his temples.

"Why do ye think she's a Healer, my lord?" Kieran glanced at her, puzzled.

"She just said she was one."

"She said nothing, Sire. The lass is nae able to speak." Kieran stared at Mercy so hard that she backed away, frightened now.

"Wait," said the taller one, leaning toward her. "Say something to me." He turned his Sight on her again.

I didn't mean to hurt you. Please, forgive me.

"I was startled by the intensity of your feelings. And I'm sorry for your terrible loss." He turned to Kieran. "You didn't hear her just now?"

"No, my lord," Kieran said. "I only heard you speaking."

When the tall young man gazed at Mercy again, she dared a bold question.

Why does Kieran call you 'sire' and 'my lord'?

He smiled at her, making him look younger. She was sure neither of them was much older than Michael.

"I am Valerian d'Alden, and Kieran is my squire. What may we call you?"

Mercy glanced at Kieran and then back at Valerian. Whatever these two were, they had shown kindness to a stranger. Her eyes filled with tears and she could no longer look into Valerian's eyes to communicate with him. She covered her face with her hands and fell to the ground, weeping.

Valerian was profoundly touched by the girl's sorrow. When she fell to her knees, he saw her long braid come into view, and he gasped.

"What is it, Sire?"

"She's one of the Brethren," he whispered. "This was their village. I *Saw* it in her mind." He thought about his dream of Gabriel, the burned buildings, the slaughtered sheep. "How did she survive?" But, of course, she had shown him how she'd slipped out before the massacre, not realizing what was about to happen.

"I dinna know, but we can't leave her here."

"Of course not." The girl wiped her face with a blood-stained apron. She appeared too young to be a Healer. Certainly too young to have witnessed such horror. Not only her apron, but her homespun dress was spattered with dried blood.

Kieran dug inside his saddlebag and produced flint and steel. "Should I set fire to the carcasses, Sire?"

"Not yet, but find some wood to pile around them and be ready to light the fire."

"Aye, my lord." Kieran glanced once at the girl and then hurried off to the sheep pens.

Valerian sat cross-legged on the ground in front of the Brethren girl. She seemed to have regained control of her emotions. He thought of Gabriel, and all those other men and youths whose names he never learned. Were they all dead? Had she alone survived?

At last she looked at him. Her eyes were so sad, but at least she didn't fear him. In truth, it appeared she had no idea who he was.

"I don't think you should stay here alone." Valerian spoke as gently as he could. "Will you come with us?"

She nodded and spoke again to his mind.

I can't stay here, but I don't know where to go.

"Rest assured, we'll find a place for you. Is there anything you'd like to bring?"

Yes. I must bring my herbs for Healing.

Valerian stood and helped her stand also. Then he followed her to the only remaining cottage, staring at the braid that hung from beneath her scarf. He didn't know hair could grow so long; it nearly reached the ground.

When she opened the door, he had to duck to enter. The single room was furnished with a table, stools, and three pallets on the dirt floor. There was a large dark stain nearby which the girl avoided. She opened a carry sack and began packing small clay pots and dried herbs from shelves in the wall. Something brushed against Valerian's head, and he saw how many herbs hung from the ceiling beam to dry.

"Would you like to bring these also?" When she nodded, he easily reached up to remove the bundles of plants from their hooks. While he handed them to her to place in the carry sack, she met his eyes.

I would have had to stand on one of the stools to reach them. It must be helpful to be so tall.

"Most of the time it's a blessing to be tall, but only if there are no low doorways or tree branches." He rubbed his head meaningfully, hoping to coax a smile from her.

She took an apron off a peg in the wall and tenderly folded it, placing it in the bulging carry sack. Then she picked it up and stood in the middle of the room, motionless. She turned back to him.

This has been my home for all my life.

"Do you want to tell me about your family?"

She briefly shut her eyes. When she opened them again, she had to blink away tears.

Not yet, not my family. But before we leave, may I tell you about the others?

"Of course." He opened the door for her and followed her to the nearest burned pile. At each one, she told him a little of the people who had lived there. He learned that she had discovered her Healing gift while assisting a woman named Faith in childbirth, that she had a cousin named Michael who'd been more like a beloved older brother to her, that a wise woman named Providence had fallen and not regained consciousness and so was spared the pain of her death. She did not mention Gabriel, though, and Valerian was reluctant to ask about him. Perhaps he was related to her. He did seem old enough to have been her father.

Valerian's righteous anger was kindled by the Brethren's tragedy. He wondered how the Horde had gotten past the garrison. Should they return now and inform Sir Walter? That might put the girl in harm's way. Valerian could send a messenger from the next village and continue on to warn Lord Reed. When they reached the gate, Kieran waited with the horses.

"Everything is prepared to start the fire, my lord."

"Thank you, Kieran. I think we're ready to go now." He glanced at the girl to make sure.

She gripped the latch of the gate, and her tears began to flow. Finally, she nodded.

"Go on, then, Kieran, and I'll help her onto my horse."

"Why don't you let me ride double with her? Gilly has carried two before, and the lass is a mere sprite, so Gilly won't even notice."

Valerian turned to speak to the girl.

"Is that acceptable to you?"

She studied Kieran's horse. Gilly nickered and gently butted her with his head. That seemed to decide her, and she nodded.

While Kieran ran back inside the village, Valerian added the carry sack to the back of his saddle.

"Have you ridden before?" When she shook her head, he studied Kieran's saddle. "Since you are wearing skirts, it might be easier for you to ride sidesaddle behind Kieran. If this doesn't work, we'll try another way."

How will I get on the horse?

"I'll lift you up, with your permission, of course."

Kieran returned and put his flint and steel in the saddle bag.

"I'm ready, Sire. Did you find out her name?"

Valerian met the girl's somber gaze and opened his Sight to her.

My former life no longer exists. It doesn't matter what you call me.

Valerian told Kieran what she said. The squire grinned.

"Well, then, if it pleases you, I would like to call ye 'Merry.' Perhaps a happy name will help ye smile again."

Her gaze became distant, and she turned back to the gate one last time. Greasy black smoke rose from the burning sheep carcasses. She swallowed, hard, and tears filled her eyes again. At last, she faced Kieran and nodded once.

"All right, lass. Merry ye shall be." He pulled himself up on Gilly and scooted forward in the saddle.

Valerian waited for Merry's permission to help her mount. He put his hands around her slender waist and lifted her up to the saddle. She grabbed Kieran's leather tunic. He glanced over his shoulder.

"Just hold me around the waist, Merry, and sit firmly in the saddle. I will nae let you fall."

Valerian stepped back and grabbed the gray's reins. "I'll keep an eye on her, Kieran, and let you know if we need to stop."

Without a backward glance, they rode down the bluff, across the bridge, and into the forest.

* * *

They traveled along the overgrown path until it intersected a wider road. Valerian kept checking on Merry to make sure she wasn't about to slide off the horse. Although she rode awkwardly, she drank in her surroundings. She'd probably never been outside her village before, so everything would be new. Kieran kept a running commentary on the weather, the trees, birds, and animals. When the squire said "tree dragon" Valerian followed Kieran's finger until he spotted the little creature scampering down the trunk of a large elm. Merry's eyes widened when she saw it and a slight smile came to her lips. Valerian was glad she wasn't a fearful sort.

They passed a few folk on the road, but since Valerian wore plain leathers, they merely nodded a greeting. Valerian much preferred traveling without the trappings of royalty. He could observe the people as they would normally behave, not just their deference to the prince of Levathia.

As the shadows lengthened it was apparent Merry was exhausted. Even though they hadn't ridden far, he remembered his first outings on horseback and how much energy he'd used just staying upright in the saddle. He couldn't imagine how difficult it would be to ride sideways while wearing a dress and holding onto a total stranger, albeit a cheerful and obliging one.

"Kieran, we must find a site to camp for the night. We won't reach Lord Reed's castle until tomorrow evening at the earliest."

"My thoughts exactly, Sire." Kieran swung his leg around, about to slide off the horse.

Merry's eyes widen, and Valerian held up a hand to stop Kieran.

"Wait! Let me help her off first." Valerian reached up and lifted Merry by the waist. She let go of Kieran and braced herself on Valerian's shoulders. He set her down in one smooth motion, but she grabbed for his arms as her legs buckled.

"Steady," he said quietly. "Until you become used to riding, it will over-tire your muscles. I well remember." He let Merry lean on him until she found her legs again.

Kieran was already gathering dead wood for a fire. He shook out sleeping furs and arranged them at equal points around the fire site. While Merry went behind the trees, Valerian and Kieran opened their saddle bags to take inventory.

"We have just two or three days' more food, my lord."

"I'm sure Lord Reed will be glad to re-provision us. If not, we have our bows."

"And I have my fishing line and hooks." Kieran appeared thoughtful. "I wonder if fish in the south are as tasty as northern fish?"

"I'd be willing to sample whatever you catch." Valerian smiled. "And you must show me how to clean and cook it."

"With pleasure, Sire." Kieran saluted.

Merry returned to the clearing, pale and worn.

"Are ye hungry, lass?" Kieran held out a piece of dried meat.

She took it and sniffed, frowning.

Is this meat?

"Yes. Is something wrong?"

Merry gave the meat back to Kieran without breaking eye contact with Valerian.

I have never eaten it.

"Never? Why not?"

We take an oath at the age of twelve that we will never take the life of any living creature.

An image of Gabriel speaking calmly to the king came to Valerian.

"I knew that, but I didn't realize it meant you couldn't eat meat."

"She canna eat meat?"

"Apparently that's part of the Brethren's Oath of Peace."

Kieran turned to Merry, chagrined.

"Ach, lass, I had no idea and dinna mean to offend you."

She gave him a tired smile.

"Can you eat bread? We have a wee bit left, but 'tis probably stale."

Merry nodded again. Kieran rummaged through his pack and pulled out a piece of flat bread.

"Here you go, Merry."

The three of them sat on the furs and shared the meal. Kieran passed around a flask of water and chattered amiably between bites. Valerian watched Kieran, amused. He was obviously smitten with the girl, but she was too tired to give him more than polite attention. Valerian felt compelled to rescue Merry from his squire's eager interest.

"If we sleep now," he reminded Kieran, "we can get an early start."

"But Sire," Kieran said with pleading in his voice. "There's still daylight."

Valerian forced a smile. "Not for long."

"Please, Sire, can we not just go a wee bit longer? I haven't had the chance to teach you the sword dance."

Valerian wanted to be stern with him, but he merely sighed.

"Very well." The last thing he wished to do was fall on his face in order to make Kieran look good in front of Merry, but he did owe Kieran his life. It was the least he could do for him.

Kieran cleared an area near the fire of twigs and leaves. Then he pulled his sword from its scabbard and laid it flat on the ground.

"May I have your sword, Sire?"

Reluctantly Valerian handed Alden's sword to Kieran, hilt first. The squire placed it on top of his own, crossed as the spears had been.

"Now, I'll stand here." Kieran took his place in the outside edge of one quarter. "And if you'll stand across from me, we can begin."

Valerian slowly moved to the spot. He glanced at Merry. She watched with the same interest she'd given the tree dragon.

"The biggest problem is we hae no music. I'll have to sing it."

"Is it a particular song? Or will any song do?"

"Ach, no, my lord. 'Tis one song only. That's what makes it the sword dance."

"I see." But Valerian predicted this exercise would not turn out as well as Kieran's training session when they had learned to use their swords.

The foot moves were not as difficult as Valerian imagined, but the timing was challenging without actual musicians to keep the beat. He found himself laughing in spite of himself. Kieran, of course, enjoyed showing off. Valerian could not be angry with him.

At last it grew too dark to see clearly by firelight, so Valerian and Kieran each wiped off their blades and returned the swords to their scabbards. Merry was visibly wilted with exhaustion, but Kieran seemed ready to talk all night. Valerian pulled him aside.

"You must rein in your enthusiasm. Can you not see that Merry needs to sleep? After all she has witnessed, I feel sure she has not slept well, if at all, for more than one night."

Kieran looked stricken.

"I'm sorry, Sire. I did get carried away and lost me head." He glanced at Merry but didn't speak again as he laid down on the furs.

Valerian knelt beside Merry and spoke quietly.

"It has grown too dark for me to *See* your thoughts. If you need anything during the night, wake me. I am, unfortunately, not a sound sleeper." She nodded and lay down on the furs Kieran had given her. When she curled on her side and tucked her hands under her cheek, Valerian covered her with another fur. As soon as she closed her eyes he bedded down close by.

Valerian lay awake, listening to the sounds of the night until he could tell by their regular breathing that Merry and Kieran had fallen asleep. He willed himself to follow them, but for some reason he couldn't stop thinking about the sisters he'd lost at a young age. Ravanna was six when she died of a fever, and he was barely three. Because his mother was expecting the younger sister at the time, it was said the babe had died of the mother's grief. Certainly she did not live more than a day after her birth. The queen had shut herself away ever since.

Why was he remembering this? Was it the sudden and unexpected contact with a female mind that had awakened such memories? He'd never had a close relationship with any woman or girl in his life. His two aunts were almost as distant as his mother, and he had no female cousins. The only women he knew were courtiers and servants at the Keep, but he'd never had any real contact with them other than polite greetings. That unspoken but very real wall of separation, what he could only term a *splendid isolation*, had kept him apart as a prince. Was that why he'd always longed to be a monk? Since he'd never really learned how to deal with people, he'd envisioned a monk's life as ideal.

He sighed. Perhaps he could have become one had his brother lived and begat an heir. Now he desperately needed to learn how to relate to every kind of person, both great and small, so when the time came he could rule wisely.

Thank the Most High Kieran had come into his life. For the first time, he had a true friend, someone he could utterly trust. Perhaps the girl Merry was a gift also, so he might learn to understand the feminine mind before he had to marry. He already felt protective of her, as if she was a sister, and he'd known her less than a day. Should she turn out to be Gabriel's daughter, he knew he would feel even more of an obligation to provide for her welfare in every possible way.

How odd he should feel such a connection to Gabriel and the Brethren, since he'd only spoken with Gabriel twice. He regretted there had been no time to sit down with the man and know him better.

At last Valerian's thoughts settled and he drifted into sleep.

When he and his men arrived at Lord Reed's castle, Caelis sent Drew and the boy with the others to the barracks. He didn't want to have to answer any nosy questions from his uncle or his cousin.

A page announced him, and he waited, pacing, in his uncle's sitting room. Lord Percival Reed was overly fond of embroidered chairs and fine tapestries. No great military mind occupied his uncle's head. At last Reed entered, smiling.

"You are welcome, nephew. What brings you south?"

Caelis received his uncle's embrace. He wrinkled his nose at the perfume the older man wore.

"I've been on patrol, uncle, and thought I'd pay you a brief visit before I return to the Keep."

"Patrol, you say?" Reed sat on a divan and urged Caelis to sit in the chair beside him. "Are the Horde on the prowl again?"

Caelis shook his head and sat on the plush cushion.

"No, but we need to stay alert for their return. I've been working with the Keep's armorer on a bow design that will be more effective in piercing the Horde's scales. I hope to give the king a demonstration soon."

"Ever bringing credit to our family, I see." Reed grinned. "Your good father, may he rest in peace, would be proud."

I doubt that. But Caelis did not say the words aloud.

He was spared further speculation on his dead father by the entrance of Reed's daughter. Hanalah swept into the room wearing a low cut red gown. Her yellow hair was arranged in a jeweled net, and her full lips were painted a deep red.

"Hello, cousin Hanalah." He admired her shapely figure.

She made a graceful curtsy and sat on the divan beside her father.

"So good to see you again, cousin. Or I should say, Sir Caelis."

Caelis was always taken aback by the contrast between Hanalah's beauty and the grating shrillness of her voice. She smiled and took her father's arm. Reed kissed her forehead.

"I have news of special interest to you," Caelis said, including them both. "Prince Valerian is in the south and expected to visit here."

Hanalah's face brightened, making her even more radiant.

"Valerian is coming here? Did he ask about me?"

Caelis laughed. His cousin always did make herself the center of every situation.

"I did not actually see him. King Orland sent him to visit all the border garrisons, and Sir Walter at the Southern Garrison just informed me that the prince was on his way here."

"How did you reach us before the prince, then?" said Lord Reed.

"He had others to visit, notably Eldred and probably Sir Rudyard MacNeil."

Hanalah pouted. Any other woman would have looked ridiculous, but the pout only enhanced his cousin's charm.

"And why would he not come here first? Are we not of more importance than some doddering old Seer and a crippled knight?"

"Now, now, my dear, you must show a little charity to those less fortunate." Reed patted her arm. "I'm sure the king will agree you would be the best possible choice to become the new crown prince's royal bride. You must be patient."

Yes, Caelis echoed silently. *We must all be patient. But I fear, my ambitious cousin, you will never be a royal bride. Your royal bridegroom isn't going to live that long.*

Chapter 17 *Thou shalt be called by a new name.*

When Mercy awoke just before sunrise, it took her a moment to remember where she was, and with whom. The fire had almost burned itself out, and she was glad to be wrapped in furs in the chilly morning air. She turned her head. Kieran lay on one side, snoring softly. Mercy smiled when she remembered how he'd been showing off, just like Michael used to do. By that alone she knew Kieran couldn't be much older than she was.

Mercy sat up, carefully stretching her sore muscles. Valerian lay on his side with his head pillowed on his arm, facing her. Asleep, he appeared more at peace than he had yesterday. Her guilt lingered for giving him such a painful headache when she forced her thoughts into his mind. Should she have tried to Heal him or would that have made the situation worse?

She closed her eyes, remembering how Kieran wanted to call her Merry. Should she tell them her real name? No, it would be best if she began to think of herself by this new name. After all, no one alive knew her as Mercy. Her throat tightened as tears spilled over her cheeks. Maybe choosing to accept this other name would help her find a new life among these outsiders. And, she reflected, it was just as much a Brethren name as the one she'd been born with.

So Mercy sadly put aside that name and became *Merry*, just as the sun's rays appeared through the trees. A new day, a new beginning. And there was heavenly light to bless the moment.

Valerian opened his eyes when the sunlight touched his face. He pushed himself to a sitting position. Kieran still slept, but Merry was awake. She sat with her face turned away from him, and she had undone her braid. From this angle, all he could see was a cascade of auburn hair. He stared, amazed at the sight of it. Merry took a comb from her carry sack and began to untangle the individual locks of hair. No wonder the Brethren kept their hair braided; it would always be in the way if they'd worn it loose.

He kept silent through the process of combing and re-braiding. The girl was remarkably quick with her small hands. When she finished braiding the hair, Merry secured it with a wooden clasp. She replaced the comb in her carry sack and rose gracefully. Then she turned, only then noticing him.

"Good morrow, Merry. I hope you slept well?"

She nodded, appearing flustered.

"Did I startle you?"

Shrugging, she came closer so he could *See* her.

You were so quiet I didn't realize you were awake.

"I would have said something, but you were engrossed with your hair. Besides, I was fascinated watching you. There are those who think *my* hair is too long." He smiled, hoping she would realize he was teasing.

Your hair is longer than the soldiers who came to our village.

Valerian ran his hands through his tangled hair. He realized it was long enough to tie back if he wished. But he was spared having to comment when Kieran leaped up, not quite awake.

"My lord! How long have ye been awake? What did I miss? Can I get ye anything?" He rubbed his eyes, clearly disoriented.

"All is well. We've just awakened ourselves." Valerian stood beside Kieran. "We ought to put away our things and get ready to leave."

"Shouldn't we break our fast, Sire?" Kieran blinked. His hair stuck up on one side, and Valerian tried not to laugh.

"If you wish it."

First Kieran refilled their water flasks in the nearby stream. He ducked his head underwater and shook it, spraying water from his hair. After that, the squire came fully awake.

Once they ate some travel bread, Kieran saddled the horses, and Valerian helped Merry up behind his squire. Then he mounted the gray and they found the road again.

The farther they traveled the more people they met on the road. Soon they came in sight of a village. Before they reached it, a woman dashed out in front of Valerian's horse, and he had to pull back on the reins to keep from trampling her.

"Please, sir, can ye help my poor son? He's fallen from that tree yonder and broken his arm."

Valerian dismounted and walked the gray off the road, Kieran's horse following. Then Valerian caught Merry's eye. When she nodded, he spoke to the villager.

"Merry is a Healer. Would you like for her to look at your son?"

The woman stared up at Merry and frowned.

"But, she's just a lass."

"Do you want our help or no?" Valerian didn't mean to sound so sharp.

"Yes, sir. Of course, sir. My boy is just over there." The woman hurried toward a nearby copse of trees.

Valerian helped Merry off the horse and handed her the carry sack of herbs. Kieran took charge of the horses as they followed the woman.

Her son sat under a stand of black oaks, a lad of seven or eight with a shock of curly brown hair. His face contorted in pain, and he cradled his right arm. As they got closer it was obvious he'd badly broken it; the two forearm bones had pierced the skin and blood dribbled from the wounds.

"I don't know what to do for an injury like this." The woman began to cry.

Merry put her hand on the woman's arm for a moment. Then she knelt beside the boy and stroked his head, trying to reassure him. Valerian squatted down opposite her in case she needed to communicate with him.

"This is Merry," he told the boy. "She can't speak, but she can help you."

The boy nodded, sniffling. Merry took one of the clay pots from her pack. Then, breathing deeply, she gently encircled the boy's injured arm with her hands. Valerian realized she intended to put the broken bones back in place, so he moved behind the boy to keep him from jumping up. When the lad tensed, Valerian bent down and spoke quietly to him.

"It will only hurt for a little while, but then your arm will be able to heal. When we're finished I'll show you the injury I received in battle. It hurt at first, but now it's healed."

The boy gazed up at him with wide eyes, but Valerian's words had their intended effect, and he set himself to endure the pain.

Merry nodded at them and closed her eyes. In one swift motion, she moved the ends of bone back under the skin. For a moment, the bleeding intensified, and then it stopped. Merry continued to hold onto the boy's arm, and Valerian watched, mesmerized, as an unearthly yellow glow emanated from her hands.

Just as Valerian felt he should intervene, for Merry's face became visibly pale, she let go of the boy's arm and opened her eyes, momentarily disoriented. She took a shuddering breath before smearing salve from the clay pot on the arm, but the puncture marks were all but healed.

The mother came forward and offered her apron. Merry fashioned a sling for the boy's arm and tied it around his waist. He pushed himself upright with his left hand and grinned.

"It don't hurt now, Ma." He turned back to Merry. "Thank you, lady." Eagerly, he faced Valerian. "Will you show me your battle scar now, sir?"

Reluctantly Valerian lifted his leather tunic and the white linen shirt underneath to reveal part of the long ax scar. The boy leaned closer and hissed through his teeth.

"What cut you so bad, sir?"

Valerian paused, remembering the pressure of the Mohorovian's ax against his abdomen, the sound of metal slicing through leather and chain mail and flesh, and the flash of fiery agony before he lost consciousness.

"A battle-ax." He pulled down the shirts to cover the scar from view.

The boy's mother fell to her knees.

"How can I ever thank you enough? What can I give you for what you have done?"

Valerian's first impulse was to raise up the woman. No one had ever knelt before him.

"You can tell us if you have heard of Eldred, an old man who recently served the king as Seer."

She frowned, thinking. Finally, she spoke.

"Nay, sir, but there is someone who might know. Sir Rudyard MacNeil recently returned from the Keep."

"Sir Rudyard lives here?" Valerian glanced at Kieran.

"Aye, in the manor house, at the far end of the village."

Now Valerian did help the woman stand.

"Thank you, good woman. That is payment enough."

Mother and son walked away. Valerian stood, but Merry had not moved from her kneeling position.

"Are you all right, Merry?"

She nodded, but he went down on one knee and peered into her eyes.

"Something is not right."

I did not fully Heal the arm this time, but even so it takes something from me to set the bones. I will be all right in a minute or two.

She tried to stand, but she lost consciousness, and Valerian barely caught her before she fell. He cradled her against his chest.

"Kieran, we must find Ruddy's house."

"What happened to the lass?" Kieran's face was full of concern.

"I think she's just spent." He pondered her words and the glow he had seen from her hands. When she Healed someone, was it at the expense of her own health? If so, she would need to be more judicious about who she helped and to what extent.

They made a strange procession through the village, he carrying Merry, and Kieran leading their horses. Two women carding wool outside a cottage stopped to stare. The rhythmic ringing of hammer on anvil ceased when they passed the blacksmith's, resuming once they moved beyond his sight. Three small boys followed, remarking on the "fine 'orses," and Valerian was especially glad not to be wearing the royal surcoat. At the far end of the village, Valerian spied a manor house just off the road.

"That must be the one." He turned to Kieran. "I don't know whether Ruddy will be glad to see me or not, but he'll be willing to help Merry, at least."

They approached the door of the wattle and daub structure. Kieran dropped the horses' reins so they would know not to wander off, and then he knocked.

A young girl answered. Her eyes widened when she saw the three strangers. Valerian spoke.

"Is Sir Rudyard at home?"

"Yes, sir." The girl nodded, staring.

"Will you tell him that an old friend has come to see him?"

"Just a moment, sir." She closed the door.

As small as she was, Valerian had to shift Merry's dead weight, now that they were standing still. The door opened again, and standing before them was the red-haired knight. He balanced on his one remaining leg and a crutch.

"Prince Valerian." His voice was gruff. "What are ye doing here, Your Highness?"

"It's a long story, which I'm happy to relate, but we must have help for the girl."

"Come in." Ruddy backed away so Valerian and Kieran could step inside the manor's hall. "Lay the lass on the cot by the fire."

Valerian strode across the spacious hall, his boots echoing on the portions of the wood floor not covered with rugs or rushes. He gently placed Merry on the fur-covered cot. By the light of the fire, Merry's face appeared ashen. Alarmed, Valerian probed her wrist for a pulse. It was rapid and shallow. He covered her with another fur draped across a nearby cushioned chair.

"What happened to her?" Ruddy hobbled closer. "Is she one of the Brethren?"

"Yes." Valerian turned to his old friend. "We found their village massacred by the Horde. She was the only survivor."

"The Horde? So near?" Ruddy frowned. He turned and bellowed, "Shannon!"

A heavy-set woman entered the hall. She cradled an infant in her arms.

"What is it, Ruddy?"

"Have that girl of yours fetch us bread and nectar."

"What's going on, Ruddy?"

"I'll tell ye after we get the bread and drink, woman."

Shannon huffed and disappeared through another doorway.

Valerian sat beside Merry on the cot and began to rub her bare feet. They felt like ice. He didn't know exactly what to do to help her, but he knew she needed to get warm.

"Why are ye in the south, Val?"

Valerian turned to Ruddy but was careful to avoid direct eye contact.

"The king sent me to all the border garrisons. My first command."

"So where are your men?" The knight crossed his arms.

"At the Southern Garrison assisting Sir Walter 'til I return. I'm looking for Eldred."

"Well, ye came to the right place. He lives here in Forestglade."

Valerian let out an audible sigh.

"I must speak with Eldred as soon as possible."

"Any particular reason?" Ruddy stared at Valerian until he met his gaze.

Without meaning to, Valerian *Saw* the older man's thoughts. His anger and bitterness assaulted him, and Valerian cringed at the intensity of it. Ruddy scowled.

"What did ye do just now?"

"I'm sorry. That's why I must see Eldred, so I can learn how to control it."

"Control what?"

"I'm a Seer." Valerian grimaced. "The gift came upon me the very hour Waryn died."

Ruddy's face reddened, and he raised his voice.

"So, Your Highness, 'tis not enough that ye cut off me leg, now ye invade my mind without permission?"

"I'm sorry, Ruddy." Valerian kept his voice as calm as possible. "I didn't intend to *See* your thoughts just then. And as for the other, I did what seemed best at the time."

While Ruddy growled, his wife and her maid entered. Shannon still carried the infant. The girl carried a tray with a flask, several cups, and a loaf of bread, which she set on a nearby table. Then she curtsied and left the room. Valerian stood and faced Sir Rudyard's wife.

"Who is this, Ruddy?" Shannon studied the three strangers.

Ruddy gestured toward Valerian but would not meet his eyes.

"This is Prince Valerian and his squire, Kieran MacLachlan."

"Your Highness." Shannon curtsied.

"This is my wife, Shannon, and our wee bairn." Though his voice was still gruff, Valerian could hear his obvious pride.

"'Tis my pleasure to meet you at last, Lady MacNeil." Valerian wondered if she knew he was the one who'd cut off her husband's leg.

"Lady MacNeil," said Kieran with a bow.

"Is your father *the* MacLachlan?" Shannon asked eagerly.

"Aye, lady. Do ye know him?"

"I certainly do. He married my mother's sister after your good mother died."

"Oh, aye." Kieran smiled sadly. "Your bonny aunt has been a great comfort to me Da."

Shannon turned her attention to Merry.

"What ails this poor girl?"

"She's overcome with exhaustion," Valerian said. "I think a day or two of rest and food will set her to rights."

"Except for meat," Kieran added. "Merry willna eat meat."

"Merry is her name?" Shannon studied her. "I see she is one o' the Brethren. She looks very young."

While they all watched her, Merry stirred and opened her eyes. She focused on Valerian first and then sat up, grimacing as she put a hand to her head. Valerian sat beside her so she could more easily communicate if necessary.

"How are you feeling?" he asked.

The room is spinning.

Kieran poured nectar into one of the cups and handed it to Valerian. He helped Merry drink from it. When she swallowed, her eyes widened.

What is this?

"It's a juice called nectar. Its sweetness will help restore you." Valerian handed her a small loaf of bread.

Merry brought it to her mouth and stopped when she saw Ruddy and Shannon. She glanced back at Valerian.

I can't eat now. It would be impolite.

Valerian sighed. Sometimes formalities got in the way.

"Merry, may I introduce Sir Rudyard MacNeil and his lady, Shannon. We are guests in their home in the village of---" He glanced at Ruddy.

"Forestglade." Ruddy hobbled closer. "Ye are welcome to stay as long as you need to recover your strength. Please, dinna wait on us. Ye need to eat, lass. You will wither away."

Merry's eyes widened when she noticed Ruddy's stump, but she quickly moved her gaze to his face. Valerian felt compelled to explain why she didn't answer.

"She is not able to speak."

"Oh?" Shannon frowned with concern. "Can she write?"

Merry shook her head.

"Poor girl! How does she communicate?" Shannon must not have expected an answer, for she turned away, distracted by her infant.

It would be difficult to explain this to her, wouldn't it? Merry shrugged.

Valerian nodded once and stared meaningfully at the bread in her hand. She bit into it. Shannon turned back to Merry.

"If you can't eat meat, what else can you eat?"

"She eats bread." Valerian realized he'd never seen her eat anything else. He met her gaze again.

Grains, herbs, vegetables.

"You must eat more than bread." Shannon frowned. "Can you eat eggs? I have chickens and ducks."

Merry frowned while she gazed thoughtfully at Valerian.

I have never eaten an egg. Isn't there a living creature inside the shell?

"Lady Shannon," Valerian said. "Merry can eat anything that comes from plants." He answered Merry quietly. "I don't believe there is a simple answer to your question, but for the sake of your conscience, if there is any doubt, you should not eat eggs."

"What about milk?" Kieran asked. "And cheese? Merry, you canna be strong on bread and vegetables alone."

She nodded at Kieran and shrugged before returning her gaze to Valerian. *We drank our ewes' milk and made cheese.*

"I can see that milking a ewe would do her no harm," Valerian said, not that he'd ever had the opportunity to milk a ewe or anything else. Other than meat, he'd never even considered where his food came from; it had always been prepared for him.

"Well, then, I'll know what to serve for the evening meal tonight." Shannon bustled out of the room, calling for her servant.

* * *

When they all sat down to a meal that evening, Valerian was surprised at Merry's appetite. Though considering what she had experienced in the last few days, he was sure she hadn't eaten during that time. And if Healing took so much energy from her, no wonder she was ravenous.

Kieran sat beside her and seemed pleased she ate so well. He eagerly refilled her trencher with everything from the table, except of course the roast venison. Ruddy pushed away his empty trencher and sat back with a sigh.

"So, Val, how long will ye be in the south?"

With only two candles on the table providing limited light, Valerian didn't have to worry about accidentally using his Sight.

"We must return to the Keep before the spring thaw." Even without *Seeing* Ruddy's thoughts, he could tell the man was uncomfortable about something.

"Before I left the Keep, the king appointed me magistrate. The day after tomorrow is the village's winter festival, and the day following I hold my first court." Ruddy cleared his throat. "Might I persuade ye to stay here 'til then? I would welcome your knowledge o' the law."

"I would be honored to help you," Valerian said, relieved. "'Tis only fair considering all the help you gave me when I struggled to learn how to use a bow and spear."

"Advice on the letter of the law is nae much repayment for all the bruises and torn muscles I suffered during your training, but I concede tae the exchange of favors." He crossed his arms, frowning. "Dinna forget the quarterstaff." Ruddy's gruffness returned, and Valerian realized it was his way of dealing with the loss of his mobility.

"How could I forget that? I *am* sorry for knocking you in the lake." Valerian sighed, and Ruddy grunted.

"Me new shirt was ne'er the same."

"Nor was my head after you cracked it." Valerian rubbed the spot on his head.

Kieran grinned. He leaned forward eagerly.

"You'll have tae tell me about that sometime, Sire."

"I will." Valerian glanced at Merry. "Some other time." She had visibly wilted. "But for now, we ought to bed down for the night. Might Kieran and I sleep in your stables?"

Ruddy glowered, and Valerian wondered what he had done wrong now.

"I am offended, Valerian d'Alden, that ye would consider me such a terrible host as all that. Thanks to your generous father, I'm well able tae offer hospitality of a better sort." He pushed himself upright and grabbed his crutch. "Follow me, all o' ye."

Valerian had to scramble to help Merry and keep up with Ruddy. The knight could move surprisingly fast with his crutch. He led them through a doorway into a narrow hall with a door on either side and one at the end. Ruddy opened the first door.

"Here is me best room, Val. I suppose your squire will be wanting to stay in here, too."

Kieran nodded and entered first.

"My thanks, Sir Rudyard," he said.

Valerian gave the room a cursory glance. There was a large canopied bed, a table, chairs, and nightstand with an ewer of water, basin, and towels.

"This is a fine room, Ruddy. You are indeed a gracious host." He nodded to Kieran. "I'll settle Merry and be right back."

Ruddy opened a door opposite that of Valerian's guest room.

"Here is a room for the lass. Our room is there at the end of the hall." He turned to leave, and Valerian stopped him.

"Thank you, Ruddy. I meant no harm in suggesting the stables. I didn't realize Father had provided so well for you, but I'm grateful for your sake."

Ruddy growled softly, the anger just under the surface.

"Dinna pity me."

"Indeed I do not pity you. I've always looked up to you, Sir Rudyard, and I always will."

The knight paused for a long moment and then hobbled toward the door to his bedchamber. Before he entered, he silently bowed.

With a sigh, Valerian turned his attention to Merry. He made sure she had everything she needed.

"I can't *See* your thoughts until morning, but if you need something in the night, don't hesitate to wake me. You don't even have to knock. I'll remind Kieran so he won't attack you, thinking you're an intruder." They both smiled at that image. "Sleep well, Merry." She nodded and closed the door.

As Valerian walked slowly back to his room, he pondered how Ruddy must feel. How did such a valiant knight, highly esteemed by the king, learn to live with the loss of his leg and accept such a new and totally different role in life?

Caelis waited alone in the guest room of his uncle Reed's castle. The clutter of too many chairs and jewel-encrusted trunks made pacing difficult, but he did not have the patience to sit on one of the embroidered chairs. He had just made up his mind to leave when there was a knock at the door. Caelis opened it.

Thrane stood with Captain Ulfred, a man Caelis had known his entire life. Before Caelis left the Keep, his cousin Lewes revealed that Ulfred was strongly in favor of a separate southern kingdom.

"Come in," Caelis told the two men. Once they entered, he closed and barred the door. Then Caelis faced them.

Ulfred, a captain of Lord Reed's guard, was about Caelis' height with a stockier frame. His plain face was unremarkable except for his gray eyes. Ulfred's gaze pierced like a bird of prey, missing nothing.

"I told Captain Ulfred about the Brethren village, Sir Caelis." Thrane leered, obviously pleased with himself.

Caelis frowned. He hadn't expressly told the men not to discuss what they'd done, but still it surprised him that Thrane would be so open.

"Then I assume you told him why." Caelis did not try to hide the irritation in his voice. Let Thrane wonder if Caelis was displeased.

"I told him about the prince's decree," Thrane said with less enthusiasm than before. "He thinks—"

Caelis held up a hand, glaring at Thrane before meeting Ulfred's unreadable gaze.

"And what do you think about it, Captain Ulfred?" Caelis studied the man's face and waited to measure his words.

"It matters little to me what a prince of Levathia decrees." Ulfred's voice remained calm, while his eyes hardened. "Though they were southerners, the pacifists would never have joined our cause." He shrugged. "It is possible we would have had to kill them anyway, if they got in our way."

Caelis nodded, pleased to hear that Ulfred was as ruthless as he remembered.

"What are the plans for the south?" Caelis asked carefully.

Ulfred's face masked his emotions, as if chiseled from stone.

"A man with great charisma named Orin Swift is quietly gathering discontented men to himself. There are more than we anticipated who desire a separate southern kingdom."

"Is that so?" Caelis lifted an eyebrow to appear interested, but all he could think was that these men were setting their sights too low. Why desire half a kingdom when the whole of it was within their grasp?

Ulfred studied Caelis before answering, as if he were a Seer. Would Caelis have any way of knowing whether or not the man could read his thoughts?

"While you and Lewes and the others at the Keep watch for opportunities to forward our cause, Swift and I and others here in the south will continue to make disciples. Once we have sufficient numbers, we will plan our course of action to bring about the desired separation."

"Even if it means war between north and south?" Caelis asked. He had to know if it could come to that.

Ulfred nodded curtly, his gaze never wavering.

"War is inevitable," he said. "The only question is when."

"Then I shall look for every opportunity to foment instability." *For my own ends, whether or not they align with yours.* Caelis smiled. *After all, you are but a captain of my uncle's guard, and I intend to be king of Levathia.*

Chapter 18 *Thine own friend, and thy father's friend, forsake not.*

Merry woke with the sun, more refreshed than she had been in a long time. She'd never slept in a real bed before. She jumped up and smoothed the covers. Once she figured out the purpose of the chamber pot beneath the bed, she decided it was a happy improvement over the outdoor necessary behind her cottage.

She poured water into the basin and bathed herself, drying off with one of the soft towels. Her clothes badly needed a washing, though she knew the blood stains would never completely fade no matter how many times she scrubbed them. After she combed and braided her hair, she tried to straighten her wrinkled scarf before tying it under her chin. Then she opened the door to her room and stepped out.

Merry crossed the hall, marveling at the high ceiling beams, and peered into one of the open doorways. She gasped when she saw it was a kitchen as large as her entire cottage. There was even an oven. Imagine, an oven *inside* one's home! She'd had to share the one village oven with everyone else.

Hoping Shannon wouldn't mind, Merry poked around in the kitchen to see what was available. Every ingredient to make her special bread was there, and Merry decided to surprise everyone, with Shannon's permission, of course. She would have to wait to ask Valerian, but all she'd need to do was get up earlier the following morning.

"Good morrow." Shannon's cheerful voice startled Merry out of her reverie. "I see you are an early riser, as I am." The woman gestured around her. "What do you think of my kitchen?"

Merry hugged herself and smiled. Then she pointed to Shannon and pantomimed rocking a baby.

"Nathan? He's still asleep, what a mercy. He woke up three times to nurse in the night." Shannon paused for only a moment. "Did you know that Nathan means 'gift'? 'Twas a blessed gift to us after waiting so long for a child. Ruddy and I have been married for ten years."

Merry smiled. She wished she could better communicate with Shannon, who seemed kind-hearted.

Shannon's maid wandered into the kitchen, yawning.

"Elsbeth, please prepare our breakfast. The men will be up soon."

The girl nodded and yawned again.

"Yes, my lady."

Merry made as if to help her, but Shannon shook her head.

"You are our guest, Merry. Elsbeth will do it. Let's go sit down while we can."

But as soon as they made themselves comfortable in the manor's hall, the baby began to cry.

"Aye, me." Shannon sighed and got up to fetch her son. Merry went with her.

The men were waiting in the hall when Merry and Shannon returned. Kieran beamed at Merry, and she ducked her head. When they all sat at the table, Shannon held Nathan and tried to eat one-handed. Merry held out her hands to take him, but Shannon shook her head.

"You must eat first, Merry. I'll let you have him when you're finished, and then I'll take my turn."

When Merry later took the infant from Shannon, she cradled him and bent her head close to better see his long lashes and his puckered mouth. There was something especially sweet about a tiny babe. Holding him brought a peace to her heart, even if for a moment.

Merry lifted her head when she sensed Valerian's gaze upon her. He regarded her with a quiet smile. Could he feel her tranquil spirit? Or was he truly peaceful in his heart, even if he had to be a soldier?

After breakfast, Shannon took Nathan back to the bedchamber to change and nurse him. Merry helped Elsbeth clear the table. The girl didn't have much to say, and Merry was grateful. Quiet companionship was especially helpful now that she couldn't talk. Would her throat ever heal? Or would she be mute for the rest of her life? She hadn't considered that possibility until now.

❖

When the women stepped out of the hall, Valerian spoke to Ruddy.

"If you don't mind my asking you, has your leg completely healed?"

"Aye," Ruddy answered, scowling. "The stump has scarred over, if that's what ye mean."

"I only wanted to make sure because you aren't using a wooden leg." Valerian hated to even bring up the subject, but he felt responsible, since he was the one who'd cut it off.

"Me uncle Torus had a wooden leg," said Kieran. "He could do all manner of things: ride a horse, shoot a bow, even throw knives." He grinned, but Ruddy did not return it.

"I canna wear a wooden leg."

Valerian glanced down at the shortened limb.

"Why not?"

"Because o' the way the leg was severed and burned, I feel constant pain, and 'tis much worse with any pressure tae the stump."

Merry stepped forward.

Please ask him if I may examine his leg.

Valerian told Ruddy what she said.

"She's a Healer, after all. I've seen what she can do."

Ruddy frowned while he massaged the leg, keeping his gaze away from Valerian's. At last, he spoke to Merry.

"Are ye sure, lass, that ye want to look at this ugly stump?" When she nodded, he untied the leather strap and pulled back the breech leg, exposing an angry puckered scar.

Valerian cringed. But Merry knelt and covered the stump with her hands. The glow appeared, and Valerian watched her face for signs she was going too far into the Healing.

Her concentration was deep, but he saw none of the strain of yesterday. Finally, she sighed and the glow disappeared. Merry sat back on the floor. After a moment, she turned her face up to him.

I think I was able to stop the pains. I hope so.

Ruddy moved the stump in several directions. His face was visibly less tense.

"I dinna know how you did that, lass, but I feel no more sharp pains. They were like wee knives stabbing me almost constantly."

Shannon came in from the bedchamber, the babe in her arms.

"Do you want to try the wooden leg again?"

Ruddy probed the stump and nodded.

"Aye, why not?"

Merry stood and held out her arms for the babe. Shannon handed her the sleepy bundle.

While Shannon left the hall, Valerian watched while Merry cradled Ruddy's tiny son. She obviously had experience handling infants. This time, when she gazed at the babe, a tear rolled down her cheek.

"Merry?" Kieran made as if to go to her, but she shook her head and fled from the room. Kieran turned to Valerian.

"Do ye think she had a babe of her own? That she was married already?"

"I haven't sensed that from her. But she isn't yet ready to talk about the family she lost." Valerian frowned. What if, young as she appeared, she *had* been married and lost a child? A chill briefly seized him. What if she had been Gabriel's *wife* and not his daughter?

Shannon returned carrying a peg leg with a padded leather cup at one end and straps sewn to the leather. She handed it to Ruddy and let him position it. He secured the straps around his thigh and pulled the breech leg down to cover the place where flesh and wood met. Then he used his crutch to stand. He put weight on the wooden leg and took a few awkward steps, still leaning on the crutch.

Finally, he lifted the crutch and walked around the hall without its support. Merry entered just as he completed a circuit around the hall. He grinned at her, his teeth gleaming beneath his red mustaches.

"Bless ye, lass. I can walk without pain."

Valerian's heart swelled. *This* was the Sir Rudyard he remembered. Was it too much to hope that the knight might someday forgive him? Was it possible to restore their former companionship?

Merry handed the infant back to Shannon. Though her eyes were red from crying, she had regained her composure.

Ruddy turned to face Valerian. The knight stood taller.

"Are ye ready tae visit Eldred? I can take ye there myself."

"Yes, I'm anxious to see him," Valerian said.

Ruddy spoke to Shannon and included Merry and Kieran.

"We might as well all go. The old man does enjoy company."

Shannon gazed down at the babe in her arms and shook her head.

"I'll stay here today, if you please. Now that Nathan is asleep, I may have time for a wee nap myself. Send Eldred my greetings."

Ruddy and Valerian walked together. Merry and Kieran followed a few paces behind. Kieran chattered to Merry as usual, but Ruddy was unusually quiet. Perhaps he merely concentrated on walking with his new leg. Valerian made sure to match his pace with Ruddy's.

Once they entered the village, everyone they met commented on the wooden leg.

"Sir Rudyard," an older man called from his seat in the square where he puffed on a long pipe. "'Tis wonderful to see yer gettin' around on yer own two limbs."

"Yes, Sir Rudyard," the blacksmith said between hammer blows. "Let me know should the leg ever need repairing."

At last they came to a small cottage. Ruddy knocked loudly, and a voice called out.

"Come in."

The four of them crowded into a cottage with a single room. It had a large window opened wide to admit light and fresh air. Seated in the only chair was King Orland's former Seer. The old man had a coverlet across his lap.

"Good morrow, Sir Rudyard." Eldred's pleasant voice quavered more than when Valerian had heard it last. "I see you have brought company."

Valerian stepped forward. He towered over the elderly man.

"Hello, Eldred. I'm very glad to see you again."

The old man peered up. His rheumy eyes widened.

"Prince Valerian? Is it really you?"

"In the flesh." Valerian went down on one knee. He locked eyes with Eldred and *Saw* his amazement that Valerian was a Seer, too.

"When did this happen?" Eldred whispered.

"Almost the instant Waryn died the Sight came upon me. I have so many questions to ask you."

Eldred nodded and glanced behind Valerian. "I will answer all your questions. But first, you should find out why your companion left us so suddenly."

Valerian turned, and Kieran whirled around.

"When did the lass leave, Sire? I didn't hear her go."

"Stay with Ruddy. I'll return as soon as I find her."

Valerian stepped outside and searched up and down the lane. There was no sign of Merry. On an impulse, he went to the sheep pen. The shaggy ewes bleated as he approached. There was a movement beyond the pen, and Valerian strode around it toward a shady grove.

When he entered the wood, he found Merry slumped against a tree. She had pulled off her scarf and twisted it in her hands. What had caused her distress? Concerned, he knelt beside her and prayed he could say the right thing to ease her discomfort.

"Merry," he began, but he got no further. She shrank from him, and he was shocked to *See* her fear and loathing. Merry pushed herself off the ground and poised to flee.

"Wait! At least tell me what I've done to cause you such grief." Valerian held out a hand in entreaty, and she turned, wiping her face with the scarf in a savage gesture.

Why didn't you tell me you are a prince?

"When we found you, I told you my name, but it is true I did not *say* I was a prince." Valerian paused to choose his words carefully. "It has been such a relief to be among people who don't know who I am and therefore treat me as an ordinary person. I didn't think about the consequences of omitting that truth. I'm sorry."

Are you the one, then? The prince who ordered the Brethren to work as slaves as if they were common criminals?

He blinked, caught off guard by her question.

"My father, the king, commanded me to decide the Brethren's punishment for refusing to fight with us. I found a solution that would allow him to obey the law yet spare the men's lives, since the penalty for disobedience to the king's edicts during a time of war is death."

Your father, the king. She shut her eyes and tears leaked out, tracking through the grime on her face. Valerian realized only then that she'd somehow gotten dirt and leaves on herself.

"Please, let me take you back and we can talk more about it."

You don't understand. Merry blinked away the tears. *Their time in the prison and after damaged their souls.*

"Who was damaged? What are you talking about?"

I don't know the details. They wouldn't tell me. My father and Michael were both so changed when they returned I scarcely knew them. She touched her cheek, and Valerian remembered seeing a bruise there when he and Kieran had first found her. Had someone struck her in anger?

"I'm very sorry, Merry. I know hardships dispirit many people, but others find peace and joy no matter what their circumstances. That's the kind of person I aspire to be." As soon as the words left his mouth, he realized those were probably not the most suitable.

She shook her head, appearing even more distressed.

That's what I don't understand. How can you be so ruthless and yet so gentle?

Valerian's eyes widened in surprise and it took a moment for him to answer.

"I have never in the whole of my life, not even once, been accused of being ruthless. Quite the opposite. Merry, neither I nor the king wanted to have to execute the men of your village, but even we have to abide by the law of the land. The law clearly states that one who disobeys the king's command must forfeit his life. I desired only to find a solution that would obey the letter of the law and avoid executing the Brethren."

Merry wrestled within herself. He *Saw* the turmoil in her mind. To his relief, she spoke again.

Gabriel tried to explain it to me.

"Gabriel?"

He said I should not hate you.

"Gabriel said that?"

He was one of those you spoke about, one who found joy and peace through suffering. She covered her face with her hands and began silently weeping again.

Valerian scanned the area. There was a tree stump nearby. He guided Merry toward it, and she allowed him to lead her for those few steps. Then he sat and pulled her to his lap. She was crying so hard she didn't seem to notice. He began to rock her as if she were a child, for that was how he saw her at this moment. What a sheltered life she must have led. First she was traumatized by having all the men taken away, and later shattered when everyone was killed. Did she not have a reason to be angry with him? How could he make things right with her?

At last her silent weeping passed as the calm after a storm. Merry took a great shuddering breath. When she met his gaze, Valerian *Saw* the light of recognition. Her eyes widened and she jumped off his lap, backing away until she stood a respectful distance from him.

Oh, God of Peace, forgive me.

"What do you think you have done wrong?" He didn't move lest he startle her into running away.

I should not have—sat on your lap. It is forbidden. She appeared stricken, and he realized what a fool he'd been.

"Then it is I who should apologize to you. I will be more careful in the future. Can we still be friends?" He smiled at her. She was a sight, covered with dirt and leaves, her hair disheveled, and her face puffy from crying.

How can we be friends? You are a prince and I am a poor maiden from a village that no longer exists.

Valerian stood and gestured to the stump.

"Merry, will you please sit here and let me tell you something?"

She stared at him for a long time. Valerian thought she would refuse to sit, but finally she nodded and walked slowly to the stump, still watching him warily. He sat on the ground beside her, close enough to *See* her but not so close as to cause her discomfort.

"I can't begin to understand your terrible grief, but I do know about loss." He paused to make certain she was listening.

"Until about four new moons ago I was my older brother's squire, just as Kieran is now my squire. Waryn was the perfect prince in every way. Everyone said so. Not much was expected of me, and so I was allowed free access to the Keep's library. My greatest joy came from studying the scrolls of history and the Holy Writ. I discussed what I read with the monks who maintain the library. I did learn to ride a warhorse and wield a spear and bow, but I have always preferred the quiet life of a scholar." He had Merry's full attention now.

Something happened, didn't it?

"Yes." Valerian swallowed, knowing it would be painful to relive that day's memories. "We were out on patrol when we were surprised by the Horde, the same monsters that must have attacked your village. I'd never been in a battle before. I didn't act swiftly enough to save my brother, and he—died in my arms." His eyes filled with tears, and he wiped them away in order to *See* Merry.

"Now I must take my brother's place, though I feel utterly unprepared, and put away my heart's desire. Forever. So in that way, I can understand your loss." The grief rose in him so sharply it took his breath away. He thought he had come to terms with it already.

Merry's face softened with compassion.

I'm so sorry for you. What a great burden you must bear. And to think I was sure my Healing gift was a burden. She shook her head.

They sat quietly for a few minutes, each lost in their thoughts. Merry gently touched Valerian's arm, and he looked up at her again.

May I tell you about my family, since you told me about yours?

"Of course."

She took a deep breath as if to brace herself.

My mother died in childbed when I was ten. With her dying breath, she made me promise to care for my infant brother. I think something died in my father's heart that day, but I was so busy caring for them I couldn't stop to think about it.

Then the men were taken, and then the Healing gift came upon me, and then they were all gone.

When she paused, he *Saw* guilt in her eyes.

Did my resentment cause their deaths? I left the gate open that morning when I ran down to the river. Would they still be alive if I hadn't done that?

"No, Merry, it wasn't your fault. If you had stayed at home you would have been killed too."

Wouldn't that have been better than living without them?

"I can't believe that." Valerian shook his head, trying to convince himself as well. "Life is precious because it comes from the Most High. He must yet have a purpose for your life."

Her eyes widened. While she pondered his words, he decided he had to know what her relationship was to Gabriel.

"Merry, you have not said what happened to Gabriel."

He was murdered also. Her face was full of pain. *He said you spoke with him.*

"On two occasions. I only wish I had known him better."

He was the leader of our village. She struggled to hold back her tears. *And I would have become his wife on my fifteenth birthday in less than three moons.*

His *wife.* She would have been his wife. Valerian's throat tightened and he had to clear it.

"Then I am doubly sorry for your loss, and for his." He gasped. The dream he'd had of Gabriel just before he and Kieran investigated the Brethren village. What did it mean? Valerian's chest twisted with a chill of guilt, though he had no idea why.

Merry touched his arm again to catch his attention.

Did you know Gabriel was a Seer, too?

"I learned so the first time I met him, at the Keep."

It was his wish that I not hate you. I wanted to blame you, but now that I've met you, I can't hate you. Merry began to pick at the dried leaves clinging to her skirts and her hair and suddenly stood up. *There's a stream just behind us. I will hurry. Will you wait?*

"Of course I will."

She ran through the trees and out of sight. Valerian stood and wiped the seat of his breeches. By the position of the sun, much time had passed since they left Eldred's cottage. Poor Kieran must be wondering what happened.

While he waited for Merry, Valerian sifted through his jumbled thoughts and feelings about Gabriel and his tragic loss, not just for Merry's sake, although it had affected her profoundly and so affected him. He wished he and Gabriel could have sat down together and discussed matters moral and religious. Valerian was certain they would have had much in common. So certain, in fact, that Valerian vowed to make Merry's welfare his primary concern.

At last Merry reappeared. She had washed her face and rebraided her hair. Her scarf and dress had wet splotches where she'd tried to clean them, and she was barefooted. With chagrin, Valerian realized that if he were to take her to the Keep he would need to outfit her for the journey. The farther north they traveled, the colder it would become.

"Shall we return to Eldred's? They're all probably wondering if we disappeared."

Merry nodded. She held up her right hand with the palm facing him. Then she met his gaze. How had he not noticed her eyes were the same shade of blue as the northern lakes?

I'm sorry for being so angry with you, she said. *I would like to be your friend, if a Brethren Healer may befriend a prince.*

Valerian smiled in relief and touched his palm to hers. Her hand was so small next to his.

"I gladly accept your friendship, and pledge mine in return." He gently squeezed her hand. "And since you cannot speak, you won't have to worry about calling me 'Your Highness.' That makes you the best kind of friend."

Without another word between them, they returned to Eldred's.

In the privacy of his guest quarters at Reed's castle, Caelis opened his saddle bag and took out the decree written in Valerian's own hand. He reread the words and then admired his cousin Lewes' carefully applied seal below the prince's signature. Authentic enough to fool simple soldiers, but never would it fool the king, even if Valerian was no longer able to defend himself.

One of Captain Ulfred's spies had discovered the prince and his squire had left the garrison and were traveling alone. This was the perfect opportunity for some accident to befall them, and no one would be able to trace the "accident" to Caelis. It was gratifying to know so many other southerners were as disgruntled as Caelis that the ruling house of Levathia had been the same for three hundred years, a family from the north. What did they know of the south's affairs? What did they care? It was past time for a change in leadership. But first Caelis had to get rid of the heir. Now that Waryn was gone, Caelis had no more guilt about his actions. He'd been willing to whole-heartedly support that prince, but never the current one or the king.

Caelis replaced the stolen royal decree in his bag and pulled out the two scalps he had taken in the massacre. Although he'd enjoyed his daydream of throwing these down at the foot of Orland's throne while pointing the finger at Valerian, if Caelis could eliminate his rival here in the south, there would be no need to keep either the scalps or the decree.

Then Caelis could ride back to the Keep with a lighter load, in more ways than one.

Now that Ulfred had given him a name, Caelis would contact Orin Swift, the leader of those plotting rebellion, and ask him to send someone skilled in the art of assassination.

Chapter 19 *The grey head is a crown of glory, if it be found in the way of righteousness.*

When Merry followed Valerian into Eldred's cottage, Ruddy and Kieran had already left.

"Even Kieran has gone?" Valerian sounded surprised.

Eldred laughed, and Merry smiled at his mirth.

"I had quite a time convincing your squire that he should return with Sir Rudyard, that you had in fact ordered him to stay with Ruddy. Kieran was quite reluctant to leave until you returned."

"I would like to have seen how you accomplished that," Valerian said. "I'm sorry I put you in an awkward situation."

"Not at all, my prince. I believe you and I both have many pressing questions that need answers before we lose our daylight. But first, I would like to meet this young woman."

Valerian turned and beckoned her closer.

"This is Merry. Kieran and I found her two days ago at the Brethren village. Everyone had been killed. It seems to have been the Horde."

"Yes, Kieran related the incident to me." Eldred grew somber. "Come closer, dear girl, and let me *See* you. You're not afraid of Seers, are you?"

Merry curtsied and went forward. She knelt on a blue wool rug directly in front of the kindly elder and stared into his pale eyes. When he *Saw* her thoughts she tried speaking to him as she had Valerian.

I'm sorry that I left so suddenly earlier.

But he did not answer and she was puzzled.

"I am sorry you are so distressed, my dear. It appears you have suffered greatly in the past little while. I offer my condolences, though I understand words are not much comfort."

Merry grasped his gnarled hand with a grateful squeeze. He smiled at her, which made his eyes sparkle. She liked him very much.

"I have long desired to find out more about the Brethren," Eldred continued. "I had thought to ask you, but I didn't want to add to your distress. And then Kieran told me you are unable to speak, so that would make answering questions rather difficult."

"Merry and I have discovered she can speak to my mind," Valerian said. "Perhaps when she is ready I might be of assistance."

"She can speak to you?" Eldred's eyes widened. "Then perhaps she can to me also." He turned his Sight on her again.

Merry spoke slowly and clearly in her mind.

I would be happy to tell you all I know about the Brethren. I don't want them to be forgotten.

He did not react to what she said. Apparently he could only *See* her frustration, not hear the actual words.

"If you're trying to communicate with me, I'm not hearing anything." Eldred gestured to Valerian. "Go ahead, let her talk to you, and I will try to understand what is happening."

Valerian went down on one knee on the rug beside Merry. She stared into his eyes, and Eldred leaned closer to them.

How can you hear me and Eldred cannot?

"I don't know, but I wish he could, for your sake. Was Gabriel able to hear you?"

Merry remembered their one time of intense sharing, but it was of emotions and images, not actual words.

No, he could only See me as Eldred does. What's the difference between us, I wonder?

"I still can't hear her." Eldred sounded disappointed. "This is something I've never heard of. To my knowledge, only the great dragons can communicate mind-to-mind. Are you part dragon, Merry?"

Valerian smiled at her, and she lowered her head when her face warmed.

"She's a Healer," he said. "Could that have something to do with it?"

"No, but as a Healer she may be especially empathetic and open to such mental communication." The old man sighed. "Too bad we don't have a dragon to test that theory."

Merry's eyes widened. Was it possible to speak to a dragon? She would like to try that!

"However," Eldred continued, "I would like to test another theory of mine concerning the Brethren. Do you know how they came to be, my prince?"

"I honestly didn't know much about them until the men were brought to the Keep." Valerian exchanged a meaningful glance with Merry.

Eldred stroked his beard, pausing before he continued.

"You know what good friends your grandfather and I always were."

"Yes." Valerian's voice sounded wistful. Merry glanced at him, but he was focused on Eldred.

"Our one disagreement concerned his grandfather, King Sigmund." He raised his brows, waiting for a reaction from Valerian.

"He was the one who abdicated the throne to enter a monastery."

"That's what your grandfather believed, because that's what *his* father told him. Do you realize King Emeric never knew his father, Sigmund? So *he* only knew what he'd been told."

Merry had a hard time following the names, but Eldred's passion for the subject made it fascinating to her.

Valerian sat back on the rug and crossed his legs.

"So, Eldred, what is your theory?"

Eldred stared at Merry for so long without *Seeing* her that she started fidgeting. When he spoke his voice was solemn.

"I believe King Sigmund changed his name to Absalom and founded the Brethren."

Merry gasped. She turned to Valerian and met his gaze.

I know that name. She closed her eyes and tried to put the names in order before she told him. When she opened her eyes, Eldred waited so eagerly she hoped she could help him. She extended her fingers and ticked off the names as she told Valerian, beginning with herself.

I am the eldest of my mother, Melody, who was the youngest of her father, Uriel, who was the eldest of his father, Manuel, who was the eldest of his father, Absalom. We were always told his name, Absalom, means 'Father of Peace.' We lived in the 'Village of Peace.'

Valerian related her words to Eldred. The old man sat back in his chair, thinking.

"So we know there was an Absalom, but whether or not he was the same person as Sigmund is not certain." He pointed to a small desk in one corner. It contained pigeon holes stuffed with scrolls. "I had the monks copy several portions of histories before I left the Keep. I will pore over them and let you know if I find any mention of our elusive Sigmund."

"Would you like for me to take one or two with me to Ruddy's house and help you look?"

Merry wondered at the eagerness in Valerian's voice until she remembered his heart's desire was to be a scholar or a monk.

"I would like that very much. Before you leave, was there something you wanted to ask me about the Sight?"

While Valerian and Eldred discussed ways to *See*, or rather not *See* the thoughts of others, Merry went to the far wall to study a tapestry that had caught her eye. The brightly colored threads shimmered in the late afternoon light coming through the window, but it was the picture that fascinated her. A huge beast, surely a dragon, dwarfed two soldiers holding spears and shields. The blue and green dragon had reared up on its hind legs with wings outspread and orange and yellow flame spewed from its mouth. The two soldiers were dressed like Valerian and Kieran but wore some kind of protective hat on their heads. The tapestry was beautiful, even though the subject was frightening.

Valerian mentioned her name, and she turned back to them.

"I do feel that being able to hear Merry's words has made it easier for me to focus on what is important when I *See* the thoughts of others." Valerian glanced at her, and she smiled. She was glad she could make something easier for someone.

"Thank you for your suggestions." Valerian stood then. "I only wish you had still been at the Keep when the Sight first came to me. It was quite—unsettling."

"How well I remember when it came to me." Eldred pointed to the desk. "Don't forget to take one or two of those scrolls with you."

Valerian picked out two of them and turned back. He was beaming.

"When I finish these, may I take more after I return them?"

"Of course, of course. But you should get back to Sir Rudyard's lest your poor squire have a nervous fit or something." He waved them toward the door.

Merry came near to Eldred. He was so like her grandfather. She leaned down and kissed his leathery cheek. He touched the place with a trembling hand.

"Why, thank you, Merry. You must come back as often as you can."

While they headed back through the village, Valerian indicated the scrolls in his hand.

"You know, Merry, if King Sigmund really did change his name to Absalom and found the Brethren, that means you and I are cousins. Distant, of course, first cousins four or five times removed, something like that, but family nonetheless."

She gazed up at him, pleased.

Then I hope they are one and the same, for I already feel as if we are connected in some way. She smiled sadly. *It would mean you and Michael were cousins, too. Our mothers were sisters.* She paused. *You would have liked him, before he changed.*

While they walked the rest of the way to Ruddy's house, Merry added silently, *and you would have had one more cousin. Rafael.*

While a single candle burned and grew shorter, Valerian pored over the first scroll. Beside him on a pallet Kieran snored, oblivious to the world. He knew he should follow Kieran's example, but he was engrossed with the history of Prince Sigmund and his father, King Lionel, fighting an invasion by Vandals from the south.

Valerian had nearly reached the end of the scroll when he heard a baby's distressed cry. He stood, listening. He didn't know much about infants, but that cry sounded more urgent than usual. He glanced down at Kieran, but he slept on.

Picking up the candle, Valerian opened the door and peered down the hall. Merry came out of her room and moved toward the sound. She had thrown a fur over her shoulders, for she wore only her white underdress. She held her carry sack with her medicines. Valerian quietly closed the door behind him and followed Merry.

When she reached Ruddy's bedchamber at the end of the hall, she knocked. By the time Valerian arrived Ruddy had opened the door. He also held a candle.

"Come in," Ruddy said, his voice strained. "Something's wrong with the babe."

Valerian followed Merry inside. Shannon cradled her son, crooning to him, but his shrieks did not abate. Even by candlelight his face appeared red. Shannon's eyes were wide with fear. Merry placed her hand on the child's small head and gasped.

"What do you need?" Valerian asked. But when she met his gaze, he remembered that it was too dark to *See* into her eyes. "Can you show me?"

She pantomimed pouring and drinking and he guessed, "Water?" She nodded.

Ruddy pointed to the bedside table.

"Is that enough?"

Valerian picked up the ewer and sloshed the water. Merry nodded and ground something in her mortar that released a sweet scent like honeysuckle. She added water, stirred it, and then started to tear off part of her underdress.

"Wait!" Valerian stopped her before she ripped the garment. "I'm sure Ruddy has a clean cloth in here."

"Aye, here's one." Ruddy stumbled to the bed and pulled a handkerchief from under a pillow. He tossed it to Valerian.

Merry soaked the material in her mixture and held it to the infant's mouth. When he would not stop wailing to suck on it, she twisted the cloth, squeezing the liquid into his mouth. He choked and coughed, spitting out the medicine, which only intensified his screaming.

Even without his Sight Valerian could see the desperation in Merry's eyes. He realized what she wanted to do.

"Go ahead," he told her. "I will watch and make sure you don't go too far." He positioned himself so he could better see her face in the dim light.

She gently placed her hands on either side of the babe's small head and closed her eyes. She grimaced once and then concentrated. Gradually the infant's distress receded and his cries lessened. He gave one last sob as his eyelids drooped. He now slept peacefully.

Merry took a deep breath and opened her eyes. She appeared a little unsteady on her feet, so Valerian found a chair and helped her to it. Ruddy went to Shannon.

"The wee one looks to be fine now, thanks to Merry." He stared at his infant son with great relief. "Thank you, lass."

Shannon turned to Merry with tears in her eyes.

"Saying 'thank you' does not seem like nearly enough, but I thank you from the bottom of my heart. His fever seemed dangerously high."

Merry nodded. Valerian guessed from her somber look that the babe had been in greater danger than even Shannon realized. He helped Merry back to her room and would not leave her until she'd climbed into the bed.

"When there is daylight enough," he said quietly, "you'll have to tell me what really happened in there."

Wearily Merry nodded and tucked her hands under her cheek. When her eyes closed, Valerian shut the door.

He wanted to return to the scroll and finish it, but he decided he'd better get some sleep, too. Even after snuffing the candle and making himself comfortable in the bed, his thoughts would not let him sleep. He thought about Merry's incredible Healing gift. He could envision great trouble for her as more people discovered it. She would be in such great demand that her life would be at risk.

If only he or Eldred could find proof she was a royal cousin, then his father could make her his ward. She would be protected for the rest of her life both from unscrupulous people who would see her gift as a means of gaining wealth and from the press of desperately sick and injured people who would endanger her health.

But even if she was not a royal cousin, he had already pledged, as a memorial to Gabriel, to watch out for her. He would do all in his power to keep that promise.

❖

Caelis found Hanalah in the castle garden. She left her maid and glided toward him.

"Hello, Caelis." The rose colored gown she wore clung to her and outlined her shape.

Caelis' eyes were drawn to her voluptuous figure.

"Hello, cousin. Where is my uncle?"

"Father is hunting with a small party. Did he not ask you to go?"

"Perhaps he did, but I was occupied." Caelis sat on a bench in the shade of a large tree. Hanalah came closer.

"And what could be more important than hunting with Father?" She sat beside him, pressing her thigh against his.

"There is other sport beside hunting deer." His gaze was drawn to her plunging neckline. Her perfume wafted toward him, made him heady.

"What sport is that?" She stared boldly at him.

"Sport that you will never know with this prince you wish to marry." He glanced back to make sure the maid wasn't watching and leaned closer. She brought her lips almost to his.

"Why do you say that?" Her breath was warm and sweet.

"Because when you want pleasure from him, he will instead read to you from the Holy Writ." Caelis growled in his throat. "Didn't you know Valerian's only desire is to be a monk?"

"It doesn't matter what he used to want." She straightened, smiling in that way that both infuriated and intoxicated Caelis. "He will not be able to resist me."

Caelis stood, tightening his fists. Hanalah rose from the bench and slid her hands around Caelis' arm.

"Why, cousin, you are not jealous, are you?" Her eyes sparkled with mirth.

Of course, he was jealous! It was bad enough the whelp had taken Waryn's place; must he take Waryn's intended bride, too? Not if Caelis could prevent it. And he *would* prevent it.

Regaining control of himself, Caelis stepped back, took Hanalah's hand, and chastely kissed it.

"I want only what you deserve, dear cousin, and that is to be queen someday." Now he stared boldly at her and was gratified to see her smirk of triumph change to uncertainty. Then she curtsied, breaking eye contact, and returned to her maid.

Caelis let her go. He inhaled deeply and squared his shoulders.

"Go, cousin, dream of ensaring your princeling," he murmured to the air. "But you will *never* be queen." Then Caelis strode from the garden, more determined than ever to bring his plans to fruition.

Chapter 20 *Every wise woman buildeth her house.*

After Healing the babe in the middle of the night, waking early was more difficult than Merry anticipated. But she was determined to make her special bread for Shannon and Ruddy, and Valerian and Kieran, too.

Not until she'd made the dough and covered it to let it rise did she hear stirrings from the back of the manor house. She walked into the hall just as Shannon entered from the doorway to the sleeping chambers, carrying Nathan.

"Good morrow, Merry. Have you been awake long?"

Merry nodded, smiling. She saw with relief the baby's healthy color.

"I can't thank ye enough for your help with Nathan." She gazed down at him, her face full of tenderness.

Merry wished she could speak to the older woman. She beckoned, leading Shannon to the kitchen.

"What have ye been up to in the last hours?" Then Shannon saw the dough and nodded. "Baking bread, I see. Aren't you coming with Ruddy and me to the winter festival? There will be more food than we can possibly eat. Since Nathan is well now, I plan to leave him here with an old dame from the village who prefers a quiet evening. Elsbeth, of course, looks forward to the festival."

Merry shrugged. She would rather stay here and tend the babe herself, but there was no way to tell Shannon until Valerian had awakened.

"Something else that happens during winter festival is the competition. There are several categories to enter, and judges award first, second, and third place in each category. This year I'm entering a needlepoint that Ruddy made a frame for." Shannon went back into the hall and opened a large carry sack. She lifted out a framed picture.

Merry gasped. It was smaller than Eldred's tapestry, but there was a similar fire-breathing dragon confronted by a lone soldier on horseback. The details were painstakingly rendered with shimmering colored threads. It was beautiful, and Merry had no way to tell Shannon how much she admired it.

"I started on this before Nathan was born, even before Ruddy was injured. At first I was afraid it would hurt him more to look at a reminder of what he'd been, but I think in time he will be glad to remember. After all, no one can take away the memories of his service to the king and all the great deeds he performed as a knight." Shannon grew quiet, and Merry saw tears in her eyes.

She laid a hand on the woman's arm, frustrated that she could not offer words of comfort.

"Thank you, Merry." Shannon wiped her eyes. "Has your dough risen enough, do you think?" Merry nodded. "And you've fired the oven? Then why don't you finish your bread and I'll drag Elsbeth out of bed to make some porridge."

Merry returned to the kitchen and found the large oven paddle. She punched down the dough and divided it into twelve small sections. She rolled out three of the pieces into long thin ropes and braided them together, placing the loaf on the paddle. When she finished she grabbed the handle and pushed the paddle with the four braided loaves into the hot oven.

She was cleaning the work table when Shannon and Elsbeth entered the kitchen. Merry held out her hands to Shannon, and the woman gave her Nathan so she could help with breakfast.

"The men are stirring, so we need to get food on the table. Your bread smells good, Merry." Shannon pulled out the paddle to check. "What beautiful loaves! They're nearly done." She pushed them back into the oven and turned to Merry.

"One category in the festival's competition is baking. Why don't you enter your bread? If they taste as good as they look, you're sure to win a prize."

Merry shook her head. She had meant for the bread to be eaten here. But Shannon persisted.

"You don't have to enter all four. We can eat two and you can take the rest to the festival."

Valerian appeared in the doorway.

"Good morrow, ladies. What smells so delicious in here?"

Merry rushed over to him, wringing her hands.

I made some bread, and now Shannon wants me to enter it in a competition at the festival. But I can't go to a festival dressed like this.

He spoke to Shannon.

"Lady MacNeil, where in the village might we find some clothes for Merry?"

"That's easy, Your Highness," Shannon said. "Right here."

"What do you mean?"

"I mean that I was a wealthy merchant's only daughter and he spoiled me with more clothes than I could ever wear. I used to have a young girl's figure, and some of those clothes are sure to fit Merry. We have a few minutes before the porridge is ready. Come, let's find something pretty for you to wear to the festival tonight."

Merry's eyes widened. She met Valerian's gaze.

I have never worn anything fine in my life. It's a little frightening.

He leaned closer to her and spoke in a calming tone he'd used with her before.

"I don't think you have to worry about fine clothes changing who you are inside."

I hope you're right about that. Though she was still apprehensive, she appreciated his encouragement nonetheless.

"Come, Merry." Shannon beckoned from the doorway while speaking to her maid. "Take that bread out of the oven now, Elsbeth, and don't forget to stir the porridge."

While the ladies were occupied, Ruddy and Kieran joined Valerian in the hall. Elsbeth made a lot of noise setting the table. Finally, Shannon appeared with a satisfied smile, cradling her sleeping infant.

"Are you gentlemen ready to meet our new lady?"

Valerian shared a glance with Kieran, who grinned. Ruddy gestured impatiently.

"Well, bring her in, woman."

Shannon turned back and beckoned.

"Come, Merry, don't be shy."

But she hesitated on the threshold, her head down. When she stepped into the room Merry lifted her head as she came forward, slowly.

Valerian could only stare at her, stunned. She wore a pale green overdress with cut sleeves that revealed a new white chemise underneath. Instead of her stained scarf, a white cap with embroidered trim was tied under her chin. On her feet, she wore green slippers.

He had never before realized what a transformation a change of clothing could affect. The uncertain village maid was no more. Merry had become a poised and lovely noblewoman. But now that he thought about it, her grace, her innate nobility had always been present. He'd just never noticed as he did now.

When she came close enough, she met Valerian's stare.

I have never worn shoes before. They are so soft, it's like walking on a cloud.

He smiled at her child-like delight. It was one of the qualities he liked most about her.

Kieran overflowed with admiration.

"Ye look absolutely beautiful, Merry."

She blushed, which only increased the effect of her new appearance.

"Yes," Valerian conceded, glad Merry could not read his thoughts, for he couldn't say what he really felt, that he would never look at her the same way again. "You wash up rather nicely."

Merry cocked her head, perplexed.

Are you teasing me?

"Of course I am."

Kieran pulled out the bench for Merry, but she made as if to go to the kitchen.

"Sit down, Merry," said Shannon. "Elsbeth will bring your bread."

"Ye made bread, did you, Merry?" Kieran grinned.

She nodded and sat on the bench. Kieran sat beside her and Valerian on her other side. Elsbeth brought in a platter with two of Merry's braided loaves. They were golden brown.

"What unusual bread," said Ruddy. "I wonder how ye did that, lass." He poured water into a cup for Valerian and handed it to him.

Valerian glanced down at Merry, and she met his eyes.

I braided the dough the same way I braid my hair, with three strands.

"It puts me in mind of the Trinity," Valerian said. "Father, Son, and Holy Ghost."

She nodded, and he *Saw* her surprise that he knew about the Trinity.

That's why our braid has three strands.

Shannon held a long knife with a serrated blade poised over one of the loaves.

"Oh, Merry, I cannot bear to cut into such a work of art. You may have to slice it."

Merry stood and held out her hand for the knife. Valerian watched her deftly cut one loaf into five equal sections, then the other. She set the knife on the table and sat down again.

Valerian picked up a piece of bread. It was still warm, and the most delicious aroma wafted from the soft center. He took a bite, and it almost melted in his mouth with a faintly sweet taste. He chewed slowly, savoring the texture, as well as the flavor. Kieran sighed happily.

"This is delicious, Merry," said the squire. "I can die a happy man."

Merry ducked her head, but Valerian saw her pleased smile.

"Yes," said Shannon thoughtfully, "you must enter this bread in the competition. But tell me, how did you manage that hint of sweetness?"

Valerian waited until Merry met his gaze.

Please tell Shannon it's a bit of honey.

Ruddy didn't say a word. He just started on his second thick piece. Shannon got his attention.

"What do you think of the bread, Ruddy?"

He didn't answer until he finished chewing the bite in his mouth.

"What do you think I'm thinking, woman? I'm thinking you should learn how to make this bread!"

❖

Caelis entered the barracks in Lord Reed's castle and saw his men lounging around, some drinking ale, others playing games of chance. In one corner, Drew sat with the boy from the Brethren village. Caelis started toward them when one of the others caught his attention.

"Sir, there's someone to see you. He says you were looking for him." The man indicated an alcove to the side of the larger room.

Caelis frowned until he realized who it had to be. He stepped into the alcove and saw a man sitting on a stool with his back against the wall. He stood, and Caelis had to look up to meet the man's gaze.

He had a weathered face, worn leathers, and riding boots that had seen much use. His thin hair didn't completely cover the thick scar where his right ear had once been.

"Are you Sir Caelis?" His voice was raspy.

"Yes. Are you from Orin Swift?"

The man nodded once. He stared boldly at Caelis.

"He said you'd pay well."

"Twenty gold pieces," said Caelis.

"Who's the mark?"

"Prince Valerian." Caelis studied his face.

"Swift didn't say it was a royal," the man said with a frown.

Caelis lowered his voice.

"Swift did say he would find someone who sympathized with our aims. Are you with us, or no?" For a moment, Caelis thought the man would refuse. But at last he nodded.

"I don't know him by sight."

Caelis made sure no one was listening.

"He is your height but slender, long dark hair, beardless. By now he's probably in the village of Forestglade with his squire, Kieran MacLachlan, who is shorter but also has long hair. Take care of them both."

"What method? And what proof do you require?"

"MacLachlan, doesn't matter. But the other, bring me his head. You may cut up his body into small pieces and feed them to the crows."

He smiled. "When you bring me his head, I will give you the twenty gold pieces."

They struck hands, and the one-eared man left without a word.

Chapter 21 *Every man should eat and drink, and enjoy the good of all his labour.*

Vendors hawking all manner of food and drink, clothing, and household items lined the perimeter of the village square. Large torches stuck in the ground at regular intervals provided ample light in the early evening. Merry's senses were assaulted by hundreds of villagers eating, drinking, laughing, singing, and dancing to a lively tune played on drum and pipe and some kind of stringed instrument. It was similar to the Brethren's celebrations but on a much larger and louder scale.

A big dog ran past, jostling Merry's basket. It carried a hunk of meat in its mouth. A young girl ran after it, shouting for the thief to stop. Then a man approached wearing a strange garment around his neck. As he came closer, Merry gasped. A small reptile sat on his shoulder with its long tail wrapped around his throat. Merry pulled on Valerian's arm to get his attention.

"That's a burrowing dragon," Valerian said. "They're similar to the tree dragon you saw, but they live in the ground."

Merry watched the little dragon until the press of taller people hid him from her sight. She imagined a dragon riding on *her* shoulder. Maybe someday she would see one up close and even touch it. She met Valerian's gaze.

Can you hear me tonight?

"Yes, surprisingly." When he smiled, the torch light reflected in his dark eyes.

"Merry," Shannon said. "I see the booth to enter the competition."

While Shannon dragged her away, Ruddy said, "And I spy an empty bench where I shall plant myself."

Merry stood behind Shannon in a line of women. After a few minutes, Shannon explained to someone about her embroidered picture, and then brought Merry forward.

"This is Merry, and she wants to enter her bread."

An older man with a neatly trimmed gray beard sat at a small table writing symbols on a piece of parchment. He peered into Merry's basket at the two loaves.

"Hmm, I've never seen anything like it." He brought his nose closer and inhaled, smiling. "Does this bread have a name?"

Merry turned to Shannon for help, but Ruddy's wife had already moved on to a nearby booth where the vendor was selling colorful scarves. The man wrote something else on the parchment.

"I'll call your entry 'braided loaf' if that's all right with you," he said.

Merry waited until he glanced up again and nodded. Fortunately, he moved on to the next person so Merry searched for Shannon, but the woman had blended in with the crowd. Fear knotted Merry's stomach, but she scolded herself and tried to retrace her steps.

"Merry!" Valerian and Kieran stood nearby, waving, and she hurried to join them.

"Where is Shannon?" Ruddy sat on a bench just behind Kieran. He frowned at Merry, and she shrugged. "Never mind, it is nae your fault, lass. The woman tends to wander away, distracted like."

Then the music changed, growing louder. Kieran's face brightened.

"Ach, Sire, the music is calling to me feet."

"Go on," Valerian said. "Show everyone how it should be done."

But Kieran turned to Merry.

"May I have this dance?"

Startled, Merry stared at Valerian.

Please tell him I don't know how.

"Merry doesn't know how to dance," he told the squire.

Kieran appeared shocked.

"How can that be? Would ye like to learn?"

Merry's first thought was to refuse him, but she *had* always wanted to try, especially after Michael told her he had seen people dancing when he went to the trading post with his father. Her throat tightened. What would Papa have said? She swallowed and let out the breath she'd been holding. Papa was no longer here. She could dance if she wanted to.

Merry nodded. Kieran grinned and held out his hand. She let him take hers, and he pulled her into an open area where several couples were already stepping together. While Merry watched them, her chest tightened and she caught her breath, almost running away. But reason returned. She *wanted* to learn this.

Kieran kept holding her hand as he turned to face her, waiting for some cue in the music. Just as the other couples stopped to face one another, he spoke up.

"All right, Merry. Now I bow and you curtsy." They did so, and Merry forgot about the others while she concentrated on Kieran's words and her feet.

He patiently led her through the dance steps, and Merry began to see the pattern. It wasn't as difficult as she feared it would be. By the third verse, she could follow the steps exactly. Now she could enjoy the music and the flow of smiling people together. The joy in Kieran's face lifted her spirits as much as the happy music.

On the song's final note, she curtsied one last time to Kieran, and he kissed her hand. Delight shone in his eyes.

"You learn quickly, Merry. Are ye sure you've never danced before?"

She mouthed the words *thank you*, hoping he would understand. Then the musicians began a faster tune, and Kieran led her back to Valerian.

"I dinna think you're ready for this one, Merry, so just watch me."

Kieran bounded back to the empty space, since the former couples had drifted into the crowd. Apparently no one else was willing to try the fast dance.

With his fists on his hips, Kieran began a series of complicated foot moves. Merry was sure he would trip, but he never missed a beat. Soon he was spinning his whole body to the back, to the front, while continuing to move his feet, and Merry didn't understand how he kept upright. She would have become hopelessly dizzy.

While the music gradually played faster and faster, Kieran added leaps and even spins in the air. Merry glanced at Valerian. He was as entranced as she was. The crowd around the circle grew, and many clapped along with the music, encouraging Kieran's amazing footwork.

The song ended on a triumphant note as Kieran did a back flip and landed on his feet, lifting his arms in exultation. He grinned, accepting the wild applause and cheering.

"What a show-off!" Valerian shouted into Merry's ear. But his face revealed his pride in Kieran's abilities.

After that exhibition, Merry wouldn't have been able to dance with Kieran again even if she wished it. He was surrounded by several young women, all full of admiration, who monopolized him for the rest of the dances.

Merry would have been content just to watch, but when another slower song began, Valerian turned to her.

"I am nothing to Kieran, but this is a simple dance that I know well and can teach you, if it be your pleasure to stand up with me."

Merry met his eyes and nodded.

I would like that very much.

Valerian led her to the dance area. Kieran was partnered with a pretty dark-haired girl.

"This is different from the one you did with Kieran. The count is by threes and I am supposed to hold you at the waist."

If you lead, I will follow.

The music changed, and Valerian bowed while Merry curtsied. Then he put his left hand on her waist and held his right palm up.

"Put your hand in mine." She did so. "Now, right--two--three, left--two--three, turn around."

Once Merry understood the simple pattern, she could let go and enjoy the carefree moment of the music and the dance. It was a different peace than she was used to feeling, but the steady rhythm calmed her soul.

Then Merry blushed when she suddenly realized she was *dancing* with the prince, though apparently no one in the village recognized him. How could they not notice he was someone special? And yet, even though he was the prince, the son of the king of all Levathia, Merry was comfortable with him, as if she'd known him always. When she peered up at Valerian, he was lost in his thoughts, so she did not intrude with hers.

❖

It pleased Valerian that Merry was so willing to try new things. She quickly caught on to both dances. Even this simple one had taken him months to learn well. Of course, at the time he had been a page and much more interested in reading history and philosophy. During that time, he'd been assigned to Lord Reed for a summer and had first met his daughter.

While Valerian continued to lead Merry through the verses of the dance, he couldn't help but compare her with Hanalah. While Merry had not Hanalah's bold beauty, she possessed a tranquil spirit and a quick, eager mind coupled with an amazing depth of character and maturity, considering how sheltered her life had been. He had to admit he was growing quite fond of her company, and he rued the day he would have to marry Hanalah and give up his friendship with Merry. By then he hoped she would be settled in her new life, though he knew he would always feel responsible for her.

Valerian gazed down at Merry as the dance came to the final notes. "Now we stop, and now one more bow and curtsy." The music ended, and she smiled.

Thank you for teaching me this lovely dance.

"It was my pleasure." He smiled at her blush, and on impulse kissed her hand.

They walked back to Ruddy and found that Shannon had joined him on the bench.

"I miss our days of dancing, Ruddy and me," Shannon said wistfully.

"Let me get used to this wooden leg, woman, and perhaps we will dance yet again." Ruddy grimaced. "'Twill have to be a slow one, nae one of those beastly frolics young MacLachlan prefers."

There were just a few more dances, and then someone announced that the winners of the competition were to be displayed on trestle tables. Shannon jumped up.

"Come Merry," she said. "Let's see how we fared."

Merry glanced at Valerian but didn't get a chance to speak to him, for Shannon pulled her into the crowd. Valerian sat beside Ruddy on the bench, watching until the two women were swallowed by the crowd.

"Tell me about your court tomorrow," he asked the knight. "Do you have many cases?"

"Thankfully, no. Two instances of thievery, one claim of false weights, and one assault." Ruddy grimaced. "The assault case is a charge by a wife against her husband. It proves tae be potentially challenging."

"Does each village have its own magistrate?" Valerian's gaze drifted to three men having a heated discussion beside the wine seller's booth.

"The king told me that every village of more than one hundred people has its own," Ruddy said. "But two wee villages nearby have no magistrate. King Orland gave me jurisdiction over them as well. 'Tis from one of these that the assault case comes." He sighed. "Because I dinna know these people personally, I've had tae call witnesses from their village."

"Count on me, Ruddy, to help in any way I possibly can." Valerian stood and scanned the crowd, searching for Merry and Shannon. Briefly, he met the eyes of a tall, rough-looking man who was missing an ear. In contrast to the laughing people around him, the man did not appear to be enjoying himself. Then Valerian became aware the laughter of some of the people had changed to the loud braying that accompanied drunkenness. He'd heard it often enough at the Keep.

"Ruddy, I'm going to find Merry and your wife. Some in the crowd have had a little too much to drink."

"I thank ye, Val. I've had about as much o' this celebration as I can handle."

Valerian took off in the direction of the trestle tables where he spotted the stout form of Lady MacNeil and the smaller Merry beside her. The man with one ear stood nearby, watching them also, but at Valerian's approach, he vanished into the crowd. Merry stared up at Valerian.

My bread won first prize. He *Saw* her mixed pleasure and embarrassment.

"You certainly deserved to win. I've never tasted bread so delicious." Valerian smiled when Merry ducked her head. Then she met his gaze again.

Shannon's needlework won third. I think she is disappointed.

Valerian searched the table for the needlework entries. He compared the first and second place winners to Shannon's.

"I understand why she's disappointed. Hers is far superior."

Shannon must have heard him.

"Thank you, Sire," she said. "Perhaps the judges thought a knight battling a dragon not a fit subject for needlework. But I did it for Ruddy."

Valerian inclined his head to her. Though not a pretty woman, Lady MacNeil was fiercely loyal to Ruddy, and he would always appreciate her for that. Then his thoughts were interrupted by more drunken laughter nearby, so Valerian urged Merry and Shannon to come with him.

"We won't be able to claim our prizes until tomorrow anyway," Shannon told Merry. "Your bread, of course, will have been eaten by then, but I'll collect my picture and you can help me hang it up for Ruddy."

Keeping an eye on the drunken men, Valerian gestured for the ladies to precede him. They made their way back to Ruddy and Kieran and then returned to the quiet manor house.

Caelis strode into the woods near his uncle's castle, carrying his crossbow and a handful of bolts. His skin felt too tight, as if it would burst from his anticipation. Soon he would have the whelp's head and could take it to King Orland, along with the body of the unnamed assassin who had killed the prince. Then the grieving king would have no choice but to name Caelis heir.

"Sir Caelis?"

He stopped at the unexpected voice of one of his men and turned to face him. Young Norris was probably not much older than cousin Lewes, but Lewes had assured Caelis of his loyalty.

"What are you doing here, Norris?" Caelis frowned at him.

Norris wrung his hands. Beneath a shock of dark hair, his brown eyes were troubled.

"Is it true you sent an assassin to kill the prince?"

Caelis clenched his jaw before answering. He set down the crossbow and the handful of bolts.

"How did you know that?"

Norris swallowed noisily and broke eye contact. In a branch overhead a bird cackled.

"I was walking through the room when you were speaking to the one-eared man." He held up his hands, pleading. "I swear I didn't mean to hear."

"Then why are you questioning me?" Caelis lowered his voice. "Didn't I tell you never to question me?"

Norris took a step back, his eyes darting left and right.

"Yes, sir, but you never mentioned killing the prince. I thought we were working toward southern independence."

Caelis pulled his hunting knife from the sheath on his belt. Norris turned to run, but Caelis was upon him, knocking the younger man to the ground. Caelis grabbed a hank of hair and jerked up his head. Before Norris could take a breath to cry out, Caelis slit his throat.

"I told you," Caelis said as he pushed himself to his feet. "Never question me."

Chapter 22 *A false witness will utter lies.*

Merry lay in her comfortable bed, hugging to herself all of yesterday's memories. She had worn her first pretty dress, and she'd been surprised that wearing it had made her *feel* pretty, too. She had won a prize for her bread, even though the greatest prize for her had been to watch the enjoyment on everyone's faces when they tasted what she'd made with her own hands.

But more amazing still was having the opportunity to learn not one, but two dances. Kieran and Valerian were both good teachers, and it was impossible to choose which one she had most enjoyed dancing with. Although they were very different young men, not only from each other but compared to the Brethren, their companionship helped fill the emptiness in her heart.

Later today, she and Shannon were to fetch the prizes for their entries in the competition. What kind of prize would hers be? She had never received any kind of honor or recognition, and it was thrilling to imagine the possibilities.

Merry got out of the bed and smoothed the covers. For a moment she considered putting the pretty dress on again, but she didn't want to soil it in the kitchen. Besides, Shannon had not told her she could keep it, only that she could wear it to the festival. After they brought home their prizes Merry would brush off the dress and take it back to Shannon.

She combed and braided her hair and reluctantly put on her old clothes with the indelible stains. Those blood stains were a constant reminder that all she loved was now dead.

Valerian decided to wear the royal surcoat to Ruddy's court. He recognized he had the opportunity not only to aid Ruddy in matters of law, of which Valerian was considered a scholar, but his presence as Crown Prince of Levathia would help the knight establish his authority here, especially for those who might think a wooden leg was a sign of weakness. Yet while Kieran tied the laces on the sleeves, it was hard not to think that he was being imprisoned inside this garment.

"Kieran?"

"Yes, my lord?" He yawned.

"While Ruddy and I are at court this morning, I want you to be especially vigilant. I know some in the crowd could become unruly if they do not like the judgments rendered."

Kieran stifled another yawn.

"Of course, Sire. I will be my usual vigilant self as soon as we eat something."

Valerian nodded, suppressing a smile at Kieran's sleepiness.

"I'll see if anyone else has awakened yet," he told his squire.

When he entered the great hall, Merry came in from the kitchen wearing her stained apron over the old homespun dress. A smear of flour on her face made her look endearing. But when she saw him dressed in the royal purple, she froze. He came near enough to *See* her.

"What's the matter, Merry?"

You look like a prince today. She curtsied and would not look up at him again.

"Merry." He made his voice as gentle as he could. "I am a prince every day. But a prince is still a servant to the king and ever to the Most High."

She raised her eyes a little and studied the dragon emblem on the surcoat. Made of spun gold thread, the dragon was *rampant*, raised upon its hind legs, and breathing fire. Finally, she spoke.

Is the dragon the symbol of your family?

"Yes. Alden the Great, who founded our royal line three hundred years ago, was called the Dragon King. He chose this emblem for the house d'Alden."

Merry reached behind her and pulled her braid over her shoulder. She lifted the end to show him the wooden clasp. He hadn't paid attention to the painted design: a small blue flower on a white background.

This is a balmflower, my father's emblem.

"Was your father a Healer, too?"

She nodded and let the braid fall. Tears filled her eyes.

"I'm sorry, Merry. I didn't mean to cause painful reminders."

She wiped her eyes and gazed into his.

It's not your fault. Everything brings painful reminders. I only hope the grief will lessen in time so I can make a new life somewhere.

"The strength of your grief shows the depth of your love. I think we carry some grief with us always when those we love go before us." Valerian swallowed to ease the sudden tightness in his throat. If only he could see Waryn one more time to tell his brother how much he did love him, and how sorry he was that he hadn't saved him.

When he glanced back at Merry she wore a slight smile.

"What is it?"

Not only are you a prince and a Seer, you are a Healer with your words.

He shook his head. She gave him too much credit.

"If I'm sometimes able to speak the words most needful, it's only because I've read so widely from the writings of those much wiser than I."

Valerian would have liked to continue their conversation, but at that moment both Kieran and Ruddy entered the hall. Ruddy was dressed in a fine linen shirt with a black velvet vest and breeches. He wore a silver chain of office around his neck. Though he walked with the wooden leg, he used a cane for balance.

"Sir Rudyard, I am pleased to see you on this fine morning." Valerian smiled at his friend.

Ruddy made an awkward bow as he leaned on the cane.

"Your Highness. I trust you slept well?"

"Very well, thank you." Valerian turned to Merry, who backed away and briefly met his gaze.

I feel like a scullery maid in the presence of all this finery and polite manners. I had better finish making breakfast. At that, she fled to the kitchen.

"What ails the lass?" asked Ruddy.

"Clothing," said Valerian. "Or rather, a lack of appropriate attire."

"Shannon has six trunks full o' clothes she canna wear," Ruddy said with passion. Apparently this was a longstanding conflict with his wife. "I'll make sure she gives Merry an entire new wardrobe. It's the least we can do after what she did for our son."

*　　*　　*

Valerian sat beside Ruddy at a table set up in the village square. On Ruddy's other side a scribe recorded the proceedings, and standing nearby was the blacksmith, who acted as bailiff for the day. The "courtroom" had served as the dancing area during last night's festival. Now, however, the mood was quite different.

Ruddy had already pronounced judgment in the first three cases. One accused thief had been dismissed for lack of evidence, and the other ordered to restore threefold the amount of eggs he had stolen from a neighbor's henhouse. The merchant who used false weights was sentenced to three days in the pillory. Even now, two men were leading the weeping man across the square to the wooden device. Several children ran after holding clods of dirt, an egg, and an overripe fruit to throw at their hapless victim.

Valerian had never been so thankful to be a Seer. He hadn't realized until today how useful this talent would prove to be in determining a person's guilt or innocence.

As the final case came forward, Valerian studied the complainant and the accused. The stout woman wore a bandage on her face and folded her hands piously across her ample girth. Her slight, bewildered husband appeared frightened. Ruddy spoke to the woman.

"Step forward and state your name and village."

The woman minced closer to the table.

"Hildara from the village of Pennybridge." She spoke with a haughty tone. When she shifted her eyes to Valerian he *Saw* her contempt for both he and Ruddy as northerners.

"State your case, Hildara of Pennybridge."

She lifted her chin and glared down her nose at Ruddy.

"I have been married to this man for four years. During that time, he has mistreated me, and recently he has turned violent. He cracked my head with a mallet." She cupped the side of her bandaged head.

"What was the provocation?" Ruddy folded his hands on the table.

The woman drew herself up, clearly offended.

"There was no provocation. I was minding my business when he came up from behind and hit me. I lost consciousness."

Valerian glanced at Ruddy for permission and leaned forward.

"If he came from behind, how do you know who hit you?" he asked the woman. When she glanced at him again, Valerian *Saw* that she had fabricated the whole tale.

"Well." She paused to choose her words. "When I came to myself, he was standing over me with the hammer, threatening to hit me again."

"What kind of hammer did he use? Wooden or metal?" Valerian kept staring at her.

Sweat beaded on her forehead, though the morning was cool and the sky cloudy.

"Why, it was metal."

"If you were struck in anger with a metal hammer to the side of the head, then you should not be alive. A metal hammer is a weapon of war, you know." Valerian rested his chin on his palm.

The woman wiped her hands on her dress.

"Perhaps it wasn't metal after all. Yes, now that I consider again, it was a wooden hammer."

"What is your husband's occupation?" At Valerian's change of subject, she blinked.

"A tailor."

"And he has a wooden hammer because?" He raised his brows, inviting her answer.

She opened and closed her mouth without answering.

"Perhaps a tailor uses a wooden hammer to beat out the cloth before he stitches it." Valerian smiled. He heard a few chuckles in the crowd that had gathered.

"Remove your bandage, Hildara of Pennybridge," Ruddy ordered, "so we may see the damage caused by this wooden hammer."

For the first time she became frightened. She shook her head.

"My lord, please, I can't remove the bandage or the bleeding will start afresh."

"Bleeding?" Ruddy frowned. "Did the hammer actually pierce the skin, then?"

"N-no, my lord. But it made a powerful fierce bruise, it did."

"Then let us see it."

The blacksmith stepped forward and pulled off the woman's bandage. There was no sign of injury. Those in the crowd who could see murmured among themselves.

Ruddy leaned close to Valerian and spoke so only he could hear.

"If you will show her to be lying by way of your Sight, then it should put the fear o' God into some of these people."

Valerian rose to his full height. The royal dragon was visible to all. The woman trembled now.

"Hildara of Pennybridge, come forward." She moved closer to the table. Valerian locked eyes with her. "Answer me truly: Did your husband strike you with a wooden hammer?"

The woman didn't answer right away, but finally she nodded.

"Yes, my lord."

"You are bearing false witness against your husband. I am a Seer, Madam, and know that you are lying." Valerian made his face as stern as possible. Several in the crowd began to point and whisper.

Hildara covered her mouth with her hands. Her eyes grew wide.

"I see you know the penalty for bearing false witness." It made Valerian sick in his stomach to think about it. In his heart he felt it cruel; with his rational mind he realized the punishment needed to be harsh in order to act as a deterrent to others.

But the woman's husband stepped forward and fell on his knees. He clasped his hands together.

"Your Highness! I plead for mercy on behalf of my wife." For a man of such slight stature, he spoke with a strong voice.

"You would ask mercy for someone who tried to destroy you?" Valerian frowned.

"She is my wife, for better or for worse. Her madness comes and goes. If you cut out her tongue, I believe it would break her mind. Is there not a lesser punishment that would serve to teach her a lesson without permanent damage?"

Valerian was moved by the man's plight. For his sake he was willing to grant mercy. He leaned down to confer with Ruddy.

"What think you?" whispered Ruddy.

"I think the poor man has suffered enough." Valerian glanced again at the longsuffering husband. "Either the pillory or a dunking should be sufficient punishment. And you will be forewarned about her in future."

"Let me pass sentence then." Ruddy pushed himself up to stand beside Valerian. "The prince has heard your plea, and has recommended leniency. For the crime of bearing false witness, I sentence Hildara of Pennybridge to three days in the pillory."

"Thank you, my lords." The man came forward and bowed, first to Valerian and then to Ruddy.

His wife fell to her knees and covered her face, moaning. The same two who had taken the merchant to the pillory lifted the woman and placed her on the other side of him.

While Valerian cast his gaze across the sea of people, watching individual reactions from the villagers, he glimpsed the one-eared man again before he withdrew into the crowd. Valerian promptly forgot the tall man when he overheard two older men talking nearby.

"I never figured a northerner to care about what goes on here in the south, 'specially not in our small village."

"Those young rowdies who're stirring up trouble ought to hear about this prince and the new magistrate. Maybe they'll bring law and order to the south again."

While the two men walked away, Valerian thought about the conversations he'd overheard at the Keep regarding the south's attitude toward the north. He hadn't realized then how large Levathia was, and that the southerners might have a reason to be disgruntled, believing the king's seat of government in the north was too far away to be effective in maintaining order.

When he returned to the Keep, Valerian would report what he'd seen and heard to his father. There had to be a way to more equally and fairly govern the south.

Chapter 23 *I sleep, but my heart waketh.*

After Valerian and Ruddy left for the village, Shannon took Merry to her bedchamber. She laid the baby on the canopied bed and turned to one of the trunks lining the wall.

“Ruddy doesn't understand why I have kept all these clothes I can no longer wear.” She opened the lid of the trunk and sighed. “I thought I would have several children by this time, and at least one of them a daughter. But 'tis not the will of the Most High that I should bear many children. I must be grateful for the one I have, and that Ruddy's life has been spared.”

She lifted a bundle of neatly folded russet fabric.

“Ah, I had forgotten about this. I never had the chance to wear it, Merry, but I always loved the soft material.” She opened the fabric and held up a tunic and split riding skirt. “With your reddish hair, this color will be especially attractive on you. See if it fits.”

Merry removed her homespun dress and pulled the soft tunic over her chemise. She studied the riding skirt and figured out how to step into it and tuck in the bottom of the chemise. The outfit felt as if it had been made especially for her. Then she realized that while wearing a split skirt she would not have to ride sideways behind Kieran. She could properly and modestly straddle the horse.

Merry hugged Shannon, wishing again that she could thank her. Shannon returned the hug and then held Merry at arm's length.

“I want to say this to you, and I don't want you to refuse.”

Dread rose in Merry's throat. What if it was something she *had* to refuse? But Shannon continued before she could answer.

"I will never be able to wear these clothes again. I may never have a daughter with whom to share them. So I want to give you these riding clothes, and the green dress, and the chemise, and the cap, and anything else we might find today."

Merry's eyes filled with tears. No one had ever been so generous to her, and Shannon could not have known that Merry had always dreamed of wearing pretty things. She hugged her again and burst into tears. Shannon held her close and let her cry herself out.

After washing her face, Merry tried on many beautiful dresses, most of which were either too ornate or too large for her to wear. There was one other simple dress in a darker shade of green that fit Merry well, and a black riding skirt.

"This one appears made for serious riding." Shannon fingered the sturdy fabric. "You might as well take it, too. You'll be riding a long way, and I'm sure I will never sit upon a horse again."

Nathan woke, demanding to be fed. Merry left Shannon to nurse him and went to show Kieran her new dress.

Just as she closed Shannon's door, she stopped, feeling a twinge of guilt. Was she being vain? Would she let the young man's admiration turn her head? What would Gabriel think? She knew what Papa would have said. But Papa was no longer here to scold and criticize her. And if Gabriel *were* here, Merry was certain he would have admired her, too.

* * *

Merry sat across from Kieran at the trestle table while he told her a story about his brothers. When Shannon entered with Nathan, Merry glad turned her attention to them, because Kieran's story was so full of people she didn't know and events unfamiliar to her that she was having trouble following him. Merry held out her hands for the baby, and Shannon gratefully gave him to her.

Shannon sat on the bench while Merry rocked Nathan. The baby's eyelids drooped, his mouth went slack, and he relaxed into a deep sleep. Kieran leaned his head against his hands.

"Ye know how to work magic on the babe, Merry."

"She certainly does." Shannon smiled. "I wish you all could stay longer. But the prince says he wants to leave tomorrow. Did I hear him right, Kieran?"

"I think he is anxious to get to Lord Reed's and get it over with so he can return tae his men at the garrison."

"So he's not looking forward to visiting our noble Lord of the Southern Woodlands, is he?" Shannon smirked. Merry got the impression Lord Reed was not well liked.

"Oh, he can tolerate Lord Reed for one night, but 'tis seeing his daughter that he dreads." Kieran winked.

Shannon put her hands on her hips.

"What are you not telling me, squire?"

He stared at the ceiling and began to whistle. Merry felt she was missing out on some private joke.

"Ach," Kieran said. "'Tis no secret I suppose. Lord Reed wants Prince Valerian to marry his daughter. The king wishes it, too."

Shannon's eyes widened, and she clasped her hands in delight.

"So there's to be a royal wedding? Do you know when? Perhaps Ruddy and I will be invited!"

Merry didn't hear Kieran's answer. She suddenly became ill and pushed back from the table, careful not to wake the baby.

"What's the matter, Merry?" Shannon leaned closer. "Do you want me to take Nathan?"

Merry nodded and eased the precious bundle into Shannon's arms. Then she fled from the hall and into the yard, desperate to find a quiet place.

The sound of a rake came from the stables. Merry ran inside, passing a stable boy cleaning out a stall. Farther down Kieran's horse stuck out his head and nickered. Merry stopped and stroked his cheek, glad that he remembered her.

In the next stall, Valerian's horse stamped a hoof but didn't come to investigate. The gray didn't have as much personality as the brown. That seemed odd. Merry guessed a prince would have a better horse than his squire. Perhaps the gray had qualities not apparent to her.

That started her tears. Why was she so unhappy anyway? Valerian was a prince. He was *the* prince and would have to marry where his father, the king desired, just as her father had arranged a marriage for her. Valerian's choice of wife would be infinitely more important than her choice of a husband had been, for wouldn't his wife be queen someday when he became king?

And just as she would have had to give up her friendship with Michael when she and Gabriel married, she would no longer be able to have such a close relationship with Valerian. But he alone could hear her words! Not even Eldred, another Seer, could do that. She would be totally cut off from the rest of the world when Valerian married this daughter of Lord Reed.

Desperately she placed her hands on her throat and tried to feel what was wrong, but apparently it wasn't possible to Heal herself. She swallowed, hard, and tried to make a noise in her throat. Nothing happened. Her tears flowed freely.

Kieran's horse nuzzled her. Merry opened the door to Gilly's stall and went inside. The straw poked at her bare feet, but she ignored it. A brush hung from a peg, and Merry took it down. Timidly at first and then harder when Gilly leaned into it, she brushed all of him that she could reach. Fortunately, she didn't have to see in order to brush him, for her tears would not stop flowing.

On the way back to the manor house with Ruddy, Valerian was sorry to see how the royal surcoat put that wall of separation between him and the villagers. It had been so nice to go among them as one of them. Now each person stopped what they were doing to bow or curtsy. Not one of the adults would meet his eye; only the children were unimpressed by the dragon emblem and the one who wore it.

Kieran met them at the edge of the road. Valerian *Saw* concern in his eyes.

"What is it?"

"Merry is distressed about something. The lass ran out of the house a little while ago. I watched her go into the stables, but she hasn't come out again."

"Did you try to talk to her?" Valerian glanced at the stables.

"No, Sire. She must have wanted to be alone."

"Go on in with Ruddy. I'll find out what's bothering her. Then I want to get out of this surcoat as quickly as possible."

"Aye, my lord." Kieran bowed and ran to catch up with Ruddy.

Valerian nodded to the stable boy when he entered the building. He peered into each stall, whether occupied or not. When he reached Kieran's horse, he peered over the half door and saw Merry brushing the bay.

"Merry!" He opened the door.

She turned so quickly the brush flew out of her hand.

"Let me get that. You shouldn't be standing so close to a horse with your bare feet." He didn't mean to scold her, but her feet were so small compared to the horse's hooves that one misstep might have crushed her foot.

While he picked up the brush and replaced it on the peg, she left the stall. But when he came out and closed the door, she was nowhere to be seen.

"Merry? What game are you playing? I need to talk to you. Please, come here." Valerian exited the stables and found Merry sitting under a shaggy beard tree. She would not look up at him. He went down on one knee and brought his face close to hers.

"Please, tell me what happened. Why are you so distressed?" Valerian kept staring at Merry, but her face was set against him. He sat directly in front of her. "I'm not leaving until you look at me, no matter how long it takes. I am just as stubborn as you are."

They sat in stony silence for many awkward minutes. Merry wore a different dress, and Valerian absently noted how it flattered her. At last Merry sighed and closed her eyes. A tear leaked out, and she wiped it away. Then she gazed into his eyes.

I have to stop talking to you. I can't stay with you any longer. It will just be more difficult.

"Merry, what are you talking about?" Valerian frowned in confusion.

We can't be friends any more, since you are going to be married.

"Who told you that?"

Kieran and Shannon were talking about Lord Reed's daughter.

"Yes, I will probably have to marry her someday." Valerian shifted when he felt dampness leeching through his breeches. "But I hope it will be many years before that happens. Why would you think we couldn't speak because of that?"

Because it would not be proper. Merry plucked a blade of grass and twirled it in her fingers.

"Proper? I don't understand, Merry. If you don't speak to me, you won't be able to communicate with anyone."

Her eyes widened and she straightened.

I know! That is why I've been so distressed! You're the only one I can communicate my words and feelings to. She shrank back in resignation and tossed the blade of grass aside. *If I were your wife, I would not want another woman speaking to your mind.*

"Oh." It was so obvious now, Valerian felt foolish for not seeing it before. Someone like Hanalah would certainly be jealous of Merry. Why hadn't he considered that? What could he do?

"Merry, I respect you greatly, and I value our special friendship. I feel I can trust you as much as I trust Kieran, which is with my life. I hope you can trust me, too." She nodded. "Before I have to marry Hanalah, I'll find some way for you to communicate. I can teach you how to write, or—" He threw up his hands. "I'll search the entire world to find a Seer who can *See* your words. I will not leave you voiceless. I would rather die than to hurt you."

She wiped her eyes again before meeting his gaze.

I'm afraid it will hurt more the longer we wait. Perhaps, I should stay here with Ruddy and Shannon. I could help with the baby and in the kitchen, and it wouldn't matter if I couldn't talk. A servant is supposed to listen, not speak.

"No! You're not a servant. You are a Healer, and that complicates all of this."

What do you mean?

He took her hands between his, amazed anew at how small they were.

"I have seen the power coming from your hands. You are gifted in a way that evil men will want to use to your destruction. I must take you to the Keep so my father and I can protect you."

The Keep? She pulled her hands away.

"It's just a castle." He stopped when he realized his words were not reassuring. "Your village had a wooden palisade around it. Do you remember when it was built?"

It was long before I was born.

"Inside those wooden walls was your whole village." She nodded. "A castle is like a village inside stone walls. Instead of separate cottages, there's a large stone building where people live in individual apartments or in community rooms, like a barracks. There are kitchens even bigger than Lady MacNeil's." He smiled when her eyes widened. "You can grow your

Healing herbs in the gardens. And there are stables. You can meet my horse at last." From the stables a horse whinnied as if in agreement.

Is the gray not yours?

"No. My horse is black and even taller. His name is Theo. I named him after my grandfather, who was King Theodoric. Poor Theo went lame just after we left the Keep so Kieran took him home and brought me the gray."

I hope Theo is all right.

"I'm sure his leg is fine now. I only hope he hasn't forgotten me."

He will not forget you. You are not forgettable.

Valerian had to look away from the intensity of her gaze. He stood and held out a hand to help her stand. Valerian should have let go of her hand, but he didn't want to. He felt a strong urge to take her in his arms. But he fought the desire, very glad Merry could not *See* his thoughts in that moment. He tried to think of a flippant comment, but his emotions were too powerful.

He cleared his throat and released her hand.

"We should go back now. Kieran was concerned about you."

Merry nodded and turned toward the manor house. As he followed her, he remembered his grandfather's words while he was teaching Valerian battle tactics years ago.

"The obvious dangers are not the most deadly. The ones you least expect will kill you."

Valerian had not considered the one danger he should have seen coming. He never expected that he might fall in love with Merry.

Chapter 24 *The words of the wicked are to lie in wait for blood.*

After Merry entered Ruddy's hall, Valerian continued to the back so Kieran could help him out of his ornate purple surcoat. She felt sad watching them, for she knew their brief time of lighthearted friendship was over.

Of course, Valerian meant what he said. He was truthful in all of his dealings. She knew that he *wanted* to keep his promise to help her communicate. But he was a prisoner of his rank and position and could not control his own destiny. For so long Merry had envied those of noble birth, believing their lives were easy compared to her own. But no one could escape life's difficulties; they just came in different forms.

She bit back her tears, weary of crying. There was no more relief to be found there. Her life had been spared, but she still did not know why. She could not speak, except to Valerian's mind. She was a Healer, though she had no one to advise her on how to keep from overextending herself. Valerian wanted to take her to the Keep, the place where the men in her life had suffered in the dungeon. What would happen to her there? Could she really make a place for herself among those people?

Merry sighed. Though she didn't want to, she needed to be honest with herself. She could have faced any kind of future knowing she had Valerian's companionship. It was the certainty of its loss that made her heart so heavy.

"Hello, Merry." Shannon came out from the kitchen. "Are you hungry?"

Merry shook her head. She couldn't imagine ever eating again.

"Kieran said Valerian wants to go to Eldred's. Are you going with him?"

Merry shrugged. She would like to see Eldred again, but she didn't know if Valerian wanted to speak with him alone. What a burden it was to be used to speaking and no longer be able! But it was no use getting frustrated with Shannon or anyone else. Even Valerian couldn't truly understand how much she depended on him.

The three men came into the hall. Valerian had changed into his plain tunic and Ruddy into his work shirt. Both Valerian and Kieran wore their swords on their belts. In his hand Valerian held two scrolls.

"Are any of you hungry?" asked Shannon.

"Aye, Lady MacNeil," said Kieran with a grin.

"But you are always hungry." Shannon sounded pleased.

Merry envied Kieran's ability to accept things as they were and not let life's woes interfere with his enjoyment of simple pleasures, like eating and dancing. She smiled. And sleeping. He could probably sleep through the worst thunderstorm.

"I'll eat, woman." Ruddy sat heavily on the bench.

"Thank you, Lady Shannon," said Valerian, "but I must see Eldred first." Merry felt his eyes upon her and glanced his way. "Will you come with me, Merry?"

She nodded.

"Oh, Merry, we have not collected our prizes from last night." Shannon turned to Valerian. "Your Highness, would you be so kind as to take Merry to the square when you are finished at Eldred's?"

"Of course, Lady MacNeil." He beckoned to Kieran as he and Merry left the hall. Kieran followed them outside.

Valerian glanced back to make sure they weren't overheard.

"I'd like for you to sound out Ruddy while Merry and I are away."

"What about, Sire?" Kieran cocked his head, curious.

"Make sure he has all he needs. I don't think he would tell me if he lacked something, because of his fierce pride. He might let it slip to a fellow Highlander, though."

"Oh, aye, Sire. We Highlanders have ways to ken these things." Kieran placed his finger beside his nose in an arcane gesture.

Valerian clapped him on the shoulder.

"I have no doubt of your ability," he said.

Merry and Valerian walked in silence to Eldred's cottage. There were so many things she wanted to ask him, but it didn't seem the time or place to pester him about details of the journey to Lord Reed's, and the garrison, and the Keep. She would have to adopt Kieran's philosophy and experience each day as it unfolded.

Valerian knocked on Eldred's door and opened it when they heard him say, "Come in."

They went inside and found the old man sitting in the same chair with the same coverlet across his lap. He smiled at them.

"Come closer, Merry. You too, Valerian. I have news for you."

Valerian replaced the two scrolls in the desk.

"I was only able to finish one of them."

"No matter, my prince. I have found the information I've been seeking." Eldred reached down and picked up a scroll lying beside his chair. "Open this and begin reading about halfway down."

Valerian carefully unrolled the parchment and scanned the writing. Watching him, Merry decided she would ask him to teach her how to read those symbols. Maybe she could learn to write them, too.

"So, it's true." Valerian let the parchment roll back and handed it to Eldred. "King Sigmund did not enter a monastery; he changed his name and founded the peaceful Brethren." He stared at Merry.

She gasped, realizing the import of those words.

Then we are *cousins.* She clasped her hands in a silent prayer. *Perhaps your wife will not mind if you speak to me, since we are family. Does she have a sister? I always wanted a sister. Do you think she will like me?*

"I hope so, Merry." Valerian's smile was sad.

Eldred sighed, and they both turned to look at him.

"I do wish I could hear your thoughts, Merry. Perhaps the Sight fades with age, as eyesight does. You're going to leave me, I hear."

She nodded and knelt beside him, resting her hand on the arm of his chair. He took her hand in both of his, and she felt them shaking, just like her grandfather's hands used to do.

"The idea of going to the Keep must seem a little intimidating to you, but I lived there a very long time, and I can tell you that you will learn to be comfortable there." He smiled. "There is so much activity going on every minute of the day and night, but there are quiet times, too, and places for you to be alone when you need it. Isn't that so, Valerian?"

"Yes, you're right."

"My prince, what have you got on your belt? Is that what I think it is?"

Valerian slipped the blade from the scabbard and held it closer so Eldred could better see.

"A sword." Eldred's voice was reverent. He let go of Merry's hand to touch the hilt.

"Not just any sword. This belonged to Alden himself."

"Where did you find it?"

Valerian replaced the sword in the scabbard.

"In the Keep's armory. There were two blades in an old, old trunk. Kieran has the other one. We've been learning how to use them. I have an idea they may be effective against the Horde's battle-axes."

"There is much forgotten lore about these elegant weapons. Perhaps you can learn more in the Keep's library."

Valerian's smile lit his face, and Merry was reminded of his love of learning.

"I plan to look when we return."

Eldred turned to Merry.

"Though I wish I had more time to spend with you, I must bid you both farewell."

She stood and kissed him on the cheek. He sighed.

"I could get used to that, my dear."

She curtsied to him. It was the only way she could think of to let him know how she felt about him.

"If you would wait just outside, I have one more thing to tell the prince."

Merry nodded and glanced up at Valerian.

I won't wander off. I promise.

"Thank you. I'll be there shortly."

At the door Merry turned back to Eldred one last time. Then she stepped outside and closed the door behind her.

❖

As soon as Merry left, Eldred handed Valerian a sheet of parchment folded and sealed with the old Seer's emblem in red wax.

"What is this?" Valerian fingered the seal.

"I've written out all the evidence for King Orland proving what really happened to his great-grandfather Sigmund. And I've proven Merry's lineage through him so there will be no question of her royal blood."

"Thank you." Valerian tucked the letter into his tunic's hidden pocket. "I shall personally give this into my father's hand."

"One thing more before you go, my prince." Eldred leaned closer. His eyes bore into Valerian's. "I have reason to believe Merry is unique in her talent of speaking to your mind. That, coupled with her rare gift of Healing, makes her doubly precious. Please take special care of her."

"You know I will, Eldred. I've promised the Most High to guard her with my life."

Eldred sat back, satisfied.

"Good, good. I only wish she could speak to me, as well."

"Yes, so do I." *But probably not for the same reasons*, he mused. "I hope I will see you again. The Keep is not the same without you."

"And I am not the same without the Keep. But the southern climate is much easier on these old bones." Eldred held out his gnarled hand and Valerian grasped it. "May the Most High be with you, Your Highness, and prosper all your dealings."

Valerian inclined his head in order to show his respect for the aged Seer.

"And you also." Then he turned and left with no delay. There were few things he disliked more than emotional partings, especially when it was quite possible he would never see the man again in this life.

True to her word, Merry stood waiting outside.

"Shall we find out what you have won for your bread?" Valerian held out his arm for her. She stared at it, momentarily confused, but then she slipped her hand under his elbow and tentatively took hold of his sleeve. He gazed down at her.

"This is just a polite way for a gentleman to escort a lady. It lets passersby know she is under his protection."

I saw people walking like this at the festival. I wasn't sure what it meant more than just being together. Her face grew thoughtful. *I have a lot to learn, don't I?*

"As do I."

When they reached the square, the "courtroom" had been replaced by hawkers selling produce and handcrafted items. Valerian spotted two men at a table who looked as if they might have been involved in the festival's competition. He steered Merry in their direction and stepped up to the table.

"This is Merry, whose bread won first prize last night."

The smaller man studied her and nodded.

"Oh, yes. Your delicious braided bread will ever be remembered in the history of our festival." He searched through one of the baskets on the table and pulled out a blue and green linen scarf. "I realize this has nothing to do with baking, except to keep your hair out of it." He handed the scarf to Merry. She took it from him with a look of delight on her face. Then she curtsied.

The man asked Valerian, "Does she not speak?"

"Unfortunately, no," he replied.

Merry touched his arm, and he met her eyes.

Don't forget about Shannon's prize.

"Oh, yes. We are also here to collect Lady MacNeil's third place prize for needlework."

The man gave Merry an embroidery hoop to take back to Shannon, as well as her framed picture of the dragon and the knight. Merry slipped the hoop over her wrist so she could hold the picture and still take Valerian's arm again.

"I would like to make a short detour to show you some flowers I saw yesterday," he said. "Nothing blooms this time of year in the north. Perhaps you can identify these for me."

I will try. You are right, there aren't many flowers in winter here. But when spring comes, there are so many the ground is thick with blooms in every color of the rainbow.

"I would like to see that someday."

They headed in the direction of Ruddy's house, but took a path off the road that wound through the trees. A burbling creek ran nearby. The air was pleasantly cool.

They had just reached the border of Ruddy's land when strong hands whipped a garrote across Valerian's throat, jerking him back. Though he couldn't breathe, Valerian grabbed at the assailant's corded arms and tried to bend over to pull him off balance. But the man was too solid and too strong. When Valerian stomped on what he hoped was the man's foot, the assailant only tightened the cord, crushing Valerian's throat. As his vision began to darken, Valerian saw the horror in Merry's eyes.

Chapter 25 *I found him whom my soul loveth*

Merry whirled around and gasped. A tall burly man choked Valerian from behind with a stout cord. Already his face had lost color. Though he struggled mightily, he was about to lose consciousness. Merry took a step forward and lifted her hands, but what could she do? Did her Oath of Peace really mean she was helpless to prevent Valerian's murder? But how could she stand here and watch him die?

Then Kieran appeared with a sword in his hand. The blade flashed, and the attacker cried out. Blood spurted from the big man's leg. He let go of Valerian and bent over. Merry jumped forward to break Valerian's fall and glimpsed a fountain of blood as the stranger collapsed to the ground.

Merry shuddered and had to force that image from her mind so she could turn Valerian on his back. His face was blue. She probed his bruised throat. His windpipe had been crushed, and he wasn't breathing. She focused all her Healing energy on the place to repair the damage and restore circulation.

"Merry!" Kieran's voice sounded as if he were far away. "You've Healed him." His hands pulled hers away from Valerian's throat.

No, no! She tried to shout, but nothing came out. When she opened her eyes, Valerian's injuries were gone. But he still wasn't breathing.

Something Papa had shown her leaped to her mind. She slipped out of Kieran's grasp and gently pulled back Valerian's head until his lips parted. Then she pinched his nostrils closed and covered his mouth with her own, pushing air into his lungs. She kept breathing for him until she thought she would pass out, but his chest spasmed and he sucked in a deep breath on his own.

Merry sat back, trembling with exhaustion. Tears of relief poured from her eyes.

"You did it, Merry. Praise the Most High for your gift!" Kieran helped Valerian sit up.

"What happened?" Valerian's voice was barely audible. He put a hand on his throat.

Kieran stayed beside him on one knee.

"I saw you coming toward the house, but then ye kept walking, so I decided to meet you. And 'tis a good thing I did. This brigand came from nowhere and garroted you. I pulled out me sword and cut one of his legs, since he was too close to risk stabbing him and maybe hitting you, too. He let go of you and so I—" Kieran grimaced and turned away, vomiting into the grass. When he turned back his face was pale. "Do ye know, 'tis the first man I've killed." His voice lowered. "I think we can now say the blade is sharp enough tae use in battle."

Valerian swallowed and tried to speak a little louder.

"Is he missing one ear?"

Kieran glanced back at the body.

"Aye, my lord. This be the one you saw at the festival. Why was he trying to kill you, I wonder?"

"I would be more interested in knowing if someone sent him to kill me." Valerian turned his attention to Merry. "Did you Heal me? He strangled me so hard I know there must have been some damage."

Merry nodded and wiped her eyes.

"She saved your life." Kieran's voice was full of awe. "After she Healed your throat, ye still weren't breathing, so she did that too."

"What do you mean?" Valerian met Merry's gaze. "What did you do?"

I breathed for you, as Papa once showed me. I couldn't let you die.

Valerian sat, stunned. Kieran stood and picked up his fallen sword. There was blood on the blade. He pulled out a cloth, cleaned it, and replaced it in the scabbard.

"Shall I fetch some help to get you both back to the house, Sire?"

"No, I'm all right now. I will help Merry. You can bury the body or leave it for the scavengers." Valerian did allow Kieran to help him stand, and the squire hovered beside him as if reluctant to leave.

"Are you sure ye don't need help, Sire?"

"Quite sure."

"Then I'll run and ask MacNeil if he has a preference about what to do with the remains." Kieran saluted and ran toward the manor house.

Valerian held out a hand to Merry.

"Can you stand? Are you well?"

She nodded and let him lift her up.

Energy has been taken from me, but not as much as before. Merry did not look away from his eyes. *I was so afraid I had lost you.* She began to tremble.

"You are so giving, Merry. Mind to mind, and now breath to breath. I feel more and more a part of you." Valerian leaned forward and kissed her gently.

When he pulled back, she stared at him, afraid to look away lest this prove to be a dream. How had he become so dear to her in such a short time? She felt as if they'd known one another always. She *was* a part of him, and he was part of her.

Her heart wanted to burst, and she hugged him, feeling his arms enfold her. She leaned her head against his chest, listened to the beating of his heart. Merry had never felt more alive than she did in this moment. It didn't matter that he would have to marry someone else someday, that her future was a great unknown. Right now in this place and time she could stand here in his arms and love him with her whole heart. That was a gift no one could take from her and a memory no time would erase.

Merry moved away first. Valerian's face mirrored her own feelings, and she smiled.

"I'm sorry," he said quietly. "I probably shouldn't have done that."

She took his hands in hers.

Don't be sorry. I'm not. We have this moment together, and that is enough for me to last my entire life.

He kissed her hands and gazed at her with such tenderness as she'd never seen before. It greatly moved her to be the object of such love.

"You are extraordinary, Merry, do you know that?"

Perhaps, but it feels a little awkward to be making such declarations with a dead man as our witness.

Valerian frowned, troubled, and embraced her again.

"All the more reason to declare myself to you now, while I can." Standing there in his arms, Merry wished he would kiss her once more, for they might never have another opportunity. After all, they were to see his intended bride tomorrow.

He must have had the same thought, for he pulled away and gazed into her eyes. Then he gently cupped her face in his hands and brought his warm lips to hers. The kiss was sweet and restrained, a moment of intimate sharing, but as far as Merry was concerned, it was perfect.

Now that, she told him when they parted, *is a very good way to communicate.*

A smile illuminated his face, making him beautiful. Perhaps that wasn't the right word to describe a man who was a prince, but he *was* noble and beautiful, both outwardly and in his soul.

They pulled apart when they heard footsteps. Merry's face grew warm as Kieran stepped out from the trees. How much had he seen and heard? Well, no matter, she trusted him to keep it to himself.

He glanced from Valerian to Merry and back, puzzled. But if Kieran suspected anything, he didn't mention it. He nodded to the body on the ground.

"MacNeil says we ought tae bury it. He'd rather not attract scavenger dragons." He held up a spade. "What about that hole over there? It looks like an old burrow. Then all I'll need to do is fill it in with dirt and rocks."

Valerian shared one last glance and smile with Merry before speaking to Kieran.

"Here, let me help you." Valerian walked to the body. "Before we bury this, we ought to see if there is any way to identify who he was."

While they were occupied, Merry picked up Shannon's picture and embroidery hoop where she'd dropped them. Then she turned away from the gruesome corpse and hugged herself. She knew she was probably being a fool, and that someday she might wish she had acted otherwise, but she had learned too well in the last few months how fragile life was. For the remainder of her days, she would always regret not having made things right with Papa and Michael before they died. She never again wanted to regret *not* having spoken or acted when the opportunity presented itself.

While they walked back to Ruddy's house, Valerian held out his arm for Merry to take. She did so, gazing at him with a muted echo of her unexpected ardor. He covered her hand with his own, recognizing that nothing would ever be the same again. Was he a fool for revealing his great affection for Merry? Should he try to suppress it, pretend it didn't exist?

How could he possibly deny it? They had a communion of minds and hearts, and now even the breath of life. There was no way he could have avoided falling in love with her, even if he had willed it. And, he had to admit, there was no one else in the whole world he could have trusted more, or more desired to share his intimate soul.

What were they going to do? How could he possibly marry Hanalah *now*?

He would try to follow Merry's example and accept this gift of today and worry about tomorrow if it came. After all, someone was trying to kill him. Between that and the Horde, their future was uncertain at best.

Before they stepped into the house, Merry gazed up into his eyes.

Will you please ask Shannon where I might wash my hair?

"You want to wash your hair?"

She nodded, looking sheepish.

It is rather a long process, and I don't think I'll have another opportunity before we reach the Keep.

"I can only imagine what an ordeal it must be." He stroked her braid. "And you're right; this is probably your last chance before spring."

He explained the situation to Shannon, who took Merry in hand. Merry gave him a parting glance. No words were necessary for him to understand that she felt as he did, and from now on each would be incomplete without the other.

* * *

"What happened out there?" Ruddy asked. His wooden leg scraped on the floor of the hall as he approached.

"Someone tried to kill me." Valerian's hand went to his throat.

"Do ye know who it was? Kieran said he had to kill him."

"I had never seen him before the festival. He was also in the crowd during your court. Tall, rough-looking, missing one ear."

"That does nae sound familiar. What will ye do?" Ruddy's face was grim.

"What can we do? Kieran and I will have to be especially vigilant. Does anyone in the village sell horses?"

"Aye. I've bought many from a man named Josiah. He's honest and fair."

"Do you have time to go with me now to buy a gentle horse for Merry? For her safety and ours, she needs her own mount."

Ruddy nodded and picked up his cane.

"Are ye coming with us, MacLachlan?"

Kieran looked to Valerian.

"Am I, my lord?"

"I think," said Valerian, "I would feel better if you and your battle-proven sword stayed here with Merry and Shannon."

"Whatever you say, Your Highness." Kieran saluted.

* * *

An hour later, they returned to the manor house. Valerian led their purchase, a small black and white gelding old enough to be especially gentle. As they came in sight of the house, Merry ran toward them wearing riding clothes, though she was barefooted. Her unbound hair flowed behind her like a reddish-brown cape. Her face lit with joy, and Valerian's heart ached to see her.

She stopped short and demurely put her hands behind her back. He met her gaze.

Kieran said you went to buy a horse. Is he mine?

"Yes, he is. He's not much to look at, but he's gentle and not too big for you."

I think he's beautiful. She sighed. *The black and white patches make his mane look striped. Does he have a name?*

"None that I was told. Ruddy, did Josiah give this horse a name?"

"I dinna think so."

Good. Merry clasped her hands. *I shall call him Stripe.*

Valerian turned to Ruddy.

"The horse has a name now. Stripe."

"It fits, lass." The knight grinned.

May I ride him now?

Valerian stared down at her bare feet.

"I thought Shannon gave you riding boots."

She did, but they're made of stiff leather and difficult to walk in. Merry bit her lip.

Valerian moved closer to her, and Stripe took a step also.

"Merry, I know you're not used to wearing anything on your feet, but it's dangerous to go barefooted around horses, and the farther north we travel, the colder it will become. You must wear those boots for protection."

Kieran came out of the house carrying a pair of boots.

"Merry," he called. "Lady MacNeil said to give these to you."

Merry mouthed her thanks and pulled them on. She appeared ready to climb on the horse right away, but Valerian stopped her.

"What about your hair?"

I was waiting for it to dry before I braided it. She pulled the hair over her shoulder and tried to smooth it.

"Do you need any help?"

Have you braided hair before? Your horse's tail perhaps?

"No, but I have watched one of the grooms. Kieran, come help me."

Merry caught his arm before she turned around.

Just divide it into three equal strands and take the outside one inside, alternating sides.

It sounded easier than it was to actually perform. He and Kieran took three times longer to braid Merry's hair than she would have taken alone. When they finally reached the end, Merry fished the wooden clasp out of a pocket in the riding skirt. Valerian fastened it to the hair, showing the emblem to Kieran.

"This is her father's symbol, a balmflower."

"Apt for a Healer," said Kieran with a nod.

Merry studied their handiwork and then curtsied. She gazed up at Valerian.

Not bad for two beginners. She smiled. *I'm ready to learn how to ride now.*

First, Valerian showed her the saddle and bridle and how to put them on. Then, he helped her put her left foot in the stirrup so she could mount. She sat astride the horse, grinning wide. It was only a matter of minutes until she was guiding the horse forward, to either side, and bringing him to a halt.

Valerian decided she'd done enough for one day. She could learn trotting and cantering while traveling.

By the time Merry had taken off the saddle and bridle, and turned Stripe over to the stable boy, the sun was low in the sky and it was time for their evening meal, the last they would share with Ruddy and Shannon. Kieran went ahead, and Valerian gazed into Merry's eyes.

"Before we lose our light, was there anything you wanted to ask?"

Thank you for my beautiful Stripe, but how are we safer if we each have a horse?

"If we are surprised by another killer or robbers or the Horde, we can get away faster with one rider on a horse. Riding double tires the animal much more quickly."

Do you mean I might get to ride a horse that is running?

Valerian heard the excitement in her mental voice.

"It's called 'galloping,' but yes, it's possible." He pretended to be stern. "Just hold on as if your life depends upon it, because it will."

She appeared thoughtful and sad. He took her hand.

"What is it?"

That sounds like what I'm doing already, holding on because my life depends on it.

He enfolded her in his arms, and she fiercely hugged him back.

"Then hold on, Merry, and never let go."

He touched his lips to her hair. It smelled of lavender, and he smiled. His heart yearned for her, but he refrained from kissing her again, because he didn't trust himself to stop there. She pulled away, as if she'd read his thoughts.

Thank you for the best day of my life.

"It has been the best for me, as well." He seized her hand and kissed it. "Shall we go in now?"

A mischievous look came to her eyes.

Let's race. Then she let go of his hand and began running. Laughing, he caught up with her and touched the door first.

It's these boots. Barefooted I would surely win.

"Then we must have a rematch soon."

Agreed.

* * *

That evening Merry sat between Valerian and Kieran on the bench. The five friends lingered over the meal and afterward. Once Shannon had to step out to take care of Nathan, but when she brought him back, Merry took charge of the babe.

Valerian glanced down at Merry often. She had such a way with the infant that her calm spilled over to him. He remembered what she had told him, how she'd mothered the baby brother who would have been only four when he died. It must have been like losing her own child. How much Merry had to grieve for!

When Kieran yawned, Valerian realized it was getting late. He hoped to make an early start for Lord Reed's. As everyone headed for the bedrooms, Valerian took Ruddy aside.

"I hope you won't be angry with me, but today when I purchased the saddle, I asked the saddlemaker if he could design a stirrup so you could ride again."

Ruddy's eyes narrowed. But the anger quickly faded, and he took a deep breath.

"I will nae lie to ye, Val. I want with all me heart to ride again, but I know it will take a lot of work. Perhaps my stable boy will help me."

"I'm sure he'll be glad to. He's a hard-working lad."

Ruddy stared at Valerian.

"Just like another lad I once knew." He bowed, leaning on his cane. "You will make an excellent crown prince, Your Highness, much better than yer brother, God rest his soul, because you have a heart of justice tempered with mercy."

Valerian was too stunned to reply for a long minute.

"Thank you, Sir Rudyard. I will endeavor to live up to the high standards you have taught me." He and Ruddy gripped one another's arms, both too moved for any more words.

❖

When Caelis entered the barracks, he found Drew playing chess with the young boy from the Brethren village. Up until now he had managed to avoid any interaction with the child.

"Drew!"

The squire jumped up.

"Yes, sir?"

"We're setting out for the Keep tomorrow." Caelis stared at the boy. Other than the girlish long hair, the child bore an uncanny resemblance to his lost brother Caeden. It might be dangerous to keep the boy, but Caelis wasn't yet ready to dispose of him.

"I'll have everything ready, sir." Drew continued to hover beside the child.

Caelis ignored him and sat down in the seat Drew vacated. The boy looked at him cautiously.

"What is your name?" Caelis spoke quietly.

"My name is Rafael. Why did you kill Papa? He was not very kind, but he was my Papa."

Caelis crossed his arms and carefully chose his words.

"I am a knight and must obey the king. The king's son wrote a decree ordering that all in your village must die. I was following orders."

"Did you kill my Sissy, too?" Rafael stared at him, not nearly as fearful as he ought to be.

"We killed everyone quickly so they would not suffer." Out of the corner of his eye, Caelis caught the movement of Drew's mouth as if he wanted to argue.

"Why didn't you kill me?" asked Rafael.

Caelis glared at Drew, daring him to contradict him.

"My squire here convinced me to spare you, which I was glad to do. After all, you look just like my little brother."

"You have a brother?" Rafael's tone was wistful.

"I had a brother named Caeden, but he drowned." Caelis' throat constricted and he had to clear it before continuing. "I wasn't able to save him."

"I am sorry," said the boy. "Do you miss him very much?"

Caelis nodded. He hadn't intended to open such an old wound, and hadn't expected the wound to still be raw.

"How old are you, Rafael?"

The boy held up four fingers and said unnecessarily, "I am four years old."

"It will be awhile before you can be a knight, but would you like to learn how?"

Rafael's face shone.

"Oh, yes! I would like to be a knight. Drew says he is learning, too."

"Yes," Caelis said with a growl in his throat. "Drew is a squire and must obey his knight." They locked eyes for a moment. "When you are six years old you can be my page, and then when you are thirteen you can be my squire."

"When can I be a knight?"

"Not until you are twenty."

The boy grew solemn again, appearing much older than his years.

"I can wait."

"Good. You have a lot to learn before then. Do you know my name?"

"You are Sir Caelis, and Drew is your squire, and I will be your page when I am six years old."

Caelis stood and wiped his hands on his tunic.

"Very good, Rafael. You are well on your way to becoming an excellent page. Now, help Drew get ready to leave early in the morning. We have a long journey."

"Yes, sir." The boy bowed and followed Drew.

Caelis watched them leave, well satisfied. It would not be difficult to attach this boy to himself, after all.

Chapter 26 *As a jewel of gold in a swine's snout, so is a fair woman without discretion.*

In the morning, before anyone else was awake, Merry crept out of her room and went to the great hall. She draped the scarf that she had won for her bread over the frame of Shannon's needlework. The blues and greens of the scarf highlighted the dragon in the picture. Merry hoped that when Shannon found the scarf, she would understand how much Merry valued the beautiful picture as well as their friendship.

Not long afterward, Merry had to bid Shannon and Ruddy farewell. She hugged the older woman and kissed the babe in her arms. Then she curtsied to Ruddy before turning to mount the patient Stripe.

"I'll miss you, Merry." Shannon came closer. "You must come again, all of you."

"We will," said Valerian, nodding at Ruddy. "You haven't seen the last of us yet." Then he mounted his horse and led the way.

Merry turned in the saddle to wave one last time. Her eyes filled with tears. Valerian must have noticed for he moved his gray closer to Stripe.

"Are you going to be all right?" He met her eyes.

I never considered I would find friendship beyond my own village.

"I have come to see true friends as one of life's greatest blessings." He glanced back. "And parting from them is never easy."

They followed the busy road, passing through two other villages by midday. After stopping to rest the horses and eat a little, Merry was ready, though not eager, to continue. Pausing beside Stripe, she stared up at Valerian.

I do want to befriend your future wife. She took the reins in her hands.

"I know you do. But please don't expect too much from her. She is not at all like you."

In what way? Merry frowned.

"She has not your goodness and gentleness." Valerian smoothed back a stray hair that had escaped her cap.

Merry smiled at him, but she quickly mounted her horse before she lost her head and kissed him in front of Kieran.

* * *

They reached the castle late that afternoon. Merry could only stare at the stone walls and towers. Red banners fluttered in the breeze, and soldiers stood guard at regular intervals. They rode through the gate, and Merry studied how it was similar to the one at her village, only heavier and larger. Grooms took their horses to the stables, and an older man greeted them.

"Good afternoon. I am Lord Reed's steward. What may we do for you?"

Valerian stepped forward. He towered over the other man.

"I am Valerian d'Alden. I am here to see Lord Reed."

The steward's eyes widened and he bowed.

"Your Highness. We are honored to have you visit. Please, follow me."

He led them into the castle. They walked through a hall similar to Ruddy's on a much larger scale. There were many tables and benches, and Merry could imagine gatherings of hundreds of people. This room could hold an entire village festival!

They followed the steward down a well-lit passageway into a lavish sitting room. It was so cluttered with furniture and tapestries and candles burning in ornate holders that Merry didn't know where to look first. The steward bowed again.

"Please, Your Highness, be seated and make yourselves comfortable. I will alert Lord Reed and bring refreshment."

Merry ran her hand over the red velvet cushion of one of the chairs and gingerly sat upon it. Valerian sat nearest the door, his back rigid. Merry had never seen him so uncomfortable. Kieran paced in front of the fireplace.

The door opened, and Valerian stood. Merry did also. They shared one brief glance before turning their attention to the middle-aged man and his daughter.

Both had yellow hair and fair skin. Lord Reed was short but muscular, in glowing good health, but Merry studied his daughter. She appeared perfectly beautiful with a full figure which she displayed to best advantage in a low cut, fitted red gown. Her full lips were painted red, like ripe cherries. She had eyes only for Valerian.

"Greetings, my prince!" Her father's voice was resonant. "I welcome you to my humble castle." He bowed graciously as his daughter curtsied. "Of course you remember my daughter, Hanalah."

"Of course." Valerian took Hanalah's hand and kissed it. Her sigh was audible from across the room.

Valerian indicated Kieran, who stood closest to Lord Reed.

"This is my squire, Kieran MacLachlan." Kieran executed a bow as if it were a dance step.

"And this," Valerian continued, beckoning Merry forward, "is my cousin, Merry."

She curtsied, trying to be as graceful as Kieran. It was a little easier in the riding skirt than in a dress.

Lord Reed's bushy brows raised. He stared at Merry.

"Cousin? I was under the impression you only had the one. Prince Andemon's son, Rupert."

While Valerian explained, Merry watched Hanalah. She scanned Merry, head to toe, and her eyes narrowed. Sadly it would probably be impossible to ever befriend such a haughty young woman.

"Yes, we have recently discovered proof that King Sigmund founded the Brethren. Merry is his direct descendant."

"The Brethren?" Hanalah's voice was shrill and grating, to Merry's surprise. "Those pacifists have royal blood?"

Valerian turned his head to glance at Merry. When he rolled his eyes, Merry had to stifle a giggle.

"Not all, Lady Hanalah, just Merry's family."

Hanalah looked as if she'd swallowed a spider.

"So do you have one of those long braids?" Hanalah reached up and raked her fingers through her shorter locks.

Merry nodded and turned around to show her the braid.

"It's so long, it looks like a rope!"

"Hanalah, dear," said her father. "Why don't you take Merry to her guest room and settle her there. We men have business to discuss."

"Very well." She sighed dramatically.

"My lady," said Valerian. "I must tell you that Merry is unable to speak."

"She's dumb?" Hanalah glared at Merry.

Valerian frowned, obviously losing patience with Lord Reed's daughter.

"She is mute and cannot make a sound." When he met her gaze, Merry saw his frustration.

Please don't worry about me. I will be fine with her, and I'll keep her away as long as I can. She hoped he took some comfort from that thought.

He nodded slightly, smiling with his eyes.

Merry followed Hanalah down a hallway, up a spiral staircase and along another hallway before they reached a sitting room that was a smaller version of the one downstairs. Unlike Ruddy's simply furnished manor house, Lord Reed and Hanalah had surrounded themselves with every trapping of luxury—enormous tapestries, carpets, ornately carved furniture, gold utensils and ornaments, and hundreds of candles burning in wall sconces and on tables, even when no eyes were present to need the light.

Hanalah sat on a plush chair with polished arms that ended in bird claws and indicated that Merry should sit in the matching chair beside it.

"So, we are supposed to become acquainted," she said in her shrill voice. "I don't understand how we can accomplish that when you cannot speak. I suppose you can answer 'yes' or 'no' if I ask you questions."

Merry nodded. Was the girl really trying to get acquainted? If so, perhaps she had misjudged her.

"So, you are Valerian's cousin." Hanalah pursed her lips. "I don't understand how he failed to mention this before." She drummed her fingers on the arm of the chair. "And you are one of the Brethren?" Merry nodded again. "Is it true you never cut your hair? Doesn't it get in your way all the time?"

Merry nodded and then shook her head. So far, this new relationship was not progressing as well as she'd like. Merry only hoped Valerian was faring better with Hanalah's father.

After Merry left with Hanalah, Lord Reed gestured for Valerian and Kieran to be seated. Servants brought in trays piled with bread, cheeses, and a few small pieces of fruit, as well as a decanter of wine and three goblets. A servant poured wine, bowed, and left the room. Kieran helped himself from the food, but Valerian sat watching Lord Reed. Fortunately, there was enough light in the room so he could *See* the man's thoughts.

"My prince, have you had a pleasant journey thus far?"

"All is well, thank you." *Except that someone wants me dead. I hope it is not you.*

He could not *See* any evil intentions in Lord Reed, however. The man was surprisingly free of guile. He enjoyed the comforts of life and hoped to have some influence once his daughter married the crown prince, but that was the limit of his ambition.

Reed worried a large ring on his forefinger.

"I dislike being too blunt, Your Highness, but I do believe in honesty."

"As do I." Even though Valerian knew what was coming, still he cringed.

"Have you and your father had a chance to discuss my proposal?"

"Not yet, Lord Reed." Valerian smiled to put the man at ease. "We have, unfortunately, been distracted by the Horde."

"Ah, yes. Please forgive me if I have been too forward. Those creatures have not been a problem in the south and so I forget how they have harassed and destroyed in the north. Your own brother, I know, was a casualty and I deeply regret his loss."

"No one mourns Waryn more than I." Valerian tightened his jaw.

"Yes, well, I didn't mean to bring up such a painful subject." Reed appeared truly contrite.

"The past cannot be changed, Lord Reed. We must live in the present and hope for tomorrow."

"Well said, Your Highness. As I once convinced your dearly departed brother, I would like to point out the obvious benefits to a joining of our two houses. You know there has ever been unrest between north and south, and joining my heir with d'Alden's heir could bring an end to that unrest."

Unlikely. He nodded. "Go on."

"I don't know whether or not your father has begun to urge you to marry and produce an heir, but that day will come, I assure you." Lord Reed smiled. "Since you and Hanalah have been friends since childhood, perhaps your union would also be a comfort to you, rather than marriage to a total stranger."

While the man extolled his daughter's supposed virtue and health and ability to bear many sturdy children, Valerian had to detach himself and listen just enough to nod and murmur in the appropriate pauses. He had never heard a man describe his daughter as a "royal brood mare" before.

When Reed paused to drink his wine, Valerian glanced at Kieran and envied his squire's ability to fall asleep anywhere, any time.

"During your stay with us here—" Reed began, but Valerian had had enough.

"Pardon me, Lord Reed, but we must leave in the morning. I left my men at the Southern Garrison and need to return to them. Part of the reason I came here was to report to you what we have seen."

Reed had a confused look on his face, and Valerian *Saw* the man's thoughts turn from anticipation to disappointment.

"Of course, Your Highness. You are busy securing our border. I will not presume upon you. Please tell me what you know."

Valerian leaned forward, fully engaged now.

"At the four other garrisons there has been no sign of the Horde. Only at the Southern Garrison have the Mohorovians made daily attacks on the walls, apparently to no purpose. At first I thought it was only the Horde making a feeble attempt at retribution before they become extinct, but something else has happened that makes me wonder if those pointless attacks are actually a diversionary tactic to deflect us from their more sinister plan."

He could tell Reed was having difficulty following him, so Valerian paused to allow the older man a moment to think on his words.

"Are you saying, then, the Horde are no longer in the north but have moved their attention here?" His eyes widened.

"I believe so, Lord Reed. Six days ago as Kieran and I were leaving the Southern Garrison, we saw fires and went to investigate. It appears the Horde massacred the entire Brethren village. Merry was the only survivor and had set the fires as funeral pyres."

Reed wrung his hands, clearly frightened now.

"What shall we do, Your Highness?"

"I recommend you put every village on the alert and have your army ready to mobilize quickly if necessary. If the Horde attacked one village, what will prevent them from attacking others? As I'm sure you know, the Brethren village was guarded by a wooden palisade. Not all the villages in your jurisdiction are so well protected."

"If only Caelis were still here, he could help us." Lord Reed stood and Valerian stood also.

"I beg your pardon?" Beside him, Kieran came awake.

"My nephew," said Lord Reed. "Sir Caelis. I believe you know him?"

"Yes, we are acquainted." This news was troubling. "What was Caelis doing here?"

"Oh, he comes every year for winter feast, since he has no other family."

"Did he come alone?"

"No, he had some men with him. Caelis said he was on patrol, trying out a new bow that he'd helped design." Reed puffed out his chest and Valerian *Saw* the pride he felt for his nephew.

"When did he leave?"

"Early this morning. Said he needed to return to the Keep. I suppose he will be traveling north while you go south to the garrison."

Valerian nodded. Perhaps it was nothing. Perhaps it was just coincidence. But he couldn't help but wonder that Caelis had been less than one day's ride from Valerian when an attempt on his life was made.

* * *

They endured the interminable evening meal as best they could. Kieran ate heartily, but Merry found little she could eat among the rich dishes. Valerian picked at his food, too distracted by the Horde as well as human murderers. Hanalah's voice grated on him, and Lord Reed's asinine remarks grew tiresome. Finally, the last course was eaten, and Valerian could graciously retire. He stood, and Lord Reed pushed himself to his feet, alarmed.

"Is anything the matter, Your Highness?"

"No, Lord Reed. You serve an excellent table, but my companions and I must get some sleep in your comfortable beds. It will be many weeks before we sleep in a real bed again."

"What will you be sleeping on, Your Highness?" Hanalah smirked.

"Most of the time, on the ground, but at the garrisons we do have cots, at least." He forced a smile.

"On the ground?" Her eyes widened and she fluttered her hand over her heart. "Like a common soldier?"

"Lady Hanalah," Valerian said more coldly than he intended, "I will not sleep more comfortably than my soldiers when we are in the field."

"An interesting concept, Your Highness." Lord Reed looked genuinely puzzled.

"Yes, and now we must bid you a good night. Come, Kieran, let us escort Merry to her room." Valerian ignored the look on Hanalah's face.

When they reached the hallway, he turned to Merry and spoke quietly.

"Are you going to be all right sleeping alone?"

Lady Hanalah does not like me, but there is nothing to fear.

"In case you need us, I want to show you where our room is so you can find us." He led Merry up the stairs and soon realized his door was down the same hall from hers. "I feel more at ease knowing that." He squeezed her hand. "Try to get some sleep, and we'll leave early."

When she closed the door, Valerian wished there were some way he could properly have her sleep closer to him. Even though he'd *Seen* no sinister intent in Reed's thoughts, he still did not want Merry out of his sight. Not when there might be others lurking with murder on their minds.

* * *

That night Valerian had troubling dreams of dragons and the Horde and human assassins. But then Merry came to him, her beautiful hair flowing unbound. She kissed him hungrily, and he responded.

Then he woke up and someone *was* kissing him. He pulled away and saw that Hanalah had climbed into the canopied bed wearing only a flimsy nightgown.

"Hanalah, what are you doing?"

"Shh, we don't want to wake your squire." She leaned closer to him.

Valerian kicked back the covers and scrambled to get away from her.

"You should not be in here. I must ask you to leave at once."

She grabbed the sleeve of his nightshirt as he slid down from the high bed.

"But I want you to love me. I want you to know what we can have all the time when you marry me. Don't you find me desirable?" She scooted closer and her gown slipped, revealing her bare shoulder.

Valerian jerked his sleeve out of her hand. The fabric ripped.

"Hanalah," he said coldly. "You must leave now. This is not the behavior of a lady, and certainly not that of a future princess."

She pouted, crossing her arms across her breasts.

"How can you send me away?"

"Very easily. Kieran!"

The squire leaped up from his cot against the far wall.

"Yes, Sire?" He walked toward the bed, rubbing his eyes.

"I need your help to remove an unwanted visitor."

When Kieran saw who was in Valerian's bed, his eyes widened. Hanalah's narrowed to slits.

"That will not be necessary. I'm going." She slid out of the bed and stormed to the door, slamming it behind her.

"How did she get in, Sire?"

Valerian tightened his hands into fists to still their shaking.

"She must have had a key. I woke up and she was already in the bed."

"That must have been quite a shock. Do ye think she might take out her ire on Merry?"

"I don't think so. She didn't mention her. But I'm not going to be able to sleep after this. You should sleep here, in the bed, and I'll watch to make sure nothing is happening down the hall."

Kieran climbed into the bed and fell back on the pillows.

"Ah, I thank ye, Sire." He closed his eyes and fell asleep almost instantly.

Valerian pulled on his breeches and boots and strapped on his sword. He quietly opened the door and stepped into the hall. After listening for several minutes, he went to Merry's room and put his ear to the door. But no sound came from there.

Still restless, he considered bringing a chair into the hall to wait out the night. But lurking in the halls in the middle of the night would make him an easier target if there were someone in the castle looking for an opportunity to kill him. So he went back to his room and locked the door. After tonight, he would make sure Merry never again had to be left alone.

Caelis glanced up from the campfire when Thrane returned. The man dismounted and strode toward Caelis. He bowed and Caelis indicated he should walk with him apart from the others.

"You're back early, Thrane."

"Yes, Sir Caelis, but I have news."

"Is our mark destroyed?"

"No, sir. The prince, his squire, and a girl arrived at Lord Reed's this afternoon."

"How could he have missed such an opportunity?" Caelis scowled.

"I saw no sign of Swift's man." Thrane shrugged. "Could he have changed his mind?"

"Not likely." He tried to think of an alternate plan.

"Sir Caelis, there is more."

"Well? Speak up, man."

"I discovered at Lord Reed's that this girl is one of the Brethren who somehow survived the 'Horde massacre' and has been discovered to be a royal cousin."

"What? Who told you that?"

"One of Lady Hanalah's maids overheard her mistress complaining about the Brethren girl."

Caelis laughed, picturing his vain cousin's probable reaction.

"She would complain. Did you see the Brethren girl? Is she comely?"

"I didn't see her close up, but what I saw could give Lady Hanalah something to complain about."

"When you say she's a girl, how young do you mean?"

"Younger than Lord Reed's daughter, but not a child."

"Marriageable age, then?" Even if she wasn't, she would be eventually.

"Certainly that," said Thrane with a lecherous grin.

A new plan came to Caelis' mind.

"I'll return. Get something to eat. I may send you out again shortly."

Caelis strode to his tent and pushed back the flap. Drew was not present, but the Brethren boy sat rocking himself in the corner. Caelis sat beside him.

"Hello, Rafael. Is anything wrong?"

"I miss my Sissy."

"I'm sure you do. Did she live in the house with you?"

The boy nodded.

"Did you see her killed that morning?"

Rafael shook his head and seemed reluctant to answer. At last, he swallowed.

"When I woke up, she wasn't there. I was going to look for her when I heard the screaming. Was she screaming?"

"I don't think so." Caelis deliberately softened his voice. "I did not see anyone who could have been your sister outside that morning."

"Then what happened to her?"

"I'm not sure. Would you like for me to find out?"

"She might be alive?" The boy's eyes widened.

"It's possible." Caelis shrugged. "But don't hope too much."

"Okay, Sir Caelis." The boy sighed.

But Caelis could see Rafael clinging to that hope. In this vulnerable frame of mind Caelis could firmly attach the child to himself, and if the Brethren girl with royal blood was his sister, Caelis would manipulate her into marrying him in order to have access to her brother. His marrying a royal could only make his conquest easier.

"Rafael?" Caelis smiled at the boy.

"Yes, sir?"

"I'm sorry we began our friendship so awkwardly. You're a fine young man, and you'll make a good knight someday."

"Do you really think so?"

"Oh, yes. And to prove it to you, I'm going to ask Drew to make a special tunic for you. Would you like to wear my lion?" Caelis opened his pack and pulled out his red surcoat with the lion rampant of his house embroidered on the front.

"Is that what a lion looks like?" Rafael touched the emblem. "It looks strong."

"They are noble beasts. Would you like to be strong and fierce as a lion?"

"Yes, sir." His voice was full of awe.

"Good. Consider it done."

"And sir, what about my Sissy?"

"Consider that done, too. I will not rest until I find her." He patted the boy's head and left the tent.

When he returned to Thrane, the man was just finishing a piece of roast venison. He stood and wiped his mouth.

"Yes, sir?"

"I have another job for you, but you'll need help."

"What is it?" Thrane's eyes brightened.

"Take Benton and find the prince. Bring him and the Brethren girl to me, unharmed. The squire too, if you can. But if he's too much trouble, kill him. We'll continue north on the road, but bring your prisoners by another route so no one sees you."

Thrane's smile was malicious.

"With pleasure, Sir Caelis."

Chapter 27 *Deceit is in the heart of them that imagine evil.*

As soon as they were out of sight of Lord Reed's castle, the road straightened, and Kieran urged his horse to a canter. Merry's horse followed without urging, and she reveled at the wind in her face, and the movement of Stripe's muscles beneath her. The hooves of Valerian's horse drummed the dirt behind her. Before the next bend in the road, Kieran pulled up Gilly, so Merry did likewise. Valerian walked his horse close to Stripe.

"That, my little horsewoman, is a canter."

I like cantering. When do we gallop?

He laughed and told Kieran what she said. The squire grinned at her.

"When we get closer to the garrison, lass, ye will have a chance to gallop, never fear."

She smiled at both of them. Riding Stripe was much more satisfying than sitting behind Kieran, just holding on.

For the next several miles, since there were other people using the road between village and the castle, they walked the horses. Merry didn't mind because there were so many interesting trees lining the road. Sometimes their branches intertwined overhead, creating a canopy that shaded them from the harsh rays of the morning sun. Thickets grew beneath the trees, and more than once Merry spotted winterberries that were not quite ripe.

They stopped near midday when they spied a stream not far from the road. They let the horses graze while they washed their faces in the stream and refilled water flasks. Then they sat together to eat a light meal from the provisions Shannon had packed for them.

"Do ye think we'll reach the garrison before nightfall, Sire?"

"I'm not sure how far we have to go," said Valerian. "But if not tonight, then by midmorning tomorrow, I would guess."

Kieran glanced at Merry, looking sheepish.

"I'll be ready to go shortly, my lord. I just need to go--behind the trees."

Merry smiled at Kieran's embarrassment. After he left them, she readied her carry sack and prepared to leave. When the squire didn't come back, she caught Valerian's attention.

Do you think he's all right?

"I think he would call for help if he needed it." He paused, listening. "But he shouldn't have needed this much time."

Please go and check on him.

"I will." Valerian followed the path Kieran had taken.

Merry sat on a fallen tree, expecting to see the two of them at any moment. But time passed and nothing happened. She began to worry. Why hadn't she heard anything?

With growing anxiety Merry stood and slung her carry sack over her shoulder. She took a few steps toward the place where she'd last seen Valerian and Kieran.

A tall stranger stepped out of the trees. He wore leathers and a large knife on his belt. When he leered at Merry, his face creased from an old scar.

"Hello, little Brethren wench. Are you looking for something?"

She whirled and started to run, but a second man came into the clearing. He was stockier, but not as sinister looking.

"Bring her," said the scarred one.

Merry tried to run, but the riding boots slowed her down. The heavier man grabbed her and carried her under one arm as if she were a sack of flour. She struggled in his grasp, but his arm was as hard as a tree branch.

After walking a short distance into the trees, the heavy-set man dropped her on the ground. Merry scrambled to her feet and scanned her surroundings. They were in a small clearing, but thickly clustered trees hid them from a view of the road. When she turned, Merry gasped. Valerian had been tied between two trees by both arms and legs. His mouth was gagged. His eyes pleaded with her, and she knew he wanted her to run. There was no sign of Kieran.

"Don't think of running, girl," said the scarred man. "If you don't do exactly as I say, I'll slit the prince's throat."

She pushed down the fear squeezing her chest in order to think clearly.

"Shouldn't we tie her up?" asked the stocky one, who seemed to be the scarred one's lackey.

"No." He raked Merry with his eyes. "She will need her hands free for what I have planned. Benton, I am hungry. I saw squirrels in the trees." He pointed to Merry. "Gather wood for a fire, and remember what I said." He pulled a wicked-looking knife from a sheath in his boot.

Merry glanced at Valerian again.

I can't leave you. She hoped he could *See* her from this distance. Then her eyes blurred with tears the entire time she collected firewood and made a sizeable pile on a patch of dirt.

"Benton will start the fire now."

Merry turned, startled by the ugly man's voice. He held the limp body of a squirrel impaled on an arrow. With his other hand, he gripped Merry's wrist and dragged her to a flat rock away from the firewood. He pulled out the arrow and laid the squirrel on the rock, unsheathed his knife, and chopped off its head. Merry flinched.

"Clean it," he said.

She froze, wondering how he meant for her to clean it. When she didn't move, he slit the squirrel's belly. The entrails bulged, out and Merry recoiled. The man grabbed her wrist again and jerked her closer.

"You disobey me, wench, and you'll wish you were never born. Haven't you ever cleaned a squirrel before?"

She shook her head.

"First, remove the entrails, then skin it so the meat will be ready to cook." He handed her his knife, but she shook her head. She opened her carry sack and took out her own small blade.

"Very well, but hurry it up." He sheathed his knife and stepped back.

Swallowing bile, Merry knelt beside the rock. She used her knife to scrape out the entrails, gagging at the odor. But she had a difficult time removing the skin. Tears kept blurring her vision and made it impossible to see what she was doing. At least the poor animal could no longer feel pain.

"You're going to ruin a good piece of meat." The man snatched the knife out of Merry's hand. "Pull up the skin while you work the blade under."

Merry gagged again when he pulled off the last of the pelt with the bushy tail attached. He thrust the slippery carcass into her hands and snapped his fingers to catch Benton's attention.

"When the fire's ready, the wench will cook this for us." He turned back to Merry. "We don't have time to build a spit, so impale it with a stick and hold it over the fire." He took a long branch and scraped the end to a point. Then he handed it to Merry. She looked at the point and swallowed.

"What is the matter with you?" Snarling, he grabbed her hand with the stick and forced the point into the squirrel carcass. Merry heard a tearing sound as the flesh was pierced, and bile rose in her throat. After the man tied the meat to the stick with a piece of twine, Merry positioned it over the flames, trying not to burn herself.

"Thrane," called Benton. "Where's the wine? I'm thirsty."

While Thrane strode over to Benton, Merry calmed her thoughts so she could remember which herbs she had in her carry sack. There was balmflower, red vein, bloodroot, and tongues-of-fire, none of which would be of any help in this situation. But she also had a small packet of dragon's bane. Though Papa had forbidden her to use it because it was so deadly, he said that a weak tea brewed with the dried leaves made a powerful sedative. If she could find a way to give some to these men, perhaps she and Valerian and Kieran, wherever he was, could get away.

She glanced up. Benton removed the stopper from a flask and took a drink. Then he set it down nearby and strode toward the trees.

"Where do you think you're going?" asked the scarred one, Thrane.

"What do you think? I've got to—" Benton glanced at Merry. "I'm going behind the trees." He turned back and went out of sight.

Thrane laughed, but it was not a happy sound.

"You always did have a chivalrous streak." Abruptly his face darkened. "Not so myself." He walked toward Valerian. "A gentle man cannot survive the cruelty of this world."

Quickly, while Thrane's back was to her, and Benton was out of sight, Merry set down the stick with the squirrel meat and fumbled in her carry sack for the packet of dragon's bane. Her hands trembled so violently she could barely open it. Then she poured the contents into the flask, spilling some. She wiped off the residue lest the men notice. Once she replaced the stopper, she swirled it a few times to speed the release of the poison into the wine. Merry barely regained her place by the fire when Benton returned and headed straight for the flask.

"You're a pathetic, insignificant excuse for a prince," Thrane was saying. "A leader must be ruthless. If you have a weakness for the suffering of others, you leave yourself open to the enemy, who will always have a weapon against you."

Even from this far away, Merry could see the anger smoldering in Valerian's eyes.

"Look at you, completely in my power. Yet your family claims divine right to rule over me. How can that be? I say only the strongest shall rule, and I am not alone in believing that."

Benton unstopped the flask and took a long drink, wiping his mouth with the back of his hand.

"You talk too much."

Thrane turned on the other man.

"It doesn't matter what he hears now. He's already dead. We just don't get the pleasure of killing him."

Merry trembled. What would she do if Thrane didn't drink any wine? She had no other way to overpower him, even if she had the nerve to use her knife against him. Benton, she was thankful to note, sat across from her by the fire. He yawned before he spoke to her.

"Don't you have that meat ready yet? I'm hungry."

Merry handed him the stick, and he prodded the squirrel meat. He unsheathed his knife and sliced off a portion, folding it over the blade and stuffing it into his mouth. He yawned again while chewing, and Merry was relieved his eyes appeared unfocused.

Thrane approached Merry. The flask lay on the ground between them. She prayed he would drink from it.

"I want some meat," he said, "and I want you to serve it to me." Beside him, Benton took another sip from the flask. "Give me that before you drink it all." Thrane snatched the flask from him and took a long drink. Then he stopped it and tossed it down to Benton without glancing at him. Merry was grateful because Benton was fast becoming lethargic and she didn't want Thrane to notice and become suspicious.

"I think, my helpless prince, that this wench means something to you, doesn't she?" He seized Merry's wrist and pulled her to him. Then he grabbed both of her arms, digging his fingers into her flesh. She flinched but did not try to get away. If she could stall him for just a little while, the dragon's bane would quickly begin its work, as it had on the other man.

"Now, at the last, you will see how a ruthless man takes what he wants." Thrane yawned. Then he crushed Merry against him and lowered his face to hers. This time she did struggle to pull away. He only laughed and gripped her more tightly. He managed to clamp his mouth onto hers. Merry's stomach heaved.

Hoping to unbalance him, she feigned a swoon, going limp in his arms. Thrane shifted his grip as he bent over her. Suddenly he let go to clutch his head with both hands. Merry fell to the ground and rolled away from him.

"My head," he moaned. "What spell have you cast over me, Brethren witch?" Slowly, Thrane toppled over and lay still beside the unconscious Benton.

Merry rushed to Valerian's side, fumbling along the way for the knife in her carry sack. First she pulled the gag from his mouth. He spat on the ground.

"Well done, Merry."

Her hands shook so badly she feared she might cut him as she sawed through the ropes binding his hands. His wrists were raw and bleeding, but she didn't have the opportunity to Heal him. Valerian took the knife from her and released his legs.

"We have to help Kieran. One of those animals smashed his head with a rock. I only hope we're not too late." He grabbed Merry's hand.

They found Kieran lying beneath a tree. Blood pooled under his head. His skin was so ashen Merry feared they *were* too late. She fell to her knees beside him and hunted for a pulse. It was weak and very slow. She glanced up at Valerian.

He's still alive, but just barely. Valerian knelt across from her, nodding for her to proceed. Then Merry took a deep breath and begged the Most High to save their dear friend.

She placed her hands on Kieran's head where the blood was slick in his curly hair. Closing her eyes, she *saw* how the rock had crushed his skull, pushing it inward to press against his brain. She opened herself to the Healing power to repair the damaged bone and tissue. Even though Merry could feel herself growing weaker, she didn't dare let up until she was sure his brain was whole again.

"Merry!" Valerian's hands gripped her shoulders. "You must come back now!"

Reluctantly she let go of Kieran and slumped against Valerian. Kieran's color was better, and he appeared to be breathing normally, though he was still not conscious.

Valerian sat cross-legged and cradled her. She shivered uncontrollably, and he warmed her with his body heat.

"I would take you back to the fire," he said quietly, "but I'm afraid to leave Kieran alone."

Merry nodded and closed her eyes. She focused on breathing deeply to bring her heart rate back to normal. At last her chills subsided, and she felt a little stronger and warmer. She met Valerian's worried gaze.

Please don't worry, love. I'll be all right.

"One of these days you may go too far in your Healing, and then what would I do?"

Merry was saved from having to answer when they heard Kieran stirring. Valerian lifted her out of his lap so he could stand and help her up. Kieran opened his eyes and pushed himself to a sitting position. He put a hand to his head and groaned.

"What happened?" His eyes tried to focus.

"You were knocked unconscious."

"By whom?" Kieran felt the place where his hair was matted with dried blood.

"Two ruffians." Valerian frowned. "They're nearby, and I must tie them up and make sure they can no longer harm us. Stay here."

As soon as he left, Merry's legs wobbled, and she fell against Kieran. Slowly she sank to her knees.

"Easy, lass. You must have Healed me. Did you?"

She nodded, checking the pulse in his neck. It was strong and sure, and she sighed in relief. Kieran took her hand from his neck and kissed it.

"Thank ye, Merry." His voice was husky. "I am humbled that you risked your life for mine."

She squeezed his hand. There was no other way to tell him how precious he was to her.

Valerian returned and squatted beside Merry.

"What did you put in that flask?"

She met his troubled gaze.

Dragon's bane. Papa said it worked as a sedative when made into a tea, so I thought putting it in the flask would do the same.

"Dragon's bane?" Valerian's eyes widened, and he turned to Kieran. "Isn't that what the Horde use to poison their arrows?"

The squire nodded, and they both stared at Merry. She began to tremble.

What happened?

"They're both dead," Valerian said. "Dragon's bane is a deadly poison, and mixed with fermented wine would probably make it act even faster."

Merry covered her mouth, horrified. Spots of light flashed around the edges of her vision.

I have broken my Oath of Peace. I have taken a life. Two lives! Oh, God of Peace, have mercy.

She collapsed and knew no more.

"What happened?" Kieran made a move toward Merry, but then grabbed his head again.

"Sit there for a while until you feel like you can stand. I think Merry simply passed out from the shock of her ordeal."

"Ordeal?" Kieran frowned.

Valerian explained how they'd been overcome by the two men, and how Merry had saved all their lives.

"And now she thinks she's broken her oath of peace." Kieran sighed. "Poor lass."

Valerian studied the slant of the sun's rays through the trees.

"We have another problem, I'm afraid. You and Merry are in no shape to ride. I've got to find a secure place for a campsite, round up the horses, and dispose of the bodies before any scavenger dragons come to investigate."

Kieran felt along his belt and gasped.

"My sword and scabbard are gone!"

"Mine, too," Valerian said. "Our assailants took them, but they must be in the clearing somewhere. I need to move the two of you up there before I look for the horses. Do you feel like you can stand now?"

Kieran took a deep breath and gingerly touched his head.

"I've got to, don't I?" he said. Valerian helped him up, and he stood swaying a little on his feet.

"Don't run off. I've got to get Merry now." Valerian gently scooped her into his arms.

"Ach, Val, I was just going to suggest we should run all the way to the garrison." Kieran tried to smile.

"For now, just hold onto my arm." They made their way to the clearing where the two men lay sprawled as they'd died. The fire had burned down. Valerian settled Kieran at a nearby tree so he could lean against the trunk. Then he laid Merry beside him with her head pillowed on his squire's leg.

"Is that the flask with the dragon's bane?" Kieran indicated the container beside the dead men. "I dinna want to accidentally drink of it."

"Yes." Valerian poured the rest of the contents into a thicket and flung the empty flask into the brush. "I'll take care of the bodies when I return. Right now, I want to build up this fire for you and then find our horses." He spied their two swords in the scabbards on top of a pile of sleeping furs and secured his to his belt. Then he placed Kieran's within his reach and gave him a flask of water.

He left Kieran and Merry with a roaring bonfire while he mounted the larger of the ruffian's horses. Fortunately, he didn't have to ride far to find their three horses grazing downstream. By the time he brought them back, however, the sun was low on the horizon.

Valerian rode into their campsite and saw Merry sitting beside Kieran, rocking herself. Kieran lifted his hands, bewildered.

"I dinna know what to do, Val. She's inconsolable."

"I know something that might help." He slid down from the horse and emptied its saddlebags. Of course, there was nothing to identify who Thrane and Benton had been working for. Unfortunately, Valerian had only briefly *Seen* Thrane's thoughts, and the man had been so full of self-importance he hadn't even thought of his master. Likewise, Valerian searched through the packs on the other horse. Then he struggled to lift Thrane's body onto one of the horses, tying it to the saddle.

"Kieran, do you feel up to helping me with this other one? He's too big for me to lift alone."

Kieran slowly stood up and nodded.

"Me head feels like it's going to stay attached now, thanks to Merry." Together they lifted Benton's body onto the other horse and secured him to the saddle. Valerian sent the horses away, hoping they would return to their master. Perhaps, it would send a strong message.

When he turned back, Merry still rocked herself, and he knelt beside her.

"It's too dark for me to hear your words, so you'll have to listen to mine." She grew still. Valerian had never seen her look so defeated. He took her hands.

"Merry, you know that obedience to the law is important to me." She nodded. "I know your Oath must be vitally important to you since it defines who you are as one of the Brethren." She flinched but gave him her attention.

"In the law of Levathia, there is a difference made between deliberate murder and accidentally causing someone's death. Surely since our common ancestor founded the Brethren there has been an incident where someone accidentally caused the death of a person or an animal?" Her brows furrowed while she thought. At last, Merry shrugged, but even in the dim light from the fire he could see the hope in her eyes.

"In the Holy Writ, the Most High makes a distinction between murder and accidental death. You acted on the knowledge you had and only intended to put the men to sleep. Isn't that right?" She nodded, but tears welled up in her eyes. "Then you did not deliberately take their lives. In fact, you provided for them a more merciful death than they would have received under the law." Her eyes widened. "It's true. They were guilty of high treason and would have been sentenced to an agonizing death."

"Yes, Merry," Kieran said grimly. "I've seen it before. Hanged, drawn, and quartered. A terrible way to die."

Valerian let her ponder his words. Her face changed from despair to calm acceptance.

"Are you better now?" She nodded but did not smile. He turned to Kieran.

"How is your sense of direction?"

"I am never lost." The squire grinned. "O' course with me head a wee bit swimmy, I might not be as reliable as usual."

Valerian glanced around the clearing. He wished they were at a higher elevation in a more defensible place.

"I want to get to the Southern Garrison as quickly as possible without traveling on the road. Do you think you could find it?"

Kieran faced the last glow of the setting sun in the west.

"The garrison is southeast from here, but I'm not sure I could find it in the dark."

"I know I couldn't, but I don't feel safe spending the night here so close to the road. Can you and Merry ride a little farther? When I found the horses, I discovered a bluff not far downriver that would make a safer campsite for the night."

"I'm willing if you are, Merry," said Kieran. When she nodded, Valerian helped her and Kieran mount their horses.

They rode slowly through the forest alongside the river. Their eyes gradually adjusted to the dim light of stars and a crescent moon, and soon the bluff loomed ahead. Valerian urged his horse up the steep incline until he reached the top. There was a cluster of trees but around the perimeter he could see the approach for a long way. He swung down from the gray. Merry and Kieran got down more slowly, and Valerian helped Merry unsaddle her horse before his own. Kieran opened the pack on his saddle and pulled out sleeping furs.

"Are we going to make a fire?"

"No." Valerian opened his pack for the rest of the furs. "I don't want to attract attention to our location. If we use all our furs and sleep close together, we'll be warm enough." He found a relatively flat area between the trees and laid two furs side by side. "Here, Merry, we'll put you in the middle so Kieran and I can make a wall around you."

She lay down, and Valerian covered her with another fur. Then he and Kieran lay on either side of her, using the remaining furs for cover.

Kieran fell asleep right away. But Valerian could tell by Merry's breathing that she was still awake, and he turned toward her. Under the trees no light penetrated. He wondered what Merry was thinking. He didn't think he had fully convinced her that she had not broken her Oath. And their ordeal at the hands of Thrane and Benton must have upset her at least as much as it had troubled him.

"Merry," he whispered. "Are you all right?"

In answer, she moved closer, and he encircled her with his arm. He was afraid to hold her too close, but he wanted her to feel safe so she might sleep. Not long afterward her head relaxed against his chest, and he smiled. At least she and Kieran would get some rest.

Valerian was reluctant to fall asleep. He couldn't stop thinking about the one-eared man and these other two. Were there more out there wanting him dead? And who was behind it? At every rustle in the undergrowth, every insect and animal sound, he imagined someone bursting from the trees, ready to kill them. He never wanted to be surprised like that again.

The guttural roar of a river dragon sounded in the distance, but after that the night grew quiet and peaceful. Unfortunately, the silence made his body relax, since he'd not slept well the night before, either.

Even as his eyelids drooped, he tried to use his Sight to look outward from himself in order to stay awake. The next thing he knew he had the sensation of floating above his sleeping form. He could see himself lying on the ground with Merry under his arm and Kieran lying on his side next to her. Then he scanned the bluff, noting the horses standing together, dozing, and beyond them the movement of a hunting owl and a hunted rodent.

With a start, he came to himself and woke up. Had he been dreaming? Or had his soul briefly left his body?

Merry stirred and turned away from him on her side. Valerian stood, made sure she and Kieran were covered with the furs, and went to check their surroundings. Once he stepped out from the trees he could see his breath misting the air by the moon's feeble light. The stars densely packed the cold night sky and winked down at the peaceful setting. If it were this cold already in the south, what would they encounter on their journey north?

❖

While he and his men drew nearer to Blackwater Garrison, Caelis looked forward to sleeping in a bed that night, even if it was just a cot. Also, he recalled that the garrison had managed to obtain a man who was a fine cook. Caelis' mouth watered in anticipation of something better than camp food.

The man riding lead today held up his hand and shouted, "Whoa!" All in their party halted. Caelis rode forward to confer with the man.

"What is it?"

He didn't answer, merely pointed ahead.

From their vantage point, the garrison and the Plains of Mohorovia stretched beyond to the east. Caelis watched, disbelieving, while the plains crawled with an innumerable company of the Horde. They swarmed toward the garrison as if they were so many warrior ants attacking a helpless worm.

The Mohorovians made living siege ladders, allowing the others to crawl upon them to the parapets. Shortly the gates opened, and the flood of creatures poured into the garrison. There were so many of them! It would have been easier to count the grains of sand on the seashore than to count these monsters. Where had they come from?

The men in the garrison could never have survived an attack like this. Fear gripped Caelis by the throat, making his heart pound so hard he suddenly felt invincible. He wheeled his horse back toward the rest of the men.

"We must ride to the Keep as fast as we can and warn the king the Horde have returned!"

"What about the men in the garrison, Sir Caelis?" The scout came alongside him.

"The garrison is lost, and we will be too if we don't get past the Horde." Drew and Rafael watched him, clearly frightened, as were the rest of the men. Caelis smiled grimly. "Come, follow me."

Chapter 28 *Love is strong as death.*

When Merry awoke, the darkness was fading. Kieran snored beside her, but Valerian's place was empty. Startled, she stood and wondered where he had gone. She decided to go look for him when he stepped from the trees. He held out a hand to her.

"Come into the light so I can *See* you."

Merry followed him to the edge of the bluff. The sun's light glowed pink below the horizon, pushing back the night. She gazed into Valerian's eyes.

Did you sleep at all last night?

"Very little. I felt I should stay awake to make sure no one took us by surprise again."

That wasn't your fault. I'm just thankful they did not succeed in their evil plans. Merry swallowed. *I'm trying to remember what you said. I think even Gabriel would not have thought me guilty of breaking my Oath.* She lowered her head and tears dripped from her eyelids.

"I'm sure you are right about that." Valerian gently lifted her chin as the sun peered over the horizon. "Gabriel would have been as pleased with your courage and quick thinking, as I am."

Why would anyone want to kill you? She hugged Valerian fiercely and he returned the embrace. He was so good and gentle. Was that the reason evil men wanted him dead? Because evil could not abide that which was good? *Oh, God Most High*, she prayed. *Please watch over this prince who wants to do what is right. The land needs him. And so do I.*

Kieran cleared his throat, and Merry let go of Valerian when the squire approached.

"Pardon me for interrupting, Sire, but the horses have wandered off. My guess is they went tae the river."

"Then we'd best go after them." Valerian grabbed Merry's hand.

*   *   *

Within the hour they were riding southeast, following the river. It grew wider the farther they traveled. As the sun rose higher in the sky, the air grew a little warmer.

Since they were no longer on the road, they had to ride single file with Kieran in the lead and Merry following him. When they reached an open field, Valerian pulled up alongside Stripe and met Merry's eyes.

"Do you need to stop?"

This looks like a good place for a rest.

"We can water the horses and refill our water flasks. Kieran!"

The squire halted and brought Gilly around.

"Yes, Sire?"

"Do you think we're getting close to the garrison?" Valerian dismounted and helped Merry down.

"The last time I could see through a break in the trees, I caught a glimpse o' the border cliff. We must be close." Kieran slid down from Gilly's saddle. "We should probably cross the river before it gets any wider. I remember it came out as a waterfall down the cliff, so the closer we get tae that spot, the faster the water will move."

Merry led Stripe toward the river. Here, at least, the current moved sluggishly, but the contour of the land and many fallen trees had made almost a pool of this section of the river. While Stripe drank, Merry kicked off her boots. Even though the water was cold, she wanted to wash her feet. She knew Valerian and Kieran would think her silly, but they were used to wearing boots or shoes and Merry had always gone barefoot.

She found a shallow place downstream from the area where Stripe now grazed. Here was a small sandy bank between thick patches of reeds. An overhanging branch gave her a hand hold. Merry had just stepped into the water when she heard a roar and a scaly head burst from the water. She had time only to glimpse the open jaws and jagged teeth before the monster lunged at her.

❖

When Valerian heard the roar, he spun around. A river dragon was attacking Merry! He ran toward her, drawing his sword just as the monster clamped down on her leg. Before it could drag her into the water, Valerian swung the blade around and drove it into the dragon's eye. It bellowed, showing bloody teeth as it released Merry's leg. Valerian lifted the sword and chopped down with all his strength upon the creature's neck, partially severing its head. Green blood spattered Valerian before the remains sank beneath the water.

Kieran was there, pulling Merry away from the river. Blood gushed from her leg, and Valerian pulled off his belt, removing the scabbard. He tightened it around Merry's thigh with a grunt, slowing the blood flow but not stopping it.

Behind them, other river dragons exploded out of the water to fight over the carcass.

"Kieran," Valerian shouted. "We have to stop the bleeding!"

Valerian lifted Merry and carried her to the far side of the clearing, into the trees. He laid her on a bed of leaves while Kieran brought the horses. The squire took Merry's carry sack off Stripe's saddle and set it on the ground.

"I know the lass has needles and thread in here," Kieran muttered. He searched the sack. "She showed them to me. Ah." He pulled out a packet and opened it. "I'll sew the gash if you'll wash it out first." He threaded a needle while Valerian grabbed a water flask and flushed the deep gash in Merry's thigh just above the knee.

She was lucky her leg was so slender and the dragon's teeth were so widely spaced. Otherwise, it would have bitten off her leg. Still, she had lost a lot of blood. Too much for someone so small.

Kieran sewed the gash as quickly as he could. Blood still seeped between the stitches, and he pressed on it with a cloth. Merry didn't even flinch, she was so deeply unconscious.

Valerian had a difficult time finding a pulse in Merry's neck. Her face was pasty white. Just like Waryn's had been when he'd died in Valerian's arms.

"Kieran." His voice caught in a sob. "She's dying."

"I'll get help from the garrison." Kieran jumped up and grabbed Gilly's reins. He swung up in the saddle, wheeled the horse around, and galloped back across the clearing.

Valerian lay close to Merry, half on top of her, to give her warmth. He took her head between his hands and touched his forehead to hers.

"I can't Heal you," he whispered. "But I'm going to hold you here if I can. Merry! Don't leave me!"

He tried as he had the night before to reach out with his Sight and touch Merry's soul with his own. She was fading, he could *See* that, and he surrounded and supported her, filling her with his strength. He was willing to give his life for hers.

Most High God, hear me! You've kept her through so many trials. Please don't take her now. Please, let me save her. Please.

He poured his vital force into her and didn't let up until he *Saw* that she grew more substantial and he *knew* she wasn't going to leave him. Then he slipped into nothingness.

The next thing he knew strong hands were lifting him away from Merry.

"No! No!" He struggled against them.

"Your Highness! Prince Valerian! It's me, Kieran. We're taking you to the garrison. Sir Walter has sent help."

Valerian forced his eyes open. Kieran's face hovered above him. They were in a wagon.

Panicked, Valerian sat up. Merry lay beside him on a pallet of furs. Though still not conscious, she had more color in her face.

"She's alive." His voice was hoarse. "Praise the Most High!" Then Valerian fell back, utterly spent.

Chapter 29 *I am my beloved's, and my beloved is mine.*

Merry opened her eyes and wondered where she was. She lay in a small bed facing a window with glass panes. The setting sun cast a rosy glow in the room. Her right leg throbbed and she forced herself upright, hissing through her teeth. Kieran sat in a chair beside the bed. When he saw her confusion, he smiled.

"I'll bring Valerian here, Merry. He's sleeping in the next room." Then he went out the door.

Merry pushed back the cover. Beneath her torn riding skirt, a bandage encircled her right thigh. Only then did she remember the river dragon's teeth and its red eyes and its roar.

Valerian and Kieran entered the room. Valerian sat beside her on the bed. He appeared so worn she grasped his hand in concern.

Are you injured?

"No, but you were. Kieran used your needle and thread to sew you up."

"I hope you dinna mind, Merry."

She turned to Kieran and out of habit answered him as if he could hear her too.

Of course I don't mind. You may use my sewing kit any time.

"She says you can use her sewing kit any time," said Valerian.

Kieran cocked his head, frowning.

"How did you know the lass said that, Sire? She was looking at me."

Merry met Valerian's gaze. He stared at her, his eyes wide.

"I didn't *See* you, but I heard you just the same." *Can you hear me now?*

She nodded, her head spinning, which caused the wound in her thigh to throb again.

I hear you the same whether you speak out loud or in your mind.

Kieran broke the silence.

"What's happening?"

"I don't know," Valerian said quietly. "Somehow I can hear Merry without having to *See* her, and she can hear me, too."

"Mind to mind." Kieran's voice was reverent. "Just like the great dragons."

"You were dying," Valerian said to Merry, "and I managed to hold you here. Could our minds somehow have become joined?"

Yes, Merry agreed, remembering. *You were with me*. She closed her eyes. *You are still with me now, much more than flesh and blood.* She tightened her grip on his hand. *We mustn't speak without including Kieran, though I would like to explore this connection further. Just think, I can speak to you even in the dark now.* She smiled happily.

"Merry! That's a real smile, lass." Kieran grinned.

Please give him my thanks for helping me be merry after all. And would you ask him how his head is feeling?

Valerian told him what she said, and Kieran nodded.

"Thanks to you, my head feels mended and whole, though me Da would tell ye 'twas ne'er whole to begin with."

Valerian laughed, and his joy mingled with her own. How could either of them ever marry another? *After all, we are already one in heart and soul and mind. All that remains is to become one flesh.*

Yes, I was just thinking the same thing. He brought her hand to his lips.

She gasped, and her face grew warm.

I did not mean to share that thought with you. We'll have to learn how to control our mind speaking, won't we?

He nodded with an understanding smile.

"Merry," said Kieran, "are ye hungry?"

Yes, I am, and I'm sure you are hungry, too.

Valerian told him what she said. Kieran shrugged.

"You know me well, do ye not? But I was just wondering if ye felt up to eating in the hall with the others."

What others? Where are we?

"We're at the Southern Garrison. After you were attacked, Kieran rode ahead to get help."

"Sorry, Merry, I forgot to tell ye that part." Kieran shrugged.

I don't know if I can walk. I do need to use the necessary, though.

Valerian glanced under the bed.

"No chamber pot. I'm not surprised, since this is an all-male garrison."

"I'll find something for ye to use." Kieran saluted Merry with two fingers. When he left the room, Merry sighed.

My love, what are we going to do?

"I know for certain I will never marry Lord Reed's daughter." Valerian's stern expression softened. "I *will* speak to my father when we reach the Keep. You are, after all, a royal cousin as well as a southerner, so he can have no objection." He smiled. *This is not how I envisioned proposing marriage to you.*

Nor I. She took a deep breath.

Then why don't we wait until you recover and I will do it properly.

Agreed. Merry liked this mind-to-mind communication. It was much faster than spoken words.

Kieran returned carrying an old bucket.

"The steward says you can have this." He set it on the floor beside the cot and frowned. "Are ye going to be able to use it?"

She nodded, laying her hand on his arm. Valerian stood.

"We'll be just outside the door until you're finished," he told Merry.

And now I can let you know, even from another room. She waited until they closed the door after them.

Slowly Merry swung her legs over the side of the cot, sucking in air at the burning pain in her thigh. She managed to use the bucket, but her leg was throbbing worse by the time she finished. While sitting on the edge of the cot, she started to remove the bandage.

I have finished, she told Valerian. *I'm looking at the wound now.*

He and Kieran came back in as she exposed the injury. The stitches ran all the way across her thigh.

Please tell Kieran he did well with the stitches. But Merry was alarmed at the angry red striation on the skin, which indicated infection. *Do river dragons have poison in their mouths?*

Valerian examined the skin.

I don't think so. Does it look like poison?

It may just be infection. Even so, it can be serious. Is my carry sack here?

"Where is Merry's carry sack?" Valerian asked.

Kieran took it from a peg behind the door.

"Is something wrong? Are my stitches too tight?"

"No, she says you did a good job. But there's infection spreading. River dragons aren't poisonous, are they?"

"No, Sire. Only scavenger dragons have poison in their mouths to help them eat rotting flesh." Kieran frowned in concern. "Can I help you, Merry?"

I need a cup of hot water, not boiling.

Valerian told Kieran what she needed, and the squire hurried from the room.

Merry took out a bundle of dried tongues-of-fire, one that Valerian had taken down for her when they first met.

Do you remember?

How could I forget? I knew you were something out of the ordinary from the beginning, but I had no idea how much you would change my life.

For the better, I hope?

In every way.

Kieran came back with a cup of steaming water. Merry crushed the dried leaves into the water and let them steep.

"Are ye making a tea?" When she nodded, Kieran asked, "is that tongues-o'-fire?"

Yes. How did you know? Valerian told Kieran her question.

"When I was a wee lad I almost died from a fever. I remember my mother giving me teas made from this herb. Is it for fever as well as infection?"

Merry nodded, smiling at the image of Kieran as a small boy with tousled black hair.

Tell Kieran he will soon be a Healer himself.

After Valerian relayed her words, Kieran shook his head.

"Never like you are, but I am interested in learning how tae help sick and hurt people. And animals."

Through Valerian, Merry explained that by the color of the infusion the tea was ready. She drank all the liquid and then pressed the sodden leaves directly on the gash.

This, she explained, *will help draw out the infection.* She took a clean cloth from her carry sack and made a fresh bandage. When Kieran's stomach growled, he laughed.

"This is hungry work, Merry. Will ye be able to go with us, do ye think? 'Tis nearly time for the evening meal."

Merry glanced down at the torn riding skirt.

This skirt is so shredded I don't think it can be mended.

"What about one of those dresses Shannon gave you?" Valerian said. "They're in my pack in the next room."

Merry sighed when she remembered there were laces in the back.

"What's wrong?"

How are your lacing skills?

Fair, but why?

I can put on the dress, but I can't reach the lacing in the back.

Oh, Merry, I'm not sure I trust myself.

You wouldn't hurt the dress even if you managed to break one of the lacings.

That's not what I meant. He swallowed, and she felt the intensity of his emotion. *If I were to lace up the dress, I would later have to unlace it for you to take it off, wouldn't I?*

Yes, but. She stopped, and her face grew hot. *I see what you mean now.*

"I have an alternative." Merry was sure Valerian spoke aloud for Kieran's sake as well as to dispel some of their more intimate thoughts. "If

Kieran and I carry you to the hall in a chair, you could hold the riding skirt together. Once you're seated at the table, it won't matter if the pieces come apart."

"This one I've been sitting in would fit under the table," said Kieran, slapping the arm of the chair beside the cot.

Merry had a thought and covered her smile, but she couldn't hide the thought from Valerian.

"So, Kieran, it appears you and I have been demoted to throne carriers."

Kieran bowed low and scooted the chair closer to Merry.

"Then arise and be seated, Queen Merry, and us lowly throne carriers shall take you to your subjects."

Valerian chuckled while she sat in the chair.

Queen Merry, he said. *I like the sound of that.* He took one chair arm and Kieran took the other. While they lifted her, Merry held on to the chair with one hand, leaving the other free to hold her riding skirt together.

When they entered the hall, many of the men were already seated at the trestle tables. Their conversation ceased at the unusual sight of a young woman coming to join them, and the even more unusual sight of the prince and his squire carrying her in a chair. Every man present stood while Merry's chair was placed at the head table. Sir Walter grinned and bowed.

"You certainly know how to make an entrance, Your Highness." The knight regarded Merry. "And who is our lovely dinner guest? I was told that your squire came for help earlier today."

Valerian took Merry's hand and cleared his throat.

"Sir Walter, may I present Merry from the Village of Peace, who we have discovered to be my royal cousin. I am taking her with us to the Keep."

"A royal cousin? How interesting." Sir Walter took Merry's hand and lightly kissed it. "Welcome to the Southern Garrison, my lady."

He called me 'my lady.' Why did he say that?

It's a term of respect. And since you are a royal cousin, it is technically what you should be called. Lady Merry.

Oh. She smiled at the knight.

"Are you recovering from your injuries?"

She nodded. Sir Walter turned to Valerian with a puzzled look.

"Merry is unable to speak, Sir Walter. However, she is able to speak to my mind, so if there is anything you'd like to ask her, I can relate her answer to you."

"Your Highness? Do I understand you correctly that you and the lady can speak mind to mind? How is that possible? I thought only the great dragons could so communicate."

Valerian locked eyes with the knight and *Saw* his thoughts. Sir Walter was definitely startled, but his respect for Valerian had grown since their last encounter. And, most importantly, Valerian could find no evidence he knew anything about the attempted assassinations.

Sir Walter's eyes widened in surprise, and he inclined his head.

"So, Prince Valerian, you are a Seer, then?"

"Yes, and Merry is a Healer."

"And one of the Brethren." The knight turned to Merry. "Then you must be the one Flint Mallory spoke about."

She nodded, but Valerian thought he heard her mental sigh.

Please tell him I wish Flint Mallory had not been so liberal in his praise of me.

Valerian related what she said to Sir Walter, who laughed.

"So, Mallory brought you more business than you'd hoped for, did he?" When she nodded, shrugging, the knight smiled at Merry, obviously charmed.

Sir Gregory entered and joined them at the head table. His squire, Terron, went to sit with Kieran and some of the other young men.

"Greetings, Your Highness. I am glad to see you again."

"All is well, I trust, Sir Gregory?" Valerian *Saw* the man's thoughts, but as with Sir Walter, there was no knowledge of the murder attempts, to Valerian's great relief.

"Very well, thank you, Sire. We are beginning to feel that we trespass on Sir Walter's hospitality."

"Nonsense," said Sir Walter. "Your men have patrolled with ours daily, and the archery contests alone have honed my men's skills considerably."

Before Valerian could introduce Merry to Gregory, Sir Walter stood up and proposed a toast to their unexpected guest. While the men heartily drank to Merry's health, Valerian hoped it wouldn't be long before he could introduce her as *Princess* Merry.

* * *

Valerian and Kieran rode out into the Plains of Mohorovia with Sir Gregory and Terron. Gregory explained to Valerian how far they'd patrolled in his absence and had not found anything except the entrances to a few old burrows apparently abandoned by the Horde long ago. Of course, the men had not gone all the way into the burrows, but the entrances, Gregory estimated, had not been used in years.

Valerian could not understand how anything lived in this desolate place. It was so different from the land beyond the rift in the earth. Had the Horde made the plains into the wasteland it had become? By their advanced weapons alone, they must have once had some kind of civilization.

Sir Gregory called a halt and turned to Valerian.

"Your Highness, I really believe the Horde must have contracted some kind of plague and been wiped out. Else there would have been some sign of them. After you left the garrison, they attacked just once more, and since then no one has spotted a single Mohorovian."

"Then perhaps, Sir Gregory, it's time we returned to the Keep with our report for the king. We'll ride back and check with the other garrisons one more time, but it appears we have good news to relate." Valerian's gut churned with uneasiness about the whole situation, but he wheeled his horse around and rode back toward the garrison with the others.

Along the way, there was an odd rock formation. Valerian guided his horse toward it. Could the Horde have set up the rocks as a marker? But no, the formation was all natural.

"Look, Sire." Kieran pointed ahead. "There's something moving on the ground between those arms of rock."

Valerian pulled up the gray and slid down from the saddle. He drew his sword, and Kieran was right beside him.

"What is it, Your Highness?" called Sir Gregory.

"I'm not sure." When Valerian reached the place, he found a young burrowing dragon, injured but still alive.

"Something must have attacked the nest as they hatched, Sire." Kieran pushed an egg shell with the toe of his boot.

"And this one survived. Do you think Merry could Heal it?" Valerian tried to ask her, but they were too far away.

"Why don't we take it to her?" Kieran sheathed his sword and pulled a cloth from his saddlebag. He wrapped it around the feebly struggling dragon and tucked the bundle inside his tunic.

They rode back at a canter. As soon as they were in sight of the garrison walls, Valerian could hear Merry again.

You're back! It was unsettling not being able to sense your presence. He had the sensation of a mental caress from her.

All is well, except we have a small patient for you.

What is it?

You'll have to wait and see.

Valerian smiled at her impatience. He and Kieran handed over their horses to a stable boy and sprinted to Merry's room. Her face lit up at the sight of them.

What have you brought?

"The only living creature we found out there." He indicated Kieran should speak.

"This wee burrowing dragon, newly hatched and injured, we know not how. Can ye Heal it?" Kieran carefully removed the cloth-wrapped bundle from his tunic and set it in Merry's lap.

She opened the cloth and gasped when she saw the little creature. It breathed with exertion and otherwise barely moved. Its yellow eyes were dull.

Oh, poor little dragon! Merry cupped it with both hands and bent closer, her eyes shut in concentration. The glow briefly appeared under her hands, and the dragon's tail lashed back and forth. With a sigh Merry opened her eyes. The burrowing dragon blinked and stared up at her with what Valerian could only describe as a worshipful look. It nuzzled her hand, and she smiled in delight.

"You did it, Merry! I'll run down tae the kitchen and see if there are any scraps to feed the wee beastie." Kieran ran out of the room.

Merry stroked the little dragon.

He feels soft, not rough like I imagined.

"Perhaps his scales are smooth in order to move quickly through his burrow. By the way, how do you know it's a 'he'?"

I just know. She gazed into Valerian's eyes. *Just as I know that you love me without ever saying the words.*

I do love you, Merry. I hope to show you in my every thought and deed and word.

I think we have gone far beyond words, love.

He leaned forward and kissed her sweet mouth. The dragon butted its head against them, and Valerian pulled away, laughing.

"It appears I have competition."

Footsteps echoed in the hallway, and Kieran appeared holding a small clay bowl.

"I got some meat scraps, Merry. I don't know if ye want to touch raw meat, but that's what the beastie would eat in the wild."

Merry peeked in the bowl and made a face. The burrowing dragon flicked out a long forked tongue in the direction of the bowl. That apparently decided her, for Merry timidly picked up a piece of the raw meat and held it out for the dragon. He grabbed it from her fingers and swallowed it whole. His tongue flicked out again in rapid succession.

This time Merry set the meat on her palm so the dragon would not accidentally pinch her finger. In no time, it had finished the scraps. Kieran moved the empty bowl to the windowsill, and the dragon curled up in Merry's lap, its belly bulging. With her finger, Merry traced the upright scales along its back.

"What will you name it?" Kieran sat back on his heels, admiring the now sleeping dragon.

I don't know. Do you have any suggestions?

Valerian stared at the reptile's protruding snout and eyes. Then he smiled at an old memory.

"Kieran, did you ever meet Sir Edmund?"

"The old knight from Westmoor? Had a laugh that would shake a mountain?"

"That's the one. He was quite jolly for a dragon-faced knight. Shave off his beard and he could have been this creature's big brother."

Then I shall call him Sir Edmund.

Valerian told Kieran what Merry said. The squire laughed.

"What a fitting name!"

* * *

Valerian was glad Merry had her new pet to keep her occupied during her recovery. She walked a little farther each day, but until she was able to ride, they would have to delay their return to the Keep. Valerian asked Sir Walter about the nearest bishop, but there was not one closer than Lord Reed's castle, and he definitely did not want to go back there. Though he would have preferred to have a priest or monk witness his and Merry's vows of betrothal, he knew nothing lower than a bishop would satisfy his father.

He would simply ask for Merry's hand now, so there would be no doubt his intentions were honorable, but they could wait until they reached the Keep to have the bishop formalize the betrothal.

Valerian watched her from the open doorway of her room. She had clipped out her stitches and left the skin open to the air. Because the day was unseasonably warm, Merry had opened the window and sat in the sunlight. Her feet were bare, her injured leg propped on a second chair. Her long auburn braid hung to the floor. Sir Edmund scampered about the room, chasing a flying insect.

Merry? She started out of her peaceful reverie and turned to face him, setting her other foot on the floor. The torn riding skirt revealed more skin than Merry realized. She must have heard his thoughts, for she brought the edges together with her hand.

Yes, Valerian?

I see you have removed your stitches. Will you be able to ride soon, do you think?

I would like to try tomorrow. I know you are anxious to get back to your father.

Yes, but I don't want to rush you. He came into the room and went down on one knee beside her.

My leg is healing well. It will not reopen the wound for me to ride.

The sooner we return, the sooner I can tell my father about you. Valerian took her hand and cleared his throat. "Merry, you know that someday I will be king in my father's place. The thought of ruling this land does not scare me quite as witless as it did before, and most of the reason for that is you." He smiled. "I want you by my side always, Merry, as my wife and someday as my queen. Being married to the King of Levathia will not be easy, but you have already proven yourself to be the bravest woman who ever lived. Will you marry me?"

Tears of joy filled her eyes.

My love, my dearest friend, of course I will. And I'll do my best to support you in every way I can. I never want to be parted from you.

Valerian resisted the urge to grab Merry and swing her around the room. Instead, he leaned forward and kissed her formally on both cheeks. Before he could pull away she caught his face between her small hands and kissed him soundly.

Sir Edmund butted against Valerian, and he grinned at the little dragon.

"Merry, love?"

Yes, my dear Valerian?

"We must remember to get a cage for this creature before our wedding night."

Agreed. Her smile was radiant.

For the first time in his life, Valerian knew perfect peace.

Chapter 30 *In a dream, in a vision of the night.*

That night Valerian's dreams began as usual with the dragons and the sword, but then Merry's burrowing dragon appeared, searching through a mound of empty eggshells. He woke up, pondering the image. After all, he had expected to dream about Merry instead.

It was nearly sunrise, so he got up and pulled on his clothes. He listened, but Merry was still asleep next door. He hated to wake Kieran, but he didn't want to ride so far out from the garrison alone.

Fortunately, Kieran came fully awake once Valerian explained what he wanted to do. They filled their water flasks and took dried meat to eat on the way. A sleepy stable boy readied their horses, and a guard opened the gate for them.

"It won't take long to find that rock formation, Sire," Kieran said.

When they spotted the rocks, they urged their horses to a faster gait. Valerian spied the nest where they'd found the burrowing dragon and dismounted. He studied the borders of the nest, two arms of rock jutting out from the main formation. He ran his hands around the edges where dirt and rocks met.

"What are ye looking for?" Kieran leaned closer.

"I'm not sure." But Valerian felt something that shouldn't have been there. Instead of the dirt crumbling in his hand, he pulled back a thick section of sod which felt like a carpet. He was reminded of a spider burrow he'd once found with a hidden "trap door" covering the entrance just like this, except on a much smaller scale.

"Help me pull this back." Together they peeled back a cleverly woven cover to a man-sized burrow entrance. *Or in this case, a Mohorovian-sized tunnel.*

Kieran peered down into the hole.

"It doesn't look very deep. Do ye want me to go in?"

"I should have thought to bring a torch." Valerian frowned. "I wouldn't want to stumble in the dark."

"In that case, I'll just see if the tunnel is big enough to walk upright, and if it's worth making another trip to explore."

"All right."

Kieran lowered himself into the hole and drew his sword. Valerian knelt at the edge, ready to pull him up quickly.

"There's room enough even for you to stand, Sire. I think ye should come and see this."

Valerian let himself down, lightly jumping to the floor of the entrance. He slid his blade out of its scabbard and held it to the ready.

But nothing immediately threatened them. What lay before them, however, nearly made Valerian's heart stop. They stood at the entrance, not of a tunnel, but of a vast underground cave, dimly lit by luminous rocks. The entire garrison could have fit inside with room to spare. And stacked as far as they could see, in numbers too vast to count, were eggs, each large enough to hold a grown man.

Valerian knew what had to be growing inside these eggs. He placed a hand on the nearest shell. It was leathery, not hard like a bird's egg. With his sword, he slit open the tough membrane. Liquid gushed out. He pulled back the cut edge, and the ugly head of a juvenile Mohorovian popped out. Though its eyes were closed, it appeared to be ready to hatch any day. Valerian cut off the head, and it fell to the cave floor with a splat.

"It's worse than I feared," he whispered. "The Horde didn't disappear; they drew back in order to breed a vast army. There are more eggs in this one cave than there are people in all of the Southern Woodlands." He met Kieran's gaze. "Even if we were to start destroying eggs now, we have only two swords. We could never kill them all before they began to emerge. By the looks of this one, they are nigh ready to hatch."

"Let's ride back, Sire, and consult with Sir Walter. He may have something at the garrison that could destroy this nest."

Valerian nodded and wiped off his blade, sheathing it.

"Boost me up, and I'll give you a hand."

Once out of the cave, they mounted their horses and galloped back to the garrison.

* * *

When they came in sight of the walls, Merry called out to Valerian.

There you are! I wondered where you'd gone. I had a troubling dream.

As did I. That's why Kieran and I went to investigate something. What was your dream?

That the whole land was devoured by horrible monsters.

If we can't stop them, your dream may come true, he answered grimly.

What?

We're almost there, and I'll explain everything.

As quickly as they could, Valerian and Kieran assembled Sir Walter and his men along with Sir Gregory and the rest of Valerian's men. Merry was there, too, dressed in her other riding skirt and boots. Sir Edmund sat in her lap. Valerian took a deep breath and folded his trembling hands before speaking.

"I had a dream last night, and being a Seer I have learned not to ignore those dreams. Kieran and I found a nest of nearly hatched eggs. When they do hatch, these Mohorovians, as numerous as the stars, will be fully grown and able to fight."

A stunned silence followed Valerian's proclamation. Finally, Sir Walter stood. His face had gone pale.

"Where is this nest, Your Highness?"

"Half an hour's ride due west. The entrance is at a prominent rock formation where we found this injured burrowing dragon a few days ago." He pointed to Sir Edmund. "I'm sure every one of you has ridden past those rocks at one time or another."

"And you're certain there are Mohorovians inside these eggs?" The knight frowned.

"Yes, Sir Walter. I cut one open to make sure. The outside is not like a bird's eggshell, but a tough leathery membrane, else it might be possible to smash them all open."

"What about boiling oil?" said one of the men. "Or pitch?"

Sir Walter turned to him, frowning in concentration.

"If there are so many of the eggs, then our limited quantity of oil and pitch will not be nearly enough." He looked at Valerian for confirmation.

Kieran stood and stepped forward.

"If I may, Your Highness, I just thought o' something." Valerian nodded at him to speak. "The entrance to this large cave is relatively small. What if we block it so the beasties can't get out once they hatch?"

Valerian gestured to Sir Gregory.

"You've seen this place. In fact, I believe the burrowing dragon's nest was taken from elsewhere and used to camouflage the entrance. What think you? Is there enough rock in that formation to seal the entrance?"

"Perhaps, Your Highness." Sir Gregory stroked his beard. "But how would we move all that rock?"

"With our strength and that of our horses," Valerian said. "We'll need every foot of rope in this garrison."

Sir Walter nodded and smiled grimly.

"Then what are we waiting for, my prince? Let's move some rock."

While the men filed out, Valerian turned to Merry.

"I'm afraid we'll have to wait until later to see if you can ride."

What if you asked one of the stable boys to help me while you're gone?

"I'd feel better if I were here, but if I explain everything to him, you should do well." Valerian offered his hand to her, and Merry took it as he led her to the horses. When they reached the stables, with activity swirling all around them, Merry gasped.

"What is it?"

When I Heal someone, I can See *the injury as clearly as your thoughts and words. I can also* See *whether or not a plant can be used for medicine. What if you take me with you and I try to* See *one of these creatures in the egg? Perhaps I will be able to tell how long it will be before they hatch.*

That's brilliant, my love. But are you sure you can ride that far and back?

We need to know so we can leave. What better way to prove it?

Valerian needed no urging to find a groom and have Merry's horse saddled and ready. He helped her to the saddle and mounted his gray.

❖

As they neared the rock formation, Sir Edmund became agitated. Merry tried to calm him, but he paced from her shoulder down to her lap and back again. She refrained from asking Valerian about it. He was already worried about the eggs, and all the way out from the garrison either Sir Walter or Sir Gregory had questions for him. Fortunately, her leg wasn't bothering her much. The deep twinges that pained her were more of a nuisance.

The horses stopped while the men studied how best to topple the large rocks. Valerian slid down from his horse and helped Merry dismount. She tried to make Sir Edmund sit on the saddle, but he leaped onto her shoulder and wrapped his tail around her neck.

"Kieran, take Merry down to the eggs while we coordinate our attack up here. We won't begin until you return."

"Aye, Sire, but I'll need one other. May Terron accompany us?"

"It's all right with me if it's all right with Sir Gregory."

Kieran jumped into the hole first, and Merry became a little queasy when Terron lowered her into it. Kieran grabbed her waist to set her gently down, and the little dragon hissed at him.

"My apologies, Sir Edmund, for having to manhandle your mistress." He went to the nearest egg. "This is the one Prince Valerian cut open. All the rest are intact, though."

Merry approached one of the other eggs. They were so large! And there were so many of them. When she laid her hands on a leathery shell, it was warm. She closed her eyes and felt the beating of the unborn creature's heart. The sound of it echoed louder and louder until it throbbed in her ears.

Then she *Saw* that this creature was interconnected with all the others, not just in this nest but from other nests in other places, some of which had already hatched. They were not separate individuals as humans were; they seemed to have a collective consciousness with one simple, driving thought: *Swarm! Spread our kind and overcome all other kinds!*

The horror of it made Merry instinctively recoil, but she forced herself to *See* as much as she could in order to help Valerian. Many of the images made no sense to her, but she hoped Valerian would be able to *See* them in her mind later and sort them out. One thing was certain: Hatching was imminent, within a day or two at most.

"Merry?" Kieran's voice brought her back from the dreadful visions. She opened her eyes and backed away from the egg, trembling.

"Are ye all right?" He sounded concerned, and once again she wished she could talk to him. She shook her head, and tears spilled onto her cheeks. There was no way to describe to him what she'd seen. Even if she could have spoken, she would have difficulty finding the words. To her surprise, Sir Edmund nuzzled her cheek with his small head.

"Kieran," said the other squire. "Prince Valerian is asking if we're almost finished. They are all set to seal the entrance."

Kieran caught her attention.

"Are ye ready to go?" When Merry nodded, Kieran boosted Terron back up through the hole. Then he laced his hands together. She stared at them, puzzled, and he grinned. "Put your foot there in my hands and I'll send you up to Terron."

Merry's eyes widened, but she trusted Kieran, and Terron lay flat at the edge, reaching down for her. She took a deep breath and stepped onto Kieran's hands. For a moment, she was suspended in midair. The burrowing dragon tightened his grip around her throat as Terron grabbed her arms and pulled her up the rest of the way.

Then Valerian's hands were lifting her up. Her eyes adjusted to the sudden bright light. Sir Walter and Sir Gregory stood nearby, expectant.

"Did you *See* anything?" Valerian asked out loud for their benefit, she assumed.

Most of it was hard to understand, but I will try to show you everything. Merry stared into his eyes so he would be sure to *See* all of her memories. Then, just as she had at their first meeting, she shared everything from her contact with the creatures in a flood of images. And like the first time, Valerian staggered back, crying out in pain. Willing hands were there to ease him to the ground. Sir Edmund hissed and flicked out his tongue. Merry's eyes filled with tears.

I'm so sorry, love. I wish I knew how to do that without hurting you.

It was worth a little pain for the information you were able to discover. Valerian rubbed his temples.

"Sire?" Kieran asked. "What happened?"

"Help me out of the way so the men can begin moving rocks and I'll explain."

Kieran and Terron each took an arm and helped Valerian stand. Then they joined the others at the ropes while Valerian and Merry and the two knights went apart to confer.

Hold me, so I can stay upright. Valerian draped his arm over Merry's shoulders, and she slipped her arm around his waist. Sir Edmund sat quietly on Merry's shoulder, to her great relief.

Is that better?

Yes, thank you. "Gentlemen, it is even worse than I feared."

Both of the older men's faces filled with concern. They did not speak while they waited for Valerian to collect himself.

"Thanks to the talents of my extraordinary bride-to-be, we know many things. This nest is not the only one. At least one other has already hatched. The Horde that you and I have fought against is an older generation who are no more. The tremendous sea of eggs they died to create represents a swarm that happens only once every few hundred years." He shuddered and Merry tightened her hold around his waist.

"The good news is that these new Mohorovians will not have enough axes and bows and poisoned arrows to use against us, if they even know where their parents left those weapons. The bad news is that they know the Keep is the seat of our government, the 'head' of our swarm if you will, and so they will be gathering against it." Valerian pointed back to the hole. "Judging by the number of eggs in that one nest, even if their only weapons are teeth and claws, they will eventually overwhelm us by the sheer mass of their swarm."

Sir Walter set his mouth in a grim line. Sir Gregory's face had gone white. He cleared his throat.

"You are remarkably calm, Your Highness, considering we are facing the almost certain destruction of Levathia."

"Not calm, Sir Gregory. Shocked and dismayed. But we have no time to lose." Valerian turned to Sir Walter. "As soon as the entrance to this nest is sealed, my men and I must ride hard to warn the other garrisons and the Keep. You should post a continuous lookout to make sure this nest stays sealed, and in the meantime warn Lord Reed to prepare the people in the south to evacuate should they see the Horde approaching. We will do the same in the north."

"Where can we go, Sire?" asked Sir Gregory, distressed. "Didn't our ancestors flee their own land to come to Levathia in the first place?"

"Yes, they did. And I don't know where we can go. I'm hoping we won't have to go anywhere." Valerian swayed on his feet, and Merry wrapped her arms around him.

What's wrong? Merry asked. *What happened?*

I saw a fleeting vision of a dragon. Not a dream, more like a waking dream. The dragon was trying to speak to me.

"Are you able to ride, Your Highness?" asked Sir Walter. "If so, perhaps you and Lady Merry should return to the garrison and rest while you can. I'll make sure you and your men have provisions before you leave."

"Thank you, Sir Walter. I believe I will accept your offer." *Why do I feel so shaky?*

Because you are trying so hard to stay calm for your men while inwardly you are reeling from this terrible news.

"Then we will see you back at the garrison, my prince." Sir Walter bowed. "If you'd like, tell the steward what you and your men need so it will be prepared when you're ready to leave."

"My thanks to you," Valerian said.

Kieran came forward, leading Stripe and Valerian's gray. Merry took Stripe's reins so Kieran could help Valerian mount. As she swung her leg around, the wound twinged again, but it went away as soon as she settled herself in the saddle.

"Thank you, Kieran," Valerian said. "You are ever the efficient squire." They shared a glance that tugged at Merry's heart; she could *See* Valerian's regret that neither of them might live long enough to be knighted.

* * *

By the time Merry and Valerian reached the garrison, Valerian had recovered from his great shock. He met with the steward about provisions while Merry went to collect her few belongings. She wanted to be ready to leave and not add anything to Valerian's burden.

Merry stared out the window but couldn't tell if the men were returning or not, so she decided she had a little more time. Gingerly she knelt beside the cot. The wound pulled a little, but the discomfort helped her focus her thoughts. She bowed her head, covering her face with her hands.

Oh, God of Peace, I ask nothing for myself. I ask for Valerian's sake that You help him find a way to save this land. He is so strong and good, please help me be unselfish and support him with my whole heart no matter what the cost. Please, please, have mercy on us.

She remained on her knees long after words failed her. Merry thought about the power of hope, even in a hopeless situation such as this one, and she clung to it with all of her being.

When Merry was able to face Valerian again and be strong for his sake, she pushed herself upright. With a start, she saw him standing in the doorway.

How long have you been here, love?

Not long. He smiled at her. *I came to see if you were ready to leave as soon as the men return.*

Yes, of course. I was just praying for you. For us.

Thank you, Merry. She sensed his overwhelming sorrow and wished she could take some of his burden on herself.

You already have, my dear lady, just by sharing it with me, though I wish none of it had to happen. He came closer.

She hugged him tightly and he returned the embrace. While she listened to his heartbeat, Merry imagined pouring her love and her strength into him to help him bear the weight of leadership.

He suddenly cried out and pulled away from her.

Valerian! What's wrong?

"The dragon," he whispered. "He *is* trying to communicate something. I think he is trying to show me how to find him."

Why would a dragon want you to find him?

"Do you remember the emblem of my family is a dragon?" She nodded. "Our first ancestor was Alden the Dragon King. I had forgotten why he was called that, but I remember now. Three hundred years ago Alden made a covenant, an agreement with the great dragons of the land. They and the men who had just sailed here were at war. Alden risked his life to end the conflict by convincing the dragons that they should live in peace with men."

If Alden could make a covenant with the dragons, then he must have been able to speak to them.

Yes, you're right. He must have been a Seer, too. Valerian gasped. "Merry, don't you see? Perhaps I was given the gift of Sight as well as the most precious gift of being able to speak to you mind-to-mind, so I could renew this covenant with the dragons. Perhaps we have hope after all."

There was a noise outside. Valerian rushed to the window.

"They're back. Come, Merry." He grabbed her hand, and they hurried to meet the men.

When they entered the garrison's yard, Merry shivered, but not because of the cloudy sky and the cold wind blowing from the north. She remembered how the dragons of Shannon's embroidery and Eldred's tapestry dwarfed the men and breathed fire. What if Valerian found the dragons and they were not willing to renew this covenant? What would happen then?

Caelis awoke with a start. It took a moment to remember where he was, since the room was totally dark. He lay on a cot in a small room of Midway Garrison. Drew and Rafael lay nearby, fast asleep. The rest of his men were in the barracks with the garrison soldiers.

They had arrived late last night, and he'd told the commander what had befallen Blackwater Garrison. Rather than evacuate, the commander seemed to think they had enough weapons and supplies to hold off the Horde when they eventually came. At the very least, the man would not decide to leave until he saw the size of the army, and Caelis was convinced that waiting would be too late.

He had to reach the Keep. He had to convince King Orland that Valerian was surely dead and that Caelis could capably lead the king's army against the Horde invasion. Perhaps he should leave now, before first light. He could travel much faster alone.

But then he thought about Rafael. Caelis still believed he could use the child's attachment to his advantage, and the boy was no trouble while traveling, to his great surprise. Drew, on the other hand, was proving to be more and more difficult. Caelis wouldn't mind leaving him behind to die, but the boy was even more attached to the squire and might not be so easily handled.

Caelis sighed. He would have to bring them both, or neither. He decided to bring them.

After waking them, he cautioned them to silence. They gathered their belongings and went quietly to the stables where they saddled their horses and led them to the gate. The sleepy gatekeeper had no reason not to let them leave, so Caelis and Drew mounted their horses, and Drew pulled up Rafael behind him. They headed north along the road to the Keep without looking back as the sun rose on a new day.

Chapter 31 *I sought him, but I could not find him; I called him, but he gave me no answer.*

After Valerian's men returned, they washed, ate quickly, and made ready to leave within half an hour. Valerian bade Sir Walter and the garrison a subdued farewell, and he and his first command headed north along the border road. Hawk rode in the lead, but this time Anson rode with him in case of trouble. They pushed their horses as hard as they dared. Fortunately, there were plenty of water sources, and they let the animals drink frequently.

When they stopped for the night beside a river, Kieran pointed to a fish as it arced out of the water and fell back with a splash.

"I never did try to catch a southern fish, Sire." Kieran's voice was subdued.

Valerian forced a smile. "You'll have another opportunity someday." *I hope.*

While the men scouted the perimeter and picketed the horses, Valerian helped Merry down from her horse. When her feet touched the ground, she hissed and stumbled a little. Supporting her, they walked around the campsite.

The leg is cramping.

I'm sorry we had to ride so hard.

Please don't apologize. I know we have to go fast. She trembled.

"What's the matter? Are you cold?" Valerian embraced her, and she nodded. "I should have asked Sir Walter if he had an extra cloak. Yours is not nearly warm enough. We'll have to improvise."

Valerian opened his pack and pulled out the sleeping furs. He picked a squarish one and laid it flat. Using his belt knife, he cut a slit in the middle.

"Let's try this." He positioned the slit and pulled the fur over Merry's head, arranging it so it hung like a herald's tabard. But it was too shaggy to look like anything other than a garment for a wild mountain hermit. He chuckled.

What is it?

You look like a barbarian princess.

As long as you will still be my prince.

The fur moved, and the burrowing dragon's head popped out at Merry's neck. It blinked its eyes.

We have woken Sir Edmund from his warm nest.

Sir Gregory strode toward him then.

"Your Highness, Cameron recommends two sentries per shift."

"I agree, Sir Gregory. Put me on first watch. And I want to awaken before the sun so we can reach Blackwater Garrison as early as possible."

"Very well, Sire." The knight went to make the arrangements.

Meanwhile, Valerian had Kieran place the rest of their furs so that Merry would lie between them and also be surrounded by the others. Merry sat down and Valerian knelt beside her.

"I must go stand my watch now. Kieran and the others will be here, and I won't be so far away that I can't hear you if you really need me."

I love that I can speak to you, even in the dark.

So do I. "I'll return in two hours. Save my place."

Kieran handed Valerian a strip of dried meat, and he stood to leave. Merry gazed up at him.

No one can take your place, love.

Valerian smiled and then turned his attention to their surroundings. He would share this watch with Hawk. They each took one-half of the perimeter and measured their pace so they would meet every few minutes for a silent "all's well."

After the last rays of the sun had disappeared in the west, the night grew cold and silent. Too silent, as if the land was holding its breath.

Valerian's gut clenched with dreadful anticipation. By the time Kieran relieved him, he felt certain he would have vivid dreams if he did fall asleep.

Valerian picked his way among the sleeping bodies. Merry lay on her side, her hair unbound like a shimmering coverlet. It pleased him to think that he could someday comb that glorious hair daily. He carefully lowered himself to the empty fur so as not to wake her. Then he reverently brought a stray lock of hair to his lips. With a sigh he lay down, facing her, and watched her peaceful face for a long time before his eyelids grew heavy and he fell asleep.

The dragon flew to him in a dream, landing within a circle of immense white stones in a field surrounded by ancient oak trees. Snow-covered mountains lay in the distance. The image was so detailed that Valerian felt as if he had stepped into the scene. He walked toward the center of the stone circle, where a large number of the great dragons waited for him. With his sword unsheathed he approached the chief dragon and bowed. But the dragon opened its mouth and inhaled, ready to incinerate Valerian with its fiery breath.

Valerian awoke, gasping for air. He sat up, trying to suppress a cough. Kieran had returned and lay fast asleep on the other side of Merry. Daybreak was still hours away.

What does it mean? Valerian wondered. *Does the dragon wish for me to find him so that I can renew Alden's covenant, or does it merely want to kill me? How can I know?*

When his breathing returned to normal, he lay down again. He didn't know how he would sleep. But Merry's hand searched for his and found it. She brought his hand to her cheek, and by that simple warm touch he relaxed and slept for what remained of the night.

* * *

He awoke as the first glow of sunrise lightened the eastern sky. The rest of the camp stirred. Merry sat up and smiled at him, and Valerian wished he had the time to braid her hair. Instead, she did the job while he rolled up their sleeping furs and handed them to Kieran.

After a quick breakfast, they resumed their pace northward along the road. The dread returned, churning Valerian's stomach. Either his silence or his uneasiness must have affected the men, for they remained silent, too.

Late in the morning, they spotted a black cloud of vultures circling ahead. Hawk and Anson crested a rise and signaled a halt. Valerian rode forward to come abreast with them and gasped. He reined his gray to stop.

The garrison was deathly quiet, its gates open. Hundreds of bodies of men and Mohorovians lay piled around the walls and inside the gates. Scavenger dragons and vultures were already at work. Valerian became sick with fear. Another nest must have hatched. How many of the swarm were still alive? And where had they gone?

Sir Gregory rode forward and joined them. His voice was somber.

"Do you think there is any possibility of survivors, Your Highness?"

Valerian shook his head, horrified at the slaughter.

"Not judging by the number of the dead." How many more scenes like this would they find? Merry moved Stripe close enough that she could reach up and touch his arm.

Oh, Valerian, I feel no sign of life from that place, except for the scavengers.

"What about the bodies, Sire?" asked another man.

Valerian wanted to scream at his helplessness, but for the sake of the others he forced calm into his voice.

"It pains me to leave those men unburied, but we must press on to Midway Garrison and pray we're not too late to warn them."

As they galloped past, it was impossible not to stare at the horror of the scene and imagine it repeated at every garrison and village and castle in the land.

* * *

They rode hard the rest of the day. Valerian had hoped to travel into the night, but the horses were spent and needed to rest. They found a high point at which to camp with a good view in every direction. Again, Valerian took first watch, and when he later fell asleep had the same dream, even more vivid than before.

They reached Midway Garrison by early afternoon, but it was too late. The same destruction prevailed, with one exception.

Valerian, there's a sign of life here.

"Sir Gregory!" Valerian rode to his side. "Merry says there's a survivor."

"Then we must find him." The knight held up a hand to signal the others.

They made their way down the road and approached the scene of destruction. Valerian tasted bile. The bodies were not in as advanced a stage of decomposition as at the other garrison, but the fierceness of the battle was evident by the terrible gashes and severed heads and limbs. Their galloping horses chased away a score of scavenger dragons, whose long low bodies moved with surprising speed.

Merry, can you tell any more about this survivor?

Only that it is a man and not a beast. Perhaps when I get closer to him, I will know.

"We are searching for a survivor," Valerian shouted. "Split up and make haste."

Valerian and Kieran stayed within sight of Merry. Valerian marveled at her calm in surveying the gruesome scene. But she had seen her village massacred; perhaps that explained her composure. Valerian had to avert his eyes from the bodies, afraid that he would throw up in front of the men.

I am close now. I feel his soul fading. Merry dismounted and searched among the bodies. Valerian joined her.

At last she knelt beside a man in a blood-soaked tunic. His eyes were closed and his shallow breathing labored. As soon as Merry touched him, he took a last shuddering breath and lay still.

I'm sorry, love. We were too late. She glanced up, stricken.

"Don't blame yourself, Merry. He was hurt too badly to save, I'm afraid." Valerian studied the immediate area to see if he could figure out what had made the killing blow.

His eyes were drawn to an object lying in the dirt. At first, Valerian thought it was a piece of rope, but something compelled him to take a closer look. He squatted beside it and saw what it was: A long braid fastened with a wooden clasp. Part of the scalp was still attached. Valerian wanted to hide it from Merry. But he didn't have that right.

Merry?

Yes?

I think you need to see this.

Merry stood and came to him. She followed his finger with her eyes. When she saw the braid, she fell to her knees. Tenderly she picked up the braid, wiped off the clasp.

No. It cannot be.

What is it?

Her gaze met his and he *Saw* her grief.

This was Gabriel's.

Gabriel's? What was his braid doing here? These men couldn't have been massacred by the same Mohorovians that killed Merry's village, could they?

"Merry, were all the people in your village scalped like this?"

Only the men. She stared at him, frowning. *What does that mean?*

"I don't know, and I'm not sure how to find out." He gently lifted her. "We must press on. I'm sorry, love."

Merry wiped the tears that filled her eyes. She opened her carry sack to place the braid inside when Valerian stopped her.

"Wait."

What is it?

"The clasp. Gabriel's emblem. That looks like a morning glory."

She nodded.

"I've seen this emblem before." He shook his head. "But I can't remember why it looks so familiar."

I'm sure it will come to you. You have much on your mind right now. Merry put the braid away and mounted Stripe.

Valerian gazed up at her for a long moment.

I never forget that you were to be his wife.

I did not choose to marry Gabriel, but I would have learned to love him. She smiled. *You are my life now.*

He squeezed her hand and reluctantly pulled away to climb back on his horse. They found the rest of the men and pressed on to the next garrison.

When they stopped for the night, exhausted, the bluff afforded such a defensible site that Hawk and Sir Gregory recommended only one sentry per hour to Valerian.

"That way, Your Highness, you won't have to watch tonight," Sir Gregory said with a yawn.

Kieran prepared the sleeping furs while Valerian drew Merry aside. She could tell something new was pressing on him, and she gave him her full attention. He cleared his throat.

"Since I first discovered Gabriel was also a Seer, I have felt a strong connection with him. Even now that he has gone on to the next life, I believe he is with me still. I can't explain it."

Perhaps because you have many of your best qualities in common—leadership, a strong sense of justice, but also mercy.

"I hope my request doesn't sound blasphemous, but I would like to wear my hair in a braid to honor the memory of Gabriel and all the Brethren. I don't want them to be forgotten."

Merry's heart swelled with gratitude.

Nor do I. That is a fitting tribute, my love.

He grabbed a hank of his hair.

Do you think it's long enough yet?

Shall I try to braid it?

Please.

First Merry found a strip of cloth in her carry sack to hold the braid together. Perhaps later Valerian could design a clasp with a dragon emblem. Whatever design he chose for his clasp, she wanted to wear it, too. Using her comb, Merry smoothed his hair. It came below his shoulders and was a little wavy, like her own, which would help keep the braid together.

Next, Merry separated Valerian's hair into three equal sections. She braided it as tightly and evenly as her own, but it was strange for the finished plait to be so short. While holding the end of the braid, Merry tightly wound the cloth around the hair, securing it. Then her chest tightened as her pride for him mingled with the grief she feared would be with her always.

Valerian reached back to feel the braid. Then he turned to face her.

Thank you. "Will it be easier to braid as it grows longer?"

Yes. She gripped his hand. *Let's keep thinking of the future, my noble lord. There is always hope.*

He kissed her gently before they returned to their place on the furs surrounded by the other men. Kieran lay snoring on Merry's right side. She could *See* Valerian's troubled thoughts making it impossible for him to sleep. The blood pounded in her temples with the fear of losing him, but she tried to keep her angst from affecting his own dark thoughts.

Valerian?

Yes? He turned his face toward her.

May I just hold you?

He put his arm around her, and she clung to him, careful not to crush the sleeping burrowing dragon. She shuddered.

Are you cold, Merry?

Mostly in my heart. Tears threatened to flow, but she forced them back.

Valerian laid his cheek against her head. She concentrated on each breath he took. Eventually, she was able to fall asleep, lulled by his rhythmic breathing.

* * *

In the morning, Merry awakened before the sun had fully risen. Her breath misted in the frigid air, but she was warm and safe in Valerian's arms. She could tell he wasn't awake yet.

Merry closed her eyes and *Saw* his terrible anxiety for the land and its people. Could she Heal his troubled mind? Or at least give him some of her strength so he could more easily think clearly and lead with confidence? Very gently, so as not to wake him, she placed one hand over his heart and opened herself to the Healing gift. The glow from her hand was bright in the predawn light, so she closed her eyes again to better concentrate.

Valerian woke with a gasp and grabbed her hand.

What are you doing?

I was trying to ease your disquiet. Did I hurt you? She shuddered.

No, but I will not have you expend yourself for that, love.

I would give you all my strength, if I could take this burden from you.

Valerian embraced her, kissed her hair. Then he pulled back to look at her face in the dim light. Merry caressed his brow, trying to erase his worry. He grasped her hand and brought the palm to his lips.

Merry. I must leave you soon.

She gasped. Her chest tightened, making it hard to breathe. When he steeled his resolve, she mentally backed away so as not to weaken that determination, though every instinct wanted only to cling to him.

He took a deep breath, and when he let it out she could *See* his calm resolution.

Everything has come clear in my mind. Our only hope is to ask the great dragons to help us. I must go alone and find them and pray I can renew the covenant Alden first made with them. Perhaps, if I take his sword they will remember.

Merry bit back her tears. She had to stay strong for him.

Must you go alone?

I'm sorry, Merry. I did not want to leave you voiceless, but the land's need is greater than our own desires.

Around them the men began to stir. The sky had lightened enough that Merry could see Valerian's face more clearly. He appeared different with his hair pulled back in the braid—older, even nobler if that were possible.

Sir Edmund rustled around inside her cloak. He poked his head out, but Merry could not tear her gaze from Valerian. She wanted to hoard every detail of his face, his voice, his beautiful mind, to save as precious memories when he had to leave. Beside her, Kieran sat up.

"My lord," he said hoarsely. "I had the strangest dream." The squire rubbed his eyes. "I dreamed of a circle of stones I saw once long ago."

Valerian grabbed his arm.

"Large white stones?"

"Aye, Sire. 'Tis the sacred place of the great dragons."

"You have been there?" When Kieran nodded, Valerian's eyes widened. His face filled with hope. "Can you take me to this place?"

"I think I could find it again," Kieran said. "But 'tis north of me home, a long way from here."

* * *

They rode hard again that day. The skies were heavy with gray clouds. When they came within sight of Gateway Garrison by mid-afternoon, it began to lightly snow. At first, Merry thought they were in time to warn the men there, but when they crested the cliff edge, a mass of Mohorovians moved toward the walls. There were so many of them! They marched relentlessly. As any were cut down by the weapons of the garrison soldiers, hundreds more stepped over the fallen. They grasped one another's limbs and tails, building ladders with their own bodies to scale the walls.

"No," Valerian cried. He whirled his horse around. "Sir Gregory."

The knight urged his mount closer.

"Yes, Sire?"

Valerian glanced back at Merry. This was it. The moment she'd been dreading.

"Kieran and I must leave you," Valerian said. "We'll ride north to find the great dragons. The Northern Garrison is along the way, so we'll warn them unless, God forbid, they've been overrun." He reached inside his tunic and pulled out a sealed document. "Take this and give it into the hand of King Orland. It proves Merry's royal blood." Then he and Sir Gregory gripped one another's arms in farewell. "I place these lives in your capable hands. Prepare the Keep for siege, and I'll bring the dragons as quickly as I can."

Valerian turned to Merry. Her belly twisted with dread. He moved his horse close to Stripe.

"I have to find the dragons, Merry."

Take me with you. If we die, I want to die at your side.

My love, I cannot. "I need you to go to the Keep with the others."

But why? Why would you send me away?

"I'm not sending you away. I want to keep you safe. Wait for me, Merry."

She gripped his hand fiercely, so afraid she would never see him or hear his thoughts again. They leaned toward one another and kissed just as fiercely. Then he backed his horse from her.

I love you, Merry. Never give up hope.

Valerian turned away, and he and Kieran galloped toward the Pass without looking back.

"Come, Lady Merry," Sir Gregory said. "We must go."

The men urged their horses along the road toward the Keep. Merry numbly held on while Stripe cantered with the rest. Her eyes filled with tears, so she couldn't see the snow growing heavier, but she the wetness touched her face. She kept her senses attuned and *knew* the exact moment when she could no longer sense Valerian's presence. Her heart broke, and she slumped against Stripe's neck, sobbing.

The snow transformed the countryside. Under other circumstances, Merry would have delighted in its purity and beauty. By the time they stopped for a brief rest, drifts were forming on either side of the road.

They led the horses into a sheltered grove beside a stream and dismounted. Merry went through the motions of taking care of Stripe and Sir Edmund, her senses as blind without Valerian as her throat was mute. Terron, Gregory's squire, approached her. He was about her age and a little taller than Kieran.

"My lady, Sir Gregory sent me to ask if there was anything you needed." His gray eyes were kind.

Merry shook her head and mouthed her thanks. But he wasn't finished.

"Forgive my boldness, Lady Merry, but I know you have no voice and can no longer speak to Prince Valerian's mind. Sir Gregory and I wish to help you communicate. Perhaps we can devise some hand signals."

Merry nodded. It was kind of Terron and Sir Gregory, but they could never know how devastating it was to lose her mind link with Valerian. She supposed it wouldn't hurt to come up with signs for important needs, though, especially if she never saw Valerian again.

She caught herself. Of course she would see him again. Wouldn't she?

During the long journey to the Keep, Caelis couldn't stop thinking about what he'd seen of the Horde. It was nearly dark on the third day when he entered the Keep's inner ward and urged his spent horse to the stables. He slid down and handed the reins to a groom. Drew did likewise and helped Rafael dismount. As soon as they entered the Keep, Caelis stopped the nearest royal page.

"Inform King Orland that Sir Caelis has returned, and wishes to speak with him."

"Yes, sir." The page bowed and hurried away.

Caelis turned to Drew and spoke severely.

"Take the boy to my apartment. Both of you clean up and eat something and wait for me there."

"Yes, Sir Caelis." Drew bowed his head.

Rafael gazed up at him with wide eyes.

"Is this our new home, sir?"

"Yes, Rafael." Caelis smiled grimly. "Drew will show you where we live. You will have your own pallet now."

Rafael sniffled and wiped his nose. Caelis wondered if he was ill.

While Drew led him away, Caelis turned his thoughts to King Orland and what he would say to him. He strode toward the great hall. The page hurried toward him.

"The king will see you now. He is in his sitting room and bade me bring you."

Caelis followed the boy up the stairs to King Orland's suite. The page opened the door.

"Your Majesty, here is Sir Caelis." Then he bowed and went off on another errand.

Orland sat in his overstuffed chair. Caelis approached and went down on one knee, bowing his head.

"Rise, Sir Caelis."

He stood and faced the king.

"Your Majesty, forgive the state of my appearance, but I have ridden long and hard and bring grave news. The Horde have returned and in greater numbers than before."

Orland frowned, studying his face.

"You have seen them with your own eyes?"

"Yes, Sire. I witnessed them destroy Blackwater Garrison. I warned Midway, leaving my men to aide them, and then rode here as quickly as I could to warn you."

"What do you propose, Sir Caelis?" The king shifted in his chair.

Caelis schooled his features into a pose of humility.

"I propose that we prepare for siege. I can continue working with Master Murray to devise weapons effective against the Horde and be ready when they come."

"How long do you estimate before they arrive?"

"Their large army cannot move quickly, Sire, especially in severe weather. I believe we have at least a month to prepare."

Orland drummed his fingers on the arm of the chair, deep in thought.

"Did you see aught of Prince Valerian?"

"No, Your Majesty, but I heard that the prince was visiting Lord Reed, Sir Rudyard, and Eldred the Seer while he was in the south." Caelis made his voice sound concerned. "I only hope the prince wasn't at Blackwater Garrison when it was overrun."

The king frowned and cleared his throat.

"We will hope for the best and wait until he returns. In the meantime, Sir Caelis, I put you in charge of shoring up the Keep's defenses and making ready for siege." He stood, dismissing Caelis. "We will call a council of war in the next few days. Be ready to give your report then."

"Yes, Your Majesty." Caelis bowed.

He turned and left the room, unable to contain a smirk. With the Horde massing between Valerian and the Keep, it was unlikely the whelp would ever return.

Chapter 32 *I will open my lips and answer.*

Valerian and Kieran pressed on through the worsening snowstorm, though they soon had to slow their pace for the horses' sakes. They took short breaks to rest the animals, but they did not stop for the night. Valerian was afraid the storm would turn into a blizzard before they reached the Northern Garrison. If that were to happen, even Kieran would be hard pressed to find their way.

Questions swirled through Valerian's mind like the blowing snow. Would the weather bar the Horde from the Keep or at least slow the swarm's advance? Would he and Kieran be in time to warn the last garrison? If they found the dragons, would the great beasts remember Alden's covenant? Or would they simply kill Valerian and Kieran so as to have two fewer human enemies?

Had he done the right thing sending Merry to the Keep? Should she have come with him and Kieran after all? The sudden absence of her presence was a hole in his heart. But how much worse for Merry! At least he could still communicate with others.

The wind picked up, howling down from the mountains and piercing Valerian's clothing like shards of ice. Shivering in his cloak, Valerian followed Kieran's lead through the deepening drifts. As the second day grew darker, Kieran had to dismount and guide his horse in order to keep to the road.

Just as Valerian was beginning to think they would have to stop for the night after all, a brief lull in the blowing snow revealed a glow ahead.

"There's the garrison, Sire." Kieran moved faster through the knee-deep snow.

They reached the gates, and the man on watch spotted them. He shouted, "'Tis the prince and young MacLachlan."

Valerian and Kieran gratefully entered the gates and were escorted to Kieran's brother. After a joyous greeting, Angus had them sit with him around a small table and sent for food and drink.

"You don't know how glad we are to see you," Valerian told him. He related the finding of the nest, the discovery it was part of a "swarm," and the destruction of the other three garrisons.

"So you've sent the others to the Keep?" Angus stroked his mustaches. "Won't the beasties go straight to it and attack?"

"Yes, but my father must be warned to prepare for siege. I hope to bring the great dragons to help."

"Ye plan to ask the dragons to *help* us?" Angus said. "Meaning no disrespect, my lord, but I'm supposing ye have a good reason for believing they will e'en listen tae you."

Valerian leaned closer and tried to project more confidence than he felt.

"I am a Seer, and part of that gift is having dreams of the future. Since my brother died, I've had a recurring dream of facing the great dragons with a sword." He patted Alden's blade at his side. "Lately I've seen the dragons inside a circle of enormous stones, which Kieran says he's seen before."

"Aye, I took the lad with me one time when we traveled that uninhabited land." Angus crossed his arms. "Pardon me, Sire, but what about the dreams makes ye think the dragons will help humans? They would rather flame us or eat us than reason with us. Humans have a history of treachery in their dealings with the beasties."

Valerian glanced at Kieran, but his squire was finishing a haunch of mutton.

"I read all the historical accounts in the Keep's library," Valerian said. "There were many references to Alden the Great and his dealings with the dragons. Did you know he made a covenant with them?"

"Aye," Angus said, frowning. "That treaty was broken not long after Alden's death. I dinna mean to discourage ye, Sire, but it worries me that ye would put so much faith in dragons."

Valerian stared into Angus' eyes and *Saw* his distress over the news about the Horde. The man also recognized, alarmed, that Valerian was *Seeing* his thoughts.

"Forgive me, Your Highness. I meant no disrespect."

"There is nothing to forgive." Valerian pushed down his anxiety and stood, staring into the flames of the fireplace. "If the dragons refuse to help us, then Levathia is lost. Those who cannot escape will die." He glanced back at Angus. "I have to find them and convince them to renew the covenant. It's our only hope."

"What Prince Valerian says is the truth, brother," Kieran said, wiping his mouth on his sleeve. "The swarm is an uncountable multitude. Lady Merry saw their purpose, which is tae destroy all living creatures."

"Lady Merry? Who is she?"

Kieran smacked his forehead.

"Ach, brother, I forgot that ye have nae met our future queen. We ourselves found her only about a month ago. She's a Healer and can speak mind-to-mind with Prince Valerian."

"You can speak tae her mind, Your Highness?" Angus raised his bushy brows. "Like the great dragons?"

"That's another reason I have hope I can speak to the dragons." *Though I would rather speak with Merry right now.*

"Well then, Sire," Angus said. "Ye and my brother ought to get a good night's sleep, and we'll hope this blizzard does nae worsen so ye might set out as soon as possible. 'Tis yet a long way from here to the place of your dreams."

Valerian gratefully accepted MacLachlan's offer. Before he lay down, he prayed the dragons would give him a chance to speak, at least. Then he also prayed for Merry's safety. His last waking thought was a wish to speak to her even at this great distance.

Merry first glimpsed the Keep when Stripe crested a rise in the road. The castle was built on the edge of a rocky bluff overlooking a large lake. The stone edifice towered over the walled village below. From this vantage point, it appeared impossible to defeat.

Each rise in the road showed Merry more detail until they came to the outer gates. Life-sized dragons were carved into each of the massive wooden halves. Guards opened them, and the horses' hooves echoed within the gatehouse. Not far away a drawbridge had been lowered over a moat. Beyond the bridge stood a second gatehouse and even taller stone walls with another dragon gate that opened to admit them.

They rode through the snow-covered yard to a long low building along the wall. Nearing the door, Merry saw and smelled a stable. Sir Gregory and the others called out greetings, and several boys and older youths rushed out to take their horses.

Merry slung her carry sack over her shoulder and handed Stripe's reins to a dark-haired lad who smiled shyly.

"I'll take good care of your horse, my lady. Just ask for Conrad when you want to see him."

She smiled at his kindness. Terron stepped forward to speak to the groom.

"This is Lady Merry. She is Prince Valerian's intended bride. And her horse is called Stripe."

Conrad's eyes widened, and he bowed his head.

"I'm honored to meet you, Lady Merry. I will take special care of Stripe. I'll put him in the stall beside Theo."

Merry perked up at the mention of Valerian's horse.

"Have you met Theo, my lady?"

She shook her head. Conrad grinned.

"When you come to see Stripe, I'll introduce you to Prince Valerian's horse."

"Terron," called Sir Gregory. "King Orland awaits."

"We'd best be going, Lady Merry." Terron indicated that Merry should precede him. "No one keeps the king waiting."

Merry's empty stomach churned, making her nauseous. She hadn't expected to meet Valerian's father like this, dressed in filthy riding clothes with a sleeping fur for a cloak, needing a bath, and unable to communicate. Her first meeting with the King of Levathia was supposed to make a good impression, with Valerian at her side to speak for her.

For Valerian's sake, Merry steeled her resolve even while she quaked on the inside. Sir Edmund crawled from his warm nest inside her cloak to sit upon her shoulder. He wrapped his tail around her neck and nuzzled his head against her cheek.

Surrounded by the men she had come to trust on their long journey, Merry entered the tall double doors and continued down a long wide hall. Torches lit their way to another set of doors carved with dragons, smaller versions of the ones on the Keep's massive gates. Two guards wearing the royal dragon on their livery opened the doors at their approach.

Seated on his throne at the far end of a cavernous room was the King of Levathia. He wore a crown upon his dark hair and a purple robe over his golden surcoat. Two men stood to either side of the throne. One was a heavy-set older man, and the other was younger, dressed as a soldier. He had yellow hair and would have been handsome, had he not been scowling.

Merry focused on the king's face. He resembled Valerian except for the severity of his countenance. Had the Brethren stood in this very chamber when they faced him?

Sir Gregory and the others stopped about halfway to the throne and bowed. Merry added her curtsy.

"Come forward," King Orland said in a deep voice.

Merry followed the men. When they reached the open area below the throne, they all went down on one knee, and Merry did likewise.

"You may rise." The king scanned their faces. "Where is Prince Valerian?"

Sir Gregory stepped forward and bowed again.

"Your Majesty, the prince and Kieran MacLachlan have gone north to find the great dragons."

King Orland stood, frowning.

"For what purpose?" His voice shook with anger.

"To ask for their help against the Mohorovian swarm."

"Their help? Their *help*?" The king stepped forward. He clenched his fists. For a moment, Merry feared he would strike Sir Gregory. "Levathia hovers on the brink of destruction, and he goes off on a fool's errand to certain death. It's a good thing he isn't here, or I would—" He stopped, fighting to control his anger. Then he gathered up his robe and reseated himself. His frown deepened.

"Sir Caelis, it appears we must accept that Prince Valerian will not return. You were right; he is utterly unreliable."

The yellow-haired man beside him, who was surely Sir Caelis, inclined his head.

"I wish it were otherwise, Your Majesty, and that you could depend upon the prince in this desperate hour, but alas, 'tis not to be."

No! Merry shouted in her mind. She pressed her hands against her throat and swallowed, fighting to make a sound. After several tries, she felt a resonance there, and at last a raspy "no" came from her lips, startling her. Sir Gregory and all his men turned to look at her in wonder.

"No," she said again. It was barely above a whisper, but she could speak again! She stepped past the astonished men and addressed King Orland. "Valerian is *not* on a fool's errand. The dragons came to him in a vision. They want to speak with him. He has every hope they will come to help us."

King Orland's eyes widened, but his anger had not abated.

"And who are you to speak to me thus?"

She banished the last of her fear and remembered who she was.

"I am Mercy, lately called Merry, of the Village of Peace. I am a direct descendant of King Sigmund. I am also a Healer, and Prince Valerian and I can speak mind-to-mind like the great dragons. I know that he will come, and he will bring the dragons with him."

"Aylmer, *See* this young woman's thoughts and tell me if she speaks the truth." The king gestured to the older man beside him.

So he was a Seer. Merry stared into his eyes and relentlessly sent images of the eggs and the massacred garrisons, and the swarm attacking. Aylmer's eyes widened and he staggered backward.

"Well? What happened? What did you *See*?"

"It is as she has said, Your Majesty." Aylmer swallowed, fearful.

Sir Gregory pulled Valerian's document from his tunic.

"The prince asked me to give this into your hand, Sire. It is from Eldred and explains about Lady Merry."

King Orland broke the seal and scanned the contents. He glanced up at Merry and back at the words. Sir Caelis stared at her, but she ignored him and focused on Valerian's father. He lowered the message to his lap.

"It appears I must call you cousin, Lady Merry. Sir Caelis has reported two of the garrisons fallen to the Horde. What more can you tell me?" King Orland turned his attention from Merry to Sir Gregory, but the knight gestured to Merry.

"I think you should hear from the lady what she and the prince have seen." Gregory smiled at her and said quietly, "I am glad you have found your voice, my lady."

Merry cleared her throat before speaking.

"Part of my gift of Healing, Your Majesty, is being able to see and feel things that would aid in Healing. I believe that my ability to speak to the prince's mind has made that gift even stronger." She swallowed again. Her voice grew more sure.

"Valerian found a nest of eggs, and using my Healing gift I discovered the Horde is swarming, something they do only once every few hundred years. The men at the Southern Garrison were able to seal up that nest, but there are others, we know not how many. Obviously they have hatched and have killed three garrisons already." Merry frowned. "They are coming here and will not stop until they have destroyed everything in their path. That's why Valerian had to go ask the great dragons to help us. It's our only hope."

Sir Caelis stepped forward, sneering at Merry.

"It is *not* our only hope. Your Majesty, with the weapons we have developed, we can hold them off here and make the Horde pay dearly for their arrogance. Have men grown soft, too weak to fight mindless beasts?"

"It is not a matter of weakness, Sir Caelis," Gregory said, projecting his voice. "Men cannot fight an enemy that outnumbers them a thousand to one."

"You exaggerate their numbers." Caelis glared at him.

"Indeed I do not. Gateway Garrison was still standing when you traveled here. We saw it attacked by such a vast swarm that it stretched to the horizon on the Plains of Mohorovia."

"Then I will make sure we have a thousand thousand crossbow bolts ready for this 'swarm' when it comes."

"Gentlemen." King Orland gestured for them to be silent. "Now is not the time to fight amongst ourselves. I am calling a council of war tomorrow morning at nine of the clock. Gather your ideas and present them there. Sir Gregory, have your men eat a hearty meal and get a good night's rest. You've earned it." With those words, he dismissed everyone.

Merry began to leave with the others when the king said, "Not you, Lady Merry." She turned back. Sir Caelis met her gaze before he exited through a side door.

A young boy wearing a dragon emblem on his tunic hurried toward King Orland. He bowed.

"What is your will, Your Majesty?"

Orland removed his crown and handed it to the boy.

"Put this away and then send one of the queen's ladies here." He paused. "What's the name of that new one, the young girl with the yellow hair?"

"Lady Gwendolyn, Sire?"

"Yes, she's the one. Bring her here."

"Yes, Sire." The page bowed and left the room.

Orland glanced down at Merry, less imposing without the crown. Streaks of gray among the darker hairs revealed his age. He winced and shifted on the throne as if something pained him.

"Are you all right, Your Majesty?" Merry took a step closer.

"Merely an old injury that pains me in cold weather."

"Where is the injury? I only ask because I am a Healer."

"My physicians say nothing can be done, that I must simply endure the pain." Orland shrugged.

Merry thought the king's physicians incompetent for saying that, but she would never speak the words aloud.

"If you're willing to let me look, perhaps I can help."

Orland studied her for a moment and then rolled up the leg of his velvet breeches to expose his left knee.

"As a young man I cracked it against a rock when I fell off a galloping horse."

Merry knelt beside him and cupped her hands around his knee. She closed her eyes and *Saw* the place of the old break and the bony spurs that had grown there. Merry opened herself to the Healing gift until she *Saw* the spurs disintegrate. When the bone was clean and whole, she sighed and opened her eyes.

Orland straightened the leg and bent it several times. He stood and walked a few steps. Then, humming to himself, he pivoted and danced back to the throne, seating himself with a flourish.

"I can't begin to thank you, Lady Merry. The pain is gone, and the restricted movement as well." He breathed out a sigh of contentment.

"I'm glad I could help, Your Majesty." She smiled tiredly.

"I saw a light in your hands and felt the power coming from them." He paused and met her gaze. "Truly you are gifted, my dear. I've never heard of abilities such as yours before."

"Apparently it's a very rare gift."

Orland nodded and sat back, studying her.

"You know, since you are a royal cousin, I could make you my ward."

"Valerian was hoping you would do so. He believes I need protection from those who might try to misuse my gift of Healing."

"I had not thought of that, but he is right." Orland stared more closely at her. "I was going to ask the queen to install you with her ladies, but perhaps as my ward you should have your own rooms." He looked up. "Ah, here comes Lady Gwendolyn now."

Merry stood to meet the newcomer. Gwendolyn was about her age with fair skin, and her hair was hidden under a veil. She walked gracefully, the folds of her yellow gown swirling along the floor. When she reached the foot of the throne, she made an elegant curtsy.

"Your Majesty."

"Lady Gwendolyn," said King Orland. "I want you to meet Lady Merry. She is a royal cousin, and I have just made her my ward."

They curtsied to one another. Gwendolyn smiled, and Merry lost her apprehension when she saw that it was genuine. This young lady was nothing like Hanalah.

"Pardon me, Lady Merry, but is that a burrowing dragon?" Even Gwendolyn's voice was pleasant, unlike Hanalah's.

"Yes." Merry coaxed the little dragon to her hand and held him up. "This is Sir Edmund."

"Sir Edmund?" Orland sounded surprised. "I remember him."

"Valerian said he was a dragon-faced knight and suggested the name." Merry met the king's eyes, and he laughed.

"Yes, it's appropriate."

As Merry continued to gaze at Valerian's father, she wanted to be completely honest with him, though her stomach fluttered, unsure of his reaction.

"Your Majesty?"

"Yes, what is it, Lady Merry?"

"I think I ought to tell you that the prince has proposed marriage to me, and I have accepted."

Orland stared at her, not speaking, while a spectrum of emotions passed over his face. Finally, he sighed and spoke quietly.

"An hour ago I would have been very angry that my son went against my wishes. I still feel strongly that an alliance between the House of Alden and the south is essential to bringing about a united Levathia."

"Your Majesty." Merry made her voice as respectful as possible. "I am a southerner. And I have something Lady Hanalah never will."

Orland's eyes widened, but thankfully he was not angry.

"What, pray tell, is that, Lady Merry?"

Merry straightened and folded her hands to hide their trembling.

"Though I am not yet trained in the ways of royalty, I do have royal blood, and I've been gifted by the Most High to speak to the prince mind-to-mind." She smiled as something occurred to her. "That might be a useful talent for Valerian and me to have in your court."

The king's careworn face appeared younger when he smiled.

"My dear Lady Merry, you are full of surprises." Orland held out his hand, and Merry happily grasped it. He brought it to his lips. "Though the choice of the crown prince's bride must, by law, have the consent of the Privy Council, I must say you have earned *my* approval." He clasped Merry's hand between both of his, and his face grew serious again. "Assuming, of course, we survive this attack by the Horde." He addressed Gwendolyn.

"I want Lady Merry to move into Prince Valerian's old apartment, and I want you to be her lady instead of the queen's. I will speak to Winifred myself."

"Yes, Your Majesty." Gwendolyn curtsied.

Orland spoke to Merry again.

"Tonight Lady Gwendolyn will help you settle in and fetch whatever you require. But in the morning I need you to describe the danger approaching us. Will you be able to speak to a hall full of people?"

"Yes, Your Majesty." Merry's voice quavered a little. "For you I would speak to all of Levathia, though my knees will be knocking together."

"Then be gone, ladies," Orland said with mock seriousness. "Until the morrow."

Merry curtsied and followed Gwendolyn to the door behind the throne. It opened into a narrow spiral staircase which led to a second floor.

"There are four apartments here, Lady Merry." Gwendolyn pointed to the first door. "This is the door to Queen Winifred's, and Prince Valerian's old rooms are next door. Across the hall are King Orland's rooms, and next to that the crown prince's."

"Is that where Valerian lives now?"

Gwendolyn paused, and her smile faded.

"Yes, ever since Prince Waryn died, but oddly enough Prince Valerian only spent one night there."

"Why?"

"Didn't you know he was almost killed, too?"

Merry remembered the scar Valerian had shown the boy whose arm she had Healed. She nodded.

"Anyway, these will be your rooms." Gwendolyn tried the door, and it opened. "Good, the page has unlocked it for us, and lit some candles, too."

Merry stepped into the room and immediately felt at ease. Though larger than her cottage, it was simply furnished with a table, a few plain chairs, a single woolen rug, and a tapestry on one wall.

"This was Valerian's old room?"

"This is the solar, the sitting room. Beyond is the bedchamber." Gwendolyn paused and took a step closer. "Is it true, my lady, you are to marry the prince?"

Merry nodded and swallowed noisily. She told Gwendolyn how they'd met, her ability to speak to his mind, how she'd Healed him, and how he'd saved her from the river dragon. Gwendolyn's eyes widened.

"What an incredible story, Lady Merry. I've never known two people who better deserve one another."

"Thank you." Merry smiled timidly. "I know there must be a rule about calling one another 'lady' in public, but in here can't we just use our names?"

"If you wish. Merry." Gwendolyn laughed. "Why do I feel slightly wicked for saying that?" She turned serious. "Do you have any clothes other than what you're wearing?"

"I have two dresses—" Merry stopped, aghast. "They're in Valerian's saddlebag, and he is a long way from here."

Gwendolyn patted her arm.

"Don't worry your head, Merry. You and I are nearly the same size. You can wear my dresses. I'll have a servant move my trunk in here." She rushed out the door, leaving Merry with Sir Edmund and memories of Valerian.

Sir Caelis stormed from the great hall and strode toward his room. He pounded his fist into his palm. The cheek of that Brethren girl! How dare she disagree with him in the king's presence!

She had to be Rafael's sister. Obviously, she was devoted to the prince. There was no way he could simply seduce her. Indeed, unless Valerian was dead, Caelis had no hope of marrying her and securing his place as Orland's heir. He might as well have killed the child and be rid of him.

But, might there yet be a way to use the boy to bend her to his will? Surely she had been quite attached to him. From what Rafael had told him, this sister was the only mother he'd ever known. Would she submit to him if he threatened Rafael's life?

He entered the room and found Drew and Rafael sitting at the small table where Drew was teaching the boy to write his name. They stood as he approached.

Caelis stared down at Rafael. Though he now wore clean clothing, his hair was still long and tangled.

"Is your sister's name Mercy?"

"Yes, sir." The boy's eyes widened. "Have you found her? Where did you see my Sissy?"

Caelis frowned at the memory of her insolence.

"Here in the Keep."

The boy pulled on Caelis' surcoat.

"Please, Sir Caelis, please tell me where to find her!"

Caelis grabbed Rafael's shoulders and shoved him back to the chair.

"I will tell you when I'm ready and not before. It all depends on you."

The boy's lower lip trembled, and tears welled up in his eyes. Caelis continued, relentless.

"Did I not spare your life, Rafael? Have I not protected you, fed you, clothed you over the last month? And asked nothing in return?" The boy nodded. "Then you must help me persuade your sister to marry me. Will you do that, Rafael?"

"Marry you? But she is s'posed to marry Gabriel."

"Gabriel is dead. The Brethren are all dead except you and your sister." He frowned. "You cannot have her back unless she marries me."

Rafael slumped in Caelis' grasp, defeated.

"Yes, Sir Caelis." A tear leaked from his eye and splashed on Caelis' hand.

Caelis turned on Drew.

"I'm going to the armory. I will probably be there all night. Keep Rafael here. If you need anything, send a servant. I forbid you to leave this room. Do you understand me, squire?"

"Yes, sir." Drew's voice was sullen. "Come, Rafael. Let's go to sleep. We will write more tomorrow."

When Caelis opened the door to leave, he glanced back at them. He almost wished Drew would disobey him. He would happily slit the young man's throat if he did.

Chapter 33 *Thou hast sore broken us in the place of dragons, and covered us with the shadow of death.*

Valerian and Kieran plodded through snow drifts, leading their ponies as they headed ever northward. The landscape was an unbroken sea of white. The mountains lay on their left and the plains on the right. The wind had died down, and all was quiet but cold. They seemed to be making very little progress.

"Are you certain we're moving forward?" Valerian said. "We'll never get there in time."

"When the way is clear, 'tis a two day journey. With the snow slowing us, it may take three or more."

"Will we be too late, do you think?" Valerian had never felt such impatience.

"Impossible tae say, Val. We must press on and keep hoping."

Valerian nodded and fell silent. He had too much time to think--about the Horde, about the safety of the people of Levathia, about Merry. Instead, he called to his mind everything he'd ever read about Alden and the dragons.

He knew Alden had led several ships of people from another land across the sea. They'd just begun to settle in Levathia when they clashed with the great dragons and a war ensued. In order to stop the hostilities, Alden had risked his life to treat with the dragons. He'd been able to communicate with them, so he must have been a Seer. He had made some kind of agreement or covenant, but Valerian had never read any of the details. And during Alden's time, swords were still widely used. Also,

Alden had been crowned the first king of Levathia, and because of the covenant he was known as the Dragon King.

Valerian realized he was putting a lot of faith in a covenant made three centuries ago. If he'd not had repeated contact with the dragons, and one, in particular, then this would certainly be a foolish venture. It was more a matter of *knowing* that he must do this than having reasoned it to be the best course of action.

They came to a flat section where the snow had blown away, so Valerian and Kieran were able to ride again. The ponies were as eager to move on as their riders, and Valerian let his have its head. The cleared area didn't last long, however, and they were back to trudging through snowdrifts, though not so deep that the ponies couldn't carry them.

Sometime later, they came to a rushing stream and stopped to let the animals rest and drink the cold mountain water.

"Up ahead we'll cut through the mountains." Kieran pointed ahead to a break between mountain peaks. "We need tae go slowly. As sure-footed as the ponies be, it can be treacherous even for them."

When they reached the pass, Valerian saw what Kieran meant. Because the snow had drifted, in places it was impossible to see the path, and they had to trust the ponies to find their way. In one place, it was literally one step at a time along a ledge with a sheer drop-off. Once Valerian's mount made a bad step, and because his legs were so long and the animal so short, he was able to brace against a rock with one leg while the pony found its footing again.

By the time they reached a likely place to spend the night, Valerian trembled from the cold and exhaustion. He and Kieran wrapped themselves in their sleeping furs and slept soundly.

The second day was a repeat of the first, and the third began even more slowly as a light snow began to fall. But by late afternoon, the snow was melting. Soon the ground was clear. Valerian turned to Kieran for an explanation.

"There are hot springs and pools of boiling mud in these parts," Kieran said. "'Tis why the dragons live here all seasons of the year."

They crested a hill and Valerian gasped. The circle of stones appeared exactly as it had in his dreams. But no dragons were in sight. He closed his eyes and tried to remember if they had appeared at any certain time of day consistently. The light in his visions and dreams indicated early morning.

"Kieran, we must find a place to camp for the night. At first light, I will enter the circle, alone."

They made camp in a sheltered glen. After eating their travel bread in companionable silence, Valerian bedded down on the sleeping furs. What would he dream tonight?

Merry opened her eyes and sighed. She'd slept holding Valerian's pillow, but it was a poor substitute. She wished she knew where he was and what he was doing. If only she could have touched him in her dream. But she couldn't even remember what she'd dreamed about.

Sir Edmund lay curled beside her, giving her some comfort. She sighed again, remembering how Valerian said they'd need a cage for the little dragon before their wedding night. The door to the bedroom opened, and Gwendolyn's face appeared between the bed curtains.

"You're awake. I thought you might be. How did you sleep?"

"Very well, thank you." Merry hugged the pillow. "But I will be happiest with my prince to sleep beside me."

"I hope it won't be long, Merry." Gwendolyn pointed to Sir Edmund. "How does your little dragon like the bed?"

"Much too well, I'm afraid. Might we find a small cage for him? There are times when I can't take him with me, and I don't want him to get lost."

"I'm sure there's an unused bird cage around." Gwendolyn pulled back the bed curtains. "Are you ready to wash and get dressed? King Orland wants you in the great hall at nine. I'm sure you'll want to eat first."

Merry shook her head, swallowing.

"I will be so nervous, I don't want to get sick."

"Then I shall wait, too, so we can eat together."

"I'd like that, Gwendolyn." Merry slid down from the high bed. Sir Edmund perched on the edge, watching. She glanced around the room. "But where shall I wash?"

"I have a basin of warm water ready for you."

While she washed herself, Gwendolyn laid out three dresses. Merry pulled on a clean chemise.

"Those are lovely," Merry said. "May I try the rose-colored one?"

Gwendolyn helped her with the gown, lacing up the back ties and the sleeves.

"It fits you well, Merry." She replaced the other dresses in the trunk and pulled out a veil to match the gown.

Merry undid her clasp and loosened the braid.

"Let me rebraid my hair first." Her hair swirled around her, and Gwendolyn stared.

"I have never seen so much hair in all my life. It's beautiful. Have you never cut it?"

"Not ever. I am almost fifteen, so it has had time to grow."

Merry combed and braided the hair and secured it with the clasp. Her stomach clenched and she grasped Gwendolyn's hand.

"Is it time to go, do you think?"

"Don't worry, Merry. I know you'll be fine." Gwendolyn squeezed her hand. "Meanwhile I'll take care of Sir Edmund for you."

"Thank you." Merry took a deep breath and opened the door. She peered into the hall and saw no one stirring. But as soon as she stepped out of the room, King Orland opened the door to his room across the hall. He wore his purple robe again with the crown upon his head. When he saw her, she curtsied to him.

"Good morrow, Lady Merry. Did you sleep well?"

"Yes, thank you, Your Majesty." She smiled. "Just knowing Valerian used to sleep there was a great comfort to me."

As he came closer, Orland searched her face.

"You and the prince appear to have a strong attachment to one another."

"He is a wonderful man." Merry's heart filled with pride and longing. "You must be very proud of him."

Orland lowered his gaze, and his shoulders sagged.

"Unfortunately I haven't spent enough time with Valerian. I confess I put all my hopes in his older brother, God rest his soul."

Merry reached out and squeezed his hand. Only afterward did she realize that might not be proper. She tried to let go of his hand, but he captured hers between his own.

"Then later when there is more time," she said, "please allow me to tell you about Valerian's strength and his courage and his goodness."

Orland swallowed, obviously affected.

"I look forward to it, Lady Merry. But first, we have a council of war." He kissed her hand before letting go.

When Merry entered the great hall on King Orland's arm, she gasped. The room appeared much smaller, packed with nobles and soldiers. A hush fell over the crowd, and everyone bowed. The king addressed the assembly.

"We have called you here today because the Horde has returned, and the peril is even greater than we expected.

"I call on Lady Merry from the Southern Woodlands, who has seen the threat with her eyes and also with her gift of Healing, as she will explain." He held out his hand for Merry and urged her forward.

Panic rose within her, and she tasted bile, but Merry swallowed, straightened, and let the memory of Valerian's courage sustain her. Fortunately the room was quiet, and she didn't have to speak loudly and strain her throat.

"I do have the gift of Healing, and part of that gift is being able to see inside to know what harms a body, as well as knowing which plants harm and which heal." She glanced at Orland, and he nodded. "I also have the gift of speaking mind-to-mind with Prince Valerian." Some in the crowd murmured, and Merry waited until they grew quiet again.

"The prince found a huge nest of eggs near the Southern Garrison and brought me to see if I could tell when they would hatch. As I touched one of the eggs, I saw much more than I expected. The monsters about to hatch in that nest were connected to other hatchlings in other nests. They are all part of a swarm that happens once every few hundred years. Their only thought is to fill the land and destroy everything in their path." Merry swallowed to ease her throat before continuing.

"When we traveled toward the Keep, we found two garrisons already killed by the Horde and a third under attack by an uncountable swarm, but I'm sure one of the prince's men could better tell you about that." Merry glanced at Orland again, who smiled in approval.

He called upon Sir Gregory who, Merry believed, was honest about the danger. She watched the faces of the nearest people grow more and more alarmed as he spoke.

Finally, King Orland asked Sir Caelis for a progress report about what was being done for the Keep's defense. The knight explained that every available person from the Keep and local villages was either helping to construct weaponry or store supplies within the Keep.

"The crossbow I've designed shoots bolts of wood rather than longer arrows, and in this way can penetrate the Horde's scales. With archers lining the walls, and catapults and cauldrons of boiling water and oil, we'll be ready for the Horde when they come."

After a few questions from the assembled to clarify details, King Orland dismissed them to their preparations for the siege. Merry's only wonder was that evacuation was never mentioned, even for the women and children. But indeed, with that vast swarm, where could any of them run? There was no place to hide.

While King Orland spoke with several of the nobles, Caelis found Rafael's sister standing to one side conversing with a young Highlander. If Caelis didn't need her cooperation so badly, he would happily strangle her. But she was dangerously necessary to his ambition; he needed an heir with her to make his claim to the throne legitimate in the eyes of the nobles.

"Good morrow, Lady Merry." Caelis bowed to her, and the Highlander excused himself.

Her eyes narrowed. She did not show the slightest approval of him.

"You're the one who accused Prince Valerian of being unreliable. That is the farthest thing from the truth."

"Forgive me, my lady, I was misinformed." His smile had no effect upon her, unlike most other young women.

"Excuse me, but I must go now." She turned away and walked back in the direction of King Orland.

Caelis felt an overpowering desire to pull out his knife and slit her throat, right here in front of everyone. Fortunately he reined in his anger and kept it close, smoldering. He watched how she acted so demurely around the other men, pretending shyness. They, of course, were all smitten with her charms.

Think, Caelis. She is a worthy adversary. You must use your head and find a way to turn her wiles back upon her.

For the first time since she'd contradicted him before the king last night, Caelis wanted to laugh. He wasn't going to let a pacifist triumph over him. With a final glance at her comely figure, he left for the armory.

Chapter 34 *I am a brother to dragons.*

Valerian awoke in the predawn stillness. The air was cold but pure, and he inhaled deeply to clear his head.

He had no fear. Instead he felt detached, knowing there was a good chance he was going to die and so was already letting go of this present world. A profound sadness came over him at the thought of never seeing Merry again. He forced himself to set aside the memory of their love in order to focus all his attention on the upcoming confrontation. As long as he *was* alive, there was still some hope he might succeed.

The sky lightened in the east. Valerian stood and rolled up his sleeping furs. He hadn't wanted to wake Kieran, but he needed to wear the royal surcoat, and he could not possibly tie the lacings by himself. When Valerian pulled the garment from his saddle bag, he held it up, staring at the dragon on the front. Would they remember Alden? Did dragons pass down stories and legends as humans did? If not, how could he convince them to help?

Kieran jumped up, suddenly awake. He did not speak, as if he too felt the import of the day. Valerian hated to disturb the quiet.

"I'm sorry, but I need your help with this blighted surcoat."

In silence, Kieran adjusted the garment with sure hands. Valerian tried to breathe evenly and deeply to still his apprehension. It was difficult to keep his imagination in check, for all his imaginings had one end—his death.

When Kieran finished with the lacings, he stepped back to examine his handiwork.

"I dinna see how you could look more royal, Your Highness."

"Thank you, Kieran." He *Saw* his squire's admiration and respect. It was humbling.

"Did ye dream in the night?" Kieran asked.

"If I did, I don't remember. I hope that means the dragons know I have come." Valerian grasped Kieran's arm. "If I don't return, promise me you will ride to the Keep and make sure everyone knows they must leave Levathia."

"I hope I won't be needing to keep that promise, Val." Kieran's face was solemn.

"One more thing." Valerian shut his eyes as the grief stabbed him a final time. "Tell Merry that I love her. Keep her safe."

"I want ye tae tell her yourself. That's what I'll be praying for while you're over there." Kieran pointed toward the circle of stones.

The sun peered over the horizon, bathing the stones with a reddish light. Valerian glanced at Kieran, who nodded. Then Valerian turned and walked toward the dragons' sacred place.

It was much farther than it appeared from their campsite. Eventually, he entered the stand of giant oaks. They could have been a thousand years old, gnarled and twisted by wind and weather. Beside them, Valerian felt like an insect—insignificant and short-lived.

Just as he was about to step out in the open and enter the stone circle, a bugling call pierced the air, resonating down his spine. While he watched, an enormous dragon spiraled down from the sky and landed in the center of the circle. It stood on four legs and folded back leathery wings. Its scales shimmered blue-green in the sunlight. As it walked, the dragon's long tail carved a trench in the dirt, marking its passage.

Other dragons answered as they flew toward the circle. Valerian saw why the stones were spread so far apart. He counted at least threescore of the great beasts, and more were coming down to land within the confines of the holy place.

Valerian drew Alden's sword to make it visible. Instead of holding it to the ready, he gripped the blade just below the hilt and held the point downward to show his peaceful intentions. Then, praying he could at least enter the circle before dying, he stepped out from the cover of the trees and walked the rest of the distance to the stones. He paused between two of them and opened his mind and his heart to hear the dragons.

I am Valerian, son of Orland, of the house of Alden.

With the absolute calm of one who has accepted death, he stepped into the circle. Though Valerian sensed the stares of many dragon eyes, he focused on the summoner, who must be the leader. When it brought its terrible head down close to Valerian, he could smell sulfur coming from its nostrils. Each of its great eyes was larger than his head.

You are of Alden? The dragon's voice sounded loud and majestic in Valerian's mind.

Yes, my lord dragon. I come bearing his sword. He held the blade higher, hoping the dragon might recognize it.

Other voices spoke in Valerian's mind:

This human has profaned our holy place.

Burn him! Kill him!

The leader rose up on its hind legs and roared at the others. Valerian almost dropped the sword at the deafening sound. His legs began to shake uncontrollably. He drew in a ragged breath to calm himself.

The dragon dropped back to all fours and lowered its head again, close enough that Valerian could have reached up and touched it.

Why have you come to our sacred place?

I saw you in my dreams. You bade me come.

I? I do not remember. The dragon narrowed its eyes. *You are a Seer. Perhaps it was a Seeing dream.* It tilted its head to better inspect Valerian. *You wear Alden's dragon. You carry his sword. What do you want of us?*

Valerian went down on one knee and set the sword before him.

I humbly ask, for the sake of the covenant which you made with Alden, that you renew that covenant with me, his descendant. The land is threatened with destruction by the Horde. We need your help to defeat them.

The voices began again:

Why should we help humans? They want to destroy us!

Let the Horde annihilate them, so we may have the land to ourselves once more.

This time when the leader reared up, he flamed two lesser dragons nearby. They crumpled in pain, keening. Valerian held up a trembling gloved hand to protect his eyes from the searing heat. Sulfurous fumes assaulted his nostrils.

Which of you challenges my authority?

No other dragon dared speak. Once more the leader turned to Valerian.

Are you king, then?

No, my lord dragon. I am son of the present king, Orland.

Has he had no visions or dreams that he might find our holy place?

None, my lord dragon. The Sight only came to me upon the death of my elder brother by the Horde. My dreams of you and this place began then, as well. He showed the dragon, as Merry had shown him, the great numbers of the swarm.

The Horde has been our enemy for millennia. They will destroy everything that is good.

The dragon turned again to address those assembled.

I was young when we swore allegiance to Alden, but I remember the goodness of his heart. This descendant of Alden, son of the king, also has the gift of Sight.

While the dragons discussed the matter mind-to-mind, Valerian stared at the magnificent leader. He had known Alden, had been part of the original covenant. Valerian shivered to think of that connection with the past and prayed it would be enough to enlist the support of the rest of the dragons.

He glanced down, and the gold threads of the dragon blazoned on the surcoat glinted in the morning light. For all his life, he'd been surrounded by representations of dragons, but had never realized their significance until now. His was an unbroken line from Alden the Dragon King, and now he had the great responsibility to continue that line. With Merry, he remembered. She was also descended from Alden, and she had gifts vital for Healing the land and its people. Together they could bring peace to Levathia, if the dragons agreed to help.

We have made our decision, the leader spoke to his mind. Valerian held his breath. *I have been reminded that humans have tried to deceive us in the past, claiming to be of Alden when they were not, and my own sire devised a test to prove a human's worthiness. Will you submit to this test, Valerian, son of Orland?*

I will. Beside the leader, one of the lesser dragons lashed its tail and opened its mouth, revealing long sharp teeth. Valerian shuddered. What had he just agreed to?

Then his attention was drawn back to the leader. The great dragon's eyes glittered as its powerful mind pierced Valerian's, pressing so hard Valerian gasped at the stabbing pain in his temples. It seared much worse than when Merry sent an overload of images, as if the dragon flamed the inside of his head. But his experiences with Merry helped him bear the onslaught without losing consciousness. He panted, and a moan escaped him, but he stayed on his knees, gripping the sword and swaying.

Without warning, the dragon withdrew from Valerian's mind, and at the sudden absence of pressure and pain, he collapsed. Beneath him, the ground shuddered from the movement of dragons all around him.

The human is false! Burn him!

No! The great dragon leader reared up and roared. *The human survived the test.*

Valerian pushed himself unsteadily to his feet. He met the dragon leader's gaze. Between them was a new rapport, and Valerian bowed as profoundly as his shaky balance allowed.

You are the first to ever survive the test. The dragon inclined his massive head. *I am Albinonix, First of the Great Dragons. For the sake of the land, and to honor the covenant we once made with Alden, we will renew that covenant with you, Prince Valerian, Son of Orland, of the House of Alden.*

And then Valerian fully understood his dreams and visions, as every dragon present reared up on its hind legs with a mighty roar that shook the ground. Exultant, Valerian grasped the hilt of Alden's sword and raised it with both hands. He lifted his face heavenward.

"To the honor of Lord Alden and the glory of the Most High!"

Merry lingered in the great hall, waiting for King Orland. Many of the nobles introduced themselves, but she could not remember most of their names. Some asked her questions about the Horde nest and the swarm. One heavy-set man even wanted to know more about how her Healing gift had revealed that information to her. She answered their questions, but she was growing weary, and her belly growled with hunger. Finally, the assembly dispersed, and Orland approached her with a quiet smile.

"That was a productive session, thanks to you. Siege preparations are begun, and most of the nobles have agreed to evacuate their families to the coast."

"I'm glad, Your Majesty." Merry recalled Valerian and Sir Gregory talking about the need to leave the country, if nothing could be done to stop the swarm. She suddenly became light-headed, and Orland caught her arm.

"Are you all right, Lady Merry?"

"Only tired, Sire, and hungry. I did not eat before I came."

He helped her to a chair and gestured for a page to attend him.

"Run to the kitchen and bring the lady a cup of nectar. Bring food, too." The page bowed and rushed from the room.

Nectar. Merry had forgotten about its restorative powers. Orland sat beside her in another chair, watching her closely. She was touched by his concern when he had much weightier matters on his mind.

"Having seen the Horde with your eyes and with your mind, do you think we should attempt to fight them here? Or would it be the better part of valor to build ships and take the people elsewhere?" Orland's eyes pleaded with her for reassurance just as Rafael used to do, and Merry felt great sorrow for him.

"I have no experience in matters of war, Your Majesty. I only know that time is short, too short to move an entire land of people. I have faith that Valerian will come and bring the great dragons with him."

"I would like to share your faith, Lady Merry." He fell silent.

The page returned with a tray of food and a flask with two cups. He set it upon a small table and placed it between the king and Merry. Then he bowed and moved back.

Merry ate bread and cheese and winterfruit, but did not touch the meat. If Orland noticed, he did not mention it. He poured nectar in both cups and handed one to her. Then he touched his cup to hers, and they drank in comfortable silence.

When Merry's strength returned, Orland stood and offered his arm. After they climbed the stairs to the royal wing, he turned to her.

"Queen Winifred has expressed a desire to meet you. I want to introduce you to her."

"I would be glad to meet the queen, Sire." The queen, Valerian's mother. Could they be friends, as she and his father were already becoming?

King Orland knocked on the queen's door, and a young woman opened it. Her eyes widened when she saw who stood there.

"Your Majesty." She made a graceful bow. Her dark hair was caught up in a jeweled net.

"Lady Brenna," Orland said. "I wish to see the queen."

"Of course, Sire. Please come in and make yourselves comfortable. I will fetch Her Majesty." Brenna curtsied again and hurried through another door.

Merry glanced around the room, noting the feminine furnishings. Did Valerian's parents live separately, then? Did they not have a happy marriage? Before she and Orland could sit down, a stately woman entered the room. Her face was familiar to Merry, though it was not possible they had ever met.

"Hello, Winifred." Orland's smile was sorrowful.

"Good morrow. What may I do for you?" Even the queen's voice was elegant.

Orland took Merry's hand.

"Meet my new ward and royal cousin, Lady Merry."

"Oh?" Winifred sounded surprised. "How did you discover she is a cousin?"

Orland cleared his throat.

"Valerian found her while he was in the Southern Woodlands."

"What I mean to say is can you prove her lineage?" The queen glanced at Merry and frowned. "There have been so many pretenders."

Merry was taken aback. Valerian's mother was definitely not as welcoming as his father had been. How could she approach her?

Orland huffed and balled his fists on his hips.

"I have written proof from Eldred, if you would like to see it for yourself."

Merry smiled at Orland to reassure him. Then she gave her full attention to the queen.

"Your Majesty, I am no pretender. I was content to live a simple life in the Village of Peace. But after my village was massacred, Valerian found me. Then I met Eldred, and we were able to determine that I am a direct descendant of King Sigmund, who changed his name to Absalom and became the founder of the peaceful Brethren. I must also tell you that your son has proposed marriage to me, and I have accepted, and he and I can speak mind-to-mind, like the great dragons."

Winifred's eyes grew larger at each of Merry's statements. She reached back to grab the arm of the nearest chair and lowered herself to it.

"That is an extraordinary story, Lady Merry."

Orland took the chair beside his wife.

"This is an extraordinary young woman, Winifred. She has the gift of Healing."

The queen stared at her until Merry grew uncomfortable. Merry wished she could read her thoughts as Valerian could. At last, Winifred found her voice.

"You wish to marry my son?"

"Oh, yes, Your Majesty." Merry caught herself before her enthusiasm ran away with her.

But Winifred must have seen what was in her heart.

"You love him, do you?"

"With all of my heart. He is a wonderful man. You must be very proud of him."

"Proud of him?" Valerian's mother frowned again, which was not the reaction Merry expected from her.

Orland indicated a vacant chair to Merry.

"Pray, Lady Merry, be seated and tell us what you've seen in the prince."

Merry sat facing Valerian's parents, eager to enlighten them. She began with their first meeting, how Valerian had been able to *See* her words, not just her thoughts.

"He's a Seer?" Winifred cried.

"I did not know myself," Orland said with a shrug.

Merry related their entire journey, how Valerian had cared for her, helped Ruddy with his first court, saved her from the river dragon, shown decisive leadership regarding their discovery of the Horde swarm. She explained about his dreams and visions which he'd believed were the dragons communicating to his mind.

"I might have believed them ordinary dreams, if I had not been awakened to my gifts of Healing and speaking mind-to-mind with the prince."

Valerian's parents sat, stunned, unable to speak for several minutes. Finally, the king gazed at the queen with a sad smile.

"It appears I have misjudged our youngest son."

Winifred's eyes filled with tears.

"I have been so blind," she whispered.

"We both have." He held out his hand to her, palm up. She slowly placed her hand in his, and he brought it to his lips.

Merry's heartbeat quickened. Something precious had begun, a restoration of love, and she had been privileged to witness it.

The king and queen turned their attention back to Merry. Her joy spilled over, and she could no longer contain her smile. Orland offered her his other hand, which she gratefully squeezed.

"Thank you, Lady Merry. You are truly a gift from heaven." He kissed her hand and released it, looking once more at the queen. "I must leave you now, Winifred, for I have another council meeting shortly. But, if you are willing, I would like to renew our conversation later this evening." His eyes were intent upon his wife.

Winifred smiled shyly, as if she were out of the habit of doing so.

"I would like that very much." Orland kissed her hand again, leaving the ladies to themselves.

After collecting herself, Valerian's mother focused again on Merry.

"How old are you, my dear?" Winifred straightened her skirts though she did not look away from Merry's face.

"I will be fifteen after two new moons."

"You are wise beyond your years."

"I had to become a mother to my newborn brother when I was only ten. Our mother died in childbed." Merry swallowed to ease the sudden tightness in her throat.

"Then I am sorry for you and for her." A shadow darkened Winifred's face. "I lost a baby girl at birth and also her older sister." She closed her eyes. "It appears I have not coped with my grief as well as you have."

"Perhaps when I marry your son I might call you 'mother,' with your permission, of course." Merry spoke quietly, feeling shy.

“Why, you will be my daughter-in-law, won't you?” Winifred's eyes softened, making her appear younger and more beautiful. “I would like that.” She cleared her throat. “I understand the king gave you my newest lady-in-waiting.”

“Gwendolyn?” When she nodded, Merry smiled. “We get along very well. I hope it doesn't inconvenience you.”

“Heavens, no. I have more attendants than I need.”

While Winifred called one of her ladies to bring refreshments, Merry studied the sitting room, cozy with a fire on the hearth. Embroidered cushions graced every seat. A chair in the far corner of the room held a red pillow and coverlet with a familiar design. Merry stood and walked closer. With a shaking hand, she picked up the pillow. On it were embroidered morning glories, the exact color and design as on Gabriel's hair clasp. Gabriel, who would have been her husband.

“That is my family's emblem,” Winifred said.

“It's lovely.” Trembling, Merry turned to face her. “Did you have a large family, Your Majesty?”

“I had one elder brother, who inherited our father's estate and is now Duke of Frankland, one younger sister who died of a fever, and the youngest, who was a boy.”

“Is your younger brother still alive?” The pulse pounded in Merry's head.

“I don't know, Lady Merry. He and Father had a terrible argument, and he ran away.” She paused. “We never saw him again.”

Merry walked back and knelt beside Winifred's chair.

“Forgive me, I did not mean to call unpleasant memories to your mind.”

“My dear, except for that one argument, I have no unpleasant memories of my brother. I only wish I knew what happened to him.”

Merry stared into her eyes.

“I think I know what happened to him.”

“How could you have known my brother?” She frowned at Merry.

Merry paused, choosing words she hoped would give the queen peace and not pain.

"About ten years ago, a man came to our village. He was sick and had been badly hurt by robbers. My father was the Healer and brought the stranger to our cottage to better tend to his injuries.

"The man stayed with us for many weeks, became part of our family. He learned about the ways of the Brethren and chose to take the Oath of Peace. He put aside his birth name and became known as Gabriel."

"What was his birth name?" Winifred whispered.

"I was very young, but I still remember. His name was Denis."

Winifred's eyes grew bright with tears.

"How can you be sure he was my Denis?"

"I watched him carve and paint a wooden clasp for his braid with the same emblem of morning glories as on this pillow." Her throat tightened, and she could not continue.

Winifred stared at the pillow in Merry's hands.

"What happened to him?"

"Gabriel became zealous in his new life and was a natural leader. Everyone noticed it. When my grandfather, who was the village leader, lay dying, he appointed Gabriel to take his place."

"And Father thought he would never do anything worthy." Winifred's gaze unfocused.

"That's not all." Merry paused. "Gabriel asked for my hand. I would have married him, had he lived."

Winifred turned her attention back to Merry.

"How did he die?"

Merry breathed deeply to ease the tightness in her chest and focused on the flame of a small candle.

"Gabriel, along with everyone in my village, was massacred. Valerian believes it was the Horde." She swallowed and continued in a whisper. "I found Gabriel lying in the grass with a terrible wound in his chest. He had a smile on his face." She glanced back at the queen. "Your brother had great faith in the Most High and no fear of death."

For several minutes, Winifred remained silent, deep in thought. Then she placed her hand on Merry's arm.

"Did you love him? Did you love my brother?"

Merry vividly remembered those two last happy days she'd spent with Gabriel before everything changed.

"I did. He was easy to love. But I must be completely honest with you. I did not love Gabriel as much as I love Valerian."

A tear spilled over Winifred's cheek.

"Thank you for telling me about Denis, or I should say, Gabriel." She dabbed at her cheek with the back of her hand. "I must beg you to leave me for a while, but please come back tomorrow."

"Of course I will." Merry stood and curtsied. Upon her return to Valerian's old rooms, she determined to bring Gabriel's hair clasp, if not the whole braid, to share with Queen Winifred.

In the small hours of the night, Caelis made his way through the secret passageway that led to Prince Valerian's old bedchamber. He slipped through the hidden panel in the wall and approached the canopied bed. With his eyes adjusted to the darkness, the sliver of moonlight through the window was enough to ensure that her maid was not in the room, though she was certainly in the next one. Caelis silently found an opening in the bedcurtains. Lady Merry lay on her side, clutching a pillow. How he wished he could take that pillow and snuff out her life. But she was much more valuable to him alive.

Caelis eased himself up on the bed and clamped one hand over her mouth. Her eyes flew open, and she struggled against him. He leaned close and spoke to her ear.

"You would be wise not to cross me again, my lady. I have something of great value to you, and it would be a shame for it to be lost forever."

She stopped struggling and stared at him.

"I have in my possession a young boy with blue eyes and long hair. If you promise not to cry out, I will tell you more."

Her eyes widened and she nodded. He let go of her mouth.

"Rafael? Where did you find him?" She had a desperate look on her face, and Caelis smiled; this he could use.

"Come, and I will show you." Caelis slid off the bed, found a candle on the bedside table and lit it. Then he pulled from his tunic the order written in Valerian's hand and opened it. When she climbed down, shivering in her white chemise, he showed it to her. "Do you recognize the handwriting?"

"I cannot read." She pushed back the heavy curtain of her unbound hair.

"Then I will read it to you. It says, '*I, Valerian d'Alden, by the grace of God, Prince of Levathia, do decree that the pacifists known as the Brethren, of the Village of Peace in the Southern Woodlands, must forfeit their lives as set forth in the King's Statutes for Times of War because of their refusal to fight to protect the citizens of Levathia against a hostile force invading from Mohorovia.*' And it is signed by Prince Valerian. This is his seal."

She took a step backward. "I don't believe you. He wouldn't order that."

"He would, and he did. My men and I were sent to do the deed. I could not kill your brother, however, and so I have taken care of him since that terrible day."

"Valerian would not have ordered that. I know him too well. I know his mind and his heart." She clenched her fists. "You're lying."

Caelis grabbed her shoulders and forced her back against the high bed.

"Your precious Valerian is not what you think him to be. Either he has run away like the coward he's always been, or he has been killed by the great dragons, who hate all humans. King Orland has no other heirs. If you, indeed, have royal blood, then it is your obligation, your duty to bear an heir so the line of Alden, unbroken for three hundred years, is not lost. If you want to see your brother again, you must marry me and produce that child."

"Are you mad? Do you really think I would agree to marry you?" She struggled against him.

"Yes. Because if you do not, your brother's life is forfeit."

"I will go to King Orland."

"Go." Caelis released her. "But while you are speaking with the king, I will go and slit your brother's throat."

She gasped, swaying on her feet.

"No! How can you be such a monster?"

"I am no monster. But I am a ruthless man and will take what I want. And you will not stand in my way, or you and your brother will die."

Caelis stared at her. "Well? Are you going to tell the king? Or will you do as I say and be reunited with Rafael?"

She clenched her fists.

"How do I know you really have my brother?"

Caelis pulled Rafael's old shirt from inside his tunic.

"He no longer needs this homespun. I have given him finer clothing."

Merry snatched the shirt from him and held it to her chest.

"I would have to see Rafael before I would ever agree to marry you."

"Then you will have to wait." Caelis sneered. "I must return to the armory and prepare for siege. I intend to save Levathia with weapons and tactics that will actually work, not following dreams of dragons. King Orland will be glad to marry his royal cousin to such a hero." He bowed to her and exited through the secret door.

While Caelis made his way back through the passageway, he felt a rush of exhilaration when he realized there was still a small chance she would go to the king. He reveled in that danger almost as much as he looked forward to the coming attack by the Horde.

Chapter 35 *His breath kindleth coals, and a flame goeth out of his mouth.*

Valerian and Kieran urged their mountain ponies to go as fast they could, struggling to keep up with the flight of the great dragons.

"It's no use," Kieran shouted. "The ponies canna keep up this pace."

Before Valerian could form a question to ask Albinonix, the dragon leader spoke first.

Your puny mounts can never match our speed.

Yes, my lord. Indeed, their hearts will burst if we push them like this.

There is a table of land ahead. We will meet you there. With a burst of speed Albinonix and the rest disappeared over the hill.

"Where did the dragons go, Sire?"

"They're waiting for us."

The horses crested a hill. Below them lay a plateau, lightly dusted with snow. The dragons had landed. Valerian directed his frightened pony toward Albinonix, but he stopped before they got too close. The poor animal heaved from exertion and rolled its eyes in terror at the nearness of the dragons.

Leave your beasts of burden. They will find their way home. We will carry you.

My lord, do you mean my squire and I are to ride upon you?

Yes. It has never been done, but we think it will be possible.

Valerian dismounted and turned to Kieran.

"My friend, you and I are going to ride a dragon."

"What?" Kieran slid down, his eyes wide.

"Take only what you must. Hopefully, the ponies will find their way back to the garrison."

"Aye, they will."

Valerian took his sword and a flask of water, and Kieran did likewise.

We're ready, Lord Albinonix.

My prince, you shall ride on me, and your man on Tetratorix. The dragon nodded at a lesser beast beside him, who dipped its head. *We believe you can sit at the base of our necks where the ridges are more widely spaced.*

Yes, I see a likely place. "Kieran, you will ride on Tetratorix. Watch as I climb on Albinonix."

"Aye, Sire."

Valerian approached the greatest of the dragons, who crouched down, watching him with his enormous eye. After bowing to Albinonix, Valerian carefully climbed upon his foreleg. It was tricky to mount the dragon's neck, but once seated where the neck met the shoulders, Valerian hoped he would be able to hold on, unless the dragon decided to fly upside down.

Kieran took his place on the lesser dragon's back and grinned at Valerian.

Hold on, and we will go aloft. It will feel as if we are falling.

Valerian did not understand what Albinonix meant. The two dragons made their way to the edge of the plateau. Huge muscles rippled beneath Valerian's legs. Even with the warning, he was unprepared for the power in the dragon's loins as he sprang from the edge of the drop-off and caught the air with his mighty wings. Valerian's head snapped back against the hard ridge behind him, and he instinctively gripped with his knees as well as his hands.

In no time, the dragon achieved an altitude higher than the Keep's lookout tower. When Valerian glanced below, his stomach leaped into his throat, and he had to swallow convulsively to keep from retching. He turned his gaze outward until the nausea calmed. Beyond the tiny specks of their ponies galloping across the snowy plain, a river snaked along like a silvery ribbon and vanished beyond the horizon. Then the view disappeared while the dragons flew up into the clouds, but shortly they emerged above them. The great line of snow-covered mountain peaks known as the Dragon's Backbone came into view. Valerian now appreciated that appropriate name.

Valerian's cloak whipped around his head, and even though it was colder aloft, he tugged it off. Without its obstruction, Valerian could see for miles from this height. He lifted his hands in exultation, laughing at the marvel of flying.

You are magnificent, he told Albinonix.

A rumble came from the dragon's belly, vibrating through Valerian's legs. Did the dragon laugh?

In all creation there is not our like, Albinonix said. *We are made without fear.*

In one hour, the dragons traveled the distance that he and Kieran and their sturdy ponies had taken days to traverse. The rectangular shape of the Northern Garrison was visible below, and Valerian cried out at the swarm of Mohorovians approaching.

I see them, my prince. Never fear, we can deal with those creatures.

At an unspoken signal, the dragons dove toward the massed Horde. Valerian's eyes teared in the cold wind. He blinked to see what was happening.

Beneath him the dragon's belly rumbled strong enough to shake Valerian's teeth. Albinonix descended so quickly, it appeared he would crash into the Horde's army. A burst of flame shot from the dragon's mouth, incinerating a long swathe in the ranks. Heat and sulfur fumes blew back in Valerian's face, and he threw up his gloved hands to protect his eyes. The dragon veered up and away, and Valerian had to grab hold of the ridge to keep from falling off. His heart had never pounded so strongly before, even during battle.

When he could see again, Valerian marked the dragons' strategy. Each knew the limit of his flame, and so they flew in formation to inflict the most damage with each pass. By the time Albinonix had made three passes, flaming hundreds of Mohorovians each time, the dragons managed to destroy nearly all of this swarm.

My lord, Valerian said, *did any of the Horde get inside the garrison?*

I do not believe so, my prince. I will fly closer so you can better see. He veered down toward the garrison walls.

Men on the walls cheered. Albinonix flew close enough for Valerian to recognize individuals, including Kieran's brother. When Valerian waved his hands over his head, Angus whooped loud enough for him to hear.

They are all flamed, my prince. Shall we go now to the Keep?

Yes, my lord. As quickly as you can.

With the cold air whistling past, Valerian held on as the great dragon lifted higher, leading the others west.

Merry could not sleep after Caelis left. She couldn't stop trembling. She wanted to call out to Gwendolyn, but what would she tell her? Caelis was just the sort of person to do Rafael harm no matter what Merry did or didn't do. Rafael was alive! But how horrifying to know her brother was here in the Keep under the control of that man, and she was powerless to do anything about it.

Valerian. She called out to him, knowing he couldn't possibly hear her. *I know you could not have written those words. Caelis must have used it to gain power over you.* She gasped. If Caelis and his men had killed everyone except Rafael, then they were in the south at the same time she and Valerian and Kieran were at Ruddy's house. Could Caelis have sent those men to kill Valerian? And what about Gabriel's braid? Another of Caelis' men could have dropped it, for they must have been the ones who'd scalped the Brethren.

She wept then for all the horrors this one man had caused, all the needless pain and suffering. If it weren't for Rafael, she would go straight to the king and ask him to arrest Caelis. But, how could she risk her brother's life?

What if she agreed to marry Caelis in order to buy time for Rafael, and then when Valerian came he could help her sort things out? She grabbed his pillow and hugged it close. And what if he never returned? What would happen then?

Tears splashed the pillow. Had she lost faith in Valerian? Of course, he would return. She need only wait until then and together they could deal with Caelis.

The room grew brighter, and Merry walked to the window, opening the curtains to admit the light of a new day. Merry shivered in her chemise and moved closer to the fireplace where the dying embers still held some warmth. To still the trembling of her hands, Merry braided her hair.

She started when she heard a sound like the Brethren's summoning bell. This, however, was much louder and more urgent. She rushed to the door, but Gwendolyn opened it first.

"My lady, that is the call for an emergency."

"The Horde. It must be the Horde." Merry covered her mouth, trying to hold back her fear.

"Let me help you dress so I can take you to the infirmary. Since you are a Healer, you will be needed there." Gwendolyn opened the trunk and pulled out a sensible dress. Just as she finished lacing it, a knock sounded at the door to the sitting room. They looked at one another, and Gwendolyn hurried to answer it.

"Drew? What are you doing here?" She let him in.

Merry was curious why Gwendolyn appeared so flustered about this young man until she saw his obvious admiration. But Merry forgot all of that when she saw who had come with Drew.

A cry stuck in her throat as she met her brother's gaze. Her heart pounded, and his eyes grew wide.

"Sissy?" He took a step toward her.

"Rafael." She knelt and held out her arms. He ran to her, and she held him, sobbing.

Merry stroked his unbraided hair. He felt thin, and she pulled back to look at his face. He had dark circles under his eyes. Merry sat in the nearest chair and invited Rafael to sit in her lap. Shyly he sat with her, and she rocked him, kissing his head. She glanced up at Drew.

"Thank you for bringing him here."

"It was the right thing to do, my lady." Drew bowed.

Merry shivered. This young man had risked his life bringing Rafael here.

"Gwen, bolt the door." She did so. "Will you introduce us, please?"

"Drew, this is Lady Merry, royal cousin of King Orland and future wife of Prince Valerian." Gwendolyn smiled at Drew's surprise. "Lady Merry, this is Drew. He was formerly squire to Prince Waryn and now to Sir Caelis."

Merry nodded. That explained how Drew was able to help Rafael escape from Caelis. Drew went down on one knee and placed his fist over his heart.

"If I survive the upcoming battle, I stand ready to go to the king and formally charge Sir Caelis with treason."

"I'll stand with you. I know the king will listen to me." Merry frowned. "But can you stay away from Caelis until then?"

"I know what part of the wall he plans to defend and can make sure I'm nowhere near there." Drew cleared his throat. "I'm sorry, my lady. I protested when Sir Caelis attacked your village and refused to participate, but I was not able to stop him."

Rafael reached out a hand and touched Drew's shoulder.

"You saved me."

Drew grasped Rafael's hand and smiled.

"I'm glad you have your Sissy again." He looked back at Merry. "How were you spared from the massacre? And how did you come to find the prince? Or did he find you?"

"Do you have time to hear the story?" Merry asked. "Or should you be somewhere now?"

Drew sat on a nearby stool, and Gwendolyn stood beside him, holding his hand.

"The bell means the lookout has seen something. It won't become urgent until the trumpet sounds for battle." Drew grimaced. "Prince Valerian and I were squires together for Prince Waryn. I would very much like to hear what happened."

First Merry explained how she had gone to the river before dawn on that fateful day. She skipped the details of finding and burning the bodies and began with meeting Kieran and Valerian. Even though Gwendolyn had heard much of the information, she listened almost as eagerly as Drew.

"Thank you, lady," he said when she'd finished. "I pray the prince is able to find the dragons."

Rafael stared up at her.

"Sissy, are you really getting married?"

"Yes, love. You'll like Valerian." She turned to Gwendolyn. "Let's show him Sir Edmund."

Gwendolyn ran to the bedchamber.

"Who is Sir Edmund?" Drew asked.

"Valerian and Kieran found him and brought him to me. I was able to Heal him, Rafael, so the gift works on animals as well as people."

Rafael jumped up when Gwendolyn entered the room. She held a bird cage. Merry smiled at her brother's expression when he saw what was inside.

"A dragon! May I touch him, Sissy?"

Merry opened the door of the cage, and Sir Edmund scampered up her arm to her shoulder. She coaxed him to her hand, and he sat watching Rafael, flicking out his forked tongue. When he crawled onto Rafael's forearm, the boy stood still, grinning.

"I wish I had one," he whispered.

"You do." Merry stroked his hair, hardly believing he was here.

At that moment, trumpets sounded the call to battle. Drew jumped up.

"My lady, I must go."

Merry caught his arm.

"Be careful." There was so much she wanted to say to him, but there was no time.

Drew glanced with longing at Gwendolyn.

"I'll be back. I hope." He unbolted the door.

"Wait!" Gwendolyn kissed him soundly. Drew hugged her and then walked backward out the door, watching her until the last possible moment. Gwendolyn secured the door behind him.

"Ah, Merry. Is this the end of all things?"

I hope not. "We must have hope, Gwendolyn. Let me fetch my carry sack and then you must take us to the infirmary."

"What about Sir Edmund?" Gwendolyn indicated the dragon perched on Rafael's arm.

"Bring him," Merry said, "but put him in the cage."

While she waited for Gwendolyn, Merry tried to pray, but her anxious mind could not form the words.

At the sound of the alarm bell, Caelis ran from the armory and into the castle yard. He stared up at the lookout tower, but couldn't tell who was manning it. Probably Hawk now that he'd returned; he had the longest eyes of anyone Caelis knew.

Anticipating an attack, Caelis returned to the armory.

"Keep working on those bolts," he told the apprentices at the tables. "I must supervise the placement of the soldiers." He adjusted the armored plates that Murray had designed to fit over his padded tunic. He felt invincible as he snatched up his crossbow and quiver of bolts, slinging both over his shoulder. He climbed the tower stairs two at a time and walked the perimeter of the battlements, making sure there were standing quivers of bolts at close regular intervals.

By the time he completed a circuit of the wall, the trumpet sounded for battle. Caelis climbed to the lookout tower and found Hawk on duty.

"What do you see?" he asked the young man.

"The Horde, Sir Caelis, many more than we saw attacking Gateway Garrison."

Caelis searched the valley beyond the walls. A massed army moved rapidly forward, like a swarm of ants.

"How could they have gotten here so quickly?"

"They must have run all the way from the plains." Hawk frowned. "I still do not see an end to their numbers."

Caelis had seen enough.

"We'll either stop them or die trying." He raced down the tower steps and emerged on the battlements. Soldiers rushed to their assigned posts along the wall.

"Wait 'til they're in range," he shouted to the men. "Make every shot count." Caelis glanced down in the yard to make sure the four catapults were aimed properly. He would have to hope that Sir Brandon had things well in hand, for he had more than enough to occupy his attention.

When the Horde neared the Keep, they spread out to surround the three approachable walls. Caelis saw no siege ladders, but he remembered how those at the garrison had used their bodies to make living ladders. The garrison walls were much shorter than the Keep's outer defenses, and Caelis had put all his trust in the fact that the monsters would be easier to cut down while exposed to the crossbow archers. He just hadn't realized there would be so *many* of them. There would not be nearly enough bolts, even if the archers didn't waste a single one.

For the first time, Caelis doubted they could survive this attack.

Chapter 36 *Thou hast covered my head in the day of battle.*

Shivering in the cold air aloft, Valerian exulted in the abilities of the great dragons. For the first time, he felt truly hopeful they could defeat the Horde's swarm.

Then something below chilled his heart. Though still many miles from the Keep, already the swarm was visible below. Their massed bodies shimmered like a living carpet blanketing the land all the way to the horizon.

My lord Albinonix.

I see them, my prince. I do not know if we have enough fire for such a great number.

Have they seen us?

I do not think so. What do you propose?

What if we fly ahead and meet them at the Keep, my lord dragon? I'm afraid if we begin flaming here that by the time we reach the Keep it will be too late to save my people.

An excellent idea, my prince. I will tell the others.

Albinonix communicated his intentions to the other dragons. He and Tetratorix would each lead half the dragons and approach the Keep from two sides. Valerian hated to be parted from Kieran, but it could not be helped. He caught Kieran's attention.

"We're splitting up to attack. We will meet you at the Keep."

Kieran nodded and raised a hand in farewell. Then Tetratorix split off with half the dragons, flying north. Albinonix took Valerian and the rest of the dragons south.

Flying above the clouds made it impossible to see what was happening below, but Valerian trusted the great dragon to make the best approach, and shortly they descended below the clouds.

Valerian gasped at the seething mass of Mohorovians surrounding the Keep. Their numbers were so great they'd filled the moat with their dead fellows in order to reach the high walls. Living siege ladders grew as the monsters gripped one another's arms, legs, and tails. From inside the castle yard, four catapults delivered stones into the attacking swarm, but they were pitifully ineffective.

Hold on, my prince!

Valerian gripped more tightly with hands and knees while Albinonix dove toward the Keep with the rest of the dragons. Underneath Valerian, the rumbling inside the dragon erupted in a roar as he blasted the enemy with a great spout of flame.

Merry, Rafael, and Gwendolyn descended a stairwell one level below the throne room and arrived in the empty infirmary. The low-ceilinged room was cave-like, with no windows to let in sunlight or fresh air. Fortunately torches and candles provided light, though the writhing flames made eerie shadows on the stone walls. Gwendolyn placed the bird cage containing Sir Edmund on an empty chair. Two men approached.

"What are you doing here?" asked the younger man.

Before Merry could frame a reply, Gwendolyn spoke up.

"This is Lady Merry, the king's ward, and I am Lady Gwendolyn."

The man folded his arms, frowning.

"That still doesn't explain why you are here, my lady."

"I am a Healer." Merry lifted her carry sack off her shoulder.

"A Healer?" The older of the two asked. "How can that be?"

"My father was a Healer, and the gift came to me as I was assisting in childbirth."

"We don't need a midwife," explained the younger man. "We'll be dealing with battle injuries."

Now Merry was able to speak with confidence.

"I've Healed broken bones, dealt with bleeding wounds, and sewn gashes. I'm sure I can help you with battle injuries. I even brought my own supplies."

The older one silenced the younger with a gesture, before he could speak again.

"Let her be. We can use all the help we can get." He turned to Merry. "I am Weldon, King Orland's chief physician. If you'll stay down here, it would free us to work with the acute injuries. We'll send you plenty of patients, unfortunately."

The two physicians hurried from the infirmary, and Merry took the opportunity to familiarize herself with the room and its furnishings. She and Gwendolyn found a cabinet stocked with clean cloths and empty basins.

"Gwendolyn, would you please fill two of these with water? We should have a pitcher of water on hand to give to the injured."

"I can do that, Sissy." Rafael's face was eager. "Remember how I helped you?"

"Of course, love. You're my best helper." Merry hugged him.

While Rafael left with Gwendolyn, Merry found a small empty table and used it to organize the herbs from her carry sack. When she finished, there was nothing more to do but wait.

In the quiet room, a vibration began to shake the wooden floor, increasing in intensity. What could it be? Was there an earthshake? Then the hairs on the back of her neck prickled just as a terrible howl came from outside. Had the Horde arrived?

Gwendolyn and Rafael entered the infirmary carrying three buckets of water. Rafael set his beside Merry's table, and Gwendolyn put her two nearby.

"They're here, Merry."

"Did you see them?"

"No, but I could hear them. We're surrounded." Gwendolyn's face was drawn with worry.

It wasn't long before a soldier brought them a young man, his foot wrapped in a blood-soaked cloth. The soldier laid the injured man on a cot.

"Can you help Brentley?"

"What happened?" Merry asked.

"Stone from the catapult dropped on his foot."

"Yes, I can help him."

The man nodded and hurried out.

Merry gently pulled away what remained of Brentley's leather shoe as he hissed through his teeth. The bleeding worsened.

"I need a wet cloth," she said. Rafael dipped one of the cloths in the water bucket and squeezed it out. Merry put the bloodroot in her mouth and bit down on the tough fibers while she firmly wrapped the damp cloth around the foot, taking care to realign the torn skin and tissues. Brentley moaned and flinched, but he didn't pull away.

After she'd broken up the bloodroot, tasting sap, Merry applied it to the place with the worst bleeding using firm but gentle pressure. She closed her eyes to better *See* the damage in the foot. Several bones were broken, but only two badly so. With her Healing power, she manipulated the pieces into place, but held herself back from completely fusing them.

When she opened her eyes, the bleeding had stopped. She was tired, but not drained. How could she keep Healing if too many were badly injured? Somehow she would have to hold herself back and save the actual Healing for those nearest death. With her herbs, she could stop bleeding and ease pain, at least.

Brentley opened his eyes.

"What did you do, my lady?" he asked. "Light and warmth come from your hands." Merry helped him sit up so he could see his foot.

"Your bones are set, but you must be careful not to turn the foot or put any weight on it. I'll fashion a splint for you, and you'll need a crutch to walk with for a while." She smiled to reassure him.

"But how can I fight?" Brentley glanced toward the door, distressed.

"You can't go back out there or you'll reinjure your foot."

"Where's my crossbow?" He groped around the cot.

"I didn't see one when the other man brought you in."

Rafael stepped forward with a cup of water.

"Are you thirsty?"

The young man focused on Rafael. Some of his panic eased and he nodded. Rafael helped him drink from the cup.

Merry wanted to say more, but a knight carried in another injured man whose face was not visible beneath the blood that covered his head.

"Please, help him." The knight's eyes pleaded with Merry through the slit in his helmet. "The physicians sent me here. They said there was nothing they could do." He gently laid the wounded man on a cot and took a step back. "I must return to the wall, but please save him, lady. He's my squire."

"What happened?" Merry wet a clean cloth and tried to wipe some of the blood away so she could see where to begin.

"He got too close to the edge, and one of those monsters raked him with its claws. I must go." The knight fled.

Merry gave up trying to wipe the squire's blood and cupped his face in her hands. There were three deep gashes, one of which had destroyed the left eye. It could not be saved. But his torn nose and upper lip could be repaired, and Merry opened herself to the Healing power to staunch the flow of blood, since there wasn't time to use the bloodroot on such a widespread area. Once the bleeding had stopped, she was able to gently wash off his damaged face.

"Gwendolyn! I need balmflower tea for this man. Rafael knows how to make it."

"Come, Rafael, show me what to do."

Thankfully, the squire had not yet regained consciousness, for the many stitches Merry would have to take would be painful. She threaded a needle and started to close the gash that began on his forehead. He moaned but did not waken, and Merry worked as quickly as she could. It was tricky making stitches in his eyelid to pull it over the ruined eye socket, but the poor squire would have to wear a patch over it anyway, once the injuries healed.

She had cut another length of thread and was about to start on the second gash when Rafael brought a steaming cup.

"Thank you, love. Set it on the table beside the cot, please."

Rafael did so and stood close by, watching her intently.

"Can you fix his face, Sissy?"

"I'm trying, love. He's hurt very badly, but he will live."

By the time Merry began stitching the third gash, which had torn his upper lip, the door opened again. The soldier who had brought Brentley entered.

"My lady, I came to bring Brentley's crossbow, since some of the Horde have got over the walls."

She nodded, but didn't answer.

"That's not all. You will not believe it, but Prince Valerian has brought a whole flock of dragons, and they're flaming the Horde!"

Merry startled as a mighty roar sounded just outside.

Caelis was so focused on aiming his crossbow at the Mohorovians scaling the wall that he jerked at the sound of an ear-shattering roar. Then a burst of flame blackened a swath of the Horde below. A dragon. No, an entire flight of them!

His excitement was short-lived when he saw who sat astride the largest dragon. Valerian? *No!* How had he managed such a feat? How could Caelis possibly discredit the prince *now*?

In blind rage, he loaded another bolt and aimed at Valerian. But the dragon veered away, and Caelis lost his target. Blast! Somehow he had to keep the prince away from King Orland and kill him before he could steal what rightfully belonged to Caelis.

But first, he had to stay alive. A Mohorovian head appeared between the battlements. It gripped the stone, pulling itself up to gain the wall. Caelis shot the monster in the eye, and it fell back, howling.

"We're running out of bolts," someone shouted nearby.

"Use your spears to push them from the wall." Caelis had better than a spear, however. He had the Horde battle-ax he'd used at the Brethren village. When he ran out of crossbow bolts, he would still be well-equipped against the Mohorovians. After all, only so many of them could gain access to the wall at one time. With the dragons cutting down their numbers, Caelis was sure they now had a fighting chance to survive.

He just had to make sure Valerian didn't get any credit for it.

Chapter 37 *A wise son maketh a glad father.*

When Albinonix came around to make his third pass at flaming the Mohorovians, Valerian glanced down at the wall and cried out. 'King Orland was in trouble. Several of the Horde had made it over the wall and threatened him and three other men.

My lord Albinonix, can you let me down on the wall? I must help my father, the king.

The dragon craned his long neck to where Valerian pointed and flew closer. He beat his great wings forward and lowered himself just above the nearest tower. *Crawl down to my foreleg, and I will drop you there.*

A hole opened in the pit of Valerian's stomach when he glimpsed the ground far below, but he quickly swung his leg around the dragon's ridge and moved down the shoulder. Just as he thought he would lose his balance and tumble off into the air, Albinonix grasped him with scythe-like claws and set him down in the tower.

Thank you, my lord dragon.

You are welcome, my prince. I go to flame more of the Horde. With a rush of air from the downward stroke, Albinonix launched off the tower and dove toward the massed swarm below.

Valerian pulled his sword from the scabbard and ran down the tower stairs to the battlements. He joined his father and the others, who were pressed against the wall by more than twice their number of Mohorovians.

He swung the blade around and partially decapitated the nearest one, then used the sword's momentum to plunge it into the next one's chest. The blow jarred him badly, but he did not lose his grip on the hilt. The creature lashed out with its claws, which Valerian barely avoided. He wrenched out the blade as the Mohorovian fell.

By now the others had turned on him, and the king and his companions were able to cut them down with their spears.

"Well done, Valerian," shouted King Orland. "You are a welcome sight, my son." With a ferocious grin, his father turned toward the next wave of Mohorovians scaling the wall.

Valerian followed the king along the battlements, using Alden's sword to great effect against the Horde swarm. Amazingly, even with the entire flight of dragons flaming them outside the walls, those who survived the fire continued to pile themselves against the walls to scale them. They truly had a single purpose, as Merry had *Seen.*

He deliberately kept his thoughts to himself and was grateful she hadn't reached out to him, though surely she knew he was near. Valerian needed all his concentration to support his father and keep them both alive. He did wonder briefly if Kieran was still aloft or if he had been set down to fight.

Though much time passed, Valerian did not personally see any casualties among the Levathians, except one older man knocked unconscious by a Mohorovian's vicious tail swipe. With his spear, King Orland dispatched the creature before it could strike a killing blow. One of the physicians attended the man, and Valerian didn't envy the headache he would have upon awakening.

The overcast sky obscured the sun, but it appeared to be only mid-afternoon before the swarm was decimated and the soldiers could take a break and drink some water. Valerian stood on the north wall with his father while they scanned the destruction below. The stench of burned flesh filled the air. Mountains of dead Mohorovians piled against the wall all the way to the battlements. The air was hazy from the dragons' fire. Only a few were still in the air, either flaming or catching and rending the remnants of the swarm. The rest of the dragons had landed on the Keep's towers or out beyond the battle site upon outcroppings of rock.

"Valerian." Orland's voice was full of weary triumph.

"Yes, sir?"

"You have saved us all." He turned to face him. "I've never been so proud of you."

Valerian did not know how to answer him. He simply said, "Thank you, Father."

"By the way, Lady Merry told me of your proposal."

"She *told* you? How did she do that?"

"She came right out and plainly said it. The lady is frank and forthright in all her dealings. I especially like that about her." Orland grinned. "I approve wholeheartedly of your marriage."

Valerian was dumbfounded. Not only could Merry *speak*, but his father had no objection to her.

"I must see her."

"You should find her in the infirmary," Orland said.

"If she is not busy, Father, I'll bring her to you." Moments before Valerian had been beyond weary. His strength returned with the anticipation of their reunion and hearing Merry's *voice*. He took the tower stairs two and three at a time in his haste to descend.

But when he stepped out from the tower, Caelis blocked his path.

Merry could scarcely continue stitching the injured man's facial wounds at the knowledge that Valerian was so near. But she could not speak to his mind, not now while he was in the midst of battle.

When Merry finished with the stitches, she used a small pot of healing ointment Papa had rendered and smeared a thin layer over the many stitches, all the while thinking of Valerian. How would he react when she spoke to him? Would he be pleased and surprised? She smiled in anticipation.

But the reality of dealing with Sir Caelis robbed her joy. The treacherous knight could not be allowed to continue spreading his murderous hatred. She needed to tell Valerian right away what Caelis had done so he could go with her to tell the king.

"Are you finished stitching him?" Rafael studied the young man's face.

"Yes, love. When he wakes, we must give him the balmflower tea."

"I'll do it, Sissy." He glanced back at their patient again. "That's a lot of stitches."

"The poor man had terrible injuries. He will heal, but he'll always have scars, and there was nothing I could do about his eye."

Rafael's face became solemn.

"Sissy, is that why we have two eyes, in case one gets blind?"

"That must be the reason, Rafael." Merry hugged him.

They sat on an empty cot, watching over their two patients and listening to the din of battle outside. Gwendolyn could not sit still and paced the length of the room, occasionally stopping to adjust the stack of cloths or take a sip of water.

"Why are there no more wounded being sent here?" she asked Merry. "Are they too badly injured, or are they simply dying for lack of someone to help them?"

"I'm sure Drew is all right." Merry squeezed Gwendolyn's hand. "Perhaps the great dragons are so powerful, no one else has been hurt." Her heart swelled with admiration for what Valerian had done in bringing the dragons. She couldn't wait to see them. And him.

She had just decided to risk going outside when the squire regained consciousness. He moaned and grabbed his head. Merry jumped up and firmly grasped his hands.

"You must not touch your face. Here's a healing tea for you to drink. It will dull the pain."

He emptied the cup with Rafael's help and opened his eye, focusing on Merry.

"What happened?" His voice rasped.

There was no way to soften it.

"One of the Horde slashed your face."

"My eye?"

"It could not be saved," Merry said. "I'm sorry."

His hand automatically went to his mouth.

"Wha's wrong with my lip?"

Merry sat beside him and gripped his hands again.

"You had three deep gashes in your face. I have stitched them together, and they will all heal, but you must try not to touch them until they do. I've put a salve on them to aid in healing as well as fading the scars."

The squire took a deep breath and lay back on the cot. He closed his eye, and a tear leaked out. Merry gently wiped it from his cheek. Brentley spoke up from the other cot.

"You really know what you're doing, my lady." He cocked his head, listening. "It sounds like the battle may be coming to an end."

Merry stood, half hoping, half fearful.

"Go on, Merry." Gwendolyn came to stand beside Rafael. "We can handle things here, can't we, Rafael?" He nodded. "I can't bear to look anyway. You go, but don't forget to come and tell me if Drew is all right."

"I'll send him to you." Merry kissed Rafael's head. "I know you'll be a good helper to Gwen until I return."

Merry ran from the infirmary, all her weariness gone with the joy of seeing Valerian again.

When Caelis saw Valerian leave King Orland's side and head for the tower stairs, he sent the men standing with him to the kitchens. Now, Caelis blocked Valerian's path to Merry in this cramped, isolated corner of the yard.

Valerian burst out of the tower. He stopped when he saw Caelis.

"Stand aside, Caelis, and let me pass."

In answer, Caelis raised the battle-ax still stained with Mohorovian blood.

"I think not. This day has been a long time coming. You will never pass over me again."

Valerian drew his sword and held it to the ready. He took a halting step in the direction of the Keep, then another.

"This is not the way to resolve our quarrel."

Caelis narrowed his eyes.

"You're wrong, as usual. This is the only way to resolve it." He tightened his grip on the ax. Lunging forward, he swung it down toward Valerian's head. This was going to be as easy as slaughtering the pacifists.

To his surprise, the whelp used his sword to bat the ax against the stone wall, sending up sparks. The vibration jarred Caelis' hand, and he barely kept his grip on the ax. Valerian rushed Caelis, the sword aimed at his throat, but Caelis blocked the blade with the haft, raising splinters. Valerian backed toward the tower entrance, so Caelis feinted another attack to force him into the corner. Then he kicked over a stack of crates to block the entrance.

Valerian moved out of Caelis' reach, inching toward the Keep.

"Your cowardice killed Waryn," Caelis said, "and now you are too cowardly to face me like a man."

A shadow passed over Valerian's face, but then he set his jaw, shifting his grip on the sword.

"I am not afraid to fight you."

Before Valerian could act, Caelis turned the ax and swung parallel to the ground, aiming just below shoulder level. Valerian's eyes widened. He ducked and then rolled out of the way, coming immediately to his feet. Caelis tried a lower swing to cut the prince's legs out from under him, but Valerian leaped out of the way. The prince used the turn to swing his blade backhanded. The sword scraped Caelis' shoulder armor, making his belly clench. He gritted his teeth and thrust the ax like a spear.

The point caught Valerian on the breastbone and slammed him into the wall. With a groan, Valerian swung wildly at Caelis, but the blade didn't reach him. The prince was bruised, even though the ax head's point hadn't pierced his chain mail. Caelis aimed again, higher. Gasping for air, Valerian slid to his right. The point caught his arm just below the mail sleeve, drawing blood. When the prince stumbled, Caelis swung the ax around. Valerian stepped inside the swing, but didn't lift his sword quickly enough. Caelis pushed him away with the haft of the ax. Valerian rolled to his feet again and held the sword to the ready.

Caelis faced him, catching his breath. The prince was panting, and sweat beaded his brow.

"Against all odds you have returned, and I cannot let you live," Caelis said. "But before you die, whelp, you should know that, not only will I take your crown and your place as king, I will also take your intended bride and sire a royal brat on her, by force if necessary."

"I won't let you touch her." Valerian's face twisted in anguish. He raised the sword over his head and lunged forward, hacking down with the blade.

Caelis easily blocked the blow with the haft. He laughed and kicked Valerian in the stomach. Moaning, Valerian bent over, nearly dropping the sword. Caelis brought the ax around to behead the prince, but Valerian charged into the swing, and the haft struck his back. The edge of the blade sliced through the chain mail and into Valerian's right shoulder. The prince cried out, and the sword dropped from his limp fingers. They grappled and fell, but Caelis came to his feet first. He was too close to properly swing the ax, so he kicked Valerian's ribs.

Valerian doubled up, groaning. He grabbed the fallen sword with his left hand and desperately chopped at Caelis' legs. One stroke connected with Caelis' right calf, and he backed off, grimacing. Warmth trickled down his leg, but it wasn't deep.

The prince pushed himself to his feet. He hunched over, his right arm dangling, but he still held the sword in his left hand. His back was to the armory wall, and his face grimaced in pain.

Caelis came toward Valerian, swinging the ax in tight figures-of-eight. The prince's eyes widened in alarm. He tried to lunge with the sword, but Caelis batted it away. Valerian struggled to hold on to the sword while evading Caelis' attack. Caelis followed relentlessly until the ax blade caught the sword and sent it flying across the cobbles.

Savoring the moment, Caelis leered. Valerian leaped forward and grabbed the ax with his left hand. He pushed the haft across Caelis' face, opening a cut above his eye. With a growl, Caelis twisted the haft out of Valerian's hand. The prince had to dive away from the blade, but it sliced across his chest and cut the dragon emblem in half.

Sneering, Caelis moved in for the kill.

Chapter 38 *Be ye afraid of the sword.*

Valerian tried to breathe deeply, but the burning pain from his cracked ribs and bruised chest caught his breath with a sob. His sword arm hung useless. How could he save Merry from this monster?

Caelis stepped closer and swung the ax. Valerian dodged, wincing. He had to work his way back to his sword. It was the only way to stop Caelis.

But Caelis didn't let him near the sword. He caught Valerian across the left thigh in a glancing blow. Crying out, Valerian grabbed the place and ducked the next blow. Warm blood poured through his fingers. His legs were too heavy to move out of the way, and the ax sliced his right forearm. Caelis was toying with him now.

Their eyes met, and Valerian *Saw* through the knight's madness that *he* was the one responsible for the massacre of the Brethren.

"You killed the Brethren?" he said, gasping.

"Cowards." Caelis growled and lifted the ax as if he were splitting wood. "Like you."

Valerian's left shoulder bumped against the toppled stack of crates. He was trapped.

Just like when the Mohorovian swung the ax at Waryn, time slowed down. Valerian *Saw* as if illuminated by heaven itself how he could give his life to keep this man from hurting any more innocents. As the ax head glinted in the sunlight and came toward his head, Valerian gathered what little strength remained and leaped to the left. The blade smashed into the crates and became imbedded in the wood. Caelis lost his balance and fell on top of the crates.

Yelling to block out the searing pain of his ribs, Valerian stumbled to the sword and grasped it with his left hand. He turned and planted his feet, sucking in a painful breath.

Caelis finally pulled the ax from the wood and approached Valerian with a roar. He shifted his grip on the haft, and his glove caught on the splinters. Valerian took that moment and with another yell lunged forward and stabbed Caelis in the right arm. Screaming, the knight tried to swing the ax left-handed, but Valerian blocked his hand, hard. The ax spun out of Caelis' grasp and clattered on the stone. With a final shout, Valerian shoved the blade through the gap under Caelis' left arm. Something tore in his own chest, and his vision swam, but he clung to the hilt.

Caelis frowned, and then his eyes widened. He fell to his knees in slow motion, incredulous, as Valerian wrenched his blade out. Valerian stood swaying on his feet, and Alden's sword glistened with the traitor's blood.

When Merry stepped into the yard, she gasped. There in the sky flew many enormous dragons. She couldn't tear her gaze from the graceful motion of their wings or the shimmering blue-green scales that sparkled golden in the sunlight. What magnificent creatures! Her heart swelled with pride that Valerian had brought them.

Strange there were so few soldiers milling about. Most of them crowded on the walls, staring outside the castle. Were any of the Horde left? She had no way to know.

Merry scanned the walls, searching for Valerian, when the sound of metal clashing against metal echoed off the stone. Running toward the sound, which came from the nearest tower, she cried out. Caelis was attacking Valerian! Valerian defended himself with his sword, but the slim blade appeared fragile against the massive battle-ax.

No one else was close enough to help. Merry wanted to shout at Caelis, but she feared it would distract Valerian. While she came nearer, Valerian struck Caelis a mortal blow, and the knight collapsed to his knees.

"Valerian!"

"Merry?" He slowly turned toward her with a weary smile. *I'm so glad to see you and hear your voice at last.*

You're hurt! The amount of blood on his arms and legs propelled her to run faster. Before she reached him, something moved behind him. *Caelis.*

"Behind you!"

Valerian could not turn quickly enough. Caelis' ax struck Valerian's right leg. The blade cut into the calf at an angle. Blood gushed from the terrible wound as the ax flew from Caelis' hands. Valerian fell forward, losing his grip on the sword.

While Valerian lay helpless, Caelis stayed on his knees, grimacing. How could Merry get to Valerian? Could she break her Oath of Peace to protect him? Then she stared more closely at the knight. His eyes were glazed and his face ashen. He was so near death he was no longer a threat.

Merry dropped to her knees beside Valerian. He had lost consciousness. Before she could staunch the flow of blood from his leg, something jerked her head back. Caelis had her braid! He slowly pulled her toward him, and he had a knife in his hand.

"No!" Valerian's sword lay beside her. Merry tried to pick it up, but it was too heavy. Caelis tightened his grip on her braid, yanking her back.

Then Merry saw a knife on Valerian's belt and pulled it from the sheath. She twisted against the pain in her scalp and pointed the blade at Caelis. Briefly their eyes met.

"No," she said again, gritting her teeth. "I will not break my oath, even for an animal like you." Instead, she used the blade to saw through her hair. With a final sigh, Caelis fell over and lay still, clutching her braid.

Merry dropped the knife and knelt beside Valerian again. His blood soaked into the ground. Merry took his injured right leg between her hands and cried out in anguish. The lower part was only connected by a strip of skin and tendon. Not knowing if it could be saved, she focused all her Healing energy to stop the bleeding before he died.

Once she stopped the blood loss from his leg, she turned her attention to his other injuries. His breastbone was cracked, as well as several ribs, along with torn muscles. He had many lesser cuts, but his right shoulder was torn and bleeding heavily from a slice to the bone, so she stopped that bleeding next and Healed it.

By the time she could focus on his ribs, Merry's strength was fading, but she rallied every scrap of strength to pour into Valerian. Strong hands pulled her away, and she fought them.

"No, no! I must save him."

"You have, Merry." It was Kieran's voice. "The bleeding has stopped. He lives."

She opened her eyes. Many hands moved Valerian to a litter.

"Where are you taking him?"

"To the infirmary," Kieran told her.

Merry struggled to stand.

"I must go, too. My medicines are there. And my brother and Gwendolyn and Sir Edmund." As soon as she was upright, she swooned and Kieran caught her.

"If you must, then I will carry you." He scooped her in his arms and glanced over his shoulder. "Drew, bring the prince's sword. Dinna forget to wipe the blade."

Drew. Merry squeezed her eyes shut against the vertigo of exhaustion. *I must tell Gwen about Drew.*

By the time they reached the infirmary, Merry had regained enough strength to stand. The men laid Valerian, litter and all, on the cot nearest the fireplace. The older physician entered with King Orland, and they went straight to the cot. Merry pulled away from Kieran to join them.

"It's miraculous the bleeding has stopped, Sire," Weldon was saying. "Otherwise he should have died from loss of blood."

"What about his leg?" Orland wrung his hands, frowning.

"I'm afraid it cannot be saved."

"Let me try," Merry begged. "I didn't attempt it outside because I had to stop the bleeding and Heal some of his other wounds. Please, let me try to save it."

Kieran stepped forward and bowed to King Orland.

"Your Majesty, I must protest. The lady is supernaturally gifted, but the use o' that gift always comes with a price." He stared at Merry. "I'm sorry, my lady, but if ye tried to Heal this terrible injury, I know it would kill you."

"You don't know that." Tears filled her eyes. "You could watch and bring me back before I went that far."

He lowered his voice.

"I did watch you. The Healing you've done today has already taken a terrible toll. Ye canna tell me that you feel no weakness still."

Orland laid a hand on Merry's shoulder.

"I would not have you risk your life and compound this tragedy, Lady Merry. You have saved Valerian's life. When he recovers, he will learn to deal with the loss of the leg. He has already proven his great strength and courage."

Merry covered her face with her hands and wept. She knew they were right. Oh, how she knew! But for Valerian's sake she wished there was a way to save his leg.

To her great surprise, Orland put his arm around her and led her away from the cot.

"Let Welden do his work now."

"What is he going to do?" She grabbed Orland's arm.

"I must complete the amputation, Lady Merry," Welden said. "Thanks to you I will be able to cover the stump with a skin flap to better prepare him for a wooden leg when it heals."

"Let me keep him from pain, at least." When physician and king both gave their permission, she rushed to the cot and knelt behind Valerian's head. His eyes were closed, and his skin so pale. Merry gently placed her hands at his temples and brought her forehead down to his. Closing her eyes, she drew on the Healing power just enough to keep him unconscious. She cradled him with her love and esteem, so he was unaware of what Welden did to his leg.

They drifted together in a place between wakefulness and sleep, each accepting the peaceful oneness beyond words.

At last hands pulled at Merry, insistent. She resisted, not willing to leave Valerian's mind, but she had to return to normal consciousness. When she opened her eyes, Rafael stood beside her.

"Sissy, I made some balmflower tea. Is that a good thing?"

"Yes, love. It's a very good thing." Merry kissed her brother's cheek. "As soon as he wakes a little, you may give it to him." She tried to stand, but the room began spinning, and strong arms caught her before she fell.

Kieran picked her up and set her in a chair. The king sat on a bench beside her, and Drew stood next to him. Gwendolyn handed her a cup of nectar, and Merry gratefully drank it.

"I do want you to rest, Lady Merry," Orland said. "But first I need some answers. How was Valerian so injured?"

Merry shared a glance with Drew. She took a deep breath.

"Sir Caelis."

"Caelis?" Orland frowned at Drew. "What do you know of this, squire?"

"Your Majesty," Drew said. "Sir Caelis has hated Prince Valerian ever since the day Prince Waryn was killed." He wrung his hands. Merry nodded at him to continue.

"When Sir Caelis took us south, at first he said it was to practice with the new crossbow in the field."

"Yes, yes." Orland gestured with his hands. "I already know that."

"Later, Your Majesty," Drew continued, his voice trembling, "Sir Caelis said he had a decree from Prince Valerian himself. I didn't see it, but he showed the men."

"What decree was that?"

Drew swallowed and glanced at Merry again.

"It ordered the Brethren put to death for refusing to fight against the Horde." He dropped to his knees and bowed his head. "I couldn't believe the prince would order something like that, but Sir Caelis was very…persuasive." Drew covered his face with his hands. "Though I did not kill anyone, I was not able to stop Sir Caelis. I deserve whatever punishment you decree, Your Majesty."

"Drew Campignon." He and Merry both looked up at the sternness in King Orland's voice. "A squire is not held responsible for the crimes of his knight. If Sir Caelis ordered his men to put to death an innocent village by deceit, he bears the responsibility. Where are the other men?"

"They were all killed in the south, Your Majesty. Thankfully, Lady Merry was not present when the village was attacked, and I—" Drew swallowed again and tears welled up in his eyes. "I refused Sir Caelis' direct order to kill Rafael, so his life was spared also."

"Rafael?" Orland turned to him.

Merry held out her free hand, and Rafael came to her, standing close but not crawling into her lap as he used to do.

"This is my brother, Your Majesty. Another cousin."

"I am very pleased to meet you, Rafael. How old are you?"

"I'm almost five years old." He held up five fingers.

"He will be five on May Day," Merry said.

"That is my birthday, too." Orland smiled at the boy.

"When I found everyone in my village slain," Merry explained, "I couldn't find my brother and assumed the worst."

"Thankfully you have a happy ending here." Orland indicated Drew should continue.

"While we were at Lord Reed's, Sir Caelis hired a killer to assassinate Prince Valerian, not willing to gamble everything on the possibility of discrediting him." Drew glanced at Merry, who nodded.

"I was with Valerian when a man tried to kill him," Merry added. "Kieran stopped him."

Now Kieran spoke up.

"But Merry saved his life. The assassin crushed the prince's windpipe with a garrote."

"Then we are doubly indebted to you, Lady Merry," Orland said. "Please continue, Drew."

"Later Sir Caelis sent two men to capture the prince and Lady Merry." Drew sent Kieran a sympathetic look. "He said to kill Kieran if he was too much trouble."

"I guess I *was* too much trouble. They crushed me skull, but Merry saved me, too." Kieran smiled at her.

"Where would we all be without you, my dear?" Orland squeezed her hand.

"Once we arrived here," Drew added, "Sir Caelis bade me stay in his quarters with Rafael. I don't know what he said to Lady Merry, but I feared for Rafael's safety and brought him to her this morning, against Caelis' orders."

"Caelis came to me in the night through a secret passageway and threatened Rafael's life if I did not do as he wished." Merry trembled, remembering.

"And what was that?" Orland asked gently.

"To marry him and produce an heir of Alden's lineage." She closed her eyes. "Then he attacked Valerian just now when no one was around to intervene." Her trembling increased, and Rafael leaned closer.

"Sissy?"

"Are you all right, Lady Merry?" Orland let go of her hand and caught her shoulder in alarm.

"No," she said in a choked voice. "I—I had to cut off my braid because Caelis grabbed it and would have killed me, but I had to save Valerian. All I could think was that he was going to bleed to death, and now I've lost the symbol of my Oath of Peace." She reached back and fingered the shorn ends of her hair. Tears sprang to her eyes.

Kieran went down on one knee and pulled something from his tunic. "Ye haven't lost it, my lady. I have it right here." He held her braid across his hands.

With a gasp, Merry reached out to touch it, and the world dissolved around her.

Chapter 39 *You shall pay your vows.*

Valerian woke from a pleasant dream. He'd been with Merry in a beautiful sunlit place. It had seemed so real.

Then fiery pain jolted his right leg. Valerian pushed himself to a sitting position and glanced at the bed. Something didn't look right. With a trembling hand, he pulled off the coverlet. He gasped.

NO!

His right leg was gone below the knee. Just like Ruddy's.

Valerian shut his eyes, panting. Panic gripped him. What happened? Where was Merry?

"I have some tea for you, sir."

When Valerian opened his eyes, a young boy stood before him, holding a cup in his small hands. His long hair was reddish-brown. He had eyes the same color as Merry's. Valerian automatically tried to take the cup, but his hands were shaking too badly.

"I'll hold it for you. I know how." The boy carefully brought the cup to Valerian's lips and helped him drink from it.

He hadn't realized how thirsty he was.

"Thank you." While he drank again, he studied the child's solemn yet earnest face.

"Are you hungry, sir?"

"No, thank you." The brief numbness of initial grief began to dissolve, and panic threatened to consume him. The boy turned away, and Valerian caught his arm.

"Who are you?"

"I'm Rafael. This is my Sissy." He pointed to a cot near Valerian's.

Merry slept there, her face pale and worn. Had she overreached herself trying to Heal him? Had she been injured too? He saw no bandages. And Rafael was her brother. Then Valerian's gaze drifted back to the stump that had been his right leg, and his chest tightened around his lungs, squeezing out the air.

Valerian lay back, reeling from the enormity of the loss. Was this how Ruddy had felt? And he had been the one to cut off his friend's leg.

Oh, Rudyard, forgive me. How did you manage it?

His thoughts were interrupted by Rafael's return. Valerian sat up again, and the boy placed a platter on his lap. There were meats and breads and a piece of winterfruit.

"I know you said you're not hungry," Rafael said. "But Sissy says hurt people must eat to get strong again." He waited, but Valerian did not move or answer him. "I'll get some more water now."

Valerian numbly watched him pour water from an ewer into the cup without spilling a drop. Merry had taught her brother well. After Rafael helped Valerian drink from the cup again, Valerian nodded toward Merry.

"Is your sister all right? She's not wounded too, is she?"

"She's just tired from Healing today." Rafael smiled shyly. "Did you know she saved your life?"

Valerian gazed at Merry's dear face and shook his head.

"No, I didn't, but I'm not surprised. It's not the first time she has saved me." He looked back at Rafael. "By the way, I'm Valerian."

"You are to marry my sister," Rafael said, nodding.

"Yes." *If she will still have me, one-legged and permanently damaged.* Valerian's gut became queasy at the thought, but if Ruddy could learn to manage with a wooden leg, then he could find a way, couldn't he?

He met Rafael's steady gaze and *Saw* the pain the child carried, pain much greater than the loss of a limb. Surely, Valerian could be strong enough to bear his own losses in order to comfort this boy. He forced a smile, but it twisted into a grimace.

"What do you think, Rafael? That will make us brothers."

Rafael studied Valerian and nodded.

"I liked Gabriel all right, but I think I will like you better." He leaned closer as if imparting a secret. "My Sissy likes you very much."

Valerian spoke quietly, sharing the secret.

"I hope so, Rafael, because there is no one in the world who I love better than your sister."

"Truly?" Rafael's eyes widened.

"Truly." He offered his hand. "Brother to brother, I pledge my life to your sister's happiness."

Rafael stared at the hand and timidly held his out. Valerian showed him how to grip wrists in a man's handshake. A smile briefly lifted the boy's solemnity. Then Rafael let go and pointed to the plate of food.

"You should eat now, Valerian."

"All right." Valerian smiled at Rafael's resemblance to his sister. With shaky hands, he tore off a piece of bread and ate it. Then his stomach growled, and he realized how hungry he was.

After Valerian finished everything on the plate, Kieran and Drew approached them. Valerian tossed the coverlet over his legs, self-conscious about his stump.

"I see Rafael is taking good care of you, Your Highness," Drew said.

"Yes, he's quite the good physician's helper." Valerian nodded at the boy. "He is to be my brother."

"Yes, so I've heard."

Kieran cleared his throat.

"I thought ye'd like to know, Sire, the dragons have hunted down every stray Mohorovian. They're still here. I dinna think they'll leave 'til Albinonix has a chance to speak with you."

Valerian glanced at the stump again. Indeed, it was difficult not to stare at it.

"I don't think I'll be able to walk for a while yet."

"Then perhaps we can find a way to carry you tae the lord of dragons in a dignified way. Drew and I could be your throne bearers as you and I were once Merry's." Kieran grinned, and Valerian had to smile at the memory. "But ye need not worry 'til the morning. I'm sure the beasties won't mind spending the night with us here. In fact, they seem to be enjoying all the attention."

"What attention?" Valerian wished he could go outside and see for himself.

"Ach, the lads are making sure they have food and water, and some o' the braver ones have even ventured close enough to thank them properly."

"How is that, Kieran?"

"With a bow or a salute, though one older man did pass out when one o' the dragons grinned at him." Kieran bared his teeth and widened his eyes, and Valerian laughed.

"The dragons are helping us dispose of the bodies before they begin to stink too much," Drew added.

"That's quite an unpleasant duty." Valerian grimaced. "I'm thankful the dragons are willing to help, otherwise it would take mere men a very long time to finish that job."

They lapsed into silence. Valerian watched Merry, both hoping and dreading she would awaken soon.

Merry sighed and opened her eyes. It took her a moment to remember where she was, and what had happened. She sat up too quickly and became light-headed, but she closed her eyes and rubbed her temples until the dizziness passed. Then she touched the back of her head, and her eyes filled with tears. Even though she'd had to cut the braid to save Valerian, Merry still grieved the loss of the hair.

She opened her eyes again and swung her legs over the side of the cot. Nearby lay two sleeping forms, her patients from earlier in the day. Rafael checked on Brentley, and Gwendolyn walked toward her, looking pleased.

"How long have I been out, Gwen?"

"Not long, just an hour or so."

"An hour? Oh, no." Merry swallowed her disappointment. "Have they already taken Valerian to his rooms?"

No, love, I am right here.

Merry gasped and stood, turning around. Valerian sat on the edge of another cot. Kieran and Drew stood to either side, both beaming. Though she wanted to run to Valerian and throw her arms around him, she hesitated. So much had changed since they'd parted on that fateful day. Did he still love her as much as she loved him?

Of course I do. My heart is unchanged, though my body certainly has. He glanced down at his bandaged stump. *Can you still love me as half a man?*

Merry slowly walked around her cot and knelt beside him. She kissed the bandage and then gazed up into his eyes.

You are more of a man than any I've ever known. I love you all the more for the terrible sacrifice you have made in saving Levathia.

Tears filled his eyes. She took his hands and kissed them.

My love, I'm so glad you are home. Then she did embrace him, gently at first until he pulled her to his lap. In front of their small audience, they shared a passionate kiss, triumphant over all the obstacles they'd faced in the last weeks.

When they parted, Merry sat beside Valerian on the cot, nestled as close as she could be.

"I'm sorry," she said. "We have not included the rest of you in our conversation."

Gwendolyn came forward to take Drew's hand, and they sat together on the opposite cot. Rafael joined the group, sitting on Merry's other side. Gwendolyn patted the space on the cot beside her.

"Come, Kieran, and join us," she said. He did so, impulsively kissing her on the cheek.

"Sorry, Drew. I dinna know what came over me."

"I know," said Gwendolyn, winking at Merry. "That kind of love is powerful and spills over to us mortals."

Kieran turned his attention to Merry.

"What I want to know is, how did ye get your voice?"

"Caelis made a false accusation about Valerian to the king, and I had to say something." She glanced at Valerian. "I suppose it was from dire need."

"I'm glad to know I have such a fierce advocate," Valerian said quietly.

"Never fiercer," she assured him. "Don't forget, I am part dragon, according to Eldred."

Valerian chuckled. Then his face grew somber, and he reached up to touch her shorn hair. "What happened to your braid?"

Merry's throat tightened, and she had to clear it before she could speak.

"After Caelis cut your leg, I thought he could no longer hurt you, so I started to Heal you and he grabbed my braid. He had a knife in his other hand, and he was pulling me to him." Her breath caught in a sob. "Your sword was lying there, but I couldn't lift it, so I took the knife from your belt. I could have used it on him and saved my braid, but I couldn't do it. I couldn't break my Oath of Peace, but I had to save you, so I—" Her throat squeezed shut, and she couldn't continue.

"So you cut off your braid to escape him," Valerian said quietly. *My dear, dear Merry, you have had so many losses.*

A braid is nothing compared to a leg. Forgive me, love, but I could not save it.

There is nothing to forgive. You saved my life. He gathered her in his strong arms, and Merry collapsed against him, weeping.

When she had no more tears, Merry wiped her face with her hand, and Gwendolyn gave her a cloth. She dried her tears but kept the cloth over her face.

I must look frightful.

You're always beautiful to me.

When she moved her head, a sob caught in her throat.

My head feels so light without the weight of the braid. She reached back and touched the cut ends of the hair again.

Our hair is the same length now.

Merry peered at Valerian from behind the cloth, and he smiled. With a sigh, she wadded up the cloth. The opposite cot was empty.

"Where did Kieran and Drew go?"

"To find a way to carry me to my room." Valerian shifted his leg, wincing.

"The one next door to the king's?"

"Yes. Where are you staying?"

"Across the hall in your old apartment, next door to your mother. I've met her, and I like her. I like both your parents."

"I'm glad." Valerian kissed her. "I know Father likes you very much. I haven't spoken to Mother yet."

Rafael caught Merry's attention.

"Where will I sleep tonight, Sissy? Do I have to go back to Sir Caelis' room?"

"Oh no, love. You may sleep with Gwendolyn and me. There's plenty of room."

"What about Drew?"

Merry looked at Valerian.

What do I tell him?

Valerian spoke to Rafael.

"I'll ask the king if Drew may be my squire, along with Kieran, and he can stay in my room."

Rafael fidgeted, reluctant to speak.

"What it is, love?" Merry combed her fingers through his unbound hair. It was now much longer than her own, she thought sadly.

"Do I have to sleep with the women? Can't I sleep where the men do?"

Gwendolyn laughed and tousled Rafael's hair.

"He has a point, Merry. He's not a baby."

Rafael straightened at her remark. "O'course I'm not a baby. Sir Caelis said I could be his page and then a knight someday."

A spike drove through Merry's heart. *What do I say to him?*

We can deal with that issue later. For now, and if it's all right with you, he may stay in my rooms. He's comfortable with Drew, and I hope he will grow to be comfortable with me, too.

Thank you. Merry squeezed Valerian's hand. "All right, Rafael. You may sleep with the men."

"Thank you, Sissy." Rafael grinned.

Kieran and Drew returned, carrying an unpadded chair. They set it beside Valerian's cot.

"This is from your apartment, Sire," said Drew.

"Of all the chairs, 'twas the easiest for us to carry together." Kieran wiped his brow, feigning exhaustion. "There are quite a lot of stairs 'twixt here and your rooms."

"I can just stay here." Valerian grimaced. "I don't wish to cause so much trouble."

"Ach, Sire, 'tis no trouble at all. Until you heal enough to wear a wooden leg and learn to use it, Drew and I will be your legs."

"Thank you, Kieran. I think." He made a face and turned to Drew. "I would like for you to be my squire, if you can put up with me and Kieran here."

Drew went down on one knee and brought Valerian's hand to his forehead.

"I would be honored, Your Highness." The young man swallowed.

Valerian clasped Drew's hand. "We have been through many trials, and we have gained strength from them." *He and I were squires together for my brother.*

Now I understand. Merry hoped the haunted look in Drew's eyes would fade with time.

Valerian closed his eyes.

I feel suddenly weary.

It's the loss of blood. You should sleep now.

They will want to take me upstairs.

You can sleep here tonight. I can even stay with you.

I would like that.

Merry stood and faced the squires.

"Valerian cannot go upstairs tonight. He needs to sleep now in the cot."

"You two can sleep in my room." Valerian's voice sounded far away. "Kieran, I know you've been wanting to try out the big bed. Here's your chance."

"Thank you, Sire." Kieran saluted, grinning.

Merry spoke to Rafael.

"Would you rather stay here or go with Drew and Kieran?"

"Do you need my help, Sissy?" He was torn between duty to his sister and friendship with older males. Merry knew which was most important to him now.

"I think our three patients will be too sleepy to need anything in the night. But if they do, Gwendolyn can help me."

Rafael's eyes shone with anticipation.

"Then I would like to go with them."

"All right, love. I'll see you in the morning." She hugged her brother, and he scampered from the room with the two squires.

Merry helped Valerian lie back on the cot and covered him with a fur. She kissed his mouth and then his eyelids.

Sleep well, my prince.

And you, my beautiful Merry.

Chapter 40 *How fair is thy love, my sister, my bride.*

Merry had just helped Valerian to the chair when Kieran, Drew, and Rafael burst into the infirmary. Drew came forward and went down on one knee.

"Your Highness, King Orland stopped me in the hall and told me I could be your squire." His eyes shone.

Valerian gripped his wrist.

"I'm right glad, Drew. In truth, I feel a little selfish to have the two best squires in all the land." He beckoned Rafael to come closer. "What think you, brother? We have two squires now."

Rafael met his eyes with a shy smile. Again, Valerian *Saw* a brief glimpse of what the boy had suffered since Caelis and his men had massacred the Brethren, and it twisted his heart. Somehow, he would make it up to him and try to be a surrogate father, as well as an older brother.

Before he could say more, King Orland entered.

"Good morrow, all." His father went first to Merry and kissed her hand. He kept her hand in his while he came closer. "Valerian, do you feel up to attending a celebration feast in the hall tonight?"

Merry, love, will I be able to go and not fall asleep on my trencher?

Yes. I'll stay beside you to make sure.

"I believe so, Father."

"Good! And if you feel up to exchanging vows with Lady Merry before Bishop Ignatius later this morning, he can post the banns, and we'll announce it at the feast."

Have you noticed my father is very energetic?

Yes, I have.

"That sounds like a good plan, Father. I only wish we could marry today." Valerian met Merry's gaze.

As do I.

"How long did you plan to wait, my son?"

Valerian gestured to his bandaged stump.

"I would like to be able to stand on my own foot and wooden leg when I appear before the altar with my bride."

"That is reasonable." Orland looked at both of them, well pleased. "I look forward to the blessed event."

"Blessed event? Is that what a wedding is called?"

"No, Valerian. I'm anxious to have a grandchild." The king chuckled and strode toward the door. "I will see you tonight."

"A feast." Kieran grinned. "'Tis been a while since we had good food." His eyes widened. "Ach, Drew, we have much to accomplish and little time to do it."

"What do you mean, Kieran?" Valerian asked, frowning.

The squire bowed. "We need to clean and mend your royal surcoat and prepare a bath for you, Sire."

"Not that surcoat again!"

"I'm afraid so, my prince." Kieran smiled in sympathy. "You canna appear at this feast in anything less."

"Very well." He shared a glance with Merry but spoke aloud for the squires' benefit. "I'll need a nap today."

After Kieran and Drew left, taking Rafael with them, Merry took a step closer to Valerian.

"I can help you Heal faster, you know."

"No," he said. The very thought of it troubled him. "I don't want you to exhaust yourself for something that will mend on its own."

"But I don't have to do it all at once." She stroked his hand. "I can help the Healing along a little each day. That way it won't tire me at all."

"I don't know, Merry." He gently gripped her hand.

"When I Healed the phantom pain in Ruddy's leg, it took very little energy. This would be much like that."

"Phantom pain? Do you mean it isn't real?"

"Oh yes, the pain is real. I heard my father call it that, but until I touched Ruddy's stump I did not understand." She kissed his hand before continuing. "When a limb is no longer there, the rest of the body doesn't realize it's gone. The brain keeps trying to tell it what to do."

"So, I will have those pains too?"

"Yes, love, but you will be married to a Healer who can help you block them."

Valerian stared at the bandaged stump, and fresh grief stabbed him.

It's as if I've lost an old friend.

In a sense, you have. Grief is not a bad thing, as long as we don't let it overpower us.

He cupped her face in his hand.

"How is it that you are so wise?"

She kissed him tenderly.

"How is it you won't let a wise woman look at your leg?"

Valerian sighed and held up his hands.

"Merry, I surrender."

She unwrapped the bandage and studied the injury.

"Welden did a good job on the stitches. There's a little infection though. I want to use some of the salve I put on my own leg injury." She fetched her carry sack.

Valerian lifted the stump to see the place, and shuddered. It was hideous. At least he still had the knee joint. He should be grateful for that. Ruddy had no trouble learning to walk, and he'd said that having a knee made all the difference.

Merry knelt and spread salve all over the end of the stump. Then she cupped it in her hands, and he briefly saw the glow of her Healing power. Amazingly, just that small touch helped with the throbbing ache.

Thank you, love. It does feel better.

She gazed up at him. Her shorter hair made her appear even younger the way it framed her face. He stroked its silky softness.

"I still want to grow my hair long and braid it to honor the Brethren," he said. "I hope that won't distress you."

Merry captured his hand between her own.

"Of course not. I won't ever cut my hair again either." She smiled. "Our braids will be the same length."

As soon as Merry stood, Bishop Ignatius entered the infirmary wearing his embroidered surplice and a skull cap instead of his mitre. He nodded at Merry and Valerian.

"Your Highness, my lady, I understand from King Orland that you wish for me to witness your vows of betrothal."

"Yes, Your Grace." Valerian kissed Merry's hand. "I have asked for the lady's hand and she has accepted."

Kieran, Drew, and Rafael returned, out of breath.

"Are we too late, Sire?" asked Kieran.

"No, you are just in time." Valerian longed to ask where they had been.

The bishop looked at the three young men.

"Are these your witnesses, then?"

Merry beckoned to Gwendolyn and indicated the two recovering patients on the cots.

"And these also."

Bishop Ignatius raised an eyebrow.

"An unusual collection of witnesses."

"We would have no other, Your Grace," said Valerian.

The bishop became serious and turned to Merry.

"My lady, I understand you are a royal cousin, though not so close as to prevent marriage to the prince. Is Merry the name you were christened with?"

"No, Your Grace. I was christened Mercy, but I no longer go by that name."

Mercy? What a beautiful name. "Why did you never tell me?"

Her face grew sad.

"When you and Kieran first found me, I was deeply grieving the loss of everyone and everything I knew. I thought no one alive knew me as

Mercy, so when Kieran asked to call me Merry, it seemed good at the time." Rafael hugged her.

"I'm sorry, my lady," Kieran said, chagrined. "I shouldn't have pressed ye about taking that name."

"Please, dear Kieran," Merry said. "Never apologize for that. You giving me a new name helped me find a reason to keep on living."

Bishop Ignatius cleared his throat.

"That's settled, then." He spoke to Valerian, who was still seated in the chair. "It is customary to kneel, Sire, but if you are not able—"

"We can help ye with that, my lord," Kieran said. "Rafael, will ye toss me a pillow, lad?"

Rafael brought a pillow from an unused cot, and Kieran placed it on the floor in front of the bishop.

"Come, Drew, our prince must kneel and needs us to be his supports."

Nervously, Valerian put a hand on each of their shoulders and hopped to the pillow. Leaning heavily upon his squires he lowered himself to a kneeling position. He tried to put most of his weight on the uninjured leg.

The bishop held out his hand for Merry, and she knelt on Valerian's left side.

"The vows of betrothal are as binding as the marriage vows. They should never be taken lightly, without commitment. Because you will be king someday, Prince Valerian, you and your future queen must enter into the marriage contract with greater seriousness than most couples." He addressed Valerian.

"Do you, Valerian d'Alden, agree to enter into the covenant of marriage with this woman, Mercy known as Merry?"

He bared his mind to Merry. "I do so promise, so help me God."

The bishop turned to Merry.

"And do you, Mercy known as Merry, agree to enter into the covenant of marriage with this man, Valerian d'Alden?"

"I do so promise, so help me God."

Bishop Ignatius then placed Merry's right hand in Valerian's right and bound them with his stole.

"By this handfasting, I bind you in the name of the Father, the Son, and the Holy Ghost until such time as you are able to make your marriage vows to one another before the altar of the Most High. What God has joined together, let not man put asunder."

Valerian gazed into Merry's eyes, too full of joy for words, when the bishop said, "You may kiss her now, Sire, to seal the vow."

Valerian leaned toward Merry and kissed her gently.

Then the bishop unwrapped the stole and bade them rise. Merry stepped away so Kieran and Drew could help Valerian back to the chair.

Kieran turned to Merry, looking more serious than Valerian had ever seen him.

"And now, my lady, we must take your betrothed away in order to present him in all his splendor later today." He bowed solemnly, and he and Drew lifted Valerian in the chair, bearing him out of the infirmary. Rafael led the way.

I'm sorry, Merry. Things have quickly gone beyond my control.

It's not the first time, and probably won't be the last. Farewell for now.

Fortunately this time it will not be for long.

Merry felt bereaved after Valerian left. She knew it was ridiculous, but she didn't want to let him out of her sight. After they did marry, would she finally be at peace? She came to herself and realized Gwendolyn was waiting patiently.

"I'm sorry, Gwen. I've been lost in thought."

"It's all right, my lady." Gwendolyn winked. "I just need you to check on Brentley's foot. He wants to know if he can use crutches yet." She lowered her voice. "He's heartily bored, and Tristam as well."

"Tristam?" Merry gasped. "I never asked his name." She'd been neglecting both of her patients since Valerian was brought to the infirmary.

"You've been rather distracted lately." Gwendolyn smirked, and Merry blushed.

She hurried to Brentley's cot and sat near his bandaged foot.

"I understand you're bored. That's a good sign." Merry smiled at him.

"My lady, I wish I could get out of here. Not that I don't appreciate what you and Lady Gwendolyn and Rafael have done for me."

"Think no more about it, Brentley. Let me examine your foot." Merry cupped her hands around the bandage and closed her eyes. Using the Healing power, she could *See* the bones beginning to mend. Fortunately, no infection clouded that process. She did bring together a few small fragments that she hadn't fused before and let go of the power before it could drain her strength.

"Your foot looks good, considering how badly it was crushed. If you promise not to put any weight upon it for at least a month, I can release you on crutches."

"Lady, for you I'd promise anything." Brentley brought his fist to his heart in a gesture that greatly touched her.

"Gwendolyn, bring some crutches, please."

They helped the squire pull himself up so he could position the crutches under his arms. Merry bade Gwendolyn stay with him while he practiced walking around the infirmary. She went to Tristam and sat beside him. He stared at her with his remaining eye. It was the palest blue with long dark lashes. He had been a handsome young man. Now his ruined face was marred with ugly stitches.

"How do you feel, Tristam?" Merry smoothed his short brown hair back from his forehead.

"Lady Merry, I feel fine on the outside, but my heart is not well." He closed his eye. "I must look like a monster."

"I won't lie to you. You had a terrible injury and will have scars for the rest of your life. But Tristam, those scars were honorably earned while helping to protect others. All true Levathians will respect you for what you have done. It doesn't matter what the rest may think." He peered up at the fierceness in her voice. Merry kissed his cheek on a place where there were no stitches. She knew Valerian would approve.

Tristam took a deep breath.

"There's no reason I should stay here, is there?"

"No, you're free to go. I'll take out the stitches as soon as you heal." Merry paused. "You can't wear an eye patch until then, but if you have a cloak with a hood, perhaps you could pull it over your eye to help you feel less conscious about it."

The squire nodded and forced himself to sit up.

"How long before you can remove the stitches?"

"When they begin to itch unbearably." She smiled at him. "You will know."

"All right, my lady." Tristam slowly stood, and Merry was surprised to see he was almost as tall as Valerian. "I know where to find a cloak with a hood." Then he turned and slowly walked from the room.

Merry glanced around the infirmary. Gwendolyn came to stand beside her.

"It's so quiet, so empty," Gwendolyn said.

"This battle could have ended so badly for all of us." Merry grasped Gwendolyn's hands. "I saw only part of the Horde's swarm at the garrison. Truly, Valerian saved us all. I hope the king realizes it."

"He does. That's the reason for the feast tonight." Gwendolyn scanned Merry from head to toe. "My lady, 'tis time we returned to your room. I want to help you get ready."

Merry ducked her head. "I would like to look my best for Valerian, especially if the king is going to announce our betrothal." She touched her short hair again. Her voice came out in a hoarse whisper. "I wish I could have kept my hair. I feel ugly without it."

"I have some ideas to make you show off your beauty." Gwendolyn hugged her. "I'm so glad you and prince found one another."

Merry returned the hug.

"Thank you, Gwen." She pulled back and stared at her friend. "But what about Drew? Is there something I should know?"

"Our families have wanted to join us in marriage all our lives, for reasons of land and dowry." Gwendolyn blushed. "But, thankfully, we've always had great affection for one another."

"Must you wait long? I don't know how marriages are arranged outside my own village."

"We must wait until Drew is knighted." Gwendolyn sighed. "Three more years."

Merry was grateful she and Valerian didn't have to wait that long. A few days, or even weeks, was nothing, and she should be more patient.

"May that time seem like just a few days, and may your love grow more and more."

"It will be worth the wait, Merry, I know it will." Gwendolyn blushed again and turned serious. "Now, I must get to work and ready you for the banquet."

Merry first put all her medicines in the carry sack and then left with Gwendolyn.

Chapter 41 *The dragons shall honour me.*

Valerian sat close to the fire in his bedchamber, wrapped in a towel. Kieran and Drew had helped him bathe, taking care to keep his bandaged stump dry.

For once, Valerian was glad for their help. He was still weak from loss of blood and off balance because of the missing lower leg. After Drew helped him pull on a pair of black velvet breeches, the squire carefully pinned back the extra material on the right leg, covering the fresh bandage on the stump.

Kieran pulled Valerian's finest white tunic over his head, the one with embroidered golden dragons along the neckline and sleeve edges. The trim would still be visible once the royal surcoat was in place.

"Drew," said Kieran. "Do ye know how to braid hair?"

"I've braided my horse's tail on occasion." He combed back Valerian's damp hair with his fingers. "I'll see what I can do, Sire."

Valerian watched Rafael. The boy sat nearby on a chair, swinging his legs. Rafael fingered his own hair, which was much longer than Valerian's.

When Rafael met his eyes, Valerian asked, "Would you like for Drew to braid yours, too?"

"Are you wearing a braid because you're one of the Brethren?" Rafael frowned in puzzlement.

"No, Rafael. I'm wearing a braid so no one will ever forget the Brethren. It's my way to honor them, especially Gabriel." Valerian wanted to believe that Gabriel would have recognized the honor he meant to give them.

"I was going to cut my hair short like Drew's so I could be a page," said the boy, "but maybe I should keep the braid. Do you think it will hurt Sissy, since she had to cut hers off?"

"I think you should wear a braid if you wish to. Even a page is not required to cut his hair. You won't hurt your Sissy. In fact, she told me she will not cut her hair again. I plan to have matching clasps made for our braids."

"Truly?" Rafael slid down from the chair and came to stand beside Valerian.

"Yes, truly." He smiled at the boy. "What do you think of a purple background with a golden dragon inside a wreath of balmflowers?" Valerian *Saw* Rafael picture the design in his head.

"It's a good idea. May I wear a dragon too?"

"Of course you may. After all, you're a descendant of Alden the Dragon King, just like your sister."

"You don't have the clasps yet, so how will you tie your hair?" Rafael frowned.

"Look in the bottom drawer of yonder press," Kieran said. "There should be some lengths of ribbon."

Rafael wrested open the heavy drawer. He picked out two ribbons and brought them to Valerian.

"Here's a purple one and a black one."

"Which would you rather wear, Rafael?"

"You should wear purple because you're the prince. I'll wear the black one." He handed the purple ribbon to Drew, who wrapped it around the end of Valerian's short braid.

Drew stepped to one side.

"Come and check my braiding, Rafael. The prince has got to impress your sister, you know."

"Sissy will like him no matter what, but he's s'posed to look handsome for the feast," Rafael said while examining the braid. "It looks good, Valerian. Can you do mine, Drew?"

Drew braided Rafael's hair while Kieran tied Valerian into the royal surcoat and set the princely circlet upon his head. All that remained was to pull on the left boot and carry him downstairs to the great hall. Valerian fidgeted in the ornate garment.

When Rafael opened the door for the "throne bearers" the boy said, "Oh, Sissy, you're beautiful."

Anxious to see Merry, Valerian had Kieran and Drew set down the chair in the hallway. Merry wore a green embroidered gown with sleeves just off her shoulders. Her hair was arranged under a green jeweled veil that framed her face. She smiled at Valerian, and his heart swelled with admiration and longing.

A pang of sadness squeezed his gut. Merry came closer, resting her hand on his sleeve.

"What is it?" she asked.

"I only wish I could escort you into the hall."

"That day will come, and soon."

While they spoke, eager footsteps ran toward them. A young man burst from the stairwell and saw the small group.

"Your Highness," he cried.

"What news, Flint?" Valerian caught the courier's excitement.

Flint Mallory? Merry sounded surprised.

Yes, do you know him?

He brought a message from your father to our village. I Healed his broken arm.

"You are wanted in the yard outside the doors to the great hall, Sire," Flint Mallory said with a flourish. "The king has sent me to bring you."

"Thank you." Valerian inclined his head. "We will come directly."

The king's messenger turned his gaze on Merry, and his jaw dropped.

"My lady," he said. "Pardon me, but you resemble someone I once knew."

"Perhaps, because I am that someone." She came forward so he could better see her.

"Why, it is Mercy the Healer. What do you here?"

"It's a very long story," she said. "One that will have to be told another time, I'm afraid."

While Kieran and Drew lifted him in the chair, Valerian spoke up. "The short version is that she is a royal cousin and my intended bride."

"Well, if that's the short version, I cannot wait to hear the long one."

As the sound of Flint Mallory's voice receded, Valerian closed his eyes and gripped the chair arms while his squires patiently bore him down the stairs.

When Kieran and Drew carried Valerian through the big double doors that led from the great hall to the castle yard, those that had assembled burst into cheers. Then Valerian saw Albinonix, Tetratorix, and several other dragons sitting in the yard. The rest of the great beasts perched on the walls, towers, and buildings of the huge castle complex.

Kieran and Drew set Valerian's chair on the ground just beyond the lowest step. Merry came to stand beside him and clasped his hand.

They are so beautiful, love.

Yes, the dragons are altogether magnificent.

My prince! Albinonix reared up and opened his great wings. *The time has come for us to leave you.* The great dragon went back on all fours and folded his wings across his back. Then he came near and looked from Valerian to Merry with his penetrating eyes.

Is this your mate, my prince?

Yes, my lord Albinonix. This is Merry.

I am honored to meet you, my lord. She curtsied.

Albinonix opened his terrible mouth in a dragon smile.

You must be another descendant of Alden.

Yes, my lord, I am. Merry opened her mind to the dragon leader as well as to Valerian. Albinonix tilted his head to better *See* her.

You are a Healer, are you not?

Yes, my lord.

Come. Wyvernia has injured her wing. Will you see if you can Heal it?

Valerian squeezed her hand and spoke aloud.

"Go on, love. I would not dare refuse him anything after what they have done for us. I would go too if I could." He beckoned to Kieran, who stood nearby. "Go with Merry. She has been asked to Heal one of the dragons."

Kieran trotted after Merry and Albinonix, and Valerian felt a twinge of envy that he could not go with them. The dragon Wyvernia was smaller than most of the others and a paler greenish-blue. She moved her wing toward Merry, and even from this distance Valerian could see the bent wing tip.

Then he heard Merry's exchange with the dragon and gave thanks for that ability. It helped make up for the loss of mobility a little.

I am Merry. I am a Healer. I will now See *your injury. You should feel no additional pain.*

I do not fear pain, Healer Merry. I fear not being able to fly properly.

Valerian opened himself to Merry while she Healed the wing. He *Saw* when her strength began to fail, but before he could warn her, he sensed Kieran adding his strength to hers to complete the Healing. How had he done that?

Valerian. Did you feel that?

Yes. Did Kieran's help keep you from exhausting yourself?

Amazingly, yes. Perhaps you could help me in the same way.

I hope so, Merry.

Wyvernia flexed her wing and threw back her head in exultation.

Thank you, Healer Merry. I am whole again.

Merry curtsied to the dragon.

It was our pleasure to aid you, Merry said. Then she and Kieran made their way back to Valerian's side. Before he reached the chair, Kieran grinned when Tetratorix bent down to playfully snort at the squire.

Albinonix came forward again and positioned himself before Valerian. Again he reared up on his back legs and stretched out his wings.

Prince Valerian, we will not forget the Covenant we have renewed with you. When you become king, we will return to welcome you as our new Dragon King. You and your descendants may call on us, always.

At that Albinonix pointed his head skyward and roared. The other dragons reared up with an answering roar.

Help me stand, love. Valerian pushed himself erect, and Merry wrapped her arm around his waist to help him balance on one leg.

“My sword! I don't have my sword.”

Kieran slid his blade from the scabbard on his belt.

"Use mine, Sire."

Valerian grasped the hilt and held it above his head. The thunderous sound of the dragons was made more deafening as the human witnesses added their shouts to the dragons' salute.

All grew quiet as Albinonix lowered himself and brought his enormous head down to Valerian. He could feel the dragon's hot breath as he returned the sword to Kieran and put his right hand over his heart. Then Valerian spoke out loud for the benefit of those present, as well as with his mind to the dragons.

"I pledge to you, my lord Albinonix, greatest of all dragons, that I will be faithful to our Covenant all the days of my life. I will teach all Levathians to respect and honor you for the salvation you have brought to us."

Tears came to his eyes when he realized that except for him and Merry, every human present had gone down on one knee, paying homage to the magnificent dragons.

Farewell, Prince Valerian. Farewell, Healer Merry. We shall meet again. And Albinonix reared up a final time, spread his wings, and launched himself into the air. The force of the backstroke pushed Valerian into the chair. Merry let go of him and held on to the chair's arm. As soon as all the dragons were airborne, they briefly flamed the air, living fireworks in the evening sky. The awed crowd watched until they were specks against the clouds.

"Well," said King Orland quietly as he came to stand beside Valerian. "That is a memory not soon forgotten."

"We should never forget what the dragons did for us, Father."

"No, we should not." The king turned to look at Valerian. "I'm afraid the feast will be rather dull after that display."

Valerian's heart was so full of gratitude, he smiled with all his being.

"How could it be so when the Keep is still standing, and most of its inhabitants are alive and well? We have much to celebrate."

Merry sat beside Valerian at the feast. King Orland had the chair on Valerian's other side, with Queen Winifred next to the king. The four of them were the only ones at the head table, but so many extra tables had been set up that the huge room appeared small and crowded. Merry caught glimpses of people she knew or had met, but most were strangers. Everyone ate and laughed and shouted to be heard over the group of musicians playing happy tunes.

Is every feast as loud as this one? Merry asked.

Valerian laughed at her reaction.

Most of them. This time it's a display of happiness at being alive.

I'm thankful for our mind talking. I would not be able to hear you otherwise.

He laced his fingers in hers and brought her hand to his lips. Before Valerian could reply, King Orland called for attention, and a hush fell over the room.

"Before this celebration becomes too unruly, there are a few things I would like to say." The king glanced about the hall. "Miraculously, we lost only four men in the battle with the Horde, and nearly all of the injuries were minor indeed. For this, we should give thanks as we remember our honored dead: Sir Emory Daughtry. Sir Caelis Reed. Randol of Frankland. Guy of Briarwood Village." He bowed his head in silence, and everyone followed his example.

Sir Emory was Tristam's knight, Valerian explained to Merry.

Poor Tristam. What will he do?

I don't know, but I'll think of something.

After a few minutes, King Orland broke the silence.

"The reason for this miracle, of course, is that Prince Valerian was able to contact the great dragons and convince them to help us defeat the Horde. I know we cannot outdo the tribute the dragons have already given him, but we can certainly try." Orland stood and gazed down at Valerian. "We owe our lives to you, my son. 'Tis a debt that can never be repaid."

Everyone in the hall leaped to their feet and erupted in cheers. Merry stood, resting her hand on Valerian's shoulder.

Try to smile, love, and let them honor their hero.

I'm trying, but I am uneasy receiving their praise.

Because of your brother?

He didn't answer in words, but Merry could *See* the regret he would always carry with him. She gently squeezed his shoulder.

It took several long minutes for the clamor to die down. King Orland raised his hand before speaking.

"I have one more announcement to make, and a toast." He gestured for Merry to be seated. "This very day, Prince Valerian is betrothed to our royal cousin, Lady Merry." He raised his cup. "May their wait be short before the royal wedding, and may the Most High bless their union and make them fruitful."

"Hear, hear!" There was much clashing of cups.

Over the noise, someone shouted, "And may their wait be short before the royal wedding night."

Merry's face grew warm, and she glanced at Valerian. His face had reddened too, but he laced his fingers with hers and smiled shyly.

When the king sat down, everyone else took their seats as well. The music began again, and the conversations grew louder, the laughter more boisterous. Merry could see Valerian's strength fading.

I'm sure your father would not mind if you went to your room now that he has made his speech.

I should stay a little longer, I think.

It was a good thing he did, for many of the men came to the head table, first bowing, and then wanting to thank him personally. Most of them acknowledged her as well, especially the men of Valerian's first command, and several also wanted to kiss her hand and wish her joy.

By the time everyone who desired it had come forward, Valerian was so exhausted that even King Orland noticed and beckoned for Kieran and Drew to help the prince upstairs. They lifted the chair and bore him out to more cheering from those who remained in the hall. Merry, Rafael, and Queen Winifred followed behind.

When they reached the quiet hallway leading to the royal apartments, the squires set Valerian down in front of his door. As Kieran opened it, the queen went to Valerian's side.

"My son, I want you to know how proud of you I am." Winifred's voice trembled. "I'm sorry I have not been a better mother to you. I want to be an encouragement to you and your lovely bride as you have already been to me." She held out her hands timidly. Valerian seized her hands and kissed them.

"The past is gone, Mother. Each day is a gift from the Most High to enjoy its blessings. We have much to be thankful for."

"Bless you, Valerian. Good night, my son." Winifred then kissed Merry's cheek. "And good night to you, my daughter." Reluctantly she turned away and went to her own rooms.

"That's the first time she's attended a feast since I was a child." Valerian shook his head in wonder, and Merry gripped his hand.

"You have helped her find a reason to return to life," she said quietly.

"And you have filled the emptiness of her heart by being a daughter to her." His face was full of tenderness. "Thank you."

Kieran cleared his throat.

"Pardon me, Sire, but if we dinna get ye inside, you will fall asleep sitting in this chair, and we'll ne'er get you in the bed."

Valerian held Merry's hand against his cheek.

I only wish you could lay there beside me.

It is my greatest wish, too. The nights are long and lonely without you. Merry bent down and kissed him. Then she watched until the door shut her beloved from her sight.

Chapter 42 *When he hath tried me, I shall come forth as gold.*

Merry woke with a start. She had not told Valerian about Gabriel.

"What about Gabriel?" he said quietly when they met later in his solar.

"Your mother and I made an important discovery the other day." Merry grasped his hand.

"What is that?" Valerian leaned closer.

"Do you remember when we found Gabriel's braid at the garrison, and you said his clasp looked familiar?"

"The morning glories." He gasped. "My mother's family emblem. You don't mean that he--?"

"Gabriel was your Uncle Denis. He changed his name when he took the Oath of Peace."

Valerian sat motionless, stunned, and Merry did not intrude on his thoughts. Rafael came to stand close beside her. Merry now wished she had waited until she and Valerian were alone. Or that she had told him mind-to-mind.

"What did the queen say?" Valerian whispered.

"She was glad to know what happened to her brother. He had run away many years ago."

"Sissy?"

"Yes, love?" She turned to Rafael.

"Mama died, Papa and Gabriel and Dilly died, and Caelis died." Rafael glanced at Valerian and back at Merry. "If I like Valerian, will he die, too?"

Horrified, she put her arm around him. His body tensed.

What shall I say to him? Even the squires had heard, for the room grew quiet.

Let me try. Valerian shifted in his chair. "Rafael, I'm sad for you because you have lost so much in your young life, and none of it, absolutely none of it is your fault."

Rafael's gaze was unfocused, and for a moment Merry wished she could *See* what he was thinking. Her brother met Valerian's eyes.

"So if I like you," he said, "you promise you won't die?"

Merry flinched, but she kept her peace. Valerian cleared his throat.

"I can't promise you, Rafael," he said quietly, "but I plan to be here for a long time, as long as the Most High wills."

Merry leaned over and kissed Valerian.

"You will as long as I have anything to say about it." She kissed him again.

Relief flooded Rafael's face.

"Because Sissy loves you so much," he said, "I know she will take care of you and keep you safe."

Merry had just begun to think she might have a whole day to spend in Valerian's company, when there was a knock at the door. Lady Brenna had a summons from the queen. Merry sighed and bade them all a reluctant farewell.

* * *

Over the next several days, Merry spent more time with the queen making wedding plans than she did with Valerian or even Rafael. She had Gwendolyn take Sir Edmund's cage to Valerian's rooms so Rafael could take over the care of the little dragon. Merry found herself crying with impatience every night, and she had to guard her thoughts lest they spill over and trouble Valerian. How could they live so close and still not be together? They never ate more than one meal a day in one another's company, and it seemed her sole purpose in spending time with him was to Heal his leg. There was always something needing to be done which kept them apart. At least, if they were already married, she could have his uninterrupted attention at night, even if they were too tired to do more than sleep.

One evening, when she went to Valerian's rooms to check his leg, he was deep in thought, sitting in his favorite chair. With his hair loose about his shoulders, he wore a linen shirt and tan-colored breeches. He had a scroll in his lap, but when he saw her, he let it roll back and set it on the small table beside him.

Merry pulled a footstool next to Valerian's chair. She had just sat down when Rafael walked into the room, the little burrowing dragon perched on his shoulder.

"Look, Sissy. Sir Edmund likes me now."

"I'm glad, Rafael." Merry sighed at the pleased look on her brother's face. Since Caelis' death, he seemed much more relaxed.

I agree. I don't think his association with Caelis did him any good.

Merry looked at Valerian, startled.

Do you know something I do not?

I mostly know from my past dealings with Caelis that he could be cruel, especially to young powerless boys. He gripped her hand.

Will he tell me what happened?

He may. But don't press him. Fortunately, he's young enough that given time the bad memories may fade.

Merry remembered how changed Gabriel had been by his hardships, changed for the better. She would have to pray the same proved true for Rafael.

Her brother stood close beside her. Sir Edmund flicked out his tongue, smelling her. Merry stroked the little dragon's head.

The door opened again, and Drew and Kieran entered. Kieran carried a pair of crutches.

"Sire, I found the crutches." He nodded to Merry. "Good evening, my lady."

"Good evening, Kieran." She turned to Valerian. "Do you feel ready to try walking?"

Valerian shrugged, but he couldn't hide his anxiety from her.

"I'm heartily tired of sitting around so much. Someday I'll be able to wear a wooden leg, but until that time I've got to build up my strength."

Kieran handed the crutches to Valerian and then stood back. Valerian took a deep breath and pulled himself upright. He positioned the crosspieces under his arms. But they were too short, and he had to lean forward. He took a careful step, then another, and began to lose his balance. Kieran and Drew jumped forward to steady him.

After a few minutes, he tried again. This time he found his balance. He walked to the other side of the room, made a wide turn and started back to his chair.

"Not very graceful, is it? But at least I'm moving under my own power."

When Valerian reached the chair, everyone remained silent while he carefully turned and lowered himself into it.

"Well," he said. "That was an adventure."

"They are too short, as I feared." Kieran grimaced. "Do ye want Master Murray to have some taller ones made?"

"Only if I'll have to use crutches often." Valerian sighed.

Merry gripped his hand again.

"Once you have a wooden leg and learn to balance yourself, you shouldn't need crutches often, but it would be a good idea to have them at hand." *Just think of them as a tool.*

A tool. Valerian sighed again. "Very well, Kieran."

The squire nodded, saluting.

"Then I'll speak to Master Murray, first thing."

Valerian woke suddenly, alert but disoriented. He'd had a vivid dream, but now he couldn't recall anything about it. Had the dragons appeared? Was there any threat lurking? Of course, he knew there would always be problems to solve in Levathia, whether human or otherwise.

He sat up, listening for Merry across the hall, but she must still be sleeping. No sound came from the other rooms, either. Was he the only one awake?

Using the crutches Kieran had left beside the bed, Valerian walked to the garderobe by himself. The weakness that had plagued him for nearly a fortnight was gone. There was no reason he couldn't get around, at least on flat surfaces, using the crutches.

With no stumbling, Valerian managed to dress himself and braid his hair. He opened the door to the solar and Kieran, Drew, and Rafael were putting away their cots. When they saw him, they came closer. All three wore pleased looks.

"What is it?" Valerian couldn't help but smile at them.

"Well, Sire," said Kieran. "After ye went to sleep, Master Murray himself paid a visit. Since we didna want to wake ye, he showed us what to do." He paused dramatically.

"Yes? What is it?"

"Wouldn't you like to eat first, Your Highness?" Drew stifled a smile.

"No. I couldn't possibly eat now that you've so piqued my curiosity." Valerian glanced from Drew to Kieran. Finally, he turned to Rafael. "Won't you at least tell me what's going on?"

Rafael quivered, unable to keep the secret.

"You have a wooden leg now," the boy said, grinning.

They bade him sit down. Rafael took the crutches while Kieran and Drew attached the leg to Valerian's stump, as Master Murray had shown them.

"How does it feel, Sire?" asked Drew.

"I won't really know until I stand on it." Valerian's heart pounded. *Please,* he prayed, *let me stay upright at least.*

They backed away, but not too far. Valerian took a deep breath and stood. For the first time since he'd lost the leg, he felt tall. He slowly put weight on the wooden leg, feeling for his balance. Then carefully, thinking through every movement, he took a step forward, then another. He understood now why Ruddy had been so grateful to have kept the knee joint; it did make the mechanics of walking much easier. Oh, how he had taken this freedom of movement for granted!

By the time he'd completed a circuit of the room, Valerian began to feel more confident, but not so much that he would risk walking any faster. It was enough that he could walk again. And that meant—

Valerian? Are you awake?

Yes, love. I have something to show you.

Gwendolyn is helping me dress, and I will be right over.

Valerian turned to his faithful squires and his new brother.

"I'll be back."

Rafael nodded with a knowing look.

"Sissy must be awake."

By himself, Valerian walked to the door, opened it, and stepped out into the hall. He went more slowly on the stone floor, since it was uneven in places, until he stood before the door to his old rooms. He had just lifted his fist to knock, when the door opened. Merry gazed up into his eyes.

"I think you have grown, my beautiful prince." She stepped into the hall, facing him. He held out his hands to her, and she took them.

"If I have grown, it is in my love for you." Valerian smiled. "I know it cannot be today, but now that I can walk, I'm ready whenever we can be married."

"I'll speak to the queen this morning. I'm sure everything can be made ready by tomorrow."

"Tomorrow? Truly?" The pulse pounded in his head.

"Yes. Your mother has been so happy organizing details as if I were her own daughter. I know she's kept her ladies busy every day of your recovery."

Tomorrow. He let go of her hands and gently cupped her face.

Only one more night alone. Her eyes shone with happy tears.

Valerian kissed Merry gently, as he had the very first time. He didn't trust himself to do more. Just that sweet touch was enough to send lightning through his body, and he had to let her go and take a step back. Merry must have felt the same, for she backed against the wall, her face flushed.

"'Tis a good thing we will be very busy today, I think." She smiled coyly. "It will make the time pass more quickly."

Not quickly enough. He ached to hold her in his arms, but he dared not.

"I would rather spend every moment in your company, but I must speak to the queen." Merry backed toward Queen Winifred's door, unwilling to turn away from him.

Valerian watched her until she entered his mother's rooms.

Oh, God Most High, I bless you for such a precious and beloved wife. Please help me be a good husband so her joys will always be greater than her sorrows.

*   *   *

The day did pass quickly, and the evening as well. Kieran and Drew invited the men of Valerian's first command to his rooms to share a simple meal and toast him on his last night of bachelorhood. Since the only one of the group who had been married was Sir Gregory, Valerian took him aside while the others talked and laughed together.

"Sir Gregory, I have a difficult question to ask you, and I'm not sure how to begin." Valerian had apparently worn his wooden leg too long that day, for it chafed his stump. He beckoned the knight to be seated with him in a corner of the solar.

"I think I know what's troubling you, Your Highness." Gregory smiled knowingly. "I was nervous the night before my wedding."

"You were?" Could it be there was nothing wrong with him, after all?

The knight clasped Valerian on the shoulder and leaned closer.

"It can be a frightening thing for a young man to take such a huge step as marriage."

"The commitment isn't what frightens me," he said. "Merry and I have been one in mind and thoughts for so long, we could not imagine marriage to anyone else. It's the—other part of our relationship which makes me anxious. For a variety of reasons, not the least of which being I had desired to be a monk when Waryn was heir to the throne, I am—" His face grew warm.

"Inexperienced?"

"Yes." Relief flooded Valerian. Sir Gregory was more sympathetic than he'd hoped for.

"Not to worry, Sire." The knight gripped his shoulder. "Let your great love for one another and your communion of minds and hearts guide you in the rest. You will be fine."

"Thank you, Sir Gregory." Valerian sighed. "I hope it didn't cause you sadness to talk about such things."

"Not at all, Your Highness. My wife and I were happy for the few years we had together. My only regret is the son she died trying to birth did not live either. But our daughter still lives and is happy with my sister and her family."

"That seems to be a great secret of life, to be happy with what you have and who you share your life with for as long as God wills."

"Yes, that's a good way to say it." Sir Gregory clasped Valerian's wrist. "I wish you and Lady Merry many years of happiness together. I heartily approve of your bride and my future queen."

"That means a great deal coming from someone I highly respect." Valerian inclined his head.

At last, the men were encouraged to return to their own quarters, and one by one they bade Valerian a good night.

"That was fun." Rafael yawned hugely.

"Yes, and now it's past time to sleep." Drew set up Rafael's cot. "We have a long day tomorrow."

The boy nodded and lay down on the cot, falling instantly asleep.

"I wish I could go to sleep so easily." Valerian winced, and Kieran came toward him.

"Is your leg bothering you, Sire?"

"Yes. I think I was on it too long for the first day." He winced again.

"Here, let me take it off and put some of Merry's salve on it."

Valerian closed his eyes while Kieran worked on his leg. He was suddenly weary and hoped he could sleep tonight, at least for a while.

* * *

Early in the morning Valerian sat on a stool in his bedchamber while Drew and Kieran each laced a sleeve of his new gold tunic. Although it was more intricate in design than the purple one, it wasn't as confining.

"You aren't nervous, are you, my lord?" asked Drew.

"I'm not nervous about getting married. I am, however, quite anxious about tripping and falling on my face."

"Dinna worry, Sire," Kieran said. "We will nae let ye fall."

"Thank you." Valerian met Kieran's gaze and before realizing what he was doing, *Saw* his thoughts. Though Kieran tried, he couldn't hide his anguish over Merry. Sick at heart, Valerian turned to Drew. "Would you please see if Rafael is still across the hall? I would like to ask him something."

"Of course, Sire. I've just finished this sleeve." As soon as Drew left the bedchamber, Valerian grabbed Kieran's arm.

"Why didn't you tell me you still felt that way about her? Oh, Kieran, forgive me! If I'd been paying attention, I never would have asked you to stand up with me at the altar."

Kieran went down on one knee and placed his fist over his heart.

"'Tis nothing tae forgive, Val. O' course I love her. I will always love her. But I am your squire and your friend. As one who loves ye well, I will ne'er let my feelings destroy our friendship. I want only your happiness, and I am glad to share in your great joy today."

Valerian could *See* Kieran meant what he said, and he marveled the squire could be so unselfish in such a circumstance. He wasn't sure he'd be so magnanimous if the roles were reversed.

"I never, *never* meant to cause you pain. I knew you liked her when we first found her, but somehow I failed to recognize the depth of your devotion." He shook his head, dazed. "I am humbled anew you are still willing to be my squire."

Kieran grasped Valerian's hand and pressed it to his forehead.

"I be your man, Prince Valerian, and I pledge my life in service to you, to your wife, and someday to your bairns. I will be faithful to you and your family 'til my death. So help me God."

Swallowing hard, Valerian raised him up.

"I accept your service, Kieran MacLachlan, and pledge my faithfulness to you in return. Never has a man had so noble a friend."

Drew and Rafael entered the bedchamber. Rafael wore a blue velvet tunic and breeches, and his hair had been combed and braided, secured with a blue ribbon.

"You look very handsome, Rafael." Valerian smiled at the boy. He resembled Merry more than usual today. "Are you ready for the wedding?"

"Yes." Rafael leaned closer and spoke quietly. "You should see Sissy. She looks like an angel."

Of course she looks like an angel, Valerian thought. But he could scarcely contain his impatience to see her.

"The king looks handsome, too," Rafael continued. "But you are much handsomer. Sissy will be pleased, and she will probably cry."

"Well, of course she will, you rascal." Drew grinned. "That's what women do at weddings." He turned to Kieran. "If Lady Merry has already reached the angelic state, then we are behind schedule. Do you want the boot or the leg?"

"I'll take the leg, my bonny fellow squire."

"Then I'll take care of the boot, my fellow future knight."

Valerian laughed at them and turned back to Rafael.

"Do you have a special task during the wedding?"

"I get to carry Sissy's train. It's heavy, but I'm strong." The boy straightened.

"Yes, you are. You are the bravest young man I've ever known." Valerian held out his hand, and Rafael gripped his wrist as he'd taught him. "Brother to brother, forever and always."

"Brother to brother." Rafael nodded solemnly.

Someone knocked at the door of the solar. Rafael ran to answer it, and Valerian heard Gwendolyn's voice.

"Come, Rafael. It's almost time to get your sister to the chapel."

Valerian gasped. How would he get down there in time? As if he'd read his mind, Kieran looked up from adjusting the wooden leg.

"Drew and I will carry ye down in the chair, Sire. You need to get there quickly and 'twill save unnecessary steps on the wooden leg."

Valerian closed his eyes and sighed.

"Very well. You make perfect sense, Kieran, as you always do." His eyes flew open. "The ring. Do you have the ring?"

"Right next to me heart where I always hold you and Merry both." Kieran patted the breast of his black velvet tunic.

Valerian gripped Kieran's arm. There were no more words necessary on that subject. Then Valerian also shared a handclasp with Drew.

"Thank you, my friends. I am ready now to go and meet my bride."

They lifted him in the chair and carried him for what Valerian hoped was the last time.

Chapter 43 *This is my beloved, and this is my friend.*

When Drew and Kieran reached the chapel door, Valerian bade them set him down.

"I must go in by myself now." He stood, balancing on his wooden leg. "But please, help me kneel and stand again when the time comes so I won't fall or look too awkward, for Merry's sake."

"O' course, Sire." Kieran's quiet voice was calming. "'Tis why we are here."

"You can count on us, Your Highness," added Drew.

They followed him into the chapel. Valerian paused, amazed. The women of the Keep had outdone themselves decorating so it resembled a garden. There weren't many flowers, since it was not yet spring, but baskets and wreaths of green gave the place life. *How appropriate for Merry the Healer*, he thought.

Valerian and the two squires slowly made their way to the altar and waited off to the side. Kieran found a velvet stool for Valerian to sit on while they watched the people of the Keep steadily fill the wooden benches. Valerian was especially glad they had arrived early enough so he would not have to stumble down the aisle twice in front of the entire assembly.

"Oh, no," Drew suddenly whispered.

"What is it?" Valerian's empty stomach lurched in alarm.

"I forgot your circlet, Sire. I'll run and get it." Drew dashed up a side aisle, dodging people all wearing their finest clothing.

It only took the squire minutes to return with the silver circlet in his hand. Breathlessly he placed it on Valerian's brow just as a choir in the loft began singing a joyous anthem. The murmur of conversation quieted while Valerian's uncles and aunts came down the aisle and seated themselves in the front row.

Bishop Ignatius entered from a side door and approached the altar. He wore his most elaborate robes and the jeweled mitre upon his head. He nodded to Valerian, and the four of them took their places at the altar.

"Are you ready, my prince?" asked the bishop quietly.

"With all my heart, Your Grace," Valerian said.

Next down the aisle was the queen, escorted by Valerian's cousin. Winifred appeared more beautiful than Valerian had ever seen her. He had no memory of her wearing anything other than black. Now she wore a pale lavender gown and coif, and when she smiled at him, it made her look young and vibrant again. What a transformation Merry had wrought upon his entire family.

Finally, it came time for the bride's maids. Lady Brenna came first, followed by a beaming Gwendolyn. They took their places on the other side of Bishop Ignatius. Then Valerian's gaze drifted to the back, and his heart quickened when the choir began a new anthem to welcome the bride.

Merry was truly angelic in her pale blue gown. She appeared to glide down the aisle, for the sheer veil covering her face hardly moved.

Oh my love, you are wondrously fair.

As are you, my beautiful prince.

She was almost to the altar before Valerian realized his father escorted her on his arm. It had seemed as if they two were alone in the room.

Father and bride stopped before Bishop Ignatius, and King Orland kissed Merry's cheek through the veil before giving her hand to the bishop. Then he stepped back beside the queen. Valerian smiled at his parents when Orland took Winifred's hand, and then he turned all his attention to his bride.

Even though Valerian understood the Latin Bishop Ignatius spoke, he listened half-heartedly to the institution of marriage in the Holy Writ, for he had read it many times. He gazed at Merry, awed and thankful that the Most High had spared their lives to this day. But when the bishop placed Merry's right hand in his, he listened carefully so as to repeat every phrase word for word and give full weight to his promise:

"I, Valerian, take you, Merry, to be my wife. I espouse you and commit to you the fidelity and loyalty of my body and my possessions. I will keep you in health and sickness and any condition it please the Most High that you should have. I pledge my love to you until death parts us."

Then Merry repeated the same promise in a clear voice. Valerian couldn't help but think of his wooden leg when she said the words "any condition," but he pushed the thought away and opened his mind to hers as fully as he'd ever done.

Bishop Ignatius bound their hands, his left to her right, and it was time to kneel. Kieran discreetly helped him down to the cushion and stepped back. Valerian met his eyes and nodded his thanks before bowing his head while the bishop prayed for their union to be long and fruitful. He shifted his weight off the stump just a little but did manage to listen to the words.

Then it was time for the ring. Kieran handed it to Valerian, and helped him hold it by the edge. Beginning with her thumb Valerian briefly placed it on each of her fingertips while Bishop Ignatius blessed it, "In nomine Patris, et Filii, et Spiritus Sancti," ending with the fourth finger on the "Amen." He kissed her hand, gazing into her eyes, but there were no words to adequately express his joy.

I understand you perfectly. Her gentle smile illuminated her eyes.

They remained kneeling long enough to take communion, and then it was time to stand. Again Kieran was there to help Valerian while Merry offered her support on his left. The bishop untied the stole, and Merry turned her face up to him.

I believe you are supposed to kiss me now.

Valerian made sure he was balanced on the wooden leg and slowly lifted the veil. Thankfully, Gwendolyn helped him pull it away from Merry's face. Tears shone in her eyes as he bent down and kissed her soundly. She encircled his waist to provide support for him, and they pulled apart once he heard comments from those present.

He saw Rafael then, standing between Merry and Gwendolyn. Valerian grinned down at the boy, who solemnly smiled back. Then it was time to walk down the aisle with Merry on his arm.

She matched her pace to his, and he wished he did not have to concentrate so hard on staying balanced and upright, for he would have liked to acknowledge all the many friends and family who had witnessed their vows. He supposed there would be time at the feast.

You will have plenty of time to speak to everyone, for I know the queen has prepared a feast that will last all day and into the evening.

I don't suppose anyone will go hungry today.

No, not even your ever-hungry squires.

Once they made it to the doors, they went into the great hall, which had also been festooned with garlands. There were two ornate chairs at the head table for the newlyweds. Once they reached the chairs, Gwendolyn and Lady Brenna removed the train from Merry's dress so she would be able to sit down. She kissed each of them as well as Rafael, and the three of them joined Kieran and Drew just below the head table.

This time Queen Winifred sat beside Merry, and King Orland sat next to Valerian. After everyone had taken their seats, the courses of the meal began, each one more and more elaborate. Valerian noticed Merry wasn't eating much.

Are you well, Merry?

Oh, yes. I am just too emotional to eat.

You're happy, aren't you?

Never happier, love. She slipped her hand through his arm. *Well, I will be happiest when we can finally be alone.*

So shall I. He leaned down and kissed her.

As the feast went on into the late hours of the afternoon, wineskins were passed around. Valerian couldn't help but notice how much Kieran was drinking. With each cup, his voice grew louder and his laugh more obnoxious. Sick at heart, Valerian realized his squire must be trying to "drown his sorrows." He'd heard of people doing that but never before witnessed it. It was all he could do to hold back thoughts of Kieran's sorrow and the reason for it from Merry.

At last the Keep's bard came forward with his lute. He bowed to Valerian and Merry.

"Your Highness. My lady. I have a new song to play in honor of your wedding. I did not write the words, but I put the words to music. And since I have discovered what your real name is, Lady Merry, this song is especially appropriate." He smiled at her and strummed a chord before he began.

"Some desire wealth, to hoard a great treasure,
Others make merry and seek only pleasure.
Some lust for power to fulfill their greed,
But he who finds Mercy finds true life, indeed."

The bard ended on a triumphant chord and bowed.

"May you, Prince Valerian, and you, Lady Merry, find true life and true love all the days of your marriage."

King Orland stood and raised his cup.

"On that note, let us toast the prince and his bride." Cups clashed together and more than one person had to wipe splashed wine from their face. "Now we must leave you for a little while to escort the bride and groom to their wedding bed."

Loud cheering caused both Valerian and Merry to blush as many eager hands lifted them in their chairs and carried them from the hall, up the stairs, and to their respective rooms. Kieran and Drew helped Valerian out of his finery and wooden leg and into a linen nightshirt. Gwendolyn and Brenna did the same for Merry, helped her into the bed, and opened all the bed curtains, for it had been decided the newlyweds should spend their wedding night in Valerian's old bed. Gwendolyn could more easily sleep in the queen's quarters than to find a place for Kieran, Drew, and Rafael.

So Valerian had to endure being carried one more time from his room to Merry's, surrounded by rowdy young men, the loudest of whom was Kieran. They set his chair beside the canopied bed, helped him stand on one leg, and lifted him onto it. With a shy smile at Merry he sat up and pulled the covers over his legs.

Bishop Ignatius pushed his way through the crowd and stood at the foot of the bed. He sprinkled a little holy water on it and recited a blessing in Latin that the Most High would grant their union to be fruitful. As soon as he said, "Amen," the young men sang a song which caused Valerian to blush again.

At last, everyone trailed out of the bedchamber. Gwendolyn and Brenna closed the bed curtains and then shut the door behind them. Valerian heard Kieran's voice begin another song, loudly and out of tune. Fortunately, his voice grew fainter and fainter as he followed the rest back to the great hall.

"I have never seen Kieran drunk," Valerian said quietly. "I hope he hasn't upset you." He shifted to better see Merry's face in the glow of the candles.

"I'm not thinking about Kieran tonight," she said, "nor anyone else in the whole world." She turned to face him, and her loose nightdress slipped, baring a shoulder.

Her skin was smooth and beautifully luminescent. He caressed her cheek, then gently ran his hand along her neck and bare shoulder. Valerian had never touched anything so soft before. Merry's eyes filled with joyous tears.

I am yours, my beautiful love, and you are mine. Before he could answer, she leaned closer and stared into his eyes, opening her thoughts fully to him. *I don't know what to do, but we can learn together.*

He kissed her sweet mouth and ran his fingers through her cropped hair. He heard her mental laugh.

It is a blessing, after all.

What is, love?

If I hadn't cut my hair, it would have been in our way.

He laughed aloud, sharing her delight, and gave thanks that the Most High had kept them through all manner of grief and peril so they might complete their oneness.

And as the night progressed, Valerian truly understood why in the Holy Writ this oneness was called "knowing."

The End

Thanks

An author needs a lot of help to give birth to a book, and I want to thank all my assistant midwives:

My husband Keith and my sons David and Robert, for all their love and support through multiple drafts and rewrites;

My critique partners, Pamela, Diane, Lupe, Sally, Judy, Kathleen, and John, for your insights and most of all for believing in me;

My content editor, Alex McGilvery, who saw things no one else did, and for his choreography help with a crucial scene;

My copy editor, Steve Mathisen, and my beta readers, Holly, Daniella, Evana, Robin, Cheryl, Wanda, Julie, Dani, Susan, and Marc for your suggestions and encouragement;

And for you, Dear Reader, for without you, authors would have no audience!

For more about the author visit
www.katyhuthjones.blogspot.com

Made in the USA
Charleston, SC
02 August 2015